A WEREWOLF IN TIME

A WEREWOLF IN TIME

A Clockwork Vampire #2

K.H. KOEHLER

The Monster Factory

CONTENTS

I	2
II	17
III	40
IV	57
V	72
VI	88
VII	105
VIII	124
IX	143

X	157
XI	173
XII	189
XIII	205
XIV	218
XV	232
XVI	252
XVII	268
XVIII	285
XIX	304

ABOUT THE AUTHOR

Copyright © 2012 by K.H. Koehler

All rights reserved. No part of this publication may be reproduced, stored or transmitted in any form or by any means, electronic, mechanical, photocopying, recording, scanning, or otherwise without written permission from the publisher. It is illegal to copy this book, post it to a website, or distribute it by any other means without permission.

This novel is entirely a work of fiction. The names, characters and incidents portrayed in it are the work of the author's imagination. Any resemblance to actual persons, living or dead, events or localities is entirely coincidental.

Paperback ISBN: 979-8-8692-6269-1

Ebook ISBN: 979-8-8692-6270-7

Cover art and interior design by KH Koehler Design
https://khkoehler.net

No part of this book was created using artificial intelligence.

> Calvin turned, rejecting the dark Thing that blotted out the light of the stars. "Make it go away, Mrs. Whatsit," he whispered. "Make it go away. It's evil."
> —Madeleine L'Engle, *A Winkle in Time*

> "I rule the night, it's my home, I welcome you."
> —Darkseed, "The Dark One"

| i |

Miss Eliza Booksat on a train bound for Whitby Village with two very dead but lively young men. The man sitting on the cushioned seat across from her was her boyfriend, Edwin. He was tall and lanky and redheaded pale, ugly-handsome, and he was hunched over a newspaper they had bought back at the train station in Suffolk. Long ago, he had been a vampire and a gangster. He was no longer a gangster. He *was* still a vampire.

He looked vaguely annoyed from what she could see through his curtain of longish ginger hair, his fierce amber gaze clocking around the paper as if he was reading something of great concern. Sometimes, his eyes narrowed or he bit his lip in consternation. She had half a mind to ask him what was wrong, but she didn't want to put a damper on their holiday.

The second vampire in their entourage sat on the bench beside her, playing a game on his phone. He was nearly but not quite as tall as Edwin. Since his transformation to vampirehood some six months earlier, he'd stopped dyeing his hair blond, and it had since grown in mocha with blond tips. He looked pale despite his Hispanic roots, and his dark blue eyes had brightened to near silver as vampire's eyes are wont to do. He was dressed in denim and leather. He'd even added a long black leather duster in an effort to look more like the Enforcer he was supposed to be, but, so far, Edwin was fairly oblivious to him, which was concerning.

Cesar was a new vampire and couldn't be trusted to be by himself just yet, which is why Eliza had insisted he accompany them. The new Vampire Bill that had passed in Congress only the year before had granted the undead human rights, but also human responsibilities. Edwin had grumbled about her suggestion but had ultimately given in when Eliza expressed her concerns about leaving Cesar alone in New York while they took their holiday. The last thing any of them needed was a vampire going amok and ruining it for Edwin's people.

It was perhaps not the ideal holiday, Eliza reflected, but it was certainly overdue. Recently, they had both defied death, Eliza had gained her freedom as a Poppet, and Edwin was the not-so-proud papa of a new Heir. He also had a book to finish for his editor, but writer's block had stalled him out in New York. They had also decided that if this arrangement of theirs was going to work, this relationship they had begun, it would be best if they really got to know one another outside work. Thus, they had decided it was time they got away from the insanity of the big city. Eliza suggested Vermont, a pretty little weekend B&B, but Edwin had been a bit more ambitious about their getaway plans.

He wanted a week in the English countryside. He thought it would be romantic. She had never been outside the United States, and being the adventurous sort, the prospect of travel excited her.

"Edwin," she said, sitting back with her East Anglia travel and cuisine book falling into her lap. She was getting tired of reading about the history of bogs and toad-in-the-hole. "Have you known Lord Severn a long time?"

She wanted to know everything she could about their host, also a vampire. Vampires, despite her relationship with Edwin, made her very nervous.

Edwin looked surprised but still smiled at her. "We go back a ways."

"A little ways or a long ways?" She noticed that Cesar was listening with great attention to their conversation.

Edwin shrugged and let the newspaper droop. "We were mates back in the early sixties." He reached across the space between them and patted her knee reassuringly. "I promise no big bad threatening vamps this time, love."

He said it as if she was spooked at the idea of spending a week in a dilapidated medieval castle, surrounded by vampires. The problem was—she sort of was. "And Baldy's a real trip. A genuine gangster who hails from Prohibition Chicago."

"Does he talk with an accent?" Cesar asked with interest. "Like Al Capone?"

"All you yanks sound like Al Capone to me."

Cesar frowned. "Better than sounding like the Artful Dodger with a nasal infection," he said in relation to Edwin's accent.

"Sod off."

"Edwin." Eliza frowned at him. He sometimes got very impatient with his new child.

"Sorry, love." He went back to his newspaper.

Cesar went back to his phone, looking slightly dejected like a puppy that had been kicked for showing too much enthusiasm. Eliza felt for him.

According to her travel guide, Lord Ian Severn was the oldest living vampire in all of East Anglia. He even predated the current residence, having established his castle and Court in the Sixteenth Century, while the Black Plague raged just beyond his borders. He was something of a local hero, having unified the people of Annwynn in what would eventually become known as the village of Whitby.

It was from Whitby that soldiers had been taken during the War of the Roses, and then again during Mary, Queen of Scots' rule as she ascended the throne. By then, Whitby had developed a reputation for strong, fierce, and indomitable soldiers.

Eliza studied the book in her lap. Old woodcuttings showed Lord Ian Severn on horseback, directing troops and building villages up, his wife at his side. It was difficult to tell from the carvings, but he seemed like a strong, virile vampire concerned with his people's wellbeing. She hoped it was true. The vast majority of vampires she had encountered in her life had been infantile and self-serving.

There were no modern pictures, so Eliza couldn't help but wonder what he looked like now. Surely, he hadn't changed much, except for the period clothes and horses. She found it hard to believe such an esteemed vampire had had any kind of relationship with Edwin.

Her vampire had been born a street brawler and a cur, an orphan who grew up much too quickly in the East End of London. She knew—though he'd never mentioned as much—that in his time, Edwin had been a thief, a con man, and a hustler. He'd been a condemned murderer when Lord Henry Foxley found him and turned him into his vampire Enforcer. Edwin had shed blood for Foxley. A lot of it. She was hardly the unsullied maiden herself, so she could not judge him on his survival tactics. But she knew instinctively that there was a deeply buried darkness in Edwin. He was the kind of man who might do anything, certainly not the type to form alliances with vampire heroes such as Lord Severn.

Eliza turned a page in her book as they entered a covered bridge and the coach went dark around them. When they emerged, she noted that Cesar was gone, though he returned some moments later with a full tea service.

"Thank you, Cesar," she told him, taking a cup and setting it on a Battenberg lace napkin in her lap.

"The porter said we're almost there," he announced with carefully controlled excitement. Ever since he'd begun living with them back in New York City, he'd put himself on standby for her and Edwin, fetching their tea and dry-cleaning, helping her in her job as Edwin's secretary and manager, and dusting Edwin's office—not that Edwin seemed to notice or care.

Sometimes, she felt like she had her own personal valet.

He poured a cup of synthetic blood for Edwin but hesitated in offering it. She detected a slight blush as he looked away from her oblivious boyfriend and out the window of the UV-protected windows of the train. They framed the flat, bushy grasslands that were unlike anything she had ever seen in the States.

"Let me," she offered and took the cup from him. He looked greatly relieved.

The train wended its mechanical way over the marshlands of East Anglia. In some ways, it reminded her of the American Midwest, cowboy towns, except that the trees seemed to grow lower, hugging the ground, and there was an abundance of thistle and scrubby bushes covering the moorlands. It looked wild and beautiful and untamable, with a broody cobalt sky that threatened rain but didn't quite seem ready to deliver on its promise.

They passed some farmlands dotted with small, shaggy horses, and then a great deal more open spaces full of long, rustling brown grasses where sleek foxes chased unseen things through the underbrush. There were a great many ruins—small, lonely stone cottages slowly toppling over, the remnants of blasted fortresses, and a few random stone circles like Stonehenge, only less impressive. Nothing looked especially threatening, just aloof and disconnected.

So, this was what Edwin meant when he said the English countryside was like living on an abandoned colony planet.

The porter came through to announce their imminent arrival at Whitby Village. Eliza knew it was important to Edwin and Cesar that they prepare for disembarking—a somewhat more complicated procedure when one was dead and likely to fry in the noontime light. They stood up together and Edwin leaned down and kissed Eliza on the nose.

"Will you be all right, love?"

She gave him an arch look. "It's not exactly Dodge out there, is it?"

"Not last I checked." He smiled then, the first genuine smile she'd seen since they boarded the train back at the airport, and Eliza felt a little of the tension she didn't know she was harboring lift from her shoulders.

"I'll be fine," she told him, waving him away.

"Are we really going back into those coffins?" Cesar asked worriedly.

"They're not coffins," Edwin told his Heir. "They're Hydraulic Protection Compartments. You don't want to fry, do you?"

Cesar shivered. Eliza thought he might be a little claustrophobic—eight hours in an HPC aboard a plane could do that to anyone, but plane requirements concerning vampires were still very stringent.

Before he departed, she grabbed Edwin by the cute little goatee he had grown just for her and which gave him a vaguely devilish charm, and dragged his face around to hers. "Don't scare Cesar."

Edwin frowned. "He's a bloody vampire. He should be scaring everyone else."

"Edwin."

"Yes, dear."

She kissed him a thank you.

Edwin and Cesar exited the private car, sliding the door closed behind them. Eliza sat back in her seat and enjoyed the silence, the tea, and the lovely, misty, early-morning landscape as they rounded a bend. A station on the moors loomed up ahead.

Eliza fished a pair of redesigned opera glasses from her utility bag —she secretly called them her spyglasses—and clicked them open.

Through the super-magnifying lenses, she spotted a pretty little collection of stone buildings, and, beyond it, more farmland stretching into what she feared might be infinity. Above, the sky growled, and she worried her holiday would be rained out for the week.

She sighed. Considering how cagey Edwin had been acting of late, she wondered if any of this had been a good idea. But she was unprepared for the life-changing conflict she was about to face down in the besieged hamlet of Whitby Village.

* * *

Eliza disembarked the train, swirling through steam amidst a rowdy collection of gentlemen in frock coats and women in long, rather old-fashioned skirts. She fished her mobile phone out of her pocket while glancing around the platform surreptitiously to make certain her driver wasn't seeking her out just yet.

A tall, white-haired man in a swallowtail suit stood down in the station, glancing around with a sign upraised in his gloved hands, but she couldn't read it just yet. She pushed a few brass buttons on the cleverly designed little device, and when Juliana came on the line, she found herself squealing in delight.

"Oh, it's lovely here!" she told her BFF. "So primitive and wild! I wanted to phone you because I have *no* idea if Lord Severn's castle has any kind of mobile phone reception. I could be trapped in the English countryside for a week with no Internet!"

Juliana squealed in response. "Oh, what if natives carry you off, dear!"

"Wouldn't that be exciting!"

"It would!" Juliana agreed, and the two laughed.

"But only if Edwin rescues you in the end!" Juliana added. "Not that you need it, but it would be fun. How is Edwin—and that adorable little vampire baby? Did they survive the trip all right?"

"Cesar hated the hydraulic compartment on the plane, but they have that law now about vampires…"

"I know! I said to Robbie just the other day…I said, Robbie, how dare they treat vampires like second-rate citizens? Storing them away like luggage!"

"Edwin's rather churlish now. I wonder if that's it."

"Oh, no! Your holiday ruined!"

"Edwin is *not* going to ruin my holiday!" Eliza stated emphatically. "He will have a good time even if I must force him!"

"There you go!"

"And there I must go! My driver is waiting for me. Will you give my love to Robert?"

"Of course! Have fun storming the castle!"

"I will." Eliza hung up, slung her utility bag over her shoulder, lifted her traveling skirts, and carefully stepped down onto the old cracked tiled floor of the train station. Distantly, she heard a train whistle, and the sound of it spurred her on to approach the old man holding the sign with her name on it.

"Hello, miss," the old man said. He looked positively ancient but very well groomed, and he spoke with what Edwin had informed her was a "country dialect," though almost everyone in England sounded the same to her at present. Still, it did sound slightly singsongier than what she had heard back in Heathrow Airport.

"Would it be just you, then?" he asked with some curiosity, looking around.

"Yes, it fact." She smiled nicely but didn't elaborate. Not everyone was a fan of vampires. And there were plenty, especially in a place like this, who might feel transporting vampires was a bad omen, so she chose not to mention her companions.

He took her bags in a courtly way, gave her a wrinkly smile, and led her to the car.

Well, it wasn't actually a car. It was a steam coach, a rather large one, but necessary. Not only would it be transporting luggage for three for a week, but it would also be carrying the rather cumbersome hydraulic chambers that contained her boyfriend and Cesar's bodies.

Before she climbed in, she went around to the boot and opened it to check the tags on the compartments the porters had loaded. The last thing she needed was to take the wrong vampires! But everything seemed to be in order.

"Miss?"

"Coming!" she called back.

The chauffeur—the patch on his uniform said he was "Mr. Cummings"—smiled but said nothing as he opened the back door for her. Eliza climbed inside and Mr. Cummings snapped the door shut.

"It's something of a ride, Miss," Mr. Cummings informed her as he climbed into the cab of the coach.

"I'm on holiday, so I have no timetable."

"We don't get many tourists out here, I'm afraid," Mr. Cummings said, adjusting his hat and starting up the steam coach, which rattled and roared cantankerously beneath them. "This country has a strange history."

"How do you mean?"

Mr. Cummings grinned as they started chugging up and down the slight hills. Slowly, they put more distance between the train station—and civilization—and what looked like a different planet up ahead. She could tell he liked to tell a good story. Maybe it was even one of his jobs to entertain the tourists.

"The lands around Whitby have a long, cursed history, miss. A dark history. There are creatures out on the moorlands at night, so I nae think you ought to be going out there without good reason."

"You mean vampires?"

Cummings laughed. "The Winged Ones are common these days, miss. No, I mean werewolves. Members of the Bloodthorn Pack are common in these parts. You naught want to meet one of them in the dark, miss, now would you?"

She hadn't read about werewolves in the travel books. "You mean there are scarier things than vampires out there?" Given her history with vampires, she found that hard to believe.

Mr. Cummings laughed as they rumbled past a crossroads where a wood marker said *Whitby 15 Kilometers*. "Whitby has long been the home of the Wild Hunt."

He paused for dramatics and then continued, "On those cursed nights, the unlucky may both hear and witness a great number of huntsmen afoot. The huntsmen are demons who ride on hideous night steeds, and their hounds are shapeshifters, jet black and horrible, with blazing white eyes. The children and the monks—those who walk with God—are always the first to hear them sounding and winding their horns."

Eliza felt a shiver at his tale.

Mr. Cummings lifted his grizzled chin to look at her in the rearview mirror. "They come to hunt our children and to take our souls back to hell with 'em. But many years ago, our good Lord Severn hunted the huntsmen and brought relief to our land. There has naught been a Wild Hunt since Severn Hall has stood upon its rock." He nodded his head emphatically.

Surely, that was nonsense.

Eliza wondered if he had been paid to tell every visitor the same story. She thought about probing him for more history and local color but then decided against it. She had experienced enough horrors for one lifetime.

* * *

The village of Whitby was a collection of little Hobbit houses with narrow low doors. Eliza saw fifty or sixty small white Tudor-style cottages and public buildings with thatched roofs and roads barely wider than goat paths running between them. It would have looked exactly like a medieval village were it not for the telephone poles and satellite and communication towers interspersed between the B&B's, pubs, and little tourist shops—that and the rare chain restaurant that had sprung up in some narrow back alley.

Eliza smiled and let out a small mental sigh of relief. There was something reassuring about the fact that even here, in the middle of literal nowhere, people enjoyed cable television, and Internet service, and regularly dined out on cheap fast food.

As they rumbled down the main road, passing bicyclists and people on foot, Mr. Cummings pointed out how to tell the locals from the tourists. Locals hung out in a shabby little red-lit pub called the Wolf's Head Lodge that looked straight out of an old Robin Hood movie, while the tourists stuck to the franchises and overpriced B&B's and bistros.

All of it made Mr. Cumming's story of the Wild Hunt seem even more fanciful and unlikely, which was just fine with Eliza. As they drove out of the town limits and into the vast, brown, forlorn moors once more, Eliza rubbed her shoulders and realized they ached as if she had been holding too stiff a posture for too long.

The Wild Hunt. It was silly rubbish, as Edwin would say.

* * *

The road that led to Lord Severn's castle was a bumpier ride than she expected. She wondered how Edwin and Cesar were faring. She couldn't imagine them sleeping through all the bumping and lurching.

Marshland bogs again surrounded them, cut only by long, flat plains of moorland so empty or sparse with grasses, she wondered how anything lived there. For a while, it was nothing but rolling hills of rocks and hard-packed earth. She guessed that not many people came out to see the old Lord of Whitby Village anymore. According to the travel book, Lord Severn had retreated from the world in the mid-1960s, at about the time of his wife's death. He now kept himself to the castle with only a small retinue of servants to see to his needs. He was not active in any kind of politics, and he was a Vampire Lord in name only. He no longer had anything that resembled a traditional Court.

"Miss, we're almost there," Mr. Cummings informed her.

Eliza leaned out the window of the steam coach. Up ahead, she saw only a heavy, veil-like white mist hanging over the road, making visibility so difficult that she wondered how Mr. Cummings navigated.

And then, like it was waiting there just to impress her, suddenly Whitby Hall took shape in the mist and became more distinct as they drew nearer. Eliza looked and looked again.

The castle stood high upon a natural motte overlooking a deep ravine that entirely surrounded it except for two arching bridges that connected it to the moorland. It didn't surprise Eliza that it had lasted over five hundred years. An attack on the structure at any angle would have been difficult, if not impossible. From the top of the spires and battlements, one would have been able to spot an enemy miles away across the flatlands, and surrounded by a treacherous ravine hundreds of feet deep, it would have been impervious to attack by anything that didn't have wings. It was beautifully and neatly composed, octagonal with a bailey and chemise, its brown flagstone walls aged but unbroken.

Eliza wasn't sure what she had expected—perhaps some crumbling ruin like in a Dracula movie. But this looked more like a giant, elegant French chateau.

Mr. Cummings slowed to an idle outside an extremely sophisticated modern gate system, the kind that she expected to see on the outskirts of a Westchester County estate at home in New York. There he thumbed the intercom system and announced them. A pause followed, then a rather gravelly and unpleasant woman's voice scolded him for running late. After another pause, though, she opened the tall iron spire gates for them.

"That's Megan, the castle Chatelaine, and the head of the Bloodthorn Pack," Mr. Cummings informed her with a laugh. "A spicy old ginger, she is."

"She's a werewolf?"

"Aye. That's all the Lord employs now," Mr. Cummings informed her.

Eliza looked at the old man carefully. "Are you a werewolf, Mr. Cummings?"

Mr. Cummings laughed. "I don't work at the castle, lass. I just do odd jobs." And that's all he said.

They motored up a well-paved road, over a bridge just wide enough for a vehicle or cart—no wider—and emerged into a walled, stone bailey. Eliza immediately detected the same surly voice shouting at them.

It was Megan. She stood on an enormous parapet in the bailey, arms crossed, looking very cross.

She wasn't what Eliza expected—not that she knew what to expect in the form of a surly lady werewolf. Megan stood just shy of six feet tall, her hair pinned up in a no-nonsense cockernonnie near the nape of her neck. She was naturally thick and muscular.

The popular fashions for that year were pale, feminine fabrics, a lot of mechlin bib lace, and bell sleeves. Megan, perhaps in some subconscious attempt to soften her image, had incorporated all of these into a voluminous dress with a pattern of tiny pink tea roses on it. It really didn't suit her. She just looked like a surly lady werewolf in a big, pink dress.

Her bright amber eyes tracked their progress across the bailey with almost predatory interest. "Mr. Cummings!" she shouted, waving. "You...are...late!"

Mr. Cummings pulled up to the gate of the bailey and leaned his elbow out the window. "Not like the vamps are going anywhere, miss, they beein' dead 'n' all."

"Aye, that may be so, but Lord Severn is hoping for an audience with his guests as soon as possible."

"The old fart's been around five hundred years, lass. Where's the fire?"

Eliza covered her laugh with her hand. Megan only sighed, turned, and pointed at the open bailey gate. "North gate."

Mr. Cummings rolled his eyes and drove them through, parking the steam coach as close to the entrance of the castle as he could. Eliza suspected he'd done so not for her convenience but so he wouldn't have to drag the hydraulic compartments very far.

But she was wrong. Even before she stepped outside the coach and onto the bailey, two young men of roughly the same build as Megan, and with the same bright amber eyes, appeared. At seven feet tall and four feet wide at the shoulders, they looked capable of bench-pressing the steam coach. Both gave her toothy grins and nodded their greetings to her before moving around to the back of the steam coach to retrieve the hydraulic containers. Each of the twins lifted one of the giant compartments to his shoulder, balancing it easily, and then carried it inside as if it was full of feathers.

Eliza was mildly shocked.

Megan stepped up to her and said, "My boys. Ain't they fine?"

"They are!" Eliza exclaimed, then turned to face the older, much taller, woman. She was momentarily afraid. She felt small and very breakable next to Megan. She had no doubts that Megan could carry her inside like a rag doll, if she was so inclined.

"You are Lord Edwin's consort? His Courtesan?" Megan asked with interest.

Eliza felt her cheeks burn even though it was a fair question. Before the debacle back in New York, when the Hive nearly dropped the world's largest gyro on the city, all kinds of decisions had been made. Things had changed between her and Edwin. They were *still* changing, if she was being honest. It shouldn't bother her so much that she had shared her blood with Edwin, that she had become part of his Court—by law, his property—but something about Megan's statement made her uncomfortable. "That's correct."

"How sweet!" Megan said with a grin. "He must be a very generous Lord to take you on holiday."

"We made this decision together."

Megan looked confused by her explanation but quickly recovered. Courtesans did not normally make decisions with their Vampire Lords, but her and Edwin's relationship was unique. He liked it when she pushed him around and told him what to do. She liked that he liked it. But trying to explain the dynamics of their romance to anyone was going to be difficult.

"Looks like rain," Megan sighed, looking up. And then she guided Eliza inside.

Eliza stepped inside Whitby Hall and gasped.

| ii |

The exterior of Whitby Hall looked ancient. The inside resembled a space station in high orbit.

Eliza took a few steps into the main hall and looked around. The walls of the castle were a burnished cobalt grey and outfitted with functional panels all slotted together like electronic components mounted on a giant circuit board. From the bailey, she had spotted tall, arched windows, but now that she was closer, she saw those windows were, in reality, video panels glowing faintly with relayed images from carefully spaced cameras outside. The entire castle was windowless, protected, infinitely vampire safe, day or night. A vampire could walk the halls anytime, depending on its mood and habits.

She turned round and round on her heel, finally spotting a metal staircase that spiraled up the walls of the castle to its highest spire. Small, homey electric torches and grand chandeliers had been placed here and there, along with banners, drapery, and even large, ornate portraiture, but for the most part, the castle was lit by row after row of bright blue runner lights like those that one might see on a giant space station.

Eliza looked and looked until she was dizzy with looking.

"Impressive, yeah?" said a voice at her shoulder.

She turned and almost jumped. One of the most frightening vampires she had ever laid eyes on stood behind her. He wasn't tall—he stood maybe an inch taller than she was—and was thick and muscular and dressed in a black cowl like some kind of demonic monk. He was perfectly white, with one of the smoothest bald heads she had ever seen. His blue eyes were so bright they looked like burnished aquamarines sewn into his face.

"Hey there." He spoke with broad, long American vowels, which threw her for a moment. She never would have expected to hear that in the English countryside

Eliza fixed a smile on her face while she clutched her utility bag in a deathgrip, holding it against her body as though it were a shield. It wouldn't do to look shaken in the presence of a vampire, especially now that they were an official part of the world population!

The strange vampire put out his very white and bloodless hand. "Baldy."

"Excuse me?" she asked.

"My name," he said. "It's Baldy. You do speak English?"

"Oh...yes!" she said after a moment when she had gathered her wits. She shook his powdery dry hand.

Baldy brightened. "You're American."

"So are you."

Baldy tipped his head. "Chicago."

"New York City."

"We're almost neighbors!" Baldy said, then laughed. "Not really."

"Ignore him," Megan said, sweeping past. "He thinks he's funny. He's not."

"He's charming," Eliza admitted.

"See, she likes me!" Baldy barked to Megan, making Eliza feel infinitely more at ease. He seemed like a very well-behaved vampire to her.

Megan shook her head. "You colonials."

Baldy winked at her and then, turning, suddenly linked his arm through Eliza's. "The English," he said companionably.

"Vampires," Megan called as she returned to the bailey to collect their luggage.

"Werewolves!" Baldy cried after her.

"Baldy, unhand my girlfriend," Edwin said from the doorway of an adjacent room. He was swaying a little as if he were still suffering the effects of the bumpy ride up the mountainside in the hydraulic chamber. He cracked his neck alarmingly and took a few steps toward them.

Cesar came slouching after, massaging his shoulder and stretching his wings. He looked grumpier than usual.

"But she's so warm!" Baldy said, pretending to clutch Eliza.

"She's also mine. Get your own!"

"The English. So greedy!" Laughing, Baldy let her go and moved toward Edwin with more fluid grace than she thought possible for such a stout man. The two vampires clenched and did that guy thing, boxing each other on the shoulder like men everywhere, of any species, do.

"Eddie!"

"Baldy."

"You're getting fat," Baldy said, punching him in the gut.

"You're getting balder," Edwin coughed, looking like he was struggling with not collapsing from the blow.

Baldy grinned, showing off a very impressive set of triangular, shark-like teeth, and ran the palm of his hand over his squeaky, shiny pate. "The Master has requested an audience with you as soon as possible."

"Christ, you even sound like Igor."

"Nah. I'm much more handsome and charismatic." He checked his wristwatch and gasped in terror. "Damn, I'm missing my stories.

Must dash...as the English say." After winking at Eliza, he trotted down a long, vast hall toward some unknown destination.

Edwin joined her, and Eliza set her hand on his arm. "So that's Baldy."

"He's weird," Cesar complained. "'Stories?'"

"Baldy likes soaps," Edwin offered. "*General Hospital, Eastenders*...you don't get between Baldy and his stories."

"Gay?"

"Straight as a bloody arrow."

"Okay, that is weird." Cesar gave him a surly look. "Did he always look like that?"

"Like what?"

"Count Orlock."

"Nah." Edwin lit a smoke and waved away the smoke. "But after he became a vampire, he lost all of his hair, so he just went with the image."

Cesar looked stricken and ran his hand over his lovely, well-groomed locks. "He lost his hair?"

Cesar loved his hair. Eliza had offered to cut it for him once, but she soon learned what a capital offense that was. You *never* cut a gay man's hair unless you worked in a salon. Not long after, they'd made a date of it every month to visit Eliza's hairdresser together. Cesar said he had a nice ass.

Edwin winked at his Enforcer. "Maybe you'll lose yours, too."

"Edwin!" she said.

Megan the werewolf called over to them with a good rolling "Oy!" that sounded more bark than anything human.

Everyone turned to face her.

She stood halfway up the long, curving stairs of the castle, two heavy valises under each arm. "Do any of ya tossers wanna room or do ya plan on sleepin' in the Great Hall, then?"

"Coming, mum…" Edwin said, and led Eliza away.

* * *

Their suite was lovely, sumptuous, and very English. There was an anteroom, a bathroom complete with a hot tub, and a vast bedroom suite that sported a huge, four-poster bed draped in white veils, a highboy with a basin and tureen for washing, and a false window that showed a view of whatever angle of the castle the viewer wanted.

Eliza experimented by changing the view a few times with the click-through until she found one she liked, that of the somber moorlands beyond filled with scrubby trees and long, golden-bronze grasses almost burning in the false sunset. It looked lonely and wild. Romantic—which was what this holiday was supposed to be.

They had agreed to use this time to get to know one another a little better. Eliza, at least, wanted to understand her vampire a little bit more.

Edwin came up behind her, very close, and slid his arms across her waist, pressing himself against her so she learned just how romantic he felt from the waist down.

Eliza turned, breaking his hold, and let Edwin have it. "Why do you have to do that?"

"Do what?" Edwin asked, dropping his hands to his sides and looking disappointed.

"Tease Cesar. You know how fragile he is."

"Bloody hell, Eliza, he's a vampire! I assure you that he is *not* that fragile."

"Emotionally he is. He's only a baby."

Edwin rolled his eyes. Then, with a deep sigh, went to unpack their things.

In a softer voice, she asked, "What do you hate him so much?"

Edwin started dismantling his valise. He had packed a great deal of golf clothes, she noticed. "I don't hate him."

"Yes, you do."

"Maybe." He put his finger and thumb together. "But only a little."

"Edwin...why? He's a perfectly lovely boy."

Edwin gave her a sharp look. "Well, for one thing, he's not a boy. He's not a baby, Eliza. He's a loaded gun." He looked at his clothes on their bed but seemed incapable of figuring out where to put them in their suite. She thought about pointing out the invisible wall compartments behind him—all of the old-fashioned furnishings were there merely for effect—but decided to let him suffer.

When he couldn't figure it out, he went to unpack his antique typewriter and set it on the desk in the corner. Edwin was hoping to get some words written on his latest novel while he was here—assuming they didn't spend the entire holiday in bed, because she knew how he was. "He's a vampire, love, and he's not yet fully in control of his own hunger. We don't even know what abilities he'll develop in time."

"So, why aren't you teaching him?"

"I am."

"No, you're not. For the past six months, you've ignored him completely."

"You *want* me to treat him like my Heir? You want me to do all the things a Vampire Lord does with an Heir?"

Eliza stuttered.

"Yes, exactly." He turned and went back to the dilemma of where to put his clothes.

It took Eliza exactly three-point-five seconds to pick her words, just long enough for her to draw a deep breath. "I want you to do whatever is necessary to make him a good vampire. I'm not naïve,

Edwin. I spent three years at Court, remember. I know how a Court operates."

"Eliza, I don't have a Court."

"Yes, you do. *We* are your Court, Cesar and I. And you need to start acting appropriately as its Lord. I just want you to be a good Lord to him. Not like Foxley was with you." She stopped and sighed in exasperation. "I didn't expect we'd be fighting on our holiday."

"We're not fighting. We're making decisions as a Court—no, a family. We're being painfully honest, I think."

"Then be honest with me. What's been bothering you so much? Is it this trip? This place?"

Edwin stared down at his borrowed desk, then looked up, seemed to come to a decision, and approached her. He touched her cheek tenderly. "I'm sorry, love. I promise to be less grumpy. Will that suffice?"

"You're deflecting again." She gave Edwin a hard look. "It is Lord Severn? You two weren't...?"

She stopped as she thought about that for a long moment. They had been *painfully honest* with each other six months ago, after the New York debacle. She'd told Edwin a little about her life at Court. And, in return, she'd learned things about Edwin that she'd suspected but never confirmed. But there were still some things she wondered about. She lowered her voice to a near-inaudible whisper. "Were you lovers? Not that it bothers me, but I'd like to know."

"No," he said. Then he closed his eyes. "I mean...we shared intimacy, but only because of Lady Catherine, Ian's wife."

"You were Catherine's lover?" That surprised her. The books she'd read about Lady Catherine Severn hadn't told her very much about the woman.

Edwin pursed his lips in that way he had that said he was struggling not to alter the truth too badly to protect her.

Eliza raised her eyebrows at that. "You were a *ménage a trois?*"

"It...was the 1960s. Things like that made more sense then, somehow." Edwin spread his hands. "Angry, love?"

Eliza reached up and slowly loosened his bow tie while holding his gaze. "I know you have something of a past. I'm just...I mean...did you...enjoy it? Being with Ian and Catherine?" She pulled his tie off. "Is that something that interests you? I want to know."

He looked sad but opted for the truth in the end. "What the three of us had...it was bloody amazing, Eliza. And it wasn't a kink or something perverse. It was...essentially, the first real, healthy relationship I'd ever experienced in my life. It just happened to be with two other people."

She wasn't angry with Edwin, and she appreciated his honesty. She also found it infinitely sad that he'd had to wait two hundred years to experience a relationship that wasn't utterly toxic. She cupped the back of his head, leaned up, and kissed him. Deeply. Completely.

When she pulled away, he said breathlessly against the wetness of her mouth, "That was bloody amazing, too." He slid his hands around her warm curves and jerked her closer. Baldy had been right; Edwin was becoming just a mite thicker in the middle—or, at least, his severely rangy physique seemed to be filling out. She figured that was her blood working on him.

"Give us a sip?" he whispered in her ear.

"Are you hungry?"

"Mmm."

Her hands wandered over him, going to places that seemed to make him a very happy vampire. "How about a quickie?" she suggested. She didn't want to have to undress and redress in the middle of the day.

"I love quickies," he said, and kissed her again, "One, Two, or Three?"

One was gentle. Two was more fun. Three left her needing an ice bag so she could stand up in the morning. Since they were expected for dinner in less than two hours, Eliza thought it more prudent that they go for Two.

Edwin didn't complain. He turned and lifted her, resting her rump in the window well. He eased her skirts up, slid her underthings aside, and took her hard and fast, the way she liked it. His lips brushed the mark under her ear, then snapped down on it. It opened automatically for him, bypassing the need for teeth. He began to drink from her mark even as he drove spiraling waves of pleasure deeper and deeper into her body.

It seemed a fair exchange—there was nothing wrong with making her guy work for his meal, she thought. Eliza leaned her shoulders against the glass, braced her hands on Edwin's shoulders, and enjoyed the full circuit of sensation coursing through her body.

For a seemingly long time, she couldn't have spoken even if she'd been inclined to, which she was not. Anyway, there was no need. After six months of being together, they were so in tune with each other's needs that all Edwin needed to do was to make a few low grunts to convey how hungry or full he was, and she needed only tap him lightly on the back of the neck to indicate she'd had enough of him.

He fed for about twenty seconds, then released the hold he had on her mark. He gave it a few grateful licks and then concentrated on just getting them both to climax. He turned his head and said in the shivery cup of her ear, "Am I getting fat?"

His statement was so unexpected that it almost broke their rhythm. "You're not fat, Edwin."

"Yes, I am. Twelve stone."

"I don't know what that means in American pounds, so it doesn't count."

He started to explain, but she cut him off.

"Just shut up and love me, you exasperating man," she said against the roughness of his cheek as they strained against one another.

Once they were done, he withdrew and they worked on fixing each other's clothes. "I'm going down to see our esteemed Lord. Shan't be more than half an hour, I promise." He leaned over and kissed her on the cheek. "And I'm pretty sure you've made me fat."

"You're not fat!"

He was gone in seconds.

Eliza sighed.

* * *

Baldy stood at the foot of the steps. "He's in his study," he said as Edwin reached the bottom.

He looked Lord Edwin McGillicuddy up and down. He had changed rather dramatically since last they had seen each other, even by vampire standards. Baldy had indeed become even balder, and Edwin had filled out.

He had always been such a lank fellow, more like a long-limbed, loose-jointed doll than a man, but Baldy had to admit he looked more solid these days. His hair was longer on top and a darker mahogany that Baldy remembered, wisps framing a face that would have been perfect for daytime soaps, except for his nose, which had been broken and badly reset while he was still alive. His eyes were a pale golden brown rather than the anemic amber hue he remembered. The lush red goatee he'd grown made him look like some virile, Ecclesial devil.

Baldy recalled an old wives' tale that a vampire who finds his perfect consort could replenish some of the color and vitality lost to him during his Inheritance. Miss Book certainly had brought it out in him.

Baldy rubbed his scalp in envy. "Is it bad?"

Edwin stopped with inches separating them. He looked at Baldy curiously. "Steady on?"

"Don't pull that Bertie Wooster shit on me, Ed. You know what I mean. I know the Master summoned you."

"Listening behind closed doors, are we?" Edwin asked as he made his way down a corridor. He smiled, hands in his pockets like the good old days, walking with the swagger of a pirate. "How positively *Upstairs, Downstairs*."

Baldy followed behind. "Jesus, everyone watches *Downton Abbey* now."

"Same thing."

"You're changing the subject."

"Am I? I thought you were." Edwin pushed past Baldy and opened the great double doors of the study.

* * *

Ian's study was so very…Ian. Edwin knew for a fact that the old Lord had been upgrading the castle for years, turning it into a completely automated, computer-run dirigible, but the study he had kept as it had been forty years ago. It was old and worn and homey, full of battered books and scuffed candelabrum. Edwin had no clear memory of ever seeing modern lighting in this room.

As he walked across the three-hundred-year-old oriental carpeting, he glanced up at the intricate ceiling mural of The Wild Hunt. The horseman and his fierce black dogs forever chasing the dawn.

From a seating arrangement near the well-lit hearth came a dry, almost rattling voice he barely recognized. "Baldy, some time alone with Lord Edwin, please."

Baldy looked at Edwin as if he didn't trust him. "Sure thing, boss."

"I'll fill you in later," Edwin promised his friend, patting his shoulder companionably.

Baldy turned, still looking pensive, but moved toward the open doors of the study, gathering them in his hands as he passed through and closing them behind him.

"And don't listen at the keyhole," Ian added.

Edwin smiled a little. He went around one of the big wing chairs and faced Lord Ian Severn for the first time in forty years.

He was horrified.

He remembered Ian—tall and rangy but not weak. Before he had become a vampire, and Catherine's consort, he had been a poor, local stable boy who worked with the horses. In those days, he'd had long, curling, coal-black hair and eyes so dark they looked positively Egyptian. He loved old grey tweed suits and red cravats. He'd always had impeccable tastes in clothes, though he was the kind of beautiful man who could wear anything and stun a room to silence. And yet, it was his wit and determination that had first brought him to the attention of Lady Catherine. Ian looked like a rake. He made love like one, too. In years past, he'd worn his hair long and unbound like a privateer and his eyes were always bright and dusky in his carven white face.

The man sitting in the wing chair now, an afghan and book in his lap, looked like the sixty-year-old grandfather of that same man. His skin looked dry and powdered down. His hair, thick but now steel grey, was tied into a queue at the nape of his neck, and his eyes were faded to grey. Still, he managed to pin Edwin with a hawkish intelligence that he would have recognized anywhere.

"Ian?"

"Hello, old friend. You haven't changed at all." Ian pushed himself up in his seat and his eyes traveled all over his visitor from head to toe, then back again. Once, his look had been hungry and lustful. Some of that remained, but now it was tempered by pain and years. He looked at Edwin as if he was analyzing his worth and fortitude rather than how well he would perform in his bed. "Not the rake you remember, yes?"

Edwin blinked but grounded himself. It would not do to look appalled while in the presence of another Vampire Lord. He knew hat. Lords needed to keep their composure at all times. Anything else was amateur hour. "You're still beautiful, Ian," he said softly.

Ian lifted an eyebrow. "And you're still an excellent liar, Prince."

Edwin moved forward to embrace his old friend. Ian's body felt far too frail, and when Edwin kissed the Lord on his forehead, moving aside the loose pale strands of his hair to do so, his skin tasted like old washed linen. His hair smelled slightly musty.

He drew back, resting his hand on his friend's shoulder. "How did this happen?"

Ian smiled bitterly. "'As we grow old...the beauty steals inward,'" he quoted Ralph Waldo Emerson.

"I'm serious. What's happened? Has anyone examined you?" Edwin knew there were medics specializing in the unique complaints of vampires. He knew a few who were even vampires themselves.

Ian, smiling sadly, brushed the skin of Edwin's face with his thumb as though he envied it. "They don't know."

"Is this the reason...?"

Ian cut him off. "*This* is of no consequence." Looking uncomfortable, the old vampire glanced past Edwin and his eyes settled on the seat opposite him. "The chair, Edwin, Do you remember?"

Edwin turned and glanced at it, then moved to run his hand over the worn upholstery of the armrest, the slowly disintegrating wood of the edges. "The chair," he agreed. The room's décor had changed over the years, probably many times, but Ian had kept the faded, Elizabethan wing chair, and now it stood out among all the slightly more modern furnishings in the room.

On the night he had met Ian and Catherine, he had been a vampire on the run, a hunted man lost in a wild country he barely understood, having grown up in the filthy boroughs of busy London. He'd been cold and wet and miserable, having fallen into and sloshed about through a bog. But then he came upon the warmly lit WhitbyHall and met the gracious Lord and Lady Severn.

Back then, this room had sported green and orange shag rugs, lava lamps on all the mantels, and a portable turntable record player with records of The Kinks and The Velvet Underground. That night, he sat in this very chair and shared in Ian and Catherine's drinks and the warmth of their fire and conversation. He would sit in this same chair many times more in the days that followed.

About a week after he arrived, Catherine finally propositioned him. She said he was very beautiful to look upon, and she felt he would be delicious. She wanted him. She was very candid about her needs and sexuality—one of the many reasons Edwin came to admire her. So, she wanted a fling. It seemed a fair exchange for the sanctuary his benefactors were offering him, and certainly not the first time he had exchanged sex for favors. After all, he had been born into a house of ill repute in the East End of London. In many ways, he had been born for a life of prostitution.

And Catherine herself was a handsome woman, tall and curvy and dressed in pale gowns of pearl or raw, tender pink—gowns almost devoid of color so only her long, rose-red hair and sea-green eyes seemed to glow. She told him that in her time, an era when the Bard was still unknown and struggling, fabrics were almost always white. Only the very wealthy could afford such luxuries as colored fabrics. She had not been born wealthy. She'd been a tavern wench in those days, an unwanted girl-child in a family of seventeen siblings. Her parents had been so poor and desperate that they had begun murdering their newborns for the stewpot, a sad but not unheard-of practice in her day.

Then the stranger—her future master and maker—showed up in their village one night and took a fancy to her. Her parents sold her to him for forty silver pieces ("Ten more than Jesus Christ," she proudly proclaimed). She never saw them again. She became his concubine, then his consort, and, in time, his Heir. Eventually, she became the Vampire Lady she was today.

After she told her story, she climbed into Edwin's lap, pressed herself tightly against his fluttering heart and groin, and kissed him long and hungrily. Ian had been attending the fire behind them while she spoke, and Edwin had started fretting about that. This was not the first time he'd become entangled with a married woman—they were something of a delicacy for him—but the idea of a cuckolded husband armed with a fireplace poker within striking distance did not sit well with him.

So, he was greatly relieved when Ian set the poker down, came around the chair, and leaned down to kiss the side of Edwin's neck. His mouth was cool and wet. He was as beautiful and charming as Catherine, and, in that moment, Edwin could not believe his luck in finding such beautiful people to love him. After that night, he entertained the possibility of becoming a more permanent fixture of their Court.

Catherine was gone. Edwin had never become part of their Court. Instead, Chimera had found him and dashed all his plans to pieces. Afterward, he had become a wanderer, a Vampire Lord with no Court, and a man without a country—at least until he met Eliza.

Edwin looked above the fireplace mantel where Catherine's ancient portrait once hung. Sadly, it had been replaced by a generic mural of a foxhunt.

Ian followed his look. "I could not bear to look upon her image any longer. All her pictures have been removed from the Hall. Not one remains. They have all been locked away in her laboratory. There is only so much pain one can endure."

He hesitated before continuing. "Am I evil for doing so, Edwin? A bad husband for removing Catherine so completely from my life? For wanting to forget?"

"You were never a bad husband, Ian." Edwin thought about adding that this was all his fault. They both knew that. Had he never come here, Catherine would be alive. But he did not want to speak the words. Ian, somehow, had forgiven him. He could not understand that. He would have preferred anger. The anger he could have borne. Instead, he was left with Ian's apathy, which was somehow worse.

He sat down in the chair where he, Catherine, and Ian had made love. He half expected something to happen, for the walls to crumble or the earth to open up beneath them, but nothing did. "Do you regret it? Taking me in?" he asked Ian.

"Do you?"

"Yes, of course."

"Then you are a foolish man."

Edwin shook his head. "Why have you summoned me? Is it because of what's happened to you?"

Ian, with the aid of an ornate cane, moved stiffly like an arthritic old man to a sidebar, where he'd prepared two drinks for them—real blood mixed with his vintage crop of wines. He carried the two large snifters back to the fire and offered Edwin one. "Yes. And no."

"Begin with the yes," Edwin said, accepting the glass.

"Do you know much about my history, Edwin? About the history of Whitby Hall?"

"Some. Not everything. Catherine kept her secrets."

"Catherine's name was Severn. Catherine Severn. I mean that she was born with that name. I took it as my surname after she chose me as her consort. Did you know that?"

"I suspected." The drink was good, the blood human. Or human-like, in any event. Edwin wondered if it had come from Ian's werewolves. He'd drunk werewolf blood once before, with rather comical results. He'd passed out on the floor of a speakeasy and had had to be dragged out.

"She was her own Lord long before I met her," Ian explained as he returned to his chair. "A very powerful Lady. She ruled over this region from this very castle for at least two centuries before I was ever born. She protected its people during the plague years and through the Normandy invasions. The people of Annwynn were like her livestock, and she protected them fiercely."

Ian paused and drank from his glass. "I was very honored to be chosen. Before Catherine, I was merely a stableman, a poor farm boy—like her once, no person of importance. It is rather a mystery to me why she even noticed me."

Edwin narrowed his eyes. "You were beautiful and alive, and Catherine loved you. I felt the love between you in our private moments. I experienced it, and it was one of the happiest periods of my life."

Ian nodded, accepting that. "She warned me before we married that the people wanted—no, they *needed*—a hero. She warned me that by loving her, by joining with her, I would become that hero, whether I wanted to be or not. And then she told me that it would likely kill me. But I didn't mind, because to be with her, to be beloved *of* her..."

He stopped musing and tilted his head back against his chair as if to savor the memory, the glint of the flames in the hearth reflected on his skin, making him seem almost alive again. In that moment, Edwin felt a profound connection with the man. This was what he felt with Eliza. He felt alive...exalted that he should be chosen of her, beloved of her, as silly as that sounded.

Ian set his glass down on the table beside him, the same place he had set his book. "That was how I came to be the Lord of the Wild Hunt." He looked down at his hands clenched in his lap, the rings on his gnarled hands crackling in the firelight. "The Village of Whitby loved her, you see. They turned to her in times of strife or need. So, of course, she needed a villain, someone to do the vile deeds that needed to be done. I became her champion and her villain. It was a terrible responsibility, a burden she made me fully aware of long before she took me as her Heir."

"I thought the Wild Hunt was just some local legend fodder, a way to scare children into their beds."

"It became that with time." Ian reached for the book on the table and handed it to Edwin. "You should read this. It explains everything about the Wild Hunt. But take care. It is very old."

Edwin held the book carefully in his lap. The leather was soft like a child's skin. He tried not to think about that too much. When he glanced inside, he saw the book was hand-written in a monkish old English script.

"The book covers the history of the Wild Hunt, and why it was necessary. Why it had to be done." He stared at Edwin with narrow, somber eyes, took a deep breath, and continued.

"In the time before recorded history, a Darkness crept across the face of the Earth. The Darkness has been recorded in Biblical literature many times. An emptiness that comes to possess the world when the world is without life. It is the same force that has made us, you and I, Edwin."

"The Darkness," Edwin said dubiously. "That's just some story."

"Of course it's a story. But that does not make it untrue. The Darkness lives, Edwin. It breathes. You dream about it every night, but you don't remember. You experience it every time you make love or take blood. It fills you with emptiness and longing, and, most of all, hunger."

Ian folded his hands. "The Darkness fills us. It animates us even after our bodies have long since stopped living. But the Darkness is not alone. It was never *alone*." Ian nodded slowly. "The Darkness first entered our world because it was pursuing the Light. And the Light, too, has filled vessels, though they are vastly different bodies."

"I'm not following."

"Edwin, do you know what Fae are?"

Edwin shook his head. "Fairies? Wee folk."

Ian smiled grimly. "Wee? No. Real Fae are much like us. Or rather, our mirror opposites. They are living vampires. *White* vampires."

Edwin turned a page of Ian's book and a woodcutting jumped out of him, of a man on horseback cutting down women and their babes with his sword. "The Light doesn't sound so friendly, Ian."

"The Light doesn't love you, Edwin. It doesn't love anyone." Ian paused for effect. "The Light eats people, not unlike the Darkness. The Darkness is simply more honest about its intentions. It is unapologetically hungry. The Light practices in deception. And still, the Darkness will forever pursue the Light."

"Because it seeks to destroy the Light?" he guessed.

Ian smiled grimly. "Because it loves the Light, Edwin, the way the dead love the living. Only mortal men assign the concepts of *good* and *evil* to elemental things in this world so we might better understand them. In a time before men, when the world was half-formed, there was only hunger, lust, and a primitive desire to consume. Do you understand?"

Edwin thought about that. He glanced down at the book again, then up at his friend. "How is this linked to the Wild Hunt? And what does this have to do with you and me?"

"In the early Fifteenth Century, the Light came to this region, Edwin. It came in great force and changed Catherine's people. They became...wrong."

"You mean Fae."

"They became the creatures who would become known as Fae, yes. It then fell to Catherine to eliminate them before the People of the Light attracted the Darkness—the Darkness which consumes all light, all life, everywhere, like a cancer. As you can imagine, this was a terrible burden to Catherine, who loved her people—perhaps not as a human loves their children but at least as a good husbandman loves his livestock. She was now faced with the terrible task of destroying them all. A task she could not endure, not on her own. This is why she needed a villain...why she needed me."

Edwin frowned. "But you said the Darkness loves the Light. Once it had the people—the People of the Light—shouldn't it be satisfied?"

Ian sipped from his glass. "Because you are full, Edwin, do you not still hunger for living blood? The Darkness cannot be filled, not with a billion souls of Light. Not with a million worlds. That's why it's the Darkness."

Edwin decided to shut up. He was out of his league on this—and it was starting to give him a headache. Then again, he was not a very old vampire, as vampires went. Catherine and Ian had lived centuries before he'd ever been born.

"One of the reasons she made me her consort was so that I could help her bear the terrible burden of the Wild Hunt. She also called forth the strongest warrior of the Bloodthorn tribe to be at her side, a Celtic barbarian by the name of Malcolm the Red. Together, her hound and I rode the Wild Hunt while Catherine consoled her people. She soothed them even while the Werewolf of Whitby and I slaughtered them in the hundreds. The old and infirm. The young and virile. So many people who had done nothing more than to be at the wrong place at the wrong time."

Again, Ian hesitated "I had killed before, of course. In those days, it was almost commonplace, but not like this, Edwin. Not like this." Ian touched his forehead as if he had a horrific headache. He kept his eyes shut a long time before continuing.

"In the days that followed, we discovered the terrible futility of what we had done. We had wiped out all but the children. Catherine could not bring herself to make me slay the children. Instead, we scattered them. But those children grew, and they carried the Light within themselves. We had hoped they might separate and migrate to other lands, but the children came home, one by one, and filled the Village of Whitby once more."

He drank again as if he were very parched. "The villagers who live here now are the descendants of those same children."

What an odd tale. And tragic.

"What happened to the hound? The Werewolf of Whitby?" Edwin knew that was another local legend. He even remembered it from his last stay in East Anglia. He did not know the legend was linked to Ian and Catherine.

"Malcolm," said Ian. "His name is Malcolm of Whitby."

"What happened to Malcolm?"

"We suffered an Inquisition shortly after we had driven the children away. The Church became suspicious of our activity. Catherine planned to take their questions and the brunt of their suspicions even knowing what they were likely to do to her. She considered it her penance for how she had betrayed her own people, but Malcolm would not allow it. He had come to love her as I did, you see. Our hound."

Again, Ian drank. "He confessed to the crimes, citing his condition, the bloodlust of his other self. When the Grand Inquisitor finished with Malcolm, very little was left that could be called a man. They tortured him continuously for over a year, always taking him to the very edge of death before allowing him time to heal. For one year, he lived in hell, and we were unable to free him from the Basilica and take him home. Many of my servants died in the task. Catherine herself nearly died when at last she brought him home.

"Oh, Edwin. He was such a horror that Catherine wept tears of blood over his wounds, and those tears fell upon Malcolm and healed some of the terrible things they had done to him, but it wasn't enough. Catherine and I then took turns feeding Malcolm our blood and pouring it directly into his wounds. He healed, though he remained in a comatose state. He was a werewolf, you see. He could not tolerate our tainted blood. His body simply shut down. We eventually interred him here beneath the Hall, in Catherine's lab. A sad tale, yes?"

"He is dead?"

Ian narrowed his eyes. "Not exactly."

Edwin thought about that for a long moment. Ian's tale had made him feel vaguely ill. Finally, he said, "I suppose you did what you had to do. But why summon me of all people?"

"I believe the Fae have grown strong once more. The signs are there, Edwin. The water has turned bitter. The birds have fallen from the sky all this summer. The harvest is rot. And someone has repeatedly attacked my stables and harmed my night steeds.

"You think the Fae are active again?"

Ian nodded once. "I believe the Light is here. I believe another Hunt is imminent and needed, perhaps within the next few weeks."

Edwin smirked humorlessly. "You realize I'm not a werewolf. I can't be your hound, Ian."

"I don't want you to be my hound, Edwin. I want you to ride for me. To be The Master of the Hunt."

| iii |

Eliza knew that dinner at Whitby Hall was apt to be a formal affair, so she'd chosen their wardrobe accordingly. Edwin only had one good evening suit, so he was no trouble at all. She chose a simple black beaded cocktail dress and Prohibition-inspired tiara to complement his outfit. In the States, it was all the rage to make one's dress large and garish. Teens and young adults even sewed devices and machinery to their gowns, but Eliza wasn't brave enough to wear anything like that. She had spent too many years on the run or just keeping a low profile in order to keep from being fingered as a runaway Poppet.

Edwin had returned from his audience with Lord Severn looking grim, though he did smile appreciatively at her cute little flapper-inspired dress with all of its glittery sequins. He requested a little time for his own toiletries before starting down, and she noted he was wearing his dangerous face, so she decided not to push him to explain. She had to trust he would tell her everything soon.

When she spotted Cesar in the hallway, she asked him to escort her down.

"You look gorgeous, Miss Eliza!" he exclaimed, looking her over in a way that was very subtlety interested. Not for the first time, she couldn't help but wonder if Edwin's bite had done some gentle reprogramming of his sexual preferences. But then he added, "Where's Lord Edwin?" and glanced around the castle halls.

"Sulking, I think." Eliza linked her arm through Cesar's and allowed her boyfriend's Enforcer to guide her through the castle halls, down the curving stairs, and into the drawing room full of monsters. Unlike Edwin, Cesar had impeccable tastes in fashion and liked to dress up. He wore a deep, plush blue cavalier jacket with huge military buttons and epaulets over a perfectly bare and hairless chest, loose, flowy black silk trousers, and knee-high boots turned down at the cuff, which gave him a very pirate-y appearance and ensured everyone in the room stared at him almost constantly. Cesar loved making a scene almost as much as he loved his hair—which, incidentally, he had spiked rather fashionably with a lot of gel.

They were inside the room no more than thirty seconds before Lord Ian Severn appeared. He kissed her hand and introduced himself formerly. Eliza was momentarily stunned by the sight of him—he looked ancient, and he was not what she expected. And yet, somehow, he remained beautiful and immaculately kept in the way of vampires everywhere. He looked less like a man and more like a black and white photograph of one.

Still, it took her a moment to recover and to remember to curtsey. Lord Severn stopped her immediately, his cold, beringed hand resting lightly on her arm. "You are my guest here, Miss Book. We should dispense with all of these silly formalities, yes? It is a modern era."

"Yes, of course," she answered properly. "Edwin and I are very grateful for your hospitality, Lord Severn."

"Ian. And it was no trouble at all." He turned his keen grey eyes on Cesar, who had remained silent up to this point. "Well, hello there, pup," he said as if in a conscious effort to sound more modern. "You are Lord Edwin's Heir, is that right?"

Cesar turned very red at the ears and looked away. "I don't know what to say," he whispered in Eliza's ear as if Ian couldn't hear only a few feet away. "Lord Edwin never told me what to do in the presence of a Vampire Lord."

He was sounding panicky, so Eliza laid her hand on his arm to calm him.

"In the old days, you would bend a knee to a higher-ranking vampire and offer fealty—not real fealty. Just a formality. But we won't do that tonight," Lord Severn offered. When he saw that just confused Cesar even more, he added, "I promise I don't bite, lad."

Ian stopped and assessed his own poor joke. Then he put out his hand. "Shall we be American tonight?"

"Um..." said Cesar, and put out his hand, which trembled slightly. "I'm Cesar...um, Schultz."

"Mr. Cesar Schultz," Ian said and took it. "What a very unusual name in terms of ethnicity."

Cesar prickled. This was his hot button. He was very proud of his mixed heritage. "Not so unusual when your mom was Hispanic and your dad was German."

Eliza tapped him in the heel.

"Sorry," he said, blushing even more furiously.

Really, she had never seen Cesar this high strung. "I...sorry, sorry..." He glanced down.

Eliza said, "He's a very young vampire. New to all of this."

Ian smiled, not offended. "You have more than a little fire, whelp. Part of the Inheritance from your master, I'd wager."

"Sorry," he said again, finding the floor between his feet keenly interesting.

"No worries." Ian looked at them both. "Right then. Shall we go into dinner?"

"Please," Eliza said.

Edwin suddenly appeared in the drawing room door, dressed in the formal green Kilkenny jacket and Gaelic kilt and sporran she had laid out for him, except he was tugging at his necktie, which was slightly crooked. Eliza immediately joined him and fixed it for him.

"You certainly took your time." She leaned in close. She could always tell when he shaved by the smell of the cream he used. In this case, he hadn't. "Cesar is having a meltdown and...you didn't even bother to shave? What were you doing up there?"

He pulled at his socks, clearly uncomfortable with the kilt he himself had picked out. Since he had no idea who his family was or even what part of Ireland he originated from, he'd opted for a simple black kilt instead of a regional tartan. "I had some things to attend to."

"Where?"

"Elsewhere."

"Like?"

"I was looking at a book that Ian lent me."

"You were reading a book?" She frowned, not liking how cagey he was being. "Edwin..."

He smiled broadly and moved past her to take Ian's hand. It was an old, formal vampire greeting. Edwin tipped his chin over Ian's hand like a suitor about to kiss the hand of a maiden, though he didn't go quite that far. He said something in Upyrese, the outdated language of the higher Vampire Courts. Ian answered him in kind. The language was so old it sounded vaguely Egyptian.

Then, still bent over Ian's hand, Edwin turned to Cesar. "Did you greet Lord Severn properly?"

Cesar looked flustered. "How do I do that?"

"You take a knee. I told you."

"No, you didn't!" Cesar glared at him, suddenly upset.

Ian interrupted, pulling his hand away. "Would it distress you very much, Lord Edwin, if I escorted our young whelp here to dinner? We could discuss such matters. Perhaps you would permit me to teach him the old greeting?"

Cesar went from flustered to terrified in seconds. He shifted slightly as if he wanted to take cover behind Eliza, but Edwin slapped Cesar on the rump, which propelled him a few inches forward. "Go entertain, Ian, whelp."

Now, it was Eliza's turn to glare at him. Ignoring it, he took her hand, tucked it into the crook of his arm, and walked her properly into the banquet hall. That left Ian to escort Cesar in similarly. Ian looked rather happy about that. Cesar...not so much.

Soon, they were all seated around the vast hand-hewed trestle table in the banquet hall. The enormous chamber followed the style set down by the old castle before reforms had been made. It was composed of white flagstone and covered in antique banners representing various Vampire Courts that Ian had entertained over the years. The room was lit by candlelight from the sconces on the wall and the giant wagon-wheel chandelier hanging from the ceiling, giving the enormous space the burnished golden feel of an Egyptian burial tomb.

Lord Ian sat at the head with Edwin to his right and Cesar to his left. Eliza knew from experience at Court that the right-hand side was where you placed a high-ranking guest you respected. The left was reserved for the guest a Vampire Lord had plans to seduce, but she didn't say any of this to Cesar. Eliza sat beside Edwin, and after a few moments, Baldy joined them, taking the empty seat next to Cesar. It was customary for a vampire's Enforcer to stand during dinners and formal occasions, so this was unusual. Eliza wondered if there was any significance to their seating, or if Ian was just being polite.

Megan arrived to serve dinner. Eliza felt odd when she realized she was the only person in the room being served a portion of real food. The rest of the denizens of WhitbyHall sat before empty plates, with tall, spiral glasses of the house vintage in front of them. Perhaps sensing her unease, Megan served a healthy portion of the lamb stew she had prepared and sat down beside Eliza.

"Lord Severn enjoys having the servants join him at dinner," she announced brightly.

"Will your sons be joining us?" Eliza asked. It would be delightful to have a bunch of living beings eating with her. She was feeling very singularly human tonight.

"Oh, my boys went for a run. And they're not me sons, ducky, just me boys. Me mates, as we say here. Part of the Bloodthorn Pack." She fluttered her hand nervously and looked over at Ian. "Or, rather, Lord Severn's pack."

Lord Ian, who had been explaining some intricate vampire etiquette to Cesar, stopped to explain his relationship with the Bloodthorn Pack. Whitby Hall had had a long history of being home to the local werewolf packs. Ian's wife, Lady Catherine, had protected the wolves when the Spanish Inquisition came pounding on their door. As a result, the wolves were bound by a loyalty oath to the Master of the Moor.

"Lady Catherine sounds like she was a remarkable woman," Eliza said.

"She was extraordinary. Progressive far beyond her time. Did you know she was a life alchemist?"

Eliza sat up straighter in her seat. "Did she have a laboratory?"

Lord Ian smiled briefly. "I shall have to show it to you this week sometime."

Edwin was quiet throughout the meal, which was very un-Edwin-like. Normally, he was a lively and outgoing man—and, of course, always charming. When they hung out with Juliana and Robert or any of their friends, he usually dominated the conversation, and he enjoyed being the center of attention. So, she knew something was up.

She meant to ask him when they got back to their room. But, after dinner, and after escorting her up to their suite, she saw the first of what would be a series of unexpected revelations that week.

* * *

"Edwin, someone's been in our room," Eliza said when she saw the table and formal setting before the giant stone hearth. A fire brewed happily in it, filling the room with a drowsy warmth that she knew was more than the wine she had drunk at dinner taking effect. She slid halfway out of her dinner wrap as she walked across the floor.

"Aye, I know," he said, closing and locking the door behind them. "I ordered it up."

The warmth must have hit him, as well. He slid out of his jacket, and as Eliza turned, she got a good look at his broad shoulders and chest encased in his pressed white shirt and tapestry waistcoat. Her heart fluttered momentarily; she'd never quite gotten over that aspect of Edwin. He was a little on the thin side, but tall, waspy, and strong. The kilt didn't hurt at all. Sometimes, she just looked at him and lost all ability to speak.

She could almost forgive him for his bizarre silence tonight and the fact that he was pretty obviously keeping secrets from her. *Almost.*

"This was you?" she asked. "Not that I'm not delightfully surprised, but you've given me this holiday. You don't need to go so overboard."

He smiled in his disarming little-boy way like he knew many naughty secrets and would tell her all of them in due time. Then he gave her a very deep, courtly bow, "Guilty as charged, Miss Book." After he straightened up, he stretched his wings a moment before folding them back carefully to keep from knocking any antiques off the shelves of their suite.

After that, he went to draw the chair for her to sit. "Please."

"Edwin, I just ate!"

"This isn't tea, love. It's dessert." He indicated the covered cake plates in the center of the table.

"I don't need dessert!" she said, patting her rather supple middle with a gloved hand. She had been a very good girl at dinner, dutifully passing up the beautiful fruit torte that Megan had served, to both of their disappointments. "I think we're both getting fat!"

Laughing, Edwin flopped down into the seat and made a villainous come-hither gesture. "Come to me, my pretty. Come sit in my lap."

"Really, Edwin," she sighed. And yet she came.

He took her by the waist and lifted her easily into his lap. He was a vampire, though, so it wouldn't have been a problem were she a two-ton elephant. Then he seized her chin in his hand, handling her almost roughly, and kissed her as if he were ravenous, as if he hadn't eaten at all. She forgot all about the fact that she felt like a bloated pig. She ringed her arms around his neck and settled closer against him, against his solidness and all his familiar hard plains. He wasn't warm, exactly, but she had grown accustomed to that. He *was* nicely muscled in all the right places, and she was generating enough heat for them both.

She started undoing his shirt buttons when he stopped her hand. "Dessert first."

"You are dessert."

"You saucy wench." He leaned forward and reached for the silver cake dome, revealing an English fruitcake heavy on the brandy. She recognized it as similar to the kind they'd had during their first honest-to-god date after returning to New York from being kidnapped by Lord Foxley during the *Gypsy Queen* debacle. She didn't think she would like the cake, but she had. Very much so.

Edwin broke off a piece of the fruitcake and offered it to her. She nibbled it shamelessly off his fingers. The sweetly citrus flavor was familiar and brought back wonderful memories of that celebratory night—and all of the very naughty things they did to each other when they got home.

"What else have you planned?" she asked, chewing in a rather unladylike way as she spoke. A few crumbs got on her chin, but he dutifully wiped them away with a napkin.

He then cupped the back of her head and kissed her, tasting the cake inside her mouth. It was a familiar old ritual. The first time he'd done it, it had thrown her. He had made her a dinner of steak and kidney pie and they had both enjoyed it—she directly and he vicariously through her. The memory made her squirm against him in a delightful way. That was another memorable night. They had explored each other in a variety of lovely and carnal ways.

"I've neglected you," he said. He kissed her cheek rather chastely, then ran his tongue along her lips in a not-so-chaste way. "I am sorry, lovey. Not much of a holiday, aye?"

"You don't neglect me, Edwin. But I am worried about you." She settled herself more comfortably against him, which was slightly difficult with the things happening below his belt. She set her hands on his chest to keep them apart—just for the moment. "I assumed that ever since the debacle with Foxley...you know, we'd be more honest with each other."

"When haven't I been honest?" he breathed in her ear. He was using his bedroom voice, wholly meant to distract her, but she was wise to his games.

"What haven't you told me? Is it Lord Ian? He hasn't propositioned you?" She swallowed. She wasn't sure how she felt about the idea of Edwin taking up with one of his past lovers. What if he asked her to join in on a threesome like in his old days? She didn't know Ian and she didn't think she was ready for that.

"That time is past. And our link—our Catherine—is long gone."

"Has he threatened you in some way?"

"Ian and I are old friends, lovey. And I'm a Vampire Lord." He tapped her on the nose. "He would not threaten me."

"Because you would destroy him, oh great Vampire Lord?"

"Because it would be a terrible breach of etiquette."

"And vampires will kill each other and literally scoop their rival's heart out with a spoon, but woe unto any who forget their manners."

He laughed at that, though the sound was strangely hollow as it rebounded around the room.

* * *

Ian hadn't needed to threaten Edwin. Edwin knew exactly what he wanted, what he expected, and he understood his obligations to his old friend.

"I don't want you to be my hound, Edwin. I want you to be The Master of the Hunt."

"You want me to slaughter your village for you. Kill your people."

"Yes. All of them. You and my hound, the Werewolf of Whitby."

"Ian..."

"You must be efficient where we were not, Edwin. You must erase them all, including the children..."

"Ian, I loved you. And Catherine. But I will not *do this evil thing. I cannot..."*

"And I cannot ride the hunt! The Fae came to this castle only a short time ago. They touched me, Edwin, and see what I have become. Edwin...Edwin, I am weak. Dying. I cannot be Catherine's hero..."

"And I cannot be Eliza's villain!"

Ian's face sharpened in that moment. "You owe me a blood debt. I intend to collect. One way or another."

"Ian..."

"It is the village or it is your Courtesan. Choose."

Edwin stopped feeding Eliza bits of cake and pulled her close, tucking her head under his chin protectively. She rested against him. It felt good to have her there, her heart thudding softly against his. Trusting him to keep her safe...

"Edwin..." she began. He could feel her concern as if it were his own. Their bloodlink was too strong, and it worked both ways. She slid her hands past his open shirt and found the place where his clockwork heart ticked along in its mechanical way. She kissed the side of his neck. "Will you talk to me?"

"Soon, love. Soon."

* * *

Cesar's suite was huge and posh. There were four rooms—an anteroom, a giant, mirrored walk-in closet area, a Grecian bathroom, and a bedroom so vast it dwarfed their entire townhouse back in New York.

It was all so beautiful, but Cesar did not know what to do with himself. He hadn't even unpacked his valise yet.

Instead of exploring the suite, he sat cross-legged on the huge, veiled, four-poster bed and stared at the vampirelifestyle.va. website, which was part of the vast Vampire Network online ("Your Source for Fashion, Food, Travel, & All Things Vampire!").

Almost everything he had learned about vampires up to this point was due to online research. The website he was reading was dedicated to bringing "The Dark Ones into the light of the modern era," so there was very little about greeting an ancient Vampire Lord, the Upyrese language, or any of the old customs. The network liked to avoid anything that made vampires look archaic—which, incidentally, they were.

He found these types of public relations tactics frustrating. Prior to joining the ranks of the undead, had been in the United States Air Force and had flown supplies to Afghanistan. Al-Qaida had used vampire soldiers of fortune to do their dirtiest work in the desert by night when it was so dark that you could hardly see your hand in front of your face. That left all of your other senses wide open—taste and smell and hearing. He remembered how vampires *tasted* on the almost perfectly clean desert night air—a wet, cold, evil taste like the reptile house at the zoo. He recalled the hot, meaty scent of their kills, the childlike sounds the soldiers made in the moments before their heads were ripped from their bodies, an act of violence executed so efficiently that they continued to scream even after they had died.

Of course, the vampires he'd faced weren't regular ones—if such things could be said about vampires. They weren't *civilized* vampires. They were hired mercenaries. Monsters. They were Orphans—that is, lesser vampires who had lost their masters in some way. Sometimes, they were weak vampires who would never become their own Lords, and, embittered by this fact, had turned killing into an art form like any other psychopath.

And, yet, those devils were now closer in kith and kin to Cesar than his old combat buddies. Maybe that was why he could not respond to letters or emails from his old friends, his ex-lovers, his sister, and, certainly, not his parents. He didn't really belong with the humans anymore. He belonged with *them*. He was one of *them*. He was like Edwin. And Ian. And Baldy. He was like those desert monsters that sometimes raped and mutilated his fellow soldiers if they stayed out in the desert after dark.

He was a vampire.

Vampire.

He kept saying the word to himself, but it never seemed to sink in properly. The word sounded so hollow, so foreign-sounding, so foreboding. Vampires were *them*. The enemy.

He was a soldier. He was Cesar Ramirez Schultz, and he'd served his country to the best of his ability. The other flyboys playfully cried "Hail Cesar!" and saluted him when he stepped into a room. He'd been a Naval Aviator, Ninth Division, aboard the *USS Pennsylvania*. He had liked the Air Force. It gave him purpose and direction while keeping him out of his parents' way. It was ideal.

One night, he and his boys responded to a distress call from a small Afghan village where one of their own—an Army Staff Sergeant—had snapped and slaughtered seventeen villagers before beheading the bodies, convinced they were all vampires. The miserable bastard had been seeing vampires everywhere since returning from desert combat. The following day, Cesar put in for an honorable discharge and took a job aboard the *Gypsy Queen* as a Night Supervisor at The Clocks, Lord Foxley's largest gambling casino.

Thankfully, he didn't actually see Foxley or any of his undead entourage, just plenty of greedy tourists, vacationers, and pretty eye-candy in the form of Pleasure Poppets. The work was okay, nothing life changing. He had only worked there three months when fate and hormones threw him carelessly into the path of Lord Edwin McGillicuddy. He'd been tired and horny and still a little hung-over from the weekend. Edwin had been tall and almost supernaturally gorgeous, with the most beautiful bedroom eyes he'd ever seen. The rest, as they say, was history.

He should have known better than to mix it up with vampires. Now, he could never return to his post at The Clocks or fly a plane in the U. S. Military because, even though vampires were now *technically* citizens, no one wanted them as co-workers, co-pilots, instructors, trench-mates, bunkmates, or friends. Vampires were...*them*.

He rubbed his shoulders. The idea left him numb, empty. It kept a buzzing of white static in his head. He tried to imagine his life going on and on, seeing centuries of human history and advancement. It was almost impossible for him to wrap his mind around that.

And if Edwin abandoned him and he went insane? He imagined killing others like those hired vampires in the desert, ripping the skin and blood and screams from his victims. He imagined driving mortal men to do the same. And, sometimes, he was appalled by his lack of reaction to that, his loss of empathy.

And that wasn't even the worse of it, because sometimes he imagined himself alone. If Edwin left him, if he became one of those Orphans, he might enjoy the violence. He might find that very interesting.

He stared at a picture of a mutilated soldier he had found on some anti-vampire website he'd gotten linked over to. He realized he had been staring at the nauseating picture for over five minutes and it hadn't even registered in his brain as something wrong. He quickly shut down the laptop, scooted off the bed, and reached for his jacket hanging over the back of the chair by his bed.

Shaken, he left the suite and took the long metal staircase to the ground floor. The Great Hall was empty, which was fine by him. He didn't want to see Baldy or Megan, or, god help him, Edwin. He didn't want to see anyone. He let himself out the bailey's south side door, but only because that was the way he'd come in, and it was the only exit he knew about.

The night was cool and felt ticklish against his face and naked chest under his jacket as he ambled along the rocky flagstones of the bailey. He sniffed the night air. He was alone, but he scented the faint, musky scent of horses far off. Except he knew it wasn't the horses he was scenting but their blood. It was all he seemed to smell now, the only thing that occupied his thoughts most of the time.

His eyes were particularly keen, more so than when he was alive. The world, no longer colorful, was now cast in brilliant shades of grey as if the night existed under a perpetually full moon. He easily spotted the footpath leading down the side of the escarpment, something that would have been treacherous for a human in the dark. He followed the long, winding path to a huge courtyard paved in flagstone, only this one was set up to serve as a stable.

He'd ridden horses when he was a boy and he'd gone camping in the Catskill Mountains with his dad in the time before they had come to hate each other. He liked horses, and the scent of them drew him on. But this stable was vastly different from the rustic, red-painted barnyards full of hay-chewing animals that he'd known as a boy. This one was as huge as a manor house and made of pale flagstone like the pavilion. The horses pawing about their outside enclosure were odd, shaggy beasts, thicker and sturdier than the horses he had ridden as a child, their manes hanging in long, lush braids almost to their feet. He wondered why they were out. He thought horses needed to be taken in at night. They did not see well, he knew, and it was difficult for them to avoid danger in the dark.

"They're night steeds," said a figure standing at the gate to the enclosure. "They are specially trained to be ridden by vampires at night."

Cesar moved cautiously toward Lord Severn's voice. The old vampire stood just outside the corral, feeding a huge bay stallion some sweet alfalfa. After the horse had taken the long, aromatic green grass, Severn patted its nose with his gloved hand. The horse snorted and backed up a step, but it wasn't Severn who had startled it. It was Cesar.

"He knows what you are," Severn said, turning to glance at Cesar. He was tall and aristocratically stunning in his dark, brushed suit, aged but not unattractive. He looked like an old British actor on TV. A pale, silvery-haired Christopher Lee from a Saturday morning horror movie, maybe.

Cesar felt his heart lurch. It took him a moment to respond. "You're one, too."

"But he knows me. I birthed him. I raised him. Would you like to touch him, lad?"

"I wouldn't want to spook him," Cesar said sadly, keeping his hands to himself. That was another aspect of vampirism he was slowly growing accustomed to. Small children and animals were beyond him now. He was dead and probably smelled that way. Nothing living or remotely good wanted to go anywhere near him. If it wasn't for Miss Eliza's offhand mothering, he'd probably have sunk into a deadly depression by now.

Severn gathered the leather halter in his hands. "Come. Touch him. But move slowly. He won't hurt you."

Cesar moved a few steps closer to the horse. At first, it rolled its eyes at him, a primordial response that made him worry. But Lord Severn must have been very strong because even though the stallion strained, he could not back up as Cesar set his bare hand on its quivering, velvet-soft nose.

"Gloves help muffle our scent a tad," Severn explained. "But Boyo has been around the block a fair bit. He doesn't much mind the smell of strange vampires."

Boyo strained. Cesar couldn't really blame him. He stopped touching the horse, and Severn released the halter. The horse immediately took off to the other side of the enclosure.

"Boyo doesn't like me," he said sadly.

Severn looked at him carefully. "Boyo doesn't know you."

Cesar swallowed nervously.

Severn smiled just a little. "You're a man of few words."

Cesar glanced up. Coming here was obviously a mistake.

"Are you afraid, whelp?" Severn asked.

Cesar centered himself. "No." He said it more forcefully than he'd meant.

Severn leaned on his cane. "It's true that I am a monster. But then, so are you. We're both the same thing, little vampire."

"No," Cesar insisted, shaking his head. "I don't do…things."

"What things?"

He didn't know how to respond to that. He just wanted to run away.

"Did Lord Edwin force you?" Severn asked softly as if he were calming one of his steeds. "Did he seduce you?"

Cesar felt a spike of sadness…and, under that, anger. "Leave me alone," he said, not caring if he was insulting an ancient Vampire Lord or not.

Severn narrowed his eyes wisely. "Would you like to see Lacy?"

He held very still, afraid to move—to even breathe.

"Come with me, lad, and I'll show you what a real monster looks like."Severn started into the stable.

After a long moment of indecision, Cesar followed him down the long, hay-strewn aisle.

| iv |

Eliza woke with a start sometime after midnight by her estimation. She started pawing at the bedside table before she remembered that she hadn't brought her trusty alarm clock, which, when activated in the morning, gave her a verbal, itemized list of everything she needed to do that day. After all, they were on holiday.

She sat up in bed, clutching the sheet against her chill. She was very naked, which was not her usual nighttime state. She liked her cotton nightgowns in summer and flannels in winter. But after they'd had their cake—or she had, anyway—one thing had led to another, and she and Edwin had had a lovely tumble before Edwin's clockwork heart began winding down for the night. She touched his mark under her ear. He had taken a few sips from her to quicken their lovemaking, but he hadn't fed. He'd said tonight was all about her pleasure.

He lay beside her, an unruly wave of auburn hair obscuring his face, the sheets bunched around his waist, dead to the world, both literally and metaphorically. Of course, all vampires "died" when they slept, only to rouse themselves eventually, usually at night, but with Edwin, it was the true death. He could not rouse himself even in an emergency. She would need to do that with the key she wore around her neck. He trusted her to do that every day, an amazing display of trust on his part.

But it was only after midnight, and that meant he'd had less than two hours of rest. He would need a few more for his heart to reset before she reactivated him.

She started resting her cheek against his lifeless chest when she detected footsteps in the hallway outside leading unhurriedly away from their room. That wasn't so unusual in a place this size with so many people moving about, she was sure, but she was almost certain someone had been *in their room* in the seconds before she'd awakened.

The closing of the bedchamber door had roused her, she decided while she lay silent, listening intently to the heavy steps growing faint. She thought about winding Edwin up and telling him about that, but then she wondered if she was being silly. She didn't want to come off like the neurotic governess in *The Turn of the Screw*, panicking about the things in her head.

She slid out of bed, wincing a little as she did so—she really needed an ice bag—and stood up, then shivered from the chill of the room. She went to the bureau and opened the top drawer, found the flannel nightgown she had brought, and slid it over her head. Next, she clicked on a light and looked around the room. The sudden brightness certainly wouldn't be a bother to Edwin.

The table and cake platter were as they had been when they'd retired, and their clothing was scattered about, but one thing stood out to her. She moved around the bed to Edwin's side and checked to make certain she was right.

Her little black flapper dress was gone. She made a circuit of the room, checking every placewhere she thought it might have fallen, but it was gone. Who would have taken her dress and why?

Well, this was simply too much!

Eliza found her robe and shrugged into it. Then she jammed her feet into her fuzzy moccasins and stepped out into the hallway.

The castle had a mostly open floor plan, like an enormously posh hotel back in New York. She leaned over the safety rail. The darkness of the Great Room lay far below her. A set of stairs curled upward to the next story, made of some luminescent material that emitted its own faint ghost light. The light increased when it detected the weight of a footfall, so all the stairs in the castle were alight at night if you climbed them. She saw no light from below, but from somewhere above, she could make out the faint, flickering illumination of someone ascending to the next level.

She started up the stairs in pursuit of her possible dress-snatcher, the stairs flickering beneath her silent feet. She wondered who it was she was pursuing and why they had stolen her clothes.

The stairwell spiraled up two or three floors. She passed many rooms in the interim, but they all looked dark and empty. One was probably Cesar's room, but she didn't know which one or even which floor he was on.

The flickering lights grew brighter as she caught up to the person above her—and then, abruptly, they stopped as she came upon a large figure coming down the stairwell toward her. It took her a moment to recognize it as Megan.

"Ducky, what can I do for you?" she asked innocently.

"Megan." She couldn't see much in the near-perfect dark with only the glow of the stairs to soften the edges of the woman's features, but she reminded herself that she was speaking to a werewolf who could undoubtedly see her perfectly fine in the dark. "I was wondering what was up there." She pointed to some vague place over Megan's shoulder.

"That would be the tower and storage rooms," Megan explained simply.

"There's a tower room?"

"Aye," Megan answered in a perfectly civilized voice.

"Do you often visit the tower room at night?"

"Sometimes" was all she answered.

She recalled that Megan was the castle Chatelaine. It seemed everyone here had their secrets and no intention of revealing any of them anytime soon. So, she said, "I think my gown is missing." She looked Megan over, but her hands were empty.

"Missing?"

"Gone," Eliza said. "As in…not in my room." She waited for Megan to move, but she stayed as she was, completely blocking Eliza's way up the stairs. There was no going up there tonight, she decided.

"Did you put it out to be laundered? We have that service here."

"I was wearing it up until bedtime."

Megan tilted her head. "I shall endeavor to find your garment for you tomorrow, Miss Book. I regret to say I'll be indisposed tonight."

"You're going out? At this hour?"

Megan seemed to smile, or her posture did, anyway. "It's my time to howl."

"Oh." Eliza waited, but Megan made no move to let her pass. Finally, she turned and started down the steps once more. What a very peculiar household!

* * *

Severn stopped at a stall at the end of the stables and stood looking down at the occupant.

Cesar paused. The smell of blood and other animal fluids was heavy on the air. He decided he didn't want to move any closer to the stall. The smell was sick. He did not want to look at a sick animal.

He had just decided to turn and leave when a hackle-raising howl that was nothing at all like a corny horror-movie wail sounded over the surrounding moors. It sounded so real, so close…primal.

"Jesus," he said, listening. He decided he didn't want to meet the owner of that howl, not out in the dark on his own.

"It is only my wolves," Severn said, unconcerned. "Megan has joined her boys for a midnight run."

"The werewolves."

"Are you afraid?"

"They're werewolves," he said, instinctively clutching his elbows. He had only seen one transformed werewolf back in his old combat days—a soldier who had been bitten but hadn't told anyone and had broken down in the middle of a firefight—but it had been enough for him. It wasn't so much scary as painful to watch as every bone in the soldier's body had broken simultaneously. He did not want to meet another one. He did not want to see that grotesquery ever again.

"You do realize that even as a baby vampire, you're at least twenty times stronger than the strongest werewolf?" Severn said.

"It doesn't feel that way," Cesar admitted.

"Has Edwin taught you anything at all?"

Cesar opened his mouth, then closed it. How he hated Edwin. The vapid, disinterested glances he threw Cesar's way, the short answers that answered nothing at all. And he hated himself for expecting more than that, for wanting more. At the same time, he felt an irrational desire to jump at Severn, to claw his face for saying those things about his master as if it were a personal attack on his person. He couldn't understand how he could feel so hopelessly distant from Edwin and yet remain so emotionally chained to him.

Severn narrowed his eyes in understanding. Even in the almost perfect dark, Cesar saw that. "I apologize. That was bad form. I mean no insult to your master, whelp."

"He's not my master," Cesar snapped much more angrily than he'd expected to feel.

Severn inclined his head. "Your Lord then. Your *maker*." He paused and almost smiled. "Your connection to Lord Edwin is strong. I expect you feel what he feels most of the time, if you stop to think about it. When he hurts, you hurt. When he hungers, so too do you hunger. Am I right?"

Cesar stared down at his feet and worked at not shivering. "I don't want this. I chose it, but I don't want it anymore. I want to go home." Suddenly, irrationally, he wanted to cry. He wanted to see his friends, his mom, and even his dad, even though he and his old man fought about everything when they were together. He suddenly had to hold back the tears threatening to spill from his eyes.

"Cesar. Come."

Cesar went with the old vampire, and Severn took him gently by the elbow and guided him forward so his senses were overwhelmed with the sickly sweet stink of a hurting animal. It filled his world, and it would have made him weep, had he been capable of it.

"What's wrong with her?" he asked, staring down at the quivering form lying on the straw under a heavy blanket.

"She was blinded by an intruder. Her eyes cut out."

"*What?*" he cried in outrage. "*Why?*"

"Because there are monsters in this world. Because people come here and they hurt my horses sometimes."

"But...why?"

"They want to hurt me, but they cannot. So they hurt what I love."

Cesar swallowed. Suddenly, his throat was very dry.

Severn moved closer so the front of his body was just touching the back of Cesar's. He was cold.

"Is she dying?" Cesar asked.

"Yes. The stress and blood loss have been too great. But we have done what we can to help her, to sedate her." Severn put his large bony hand on Cesar's shoulder. "I would like you to end her suffering for me."

"How?" Cesar asked, appalled.

"How do you think?"

Cesar shook his head. "I can't do that."

"It would help her. Don't you want to help her?"

"It's horrible."

Severn reached around and opened the stall door. He moved with more grace than Cesar expected. Before he even knew what was happening, Severn had guided him inside. In seconds, they were kneeling on either side of the giant animal's body. Severn showed him the place. It was not where he had expected it.

"You would hurt her if you bit her neck." He took Cesar's hand and moved it across the quivering, cooling body to the long, strong back leg, stopping at the place behind the horse's knee. "There. I promise. She won't feel anything. It will be like going to sleep for her."

He could feel the blood moving under the quivering skin. He lowered his head and placed his cheek against the spot. The pulse was thunderous in his ears. It was terrible, fascinating. He turned his head and licked a small spot.

"Don't bite," Severn said. "You'll distress her."

"I can't reach it."

Severn leaned over and produced what looked like the world's thinnest scalpel. He incised the spot with practiced ease, very deeply, and the little wound immediately filled with bright red life.

Cesar loved the horse—pitied her. But the moment he scented the blood, he realized he loved the blood more.

It took longer than he thought. Somehow, he expected it to be quick like in the horror movies, but it wasn't like that at all. He drank and stopped and drank some more. The warm blood roughed his mouth and cheeks. It made his hair stick to his face. It tasted sweet and metallic and fiery. He drank until his stomach cramped. There was still more blood, but he was full at last. He sat back and looked up at Severn watching him so intently.

"She's gone. She's been gone for a while. You did well."

The praise elated Cesar. "She's still warm," he said, running his hand lovingly over her hind leg.

"You're warmer," Severn told him, touching Cesar's bloodied cheek.

Cesar looked down at the beautiful horse, realized what he had done, and suddenly threw up in the corner of the stall. He sobbed tearlessly.

He immediately stood up and ran. He felt warmer, faster, and stronger, even after purging up some of the blood. It was nothing at all like when he finished a meal of synthetic blood, which left him drowsy but not energized. He stopped and rubbed at his cheeks, looked at the smears of blood on them, and pulled his jacket off. He felt like he was burning up suddenly, as if he had some kind of fever, but he didn't feel sick at all. He wondered what human blood was like...

Severn caught Cesar at the waist near the stable door. Cesar whipped around, his wings beating frantically at the air and his teeth bared in a defensive gesture. He came face to face with Lord Severn. Then his back slammed into the wall with enough force to shake the whole stone structure. He didn't feel a thing—no pain, certainly no fear.

Severn pressed him back against the wall. Cesar felt his heart trip the way it had one night when a friend gave him a spot of acid at a rave in downtown Brooklyn. That night, the whole room felt like it was pulsing with neon and electricity, as if he was living inside the heart of a giant video game. He hadn't liked it then, the loss of control. But now, he didn't care. Now, the night had all smooth, velvety edges, no lights, no colors, and it felt both cool and hot on his skin. He groaned at the sensation. It was as if the night was kissing him intimately all over.

He looked into the old vampire's eyes and saw darkness and depth and more darkness. He saw an unbreathable sadness unlike anything he had ever experienced in his mortal life. He should have been afraid, he thought. Surely, this was all a trap. He might be experiencing his last moments of life...or afterlife...or whatever this was.

Then Severn leaned forward, clutched his chin, and licked the blood off his cheeks.

He wasn't afraid. Why should he be afraid? he wondered. Severn himself had stated that Cesar was stronger than twenty werewolves. And, now, finally, he felt it. There was nothing to be afraid of. Death couldn't touch him; he *was* death—dark-winged, eternal. The warmth of the blood in his belly moved like whiskey, forcing sluggish power and a slow, unprecedented happiness through his body. Suddenly, nothing mattered, and nothing was outlawed. There was no fear, no loneliness. For the moment, he was truly happy.

Cesar squirmed as Severn's tongue swirled avidly over his face and lips. It was like being licked by a lovable puppy. He laughed, though there was nothing especially puppy-like about the way Severn kissed him. There was also nothing of love in that kiss. It was all hunger, all pleasure, and a little bit of pain as Severn's teeth grazed his tongue and snapped at his mouth.

It was honest. And Cesar didn't care. He had long since given up on the concept of love. And ever since his mortal death, pain had ceased being uncomfortable. It had become, instead, a curiosity.

Lord Severn held him in place while they made out like a pair of randy teenagers. He might have worried about the idea of a vampire's teeth so close to the nervous pulse in his throat, but he decided he didn't much care if Severn bit his throat out. He'd lost everyone, including himself. And Edwin was never his, not really. No one was. He was alone. What did it matter?

Severn growled like a wild animal against the sensitive spot under his ear. Cesar gasped at the sensation, the sweetness of pleasure and death so close. He fisted his hands in Ian's suit coat. It had been like this with Edwin in the beginning, the wanting and the anticipation. The drowning he had wanted so badly.

"He didn't force me," Cesar whispered so low that he didn't know if Severn could even hear him past the low groans of pleasure they were making and the blood they were smearing between themselves. "He asked."

"But you wanted it," Severn whispered in a voice not quite human. "They always want it."

When Ian's hand went to his lower half, he shuddered and withdrew. He hadn't had sex for over six months, not since the night Edwin changed him. He wondered if everything…worked all right. That was something else Edwin had neglected to explain. What if he couldn't do it? Or, what if he did it all wrong? He had no one to ask these questions of.

Severn, sensing his unease, eased back and said with a light, affectionate stroke over his hair, "And now, whelp?"

Cesar hung against the wall, his heart ticking in his throat. He was tired of being afraid. Always so afraid. "Yes," he said, finally. His teeth were sharp in his mouth. He wondered what Severn tasted like—hot, strong whiskey like the horse or chilled sweet wine like Edwin?

"Are you certain? You're no swooning maiden. I shan't be gentle with you, little vampire."

This close, Cesar was able to bury his face in Severn's long, wind-loosened hair. It smelled strangely comforting, like his pillow in the morning. He ran his fingers over the silken, silvery strands.

"I don't care," he said, amazed by the growling quality of his voice. He hardly sounded human anymore.

He *wasn't* human, he reminded himself. He was a vampire. What was there to be afraid of?

"Just take me."

Severn laughed against the shivery skin of his throat. "You American boys are a delight!"

* * *

The first thing Eliza did when she woke the following morning was to circle the room and look for the missing dress again. But it was still missing. The second thing she did was wind Edwin up.

She inserted the key, giving it six turns. The mechanism seemed to take longer than usual to make a full rotation. Then Edwin took a deep, sharp breath and lunged awake. "Blimey, I hate that," he said, falling back on the pillow. He touched his heart and squeezed his eyes shut for a long moment.

"There's been pain?" she asked with concern.

Edwin gasped. "There's always pain like a cramp letting go."

She put her ear to his chest and listened for a long moment. "There doesn't seem to be anything wrong. Unless it's what we discussed that one time."

He narrowed his eyes, which meant he either didn't remember or didn't want to.

"About your body eventually rejecting the mechanism."

"Ah." He sat up against the pillow and worked hard at keeping the concern from his face. He did not like to show her how afraid he was sometimes. It was his only conceit. Too often, Edwin liked to keep his own counsel. She expected it was part of his whole tough-guy gangster image, as well as a knee-jerk reaction he had developed while working as Lord Foxley's Enforcer for almost two hundred years. Foxley did not tolerate weakness in anyone, even himself.

"Do you think it is a possibility?" he finally asked.

"You're a wind-up vampire, Edwin. Nothing like you exists in this whole world. I don't even know what's possible." She sat back, regarding him carefully. She wasn't going to mince her words with him; she knew he wouldn't appreciate that. "I barely understand how it works. And, I'll be honest, there may come a time when we both need to return to the *Gypsy Queen* so you can have a...tune-up, so to speak."

Edwin shuddered visibly at the possibility of returning to his master, who had invented the device that kept him alive. They both knew it was unlikely that Lord Foxley would let him go as easily as he had the first time.

Then she thought about something that Lord Severn said last night. "Severn said that Lady Catherine was a life alchemist and that she had a lab. It might be worth exploring. Maybe she has some notes that might help me learn how to maintain your pacemaker without us needing to get Foxley involved."

She paused, looking deep into what she felt were troubled vampire's eyes. "I'll ask him to show me the lab today."

"Is something wrong?" he asked after a moment.

She shook her head. "I don't like him, Edwin."

"I promise Ian is a perfect gentleman. He's entirely devoted to Catherine's memory."

"That's not what I mean."

"Then what, lovey?" He took her hand.

She shrugged. "He reminds me of my own Lord in some ways. So proper on the outside, but if you were alone with him for even one moment..." She shuddered. "And the way he was looking at Cesar last night at dinner..."

Edwin smiled but it did not touch his eyes. "Cesar is a big boy. He can handle himself."

She was about to protest that, so he leaned forward and kissed her gently and thoroughly to distract her. "You always taste so good, even in the morning," she admitted. "No morning mouth. It isn't fair."

"It's just one of me many charms," he said in his best phony Irish accent.

She smiled against his mouth and tousled his hair. "We'd better get up before your *charms* delay our schedule." She glanced down at his lap.

With a longsuffering sigh, Edwin fell back on the pillows. "It's called a holiday, love." He drew the last word in the air. *H-o-l-i-d-a-y.* "It means we don't work. We have no schedules."

"*You* have no schedule," she said, going to the wardrobe and flinging it open. "Except for...what is it, golf? Which you play abhorrently. Well, I don't plan to stand around on the green all day while you chase a little white ball that keeps escaping you. I mean to see this lovely countryside."

"I don't play golf abhorrently," he sniffed.

"Excuse me. *Hideously.* Two hundred years and you can't even do eighteen holes of mini-golf."

"I do eighteen holes just fine," he said, sitting up in bed. "Old Tom Morris himself taught me in 1861, and he was the Tiger Woods of his time. Besides, I've been playing the Wii." He made a clumsy teeing-off motion to prove it.

She rolled her eyes as she sorted through the wardrobe, looking for the proper ensemble. "Very well. Chase your balls and play your golf abhorrently. Now, I plan to visit the village with Megan."

"What are you doing with Megan in town?" he asked, falling back on the bed and pillowing his head on his arms.

"I will be shopping, spending money, and having *high tea*." She turned and grinned at him, holding a long white satin garden dress against herself. She felt a delicious thrill; she had bought the dress just for this occasion. Just for tea. "Do you like it?"

"I like what's underneath it better," he said, giving her his sexy, lazy, weekend look.

"Edwin, really," she said. "I've never had English high tea before."

"Yes, you have. With me."

"That was America. I'll be doing it here in England, which makes it *real* English high tea."

Now it was Edwin's turn to roll his eyes. He sat up in bed, which made the sheet slide away. Eliza took a moment to admire the view before swinging back around to the wardrobe and checking her reflection in the mirror on the inside of the door. She wondered if she ought to wear a hat today. And would gloves be proper? She had so many questions! She would need to ask Megan.

"I still would like to know what happened to my dress from last night."

"What happened to your dress from last night?"

She told him about her cocktail dress going missing while Edwin shaved and brushed his teeth in the bathroom. She finished by saying, "Don't you think it's peculiar? Why would someone steal my dress? It wasn't even special or expensive." She looked glumly into the mirror at the whiteness of the tea gown. "I bought it used, but I really liked that dress."

"I'm sure no one stole it," he said, stepping back into the room and reaching for his crumpled trousers on the floor.

In the mirror, Eliza offered him a disgruntled look so he knew she wasn't pleased that he was putting on yesterday's clothes. She had chosen a summery grey tweed suit and the right shirt to go with it, which he dutifully reached for now.

While she showered in the bathroom, she listened to him struggling into his daywear. "It probably just got moved," he shouted over the roar of the water. "Or laundered!"

When she emerged warm and wet from the shower, a towel wrapped securely around her hair and body, Eliza told him, "Megan doesn't want me going up to the tower room."

Edwin sat down on the divan at the foot of the bed to tie his shoes. "Then don't go up to the tower room."

"What's in the tower room?"

"How the bloody hell should I know? Maybe something dangerous like the wiring or the main computer mainframe that controls the castle. Or maybe it's a psychotic hunchback they've got locked up there."

"Edwin!"

"If Megan doesn't want you near the tower room, love, then don't go near the tower room."

Eliza gave him a surly look. "Well, I mean to interrogate Megan further on the matter. I'm sure she's hiding something!" She dropped her towel and began to dress, which caused Edwin to automatically swivel around on the divan to watch her.

"I'll be in the village of Whitby until the early afternoon, then Megan and I will be back here for tea in the bailey. While you golf with Ian, will you please mention my interest in the alchemist lab? And maybe find out about the tower room?"

She was dressed within minutes, hair pinned up in a very proper coiffure, she thought. She wanted to be on her way soon!

Before she left, Edwin stepped up to her, took her by the shoulders, and kissed her on the nose. "I shall."

Eliza smiled. But she didn't mention the lingering darkness in Edwin's eyes. She suspected it wouldn't be golf the two vampires would be discussing today.

| V |

Megan was as exuberant as a schoolgirl as she drove them into the village of Whitby. She chattered on about various legends and old landmarks, and she insisted they just *had* to visit the Wolf's Head Lodge. She said it was quite dreary but full of local color.

The way she talked made Eliza wonder if there wasn't an alternative reason she was showing Eliza the sights, Primarily, to get her out of the castle for the day.

Eliza looked the other woman over. She was dressed in a huge, nightmarish chiffon dress of pale lavender pinched at the waist, with big bell sleeves. Her auburn hair was tucked up under a wide-brimmed white hat that matched her dress not at all. Eliza decided they absolutely *had* to visit the local dressmakers before they made their way back.

Megan smiled but kept checking her appearance in the rear-view mirror of the Slipstream car she was driving. It was huge and rambling, a novel vehicle from circa 1970-something, but Megan kept it in perfect working condition.

"Is the Wolf's Head where your beau works?" Eliza asked with a grin from the passenger seat.

Megan flushed bright pink, which was rather becoming on her fair, freckled face. Her brown eyes paled to wolf-amber for a moment before returning to their normal color. Eliza knew she was right.

"Oh, my, it looks like rain," she said, glancing around the countryside before turning her attention back on Eliza. She gave her passenger a nervous laugh. "Please don't say anything to Lord Severn or the others."

"Why would I say anything? And why would it be any business of theirs if you're sweet on someone down in the village?" Then Eliza thought about that. "You are a free woman? I mean, you aren't married?"

Megan's face fell, briefly. "I was, long ago. But Jonathan died."

"I'm sorry."

"It was long ago—long before you were even born, ducky." She laughed at that, then added, "We wolves age very slowly, you see. I'm one-hundred and thirty-eight years old."

"Oh, my. You *have* aged well," Eliza laughed. Megan didn't look much older than she was. "So are you...you know, *his* wolf?"

"Lord Severn's? Oh, no. I only work for him." Megan turned her full attention back to the road. They drove along for another half mile before she explained. "It's...you see, his name is Mickey. He owns the Lodge." She glanced over at Eliza. "He's not like your Edwin or anything. He's a widower and he's...well, Mickey."

"Tell me what Mickey is like," she said, hoping to encourage Megan.

Megan frowned. "Ah..."

"What's wrong?"

Megan shrugged, then looked away.

"He isn't gay?"

"No!" She turned to glance at Eliza with stricken eyes. "It's...Mickey's human, you see." Megan turned back to the road. "And I'm not."

"Ah."

"I supposed it's different in the States, more progressive. No one cares who you're with there. But here…well, everyone is very set in their ways."

"Where I come from, they care, believe me," Eliza admitted. "There's still a lot of hate in the States, especially since the Vampire Bill passed. Edwin, for instance, couldn't possibly get a regular job. Nobody wants vampires in the workforce. The same is true of Cesar. He couldn't re-join the Air Force even if he wanted to. The U. S. military won't allow vampires to serve. Don't ask, don't tell. Except, well…that's not exactly something you can hide."

Megan looked surprised. "What about werewolves?"

"The States are even stricter about shapeshifters than they are about vampires, which is funny when you think about it. I mean, vampires are *far* more dangerous, but the U.S. makes concessions for them because they *look* human."

"Vampires don't look more human," Megan said and shivered. Eliza had the feeling that the woman had seen the worst of that lot. "Vampires are the most dangerous monsters in the world precisely because they're the most human…"

Then she glanced over. "I apologize. That was thoughtless of me…"

Eliza waved it away with one gloved hand. "That's quite all right. I know exactly what you mean. Edwin can be very sweet, but sometimes I wonder what he's capable of. He's not very old, but he *is* powerful, more than he lets on."

"He's Lord Foxley's Heir, isn't he?"

"Yes."

"They say Lord Foxley is the most powerful vampire on earth. He's certainly the oldest. Twelve thousand years. Can you *imagine* living for twelve thousand years?"

"No," she admitted. "I can't."

She tried to imagine Edwin at twelve thousand years, but she couldn't even imagine him at a thousand. By then, of course, she would have been long gone. She wondered what kind of a man he would be in a thousand years. By then, would he have found someone else? Maybe several someones? The thought was fatally depressing, and she almost didn't hear Megan's next question.

"Has it worked out between you two? You and Edwin?"

"Yes," she said at once. Then she rethought that. "Usually it does. But we have our moments like every other couple, I suppose. Edwin likes to keep secrets. I like to pull them out of him."

Megan nodded and grinned. "All men are like that. That's nothing uniquely vampire-like. I wonder if Mickey has secrets."

"Does he know about you? About what you are?"

Again, Megan blushed. "I expect so. I've worked as Lord Severn's Chatelaine for over a hundred years now, and there must be stories. He must know."

"I see."

"So, even if Mickey does like me...well, I guess it wouldn't really work out, would it? I mean, he'd eventually grow old and die, and I'd just keep going, wouldn't I?"

Eliza was unsettled by how Megan's thoughts mirrored her own. "Unless...you know, you changed him. So he was like you."

Megan bit her lip. "There's a thought."

"Would you do it?" Eliza asked. "I mean...if you loved someone, would you change him?"

Megan turned off the dirt path they were on and onto the main road through town, the little, now-familiar gingerbread buildings closing in around them. "I'm not sure. I expect I would if he asked. What about you? What if Edwin offered? *Has* he offered to make you his Heir?"

Eliza swallowed hard and looked over the sugar-white, perfectly picturesque little antique shops and inns they were passing on the way to their first port of call: breakfast at Annie's Tea Shop.

"We haven't discussed it." She didn't add that that was mostly because he knew how she felt about vampires, with the exception of him. She'd attended her Lord's Court for only a year. But during that time, no part of her body had been her own. There were days when she woke up and she still couldn't believe what she had meekly accepted as treatment at the hands of her master, not that she'd had much of a choice at the time. Back then, she'd been nothing but a living blood doll, an orifice to be violated anytime and anywhere her master wished it...though the politically correct term was *Poppet*. It sounded prettier and more acceptable than "blood slave."

She had no doubt that Edwin would make her his Heir if she requested it. Juliana and Robert had discussed converting Juliana to a nonhuman state, with mixed results. Juliana had so far remained undecided, but every time Eliza saw her BFF, she could see a little more of Robert's were-leopard culture seeping into her, everything from the clothes she wore to the words she spoke and the gestures she used. She knew it was only a matter of time for Juliana. And, perhaps, herself.

She was almost twenty years old now. Edwin was nineteen when Foxley changed him—barely more than a child by modern standards. Right now, they looked like they belonged together, but in another ten years—or twenty years—things would be very different. She wondered if Edwin would want her then, or if he would merely keep her around out of pity or habit. She knew that even with her enhanced Poppet genes and slower aging, she would not be able to compete with the beautiful young men and women who would eventually turn his head.

After parking the Slipstream, she and Megan ducked inside the door of the tea shop—the doorway was only a little larger than she was and Megan had to duck very low—and discovered they had almost the entire café to themselves. Megan said that at this time of day, most of the village was busy with their farms and livestock, the lifeblood of their existence in a mostly agricultural land.

They bought coffees and croissants, though Megan seemed a little off her feed this morning. She said she was still colicky from the night before. "I shouldn't have eaten that whole buck." She covered her mouth in a ladylike way with her napkin to prevent a hiccup, then blushed. "I always make such a sow out of myself, and then I have a food hangover the next morning."

After breakfast, Megan took Eliza to the candle shop where they made custom orders, then an antiques auction located in a drafty, converted barn full of locals. They stood together in the back and watched the fierce bidding of an estate sale. Eliza noted antique highboys, Edwardian silverware, and even a pen of pigs being auctioned off to various local farmers and business owners. Eliza won an antique hair comb for herself and a stickpin for Edwin's cravat—not antiques, but more like souvenirs. She stood very still and tried not to say too much, afraid the locals would notice she was American, while Megan took her pound notes to pay for the items at the auction window, but a funny itch between her shoulder blades made her turn.

A tall and very young blonde girl of about eleven years was standing by the wall, clutching a ragged antique doll. She was watching Eliza with wide grey eyes. Eliza glanced around, but the girl seemed to be completely alone, and just about any young woman in the room could have been her mother since almost all of the women in the room were tall and fair like the girl. In fact, there wasn't a single villager who was short and dark like she was. Eliza waited, but after a few minutes, no one stepped up to claim the girl.

Concerned, Eliza scooted over to the wall and sank to one knee. "Hey, button, are you lost?"

The girl looked her over warily as if her parents had told her many times not to speak to strangers. But eventually, curiosity overcame her and she lifted her hand and reached out to touch a few spiraling strands of Eliza's inky black hair, most of which was coiled up under her hat, though a few strands had come loose. She quickly dropped her finger to Eliza's cheek. "Your skin is the same color as my mare," she said.

Eliza had to remind herself of where she was. This wasn't New York. The villagers of Whitby didn't have a lot of black girls living in town, she supposed. They were painfully sheltered. Still, there *was* TV and the Internet.

"Is that so?" she said.

The girl's eyes went wide. "Are you a savage?"

Eliza jerked back, gritting her teeth in anger. She didn't like this very rude girl so much now. But before she could respond, a woman rushed up and grabbed the girl by the shoulder, hard.

"What are you doing?" the girl's mother asked, shaking her.

"I was talking to the nice lady, mum," said the girl, pointing to Eliza. "Look at her skin! She's the same color as Chestnut."

Eliza glanced up at a tall, slender woman with bright yellow hair and somber blue eyes. She was about to explain how rude and sheltered her child was when her voice caught in her throat at the woman's expression. She looked positively frightened.

"You're not from here," said the woman.

Eliza stood up slowly, looking around. Suddenly, she was half-afraid her presence in the auction hall would start some kind of riot. But before anyone noticed the exchange, Megan pushed in front of Eliza and glared at the woman. "I think perhaps you ought to take your child and go, madam," she suggested.

The woman held Megan's eyes in a surprisingly hostile way but quickly backed away, dragging the girl with her, as any smart person would if confronted by a giant, angry lady werewolf. Eliza decided there was something to be said about giant lady werewolves.

"Locals," Megan said and spat on the floor. "Everyone lives under a bleedin' rock!" She added a few choice profanities that Eliza had never heard from a lady's mouth before but had quite a lot to do with barnyard animal testicles.

The other locals had finally noticed the ruckus.

"Congratulations on proving to a stranger what a lot of uneducated hicks you all are," she told them, then turned to Eliza. "This is the reason I don't like coming to town."

"Perhaps we should get back to Whitby Hall," Eliza said once they were back in the car.

"Absolutely not. We will not let this spoil our afternoon!" Megan proclaimed.

They stopped at the one dressmaker in town. Megan picked out a big, red travesty of a dress until Eliza suggested a more conservative A-line dress in a deep blue color that complemented her red hair and the pink in her cheeks. Eliza then removed and discarded the odious white hat and pinned Megan's hair up properly with the antique comb she had bought at the auction house.

"Oh, my," Megan said, looking at herself in the three-way mirror. She was blushing furiously, her hands on her cheeks. The blue suited her. "You are like a fashion angel, Eliza."

Eliza laughed at that.

Afterward, Megan showed her a wool factory where the town made its own yarn and then, afterward, a winery. The incident in the auction hall continued to haunt Eliza as the tour guide guided them through the vat room, but Megan seemed to read her mind. Or maybe just her face.

She shook her head and said, again, "Locals. I'm so ashamed."

Adjacent to the winery was the brewery where Lord Severn had his special house brew manufactured. Eliza was somewhat dismayed to learn that after the sheep were processed through the wool factory, they were sent onto the brewery for "milking." She hadn't known that Great Britain still used animal blood in their synthetic blood recipes.

Megan was unfazed by the process. Then again, Megan ran through the forest naked and ate bucks until she had a food hangover. Eliza ordered some bottles of wine for herself and a few bottles of the house brew for Edwin.

Megan was visibly excited when they got back into the Slipstream. She kept glancing at herself in the rearview mirror. Their last stop before returning to the castle would be the Wolf's Head Lodge.

It was a squat stone structure that looked positively medieval. Hanging over the steel-banded wooden door was a plaque with an engraved wolf's head on it and the name of the tavern. The inside was as dark as a cave, even at noontime. Authentic-looking longswords and shields decorated the flagstone walls, and there was a hearth as big as the one in *Citizen Kane*. Eliza had a fantasy of the ancient people of Whitby roasting a full boar across the fire with room to spare for a cauldron or two.

They took their seats at a table near the back, under the subtle amber glow of a modern Tiffany lamp. Barmaids in rustic costume dresses fluttered by in their long skirts, the tops of her breasts pressing against their corseted bodices.

"Oy, Susie! Two stouts!" Megan called to the barmaid behind the bar, pounding the table before her like a seaman. Then she seemed to recall her new, ladylike manners and turned to face Eliza. "Or would you prefer something more civilized, ducky? Wine?"

"No, that's fine," she told Megan. "I've always wanted to try authentic English stout."

The brew was potent. After only two sips, Eliza started feeling giddy. They sat together, snickering about the locals and waiting until after one in the afternoon when Mickey took over pub duties from Susan.

Megan seemed to grow more energized when he stepped into the room. He wasn't what Eliza expected. He was Susan's father, and he was small, stout, and completely white-haired, with a dirty apron tied around the large bulk of his belly. Then Eliza recalled that Megan was over a hundred years old; Mickey must look like a teenager to her. But he smiled warmly and greeted them at their table when he saw them.

"Canna get you pretty lasses anything?" he asked with a deep, long country brogue.

Megan was too tongue-tied to answer, so Eliza requested two more stouts. She had decided she very much liked authentic English stout.

After Mickey had gone to fetch another couple of pints, Eliza turned to Megan, who had lowered her head and was staring at her hands on the tabletop as if they were the most interesting things in the world. "Why don't you at least talk to him?"

"I can't, Eliza," she whined with defeat. "I just can't."

"Megan, he seems to think you're lovely!"

Megan pulled her glove off her left hand and looked at it. The two middle fingers of Megan's rather large hand were the same length. "I'm not lovely, Eliza. I'm...deformed."

"You are *not* deformed. And if you think that, then you may as well say the same thing about Edwin...or Lord Severn...or Baldy!"

"Well, Baldy does look kind of deformed, don't you think?"

"Megan!"

Megan grinned in response.

"Go talk to him," Eliza told her. "You must!"

"I can't," she whined.

"If you don't, I will. I'll tell him you're madly in love with him."

"You would not!"

"I would."

Megan gave her a petulant look. Then she slowly climbed to her feet, ran a hand skittishly over her hair, and started a little unsteadily toward the bar.

* * *

They played only three holes before Edwin got his golf ball stuck in Lord Severn's homemade sand trap. That was something of a record even for him. Lord Severn, standing across the trap from him, tossed him a new ball from the endless pockets of his suit coat.

Edwin caught it one-handedly.

"Handicap."

Edwin stared at the old vampire a long moment before conceding. Were he in a better and more sporting mood, he would have declined the ball, but he really wasn't into the game. He turned and glanced across the green to where Cesar and Baldy were resting under one of the well-groomed weeping willows rippling in the breeze, golf bags resting at their sides. Sunshine shone down on them all.

Cesar looked uncomfortable and kept glancing up at the sky as if someone—God, maybe—would strike him down for being out in the daylight even though he knew full well that the enhanced stratospheric UV shields that Ian owned were up. Generated by strategically placed satellites high in orbit, they directed ultra-powerful polarized shields that entirely encapsulated his estate and protected its occupants against ultraviolet light and radiation. The technology cost him millions of pounds every year just so he could spend a few hours a day out in the daylight. Baldy had briefed them all on the specifics of the relatively new technology, but Cesar didn't look overly confident in it.

"The longer you procrastinate, the more money you cost me," Ian pointed out. He stood in his natty white golf suit, hands resting on his favorite driver as he used it in lieu of his cane.

"You pay for the shields by the hour?" Edwin asked.

Ian smiled nicely. "Yes."

Edwin tossed the ball he held into the sand trap.

Ian reached into his pocket and threw Edwin a new one. "I can keep this up all day, squire."

"I intend to play a very long, very bad game," Edwin said.

"You know," said Ian, staring at his feet with a bitter smile, "Foxley used to talk of your...stubbornness. He didn't use that exact word, of course. He used more colorful language in regards to you, Edwin. But the point is, I never used to believe him. I used to think the little toerag was being melodramatic. But I can see his point. He was spot on with you." He glanced up. "You mean to be a little twat, don't you?"

Edwin rested his driver on his shoulder. "You'll get used to it. He did."

"I wanted to be kind. I've always liked you, Edwin. Loved you, even. I never wanted to be your Foxley."

"Let's talk about Foxley a moment—and kindness," Edwin said. "He kidnapped my woman, threatened me, and tried to destroy my life because I wouldn't be his bloody lapdog. I'd say you're graduating to Foxley status admirably, Ian. Except for one thing."

"What's that?" Ian stared down at the ball in his hand, looking bored by his guest's repartee.

"Foxley, for all his faults, was always honest with me. I always knew when the tosser was going to fuck me over—which was all of the time. With you, I can never tell."

"I'm hardly fucking you over, Prince." Ian smiled nastily. "You will know when I am fucking you over."

"I rather doubt that, old thing. I've had better lays in back alleys in the East End."

Ian's eyes darkened. "You owe me, *old thing*."

"Aye, I do." Edwin dropped the ball and putted it away from the sand trap. "But, you see, you surprised me. I expect deception from Foxley. I didn't expect it from you. We were friends." He was surprised by the pain in his voice. "We were more. Catherine's death changed you, Ian. It made you hard."

Ian's eyes flared with rage and anger. "I cannot ride the Hunt, Edwin. If I could, I would not have called in these markers. I would not have summoned you."

"You could have asked for my help. You could have gone to the High Courts. You could have come to me."

"And would you have ridden for me if I had come? If I had asked nicely?"

Edwin snorted and tried to concentrate on the ball. "No. But I would have tried to help you. I would have found you someone to ride…"

"Who? An Heir? A fool? Your Cesar?" Ian cast a sideways glance toward the stand of willows.

"Leave Cesar alone," Edwin growled, his teeth automatically sharper in his mouth. "He's only a baby. He has no idea what being a vampire is about. He has yet to descend into the depths of our backbiting and deception."

"You're neglecting him, Edwin. You've taught him nothing."

"He's a virgin. He's not ready." Edwin struck the ball too hard with the edge of the club and it shot past Ian's head by centimeters. Seconds later, it ripped through the willows and Cesar and Baldy flinched noticeably. They looked at each other and slowly stood up.

Edwin rested on the driver and glared at Ian.

"And you know this...how?"

"I'm his Lord," Edwin said only. "He's my Heir. I know."

Ian smiled in that disarming way he had. Edwin had loved that smile once. The smile of a hero. Now it looked like a painted-on sneer. "We lose things, Edwin. There's no stopping that."

"I'll put up a fight."

"You will, won't you?"

"What's mine is mine. If anyone wants to take that, they'll have to go through me first."

"Spoken like a true Vampire Lord at Court."

Edwin smiled as well, but he knew his eyes were black and feral. "There aren't many with the power to take me down, Ian."

"Bit confident, yes?"

"I'm Foxley's strongest Heir. It's not confidence; it's truth."

"And I think as Foxley's strongest Heir, you have the strength to ride the Hunt. It's why I chose you above all others."

"Catherine would be ashamed," Edwin said.

"Catherine is dead," Ian answered. His voice was flat and toneless as if he spoke of nothing—no one he had ever loved.

Edwin dropped his driver, went to Ian, and touched his face with only his fingertips. Ian flinched.

"My privateer. My pretty. How ugly you've become. If I could have taken her place, I would have. Perhaps it is your bitterness which has undone you." Edwin sought some remnant of the handsome young Englishmen he had known, some shadow in that once-beautiful face. Instead, he had this *shell*. "You hate me. You have never forgiven me."

Ian reached up and removed Edwin's hand. "I don't hate you, Edwin. I *need* you. Without you..." He let his voice trail off. They both knew the consequences of *that*.

"I'll ride your hunt," Edwin decided. "But only if you release them. Only if you can guarantee their safety."

"Your pretties."

"On your soul as an Englishmen. As Catherine's lover. That's the deal."

Ian looked satisfied. Not happy, because there was no happiness in this business, but satisfied. "You'll need to acquaint yourself with my night steeds."

"I know that."

"I shall summon the Werewolf of Whitby as your hound."

"I am sure you will be very thorough in your preparations."

"The ride must be soon. A few days, at most."

"Two more conditions." Edwin paused for emphasis. "The first is that you will not speak of this horror to anyone. Not Eliza. Not Cesar. If you do, I'll kill you. Do you believe me?"

Ian stared at him very seriously. "Do you love them?"

"They're my world. Yes, I love them."

Ian thought about that. "You have my word. I mean them no harm. I would never do to you what you did to Catherine. To me."

Edwin reached up and grasped Ian by the ascot. His fingers pressed deep—deep enough to dent Ian's windpipe so that the man expelled a polite cough. Edwin drew close to Ian, close enough to smell Cesar on his breath. Baldy was on his feet, alerted to his master's distress, but Cesar put his hand on his arm, halting him in mid-step.

"Number two, you will stop grooming my Heir," Edwin said.

"Cesar acts under his own will, Edwin. I am not influencing him in any way." Ian smiled nastily. "And, perhaps, after all, I love the whelp."

"You do not know what love is." Releasing the old vampire, Edwin walked off the green and back to the castle that seemed to float within its own distant mist.

| vi |

Edwin stopped in the doorway to the castle gardens, leaned against the casting, and watched his girlfriend and Megan sitting in their wood-slatted patio chairs, big white sunhats like halos on their heads, enjoying high English tea and girl gossip. There was an antique tea set between them, and a silver platter piled high with cucumber sandwiches and chocolate digestives. Cesar was busy pouring the ladies their tea.

Edwin remembered cucumber sandwiches, though he'd long since forgotten what they tasted like. He remembered being brought back to Foxley's manor house as a young, hungry mortal man—just a child, really—and bolting down the whole tray of sandwiches while the servants looked on in horror and Foxley laughed in delight. That was a very long time ago.

He watched his woman sharing some private girl moment with Megan and Cesar and smiling. For the moment, she was happy.

He liked to see Eliza happy. She had spent too many years being afraid, being small and hurt and hunted. Even after they were together, it had taken her a month before she stopped flinching unconsciously when he touched her. But because Eliza was a proper type of girl, she didn't often talk about that aspect of her life, the terrible things her Vampire Lord had done to her.

Eliza looked up from under her sunhat, smiled, and fluttered her white-lace-gloved hand at him. Eliza always smiled, and she always made it look genuine. Someone could hurt her in the worst possible way and she would still bloody smile that impregnable smile, the pain locked so far behind her eyes that it made him want to kill the world that had hurt her. It made him want to kill her former Lord— and he knew he would if their paths ever crossed.

And Ian. Most definitely Ian. He'd loved Ian once. But Ian had crossed a line. He'd threatened Edwin, and that was just fine. He expected greed and aggression among the other Vampire Lords— even his so-called mates.

But Ian had threatened Eliza and Cesar, and that was something entirely different. Edwin did not care if his enemies punched him or stabbed him or tried to kill him in any number of creative ways. He didn't care if they tortured him or humiliated him. He'd had it all done to him over the centuries, and worse. But a threat to his pretties would not go unanswered.

"Edwin, how was golf?" Eliza said, giving him the dazzling smile he loved so much.

"I played poorly."

"What else is new?" She checked the little mechanical remote that controlled the strength of Ian's shield service. "Come join us! The shields are at full strength."

He wanted to step out into the dazzling sunlight of the gardens, but something stopped him. He was afraid. He knew here in the doorway, his face was shadowed enough that Eliza couldn't see his worry lines and his clenched fists. But, out there, he would be naked and wide open to her scrutiny. And she would know. She always knew when he was upset or hiding something. The longer they were together, the harder it was for him to conceal anything from her.

Anyway, he needed to check on the tower room. He wanted to see if preparations were coming along all right. "I'll be along shortly. Baldy thinks he's found your dress, love!"

Eliza sat up. "Where was it?"

"Mixed in with the laundry."

"How did it get there?"

"I'm not sure, but I'll ask." And he ducked back inside the castle, leaving Eliza to her lovely sunshine.

***

After dinner, Megan and Baldy invited Edwin and Eliza to join their poker party in the castle's game room. They used cards that once belonged to Oscar Wilde himself, a gift from Wilde to Edwin...but Eliza stopped them dead in their tracks. She did not want a detailed summary of Edwin's historical conquests.

They played two hands—Eliza won both—before Edwin excused himself and announced he needed a walk in the countryside, which Eliza found rather odd. It was not a very Edwin-like thing to do. He was a very urbane vampire. Such things as walks at midnight in the country interested him not at all. And he liked poker. Back in New York, Wednesday nights were poker night for Edwin and a small number of his vampire and shapeshifter friends.

She almost rose from her seat to see to him, but Baldy immediately grasped her wrist. It wasn't a rough grab, but his hand was cold and made Eliza jump.

"Sorry," he said and grinned, trying to show he meant no offense. Unfortunately, his little catlike teeth made him look fearsome. "I was checking to see if you had any cards up your sleeve."

"I do *not* cheat, Mr. Baldy," she told him with great insult. "I'm simply on a winning streak."

"Eddie says you play poorly, Miss E."

"I do play poorly. Edwin says I get two aces and it's all over my face."

He looked at her mounting chips. "Not tonight. You're a regular poker face, Miss E."

The truth was that her mind kept wandering, which was why she was playing well for a change. "I'd like to be excused, please," she said.

"We need to up the ante," Megan stated, looking over the table.

"Strip poker!" Baldy said.

"Secret poker!" Megan said. "Every time someone loses, they have to reveal something secret, like Truth or Dare. It'll be grand! And embarrassing for Baldy."

Baldy looked worried. "I don't have any secrets. I was a gangster. You already know where all of the bodies are buried."

"Then you'll just have to strip, Baldy," Eliza said with a rueful smile to get him back. She couldn't help herself. For monsters, Megan and Baldy were terrific company.

"Oh, dear god, no!" Megan cried, covering her face with her hands. "Do you want all of the mirrors in the room to crack?"

Baldy stood up and shook his ass at her. "Wish I'd changed my shorts."

Megan looked up imploringly at Eliza. "Please don't leave me alone with Baldy's ass, Eliza."

Secret Poker sounded like great fun and a good way to find out some things about Lord Severn and the castle—and maybe, just maybe, what was going on with Edwin.

Baldy, who had no secrets, had to slowly remove his clothing. Megan supplanted information and history about the castle every time she folded. Eliza did well, only needing to reveal a few small and insignificant details about herself. She did not tell either of them that she was a Poppet and a former Courtesan, or even that

Eliza wasn't her given name. No one knew those things, not even Juliana. Only Edwin knew.

An hour later, she yawned for the first time and glanced over at the clock on the mantel. It was one in the morning. Since poor Baldy was down to his shorts, she decided to call it a day and excused herself.

As she started up the stairs, dimly lit by the castle runner lights, she wondered where Cesar was. He'd disappeared shortly after dinner with Lord Severn, who'd offered to show him the library. She thought about hunting them down, but Edwin was right. She was treating Cesar like a child. Surely, he knew what he was doing?

She reached their suite and stopped to listen at the door. It was dead quiet and dark. Edwin wasn't back yet. She kept going up the stairs, climbing until her legs ached and she spotted a dim light up ahead. She increased her pace as she approached the tower room, almost running full tilt when she finally found herself in the corridor that led to the tower room door.

She gripped the door latch…and found it disappointingly locked. She rattled it, cursing under her breath, then got down on one knee to peer at it in the dimness. It was just an old-fashioned doorplate, which was immensely frustrating. If it was a modern computerized system like the rest of the castle, she might have been able to manipulate it with her bizarre powers as a techkinetic. She tried peering through the keyhole, but all she saw was a fuzzy dimness.

"Edwin, *what* are you up to?" she asked no one in particular.

Someone grabbed her from behind and Eliza screamed and whipped around, suddenly finding herself in Edwin's arms. "Get lost, Nancy Drew?" he asked innocently.

"Edwin, you frightened me!" She smacked his shoulder with the palm of her hand. She'd never even heard him sneak up on her.

"I'm a vampire, love. Frightening people is in the job description."

"You're awful!"

"Yes, I am." He grabbed her by the hips and dragged her against the front of his body. "But fear is good," he said low, intimately, in her ear. His voice was little more than a low growl in his throat. He was using his bedroom voice, trying to seduce her. "It gets the adrenals flowing. Makes you feel primal."

He brushed his mouth against her cheek, then neck. He continued to hum low in his throat as if he was purring. She thought about telling him off, but he smelled like the night, and his eyes tonight were wild and hungry. The only thing that kept her from swooning in his arms was the fact that he smelled like horse sweat.

She sniffed the front of his shirt. "Have you been riding?"

He hesitated a heartbeat. "Ian has night steeds...horses that can be ridden in the dark."

"I thought you hated riding."

Edwin shrugged. "I was curious to know if I still could. Turns out, it's like riding a bicycle. You never really forget how."

She studied him carefully. "You're acting very odd, Edwin. I don't like it."

"I'll shower if it bothers you." He dragged her a little closer. "We can shower together."

"That's not what I mean—"

He cut her off. "I'm famished. Fancy a tumble?"

"Edwin...you're deflecting again."

But before she could protest further, he swept her up into his arms and carried her downstairs to their suite. Eliza screamed with laughter.

* * *

After she'd fed him and Edwin's clockwork heart ran down, Eliza lay on the mattress next to her dead boyfriend, letting her thoughts wander. Edwin had wanted Number One tonight, which was much slower and a great deal sweeter than their usual mattress tumble. He hadn't drunk very much—less than a tablespoon of her blood, by her estimation—so she didn't think he'd been especially hungry tonight. He'd just wanted a shag, a slow, sweet shag...and to get her away from the tower door.

Frowning, she climbed out of bed and slipped into her flannel pajamas and fleece robe. Despite the fire in the hearth, the room was dead cold like a metal-lined crypt. She was happy she'd listened to Edwin and packed winter gear despite it being the height of summer in East Anglia. She'd had no idea a modern and completely computerized castle could be this drafty!

Grabbing an electric torch, she approached the door. "Sorry, love, I need to find out what you're hiding," she told Edwin. Torch in one hand and tool kit in another, Eliza crept from the room.

The halls were empty and her footfalls hollow sounding as she made her way back up the stairs. Megan and Baldy must still be busy in the game room, she thought. Or maybe they wandered the castle all night long like two lost souls? Nah.

She stopped when she reached what she thought was Cesar's suite. The door was ajar an inch, just enough that she could hear low, rough voices coming from within. She sank to one knee and peered through the crack in the door.

At first, she thought Lord Severn and Cesar were engaged in some kind of battle. Their clothing was tattered, and blood speckled the shining whiteness of their shirts. Ian held Cesar effortlessly against the wall of his suite while Cesar, his magnificent bronze wings outstretched, grappled the man, his teeth deeply embedded in the tough muscle in the side of Lord Severn's neck.

Cesar groaned and drank and ripped his fingernails down the back of Ian's blood-plastered shirt, adding one more set of scratches that mended in seconds but left his shirt in ribbons. When Eliza realized what they were doing, she swallowed and felt her face flush. This was a little more violent and vampiric than the romance novels and movies covered. She turned and rested her shoulders against the wall beside the door. She was shaking, and she thought about going back to bed, but now she'd *never* get to sleep.

She darted past the door and up the stairs, sticking to the edges of the stairs where the weight sensors wouldn't activate the stair lights. The cheerless blue runner lights were her only guide as she reached the tower door—which continued to prove problematic. No matter what tools she applied, she simply couldn't undo the lock. The door probably required a ridiculously low-tech key of some kind, maybe a skeleton key like a Chatelaine likely carried. She was about to rattle the knob in frustration when she spotted a dim illumination far below.

She was afraid it might be Megan or Baldy...and if it was Megan, she didn't know *how* she would explain her presence up here again. She quickly extinguished her torch, which immediately plunged her into a thick, almost sentient darkness broken only by the somber lights along the walls. It made the faint glow from below seem much brighter. Eliza held her breath and wondered if the light would grow closer as the mysterious someone with the torch ascended.

She shivered. The dark made everything seem colder—so cold, she expected to see her own breath. "Oh, forget this." She picked up her toolkit and torch and started down the steps, feeling carefully as she descended each riser. If it was Megan or one of the boys, she'd just make up some silly excuse.

Down below, the ghost light seemed to shift erratically, like someone who didn't quite know their way around the place. Now, it looked less like an electric torch and more like the deep-sea phosphorescence of some bizarre sea creature. As Eliza moved closer to it, it seemed to shrink as if it were shifting away.

She stopped halfway down the stairs but rejected the notion of running back to her room like a frightened child. She forged on, and once she reached the ground floor of the castle, called out a tentative "Hello?"

A figure stood at the far end of the corridor ahead of her, pulsing with dim, barely-there light. It looked vaguely like a woman, but when Eliza squinted, she could make out no torch in her hand. It almost seemed as though the light was coming from the woman herself.

The little hairs on the nape of her neck lifted and brushed the back of her nightgown. "I don't believe in ghosts," she said far more bravely than she felt and took a few tentative steps down the corridor, the torch held out in front of her like a weapon. Vampires and shapeshifters existed. There was no question of that. But she was dubious, at best, about ghosts.

The creature did not move.

Eliza slowed her steps, thinking that perhaps it would be more prudent to fetch someone and explain about the intrusion than to continue on as she was.

She cleared her throat. "Whoever you are...you're trespassing here. Who are you?" She lifted her light, but the tall young woman shushed away before Eliza could catch her in its glow. In fact, she retreated with a weird, loping gait.

Eliza followed, now more curious than ever.

The castle was darker here, the runner lights fainter and fewer apart. But, finally, she saw that the figure gave off its own chilly light, and that light grew exponentially brighter the darker the corridors became. For the first time in her life, Eliza entertained the very real possibility of ghosts.

Even though it moved quickly, she had no trouble following it. They were moving into some heretofore unknown part of the castle. Down here, on the lower levels, the castle seemed more archaic and less inclined to technology. She saw bare flagstone walls and what she thought might be real mutton windows full of the pale, sad glow of the full moon. The runner lights had run out at last, and Eliza was forced to turn on the hand torch, which threw a sickly and much-too-small pool of yellow light ahead of her.

Ahead lay a long, faintly dangerous-looking stairwell into darkness. A door closed soundly at the bottom, and a draft of cold air skittered unseen debris up the stairs. Eliza shivered and soldiered on down the long, treacherous steps until she found the door, mostly by touch. A faint light glinted from beneath it—the light of the being on the other side, she figured with a shiver. But it had opened a door. Ergo, it was not a ghost.

Emboldened, she took the big metal ring latch in hand and pulled, discovering she needed to set the torch down and pull with both hands to get the heavy, banded, oaken door open, and she wasn't exactly a wilting violet. She was a Poppet with enhanced Poppet strength. The being on the other side had to be incredibly strong to open it with one hand.

Beyond the open door was a silvery, shiny, glassy wonderland glinting in the almost perfect dark. It was cold and smelled of age, water damage, and the faint, unmistakable scent of chemicals. A lab, she realized.

The lab. Catherine's life alchemy lab!

The room was a vast, dusty emporium of long trestle tables, and it housed many familiar scientific devices like Tesla coils, glass beakers, and distillation pipes. Walls and walls of shelves were filled with books, glass specimen jars, and age-petrified herbs. She flicked the torch around, trying to take everything in at once. It was almost impossible. Some of the devices she recognized, like the skinner boxes and Tesla coils. Others, like the giant, vaguely manlike metal creature standing cobwebby in one corner, were completely unknown to her. Everything was covered in a fur of thick white dust, and cobwebs as thick as shredded sheets hung from the ceiling and in every corner.

Behind her, stacked neatly beside the door, were a number of framed portraits as tall as a man and half-covered in a moth-eaten sheet. Eliza used the hand torch to nudge the sheet away, which fell with a huge plume of dust.

The first one was a painting of a noble couple in the Elizabethan fashion painted by some old European master she didn't know the name of. The man in the picture was tall and aristocratic, with blue-black hair like oily raven's feathers gathered into a queue and the most beautiful dark eyes. He was dressed in a stunningly ornate shirt open at the throat with a lot of ruffles and eyelet lace, and he was standing beside a chair, his heavily beringed hand resting upon the headrest. The woman sitting in the chair, her hands set primly in her lap, looked almost too beautiful to be real. She had a face like a white lily, rose-red hair, and green eyes so vivid it was as if the artist had deliberately exaggerated her beauty. She looked very serious and proper, though her gown was so pale and diaphanous that it was nearly pornographic. They were young-old faces, ageless, impossible to read. The faces of vampires.

Lord Ian Severn. She wondered, distantly and with a dull ache, what had happened to him, how he had come to be this *thing* he was now. Lord Ian and Lady Catherine Severn. It came as no surprise to her that Edwin had loved them. They were made for love and adoration, and perhaps even worship.

She shifted the portrait. The one beneath it surprised her more.

Edwin, as defined by a 1960's pop artist's melodramatic hand. All splattery, psychedelic yellows and reds, but it was clearly him, and the artist had painted him to resemble some dark saint. He looked out at the world with eyes so hungry that it made her shudder.

In his one outstretched hand he held a burning dove, and in his other, he grasped a pitchfork. He most certainly looked the part of the Prince of Hell, Lord Foxley's Enforcer, and she wondered if this then was Edwin's true face, or if this was nothing but the results of artistic license.

A shuffling sound made her swing around and stab into the dark with her light as if it were a sword. She had almost forgotten her visitor, who had moved to the far end of Catherine's abandoned lab and was playing with something.

Eliza followed more cautiously now. There was a dull buzzing in her ears and a prickling along her skin, something that happened only when she stood in a room heavily wired for computers. It was almost like her weird telekinetic powers were seeking out the electronic components in the lab, trying to speak to them. Catherine's computers, which Eliza would have assumed were antiquated and fallow, were mumbling to her as if they were afraid...

"Get away from there," she told the intruder.

The creature ignored her. She stood before a primitive electronic dais crudely constructed of what looked like scrap metal and galvanized by what seemed a primitive industrial gear-and-cog system, with a giant containment unit atop it. It looked like a giant mountain of spare parts. The glass unit atop the device was shaped like a bell jar and stood at least twelve feet tall. Everything was coated in a fine layer of silvery dust.

Eliza's head was buzzing worse than ever, and when she stumbled and touched the glass, her head filled with white static. In that moment, she knew exactly what the device was.

Catherine was a Life Alchemist, and such practitioners excelled in developing life where there was none—or else preserving it. The device before her was a Preservation Unit. Catherine had invented it centuries before the Industrial Revolution was even an idea. Eliza marveled at the complexity of the device even as the dull edges of a migraine started riding up the back of her skull. Not only had Catherine created a primitive suspended animation machine, but she had also rigged it to a crude computer system, and *that* system that was speaking to her now, begging her for help...

A single drop of blood trickled over Eliza's lip from her nose, but she quickly dashed it away with her sleeve.

The bell jar was fogged with age and coated with dust so it was impossible to see what it contained, but the intruder seemed to be studying the ancient, dusty controls, looking for something. Eliza, now synced with the system, decided she didn't want the creature anywhere near the beautiful device.

"I said get away!" Eliza lunged forward and raised her torch to ward off the intruder.

The stranger turned.

Eliza stopped, and for the first time in her life, she had to make a conscious effort not to wet herself. The woman was much taller than she, at least six feet, and willowyand dressed in loose, colorless robes like some kind of Druid queen. She had a magnificent model shape, high breasts, a tiny waist, and sumptuous hips. Her hair was long and pale as falling rain, her skin as flawless as glass, and her eyes were the color of a dazzling summer sky. Only the mouth ruined the image of angelic perfection. It stretched from one cheekbone to the other, a massive, lipless, inhumanely long black gash filled with a jumble of tiny white, shark-like teeth.

The creature had so many teeth that they overlapped, locking the mouth into a grim and eternal Glasgow smile. No human face could look like that, and Eliza immediately dropped her upraised torch and stumbled back, colliding with an old, rambling calorimeter while the woman—the *creature*—took an awkward step toward her, stepping into the path of her fallen light with long deer-like legs that ended in tiny hooves.

"Je-sus," Eliza said, cupping a hand over her mouth to keep from screaming.

"What are you?" the creature said, struggling to speak through its massively malformed mouth.

"E-Eliza," she stammered. "The Courtesan of Lord Edwin McGillicuddy."

The creature stopped. "Not who. *What* are you?"

Eliza didn't know how to answer that. She just squeaked out, "You first."

The creature's otherworldly glow brightened, illuminating the whole shambling figure as if it were somehow *proud* of its appearance, as if it wanted Eliza to see it. Its skin, a pure shining white, looked like glass with a moonlike glow pulsing deep within. Eliza could see the full tree-like network of its cold blue blood, the slender, fragile-looking bones illuminated like some form of X-ray, the long hair glittering like a spider's web in the rain.

It smiled, further pulling that unnatural smile into a hideous travesty, and said one word: *"Sidhe."*

The whole room seemed to breathe around it as if there were others she couldn't see—or, perhaps, that one word contained a thousand separate voices.

It pranced forward on its little hoofed feet like some weightless demon, looking suddenly testy. "What are you?" it screamed impatiently.

Eliza jumped back. "Human!"

It twisted its head unnaturally in a way no human could, moving its entire body as though it were made of rubber. "Not human. Tell me the name!"

She knew what it wanted, but she refused to say the word. "I don't know what you want me to say!"

"What power have you?" the ghastly thing asked in its acidic voice. Its phosphorescence was slowly filling the room like a bank of lit candles. Even so, small pinpoints of light flickered in different corners of the lab, and more seemed to be coming on all the time as if the lab were waking up.

On noticing this, the creature swung around in alarm. "What have you done?" it cried, sounding afraid.

"I don't know!" Eliza said, edging as far away from the Sidhe as she could.

It turned its murderous gaze back on her, and Eliza flinched.

"Techkinetic! I'm a techkinetic!"

The creature regarded her carefully as it drifted closer, its inhumanely long hand fully extended as if it meant to shake hands with her. "You command machines?"

Eliza didn't know what to say, what would save her. She only knew she didn't want that...*thing*...touching her. "I..."

The impossible blue eyes bored into her like two rivets. "Machines are under your command?"

"Yes. Sometimes. I don't know!" She glanced around the lab at the machines that had flicked on and were now blipping over ancient, dusty monitors. She noted the ticking reel-to-reels as they spun lazily in their cabinets. She needed a weapon but saw nothing at hand that she could use to ward the Sidhe off...if, indeed, she even could.

The Sidhe glanced around with interest. "You can wake the machine," said the creature and reached out to her. "You can kill the machine!"

The creature felt cold, so cold. Colder than any vampire. Not like ice, but like steel buried in ice. And strong. Eliza shirked and tried to scramble away, but the creature was already on her. She lifted Eliza easily by the front of her nightgown and dragged her back to the Preservation Unit, Eliza's slippered feet barely touching the floor. Eliza fought, but it was like being carried along by a hydraulic machine on a mission. There was no escape.

The creature threw her down on the floor before the dais.

"Destroy the Preservation Unit," the creature told her in its raspy, metallic voice, pointing toward the device with one long, thin hand.

"No." The thought seized her. The horror of killing Catherine's beautiful machine was more than she could bear. "I can't."

"Kill it or I'll kill you," the creature told her. "I'll do worse..." Her glowing cold hand reached out to touch Eliza's horrified face, the cold encroaching so it nearly burned her skin.

Eliza, too terrified to push the creature's patience anymore, scrambled up, gripping the edge of the dais to steady herself. She stared at the almost alien controls, the unfamiliar dials and switches, but she couldn't make heads or tails of any of it. She ran her hands through the dust, but nothing significant happened. A few lights flickered on, but the Preservation Unit didn't feed any pertinent information into her mind now. It was almost like it knew she meant to betray it. All she caught were vague glimpses of an ancient darkness, starbright teeth, slashes of blood—that and a ticking fear in her throat as the creature drew perilously close, her mouth gaping open like some fresh wound.

She had to do something. She glimpsed a shard of heavy iron rebar on the floor under the dais, broken off from the decaying iron staircase that rose up along the walls of the bookshelves. She ducked down and quickly picked it up. Turning, she swung it at the creature, but it passed harmlessly through her as if the Sidhe were truly a ghost, though Eliza felt a shock of cold and her teeth ached on contact.

"Destroy the machine now!" the creature screamed at her, and the force of its voice swept along the debris on the floor of the lab.

"Sod off, bitch," Eliza said, thinking how very proud Edwin would be of her. She turned, still swinging the rebar, and let it collide with the glass of the containment unit instead.

Her world exploded into chaos.

| vii |

Lord Ian Severn jerked awake.
He sat up slowly, forced himself to resume breathing, and glanced around the icy cold room. His eyes easily pierced the dark, picking out familiar shapes in the almost total pitch-blackness—the scattering of bloodstained clothing, the wardrobe, the bedside table with the laptop upon it. This was not his room, his bed, he recalled. He had merely collapsed here into his usual deathlike sleep after he and the boy had finished their lovemaking.

That had never happened to him before. For more than half a millennium, he had slept in his and Catherine's antique sleigh bed, first with Catherine and/or with various guests of interest, and then alone. He did not sleep anywhere else in the castle but there, in his securely locked and encoded bedchamber. But tonight had been different.

The room was so cold that a slick layer of glass-like condensation clung to the walls, not that it bothered him. He had not felt proper heat or cold since his death well over five hundred years ago. Neither he nor the boy had thought to start an electric fire in the hearth. They had been entirely preoccupied with the taste of blood and each other.

He shifted amidst the icy sheets and glanced down at the boy lying dead asleep beside him. He was beautiful in that strangely fabricated American way. Through exercise, fashion, and sometimes simple cosmetic modifications, the Americans strove to soften or strengthen their edges and even out their flaws so they looked as exquisite as vampires. The boy had been lovely in life, either due to genetics or modification. His Inheritance had simply brought that to full flower.

Edwin's little whelp fascinated him. He slept like the dead, his pretty, doll-like face at ease, his wings—which he had found endearingly cumbersome during their lovemaking—partially unfurled around him like two shining bronze fans.

Ian touched the lovely young face. "Little angel," he said.

He had not met a virgin vampire in more than a hundred years. He did not think they existed anymore—vampires who had never taken human life. Vampires who were, for all intents and purposes, *innocent*. Even Edwin, for all his altruistic intentions, carried the shadow of death with him, but such darkness wasn't present in this lad's face. His troubles were more worldly and mundane. Human worries. He wanted to love and be loved. He wanted to be accepted. He was at odds with what he was, and he would continue to be so until he shed his virginity. Then, and only then, would he truly be one of them.

What had Edwin said? *He has no idea what being a vampire is about. He has yet to descend into the depths of our backbiting and deception.*

The lad made him ache. He realized he wanted a baby of his own, even though such thoughts had long since fled him with Catherine's passing. But yes...an Heir. Baldy had been more Catherine's progeny than his own, and though loyal to him as his Enforcer, Ian had no emotional or sexual connection to the vampire. Baldy did not love him. And Edwin was never a part of his bloodline. The wolves were his constituents and as loyal to him as Heirs, but he could not infect them. The curse of their lycanthropy overruled any curse he could place upon them.

In the beginning, it was a game. The lad was pretty and innocent and almost laughably easy to seduce. But something had changed in the few short days since their first encounter in the stables, and it was only now that Ian was recognizing the extent of Cesar's power. Ian had sought sex and companionship—a part-time shag, as they called it now. He had not expected the tenderness that followed.

Or the power. The lad was far more powerful than even Edwin realized. But then, Lord Foxley was the fount of their strength, and one did not live twelve millennia without absorbing a terrible amount of power. Foxley had poured far too much of himself into Edwin, and Edwin, in his haste to create an Heir, had committed the same error. But then, Edwin was ruthless, erratic, and far more bloodthirsty than his pretties realized, which was why the vampires called him the Prince of Hell, the Devil. A Gaelic vampire, his nature was volatile and chaotic. A dangerous combination.

Dragging himself from the bed, Ian moved to stand naked before the highboy with the framed mirror above it. The old man in the mirror did not look as old now. There were still the lines, the stone-like pallor, the dust, but it almost seemed as though the cobwebs were coming away from his dark eyes, making them glitter like whetstones, and his long reams of silvery hair looked darker, more virile. He was changing, bit by bit.

A rustling sound made him turn. The boy was awake, sitting up in bed. He still moved awkwardly with his big wings, like some young, postulant dragon. With his seamless bronze skin and palomino hair and lovely, sluttish blue eyes, he was absolutely beautiful. Ian could not understand how Edwin managed to control himself around the lad.

"Ian? Is something wrong?" he asked in his dry, toneless American accent.

"Do you feel there is?" Ian asked in return.

The runner lights traversing the walls flickered, filling the room with a dull, cold, deep-sea light before blinking out. Ian would need to have the wolves see to the computer mainframe and electrical system, he realized.

Returning to bed, he settled on the mattress and palmed the lad's face, while something deep inside his body hurt with a dull, sad hunger.

"Should they be doing that?" the lad asked with alarm, glancing around the room. He shivered, but Ian knew it was not from cold, which the boy was practically inured to at this point.

But Ian wasn't worried about a few flickering lights just then. If all the lights in the castle had gone out, it would have made very little difference to him. He buried his face in the lad's shoulder and tasted his cool, sweet blood even through the skin. He could not mark this little pretty, of course—Edwin had already done that—so he would need to bite through as he had earlier and make a less permanent and more painful opening. He waited to see if the boy would protest, but the little vampire simply lay there, his hand in Ian's hair, listening.

"What's wrong, lad?" he asked. He found he did not want to hurt the lad, force him. He wanted the pretty to want him.

The lad's eyes shone narrowly in the dark. "Someone's turned a computer on."

"What do you mean?"

"I can hear it. Can't you? That subliminal little hum you hear when you fall asleep near your notebook."

Ian did not have a notebook. Computers, as far as he was concerned, were huge unseen systems that powered and controlled his home. That was one of the reasons he employed the wolves, who were somewhat more contemporary than the vampires.

"The entire castle is run on a computer," he said.

"I know. But I haven't heard this one yet. It's big and really old..."

Ian paused, his teeth denting the lad's sweet throat. "Catherine's lab..." he said as the realization struck him. He sat up and immediately reached for his clothes. "Someone's in Catherine's lab."

* * *

Breaking the Preservation Unit had saved her life, but only barely.

The moment the tank was breached, an explosion of fetid brown water knocked Eliza straight down and under the edge of the computer dais. The thick, broken glass followed, fiercer than the gushing cold water that now stung her eyes. A shard of glass passed right through the Sidhe's middle, seemingly with no effect, then the top half of the creature's body slid, slid farther, and then the whole thing collapsed and the water washed it away and into a corner of the lab.

The lights flickered and went dark, and Eliza, huddling in the wet if relatively safe spot under the dais, though it was likely the water had short-circuited the archaic wiring. Lost in the darkness, she scrambled around on her hands and knees in three inches of stagnant water until she bumped into the far wall of the lab. Then she turned and huddled against the wall.

Thousands of gallons of water from the Preservation Unit had gushed out, leaving the enormous bell jaw transparent, but in the dark, she could see few details of what was in it past a vague dark shape. She did spot a luminescence shimmering just beneath the surface of the water. Then the Sidhe rocketed up, not injured, but angry, its glow filling the room and illuminating the debris floating on the surface of the water that had not yet found an escape route down the grated drain in the middle of the lab floor.

"*You,*" the Sidhe said in that grating, unmusical voice like its mouth was full of marbles. It drifted across the surface of the water, its screaming face nightmarishly lit up, its hand outstretched.

"Go to hell!" Eliza was wet and cold and scared out of her mind, and she was getting tired of this thing threatening her for its own unknown reasons. She slapped around the water she sat in, looking for something she could use as a weapon even though she knew it was probably useless. If cutting the creature in half didn't kill it, she seriously doubted hitting it with a piece of flotsam would do any good. But she couldn't help herself. She wouldn't go down without a fight!

Her hand closed around a small, loose flagstone in the floor. At the same time, the Sidhe lunged at her, screaming. But before Eliza could heft her weapon and use it on the thing, something howled from within the broken Preservation Unit, a sound so primal and inhuman that Eliza groaned, dropped the stone, and pressed both hands against her ears.

The sound stopped the creature dead in its tracks. It swiveled around to take in the source of the howl—the broken Preservation Unit, which now resembled a giant cracked egg. The glass was shivering, chattering apart as the whole unit began falling to pieces, revealing...some dark creature standing on all fours and watching them.

Eliza scrunched herself against the wall, trying to make as small a target of herself as she could while the Sidhe hovered before her, its attention divided between her and the beast. Finally, it chose to focus its attention on the new creature—and Eliza saw why.

The beast watching them stood as tall at the shoulder as one of the East Anglian ponies she'd spied in town, and it was covered in long, sodden, spiky midnight blackfur. Its pale, forest-green eyes found Eliza, and though it resembled an enormous wolf, the eyes were not animal at all. They looked human. They knew. They understood. And they raged.

The creature dropped its jaw and its starbright teeth seemed to glow in the dark, along with its eyes. The growl it emitted made the floor tremble and every little hair on Eliza's body stood on end.

The Sidhe eyed the wolf critically, then pointed at it. *"You..."* it began but never finished threatening it.

The wolf moved too quickly. A streak of eyes and teeth in the dark, and suddenly the creature was upon the Sidhe, its enormous, slavering jaws clamped around the slender white throat. The wolf shook its head, and the creature crumpled as if it were made of white paper. A whitish fluid as thick as curdled cream gushed forth and painted Eliza up and down.

The Sidhe blood burned cold on her skin. Eliza immediately scrambled to her feet and started to race for the door of the lab, hoping the two monsters would stay occupied long enough for her to make her escape.

But the water was still knee-deep, and she wasn't fast enough. Nothing, she thought, was fast enough to outrun something like that! The wolf knocked her down, and for one moment, her whole world was full of musky wet fur and heat. She had a moment of profound panic—then, seconds later, a wind as sharp as a white sword passed overhead. Another Sidhe, she realized as she floundered in the water.

She turned her head in time to see the wolf jump. Airborne, it snappedits jaws over the throat of the second Sidhe. The two crashed into the far wall, the wolf driving it to the ground under its weight. The second Sidhe seemed to shatter on impact, painting the walls with its milky, stinking blood.

Eliza scrambled to her hands and knees and started crawling backward across the floor. The room was quickly draining of water, but the floor was a minefield of broken glass and debris, and she had no idea how she would ever get to the door without tearing herself to shreds. Not that she had a chance.

In seconds, the wolf was back, as vast as a lion, stalking her. It walked on all fours, but with a more ape-like gait as it crawled along on its knuckles. Its arms and hands had transformed into long, muscular, human-like appendages, and, now, it seemed to be in a kind of transitional state between man and wolf.

For the first time in her life, Eliza realized she was staring down a transformed werewolf. "Please…" she said, gulping blood from where she had bitten her tongue.

But the wolf didn't listen, or else it didn't care. It pawed toward her like some alien *thing*, head down, snout wrinkled back to reveal its enormous saber teeth. She hardly saw it move. Suddenly, it was right there, standing over her, sniffing the front of her sodden nightgown where it clung to her body. She wondered if, in the white nightclothes, it thought she was like the others, and if it would kill her now.

She felt a pang. There were so many things she'd wanted to do—and so much left unsaid between her and Edwin. Tears burned her eyes. The wolf pinned her to the floor, unrolled its enormous crimson tongue, and flickered it over her face, licking away the blood and tears. "Please," she repeated. "Don't…"

"Malcolm."

The black werewolf stopped and straightened up, turning its rigid attention on the door. Eliza watched the creature rise up on its haunches. She thought it meant to leap at the man standing in the doorway of the lab. Instead, it tilted its enormous head back and howled, its voice so loud it made all of the remaining glass in Catherine's lab sing.

It stood as a man might now, and as it did so, the black fur body seemed to crack apart, revealing what was underneath—a tender, pale human body covered in a thick, clear mucus. The pieces of the wolf seemed to slough away inch by inch, revealing one of the most handsome young men she had ever looked upon.

He was tall and kingly, and he was built like a young man used to hard manual labor—a young Viking, perhaps—and there were glyphs burned into his skin in a language Eliza did not recognize. His blue-black hair fell in damp, tangled waves to his waist. Eliza found herself acutely aware of how close she was to his groin, the pungent animal smell of him. She scrabbled back, despite the glass on the floor, and did not stop until she hit the wall beside the door. Finally, shehad put some distance between herself and the werewolf. She did not feel the burning cuts on her hand, and she barely noticed the snail's trail of blood she had left behind from the broken glass.

The werewolf noticed. He looked at her unabashedly—hungrily. His nostrils flared. He neither noticed nor seemed to care that he was naked. His attention was fixed solely on her as he took a step toward her. But, again, he stopped when he heard his name.

"Malcolm."

Finally, he turned his full attention on the man who had spoken —on Ian. The old vampire stood at the door of Catherine's lab, dressed in dark, torn clothing. He looked like he'd waged a war, and possibly lost it. "Malcolm," he said in a softer voice, gesturing with both arms outstretched toward the naked young man. "My wolf."

"My Lord," the werewolf answered. His voice growled up out of his chest like the buzz of a dangerous mechanical tool. Leaving Eliza where she huddled against the wall, the werewolf went to Ian and prostrated himself before his master.

* * *

The following morning, Eliza rose early, changed the dressings on her scratches, dressed in a summery chiffon gown and gloves, and walked solemnly downstairs to Ian's study. Megan noticed her but said nothing as Eliza took a seat on one of the divans by the big bay window. The "window" was actually one of the videos of the outside of the castle walls, the west side: summer in East Anglia, the long brown grasses shushing in the wind, interspersed with purple pasque flowers and yellow oxlip. The divan was not very comfortable, and she was still very sore from her adventures the night before, but she meant to sit here all day if need be—until she had the answers she needed.

"May I fetch you some coffee, Miss E?" Megan asked politely. She must have sensed the fission in the air because she was back to formalities with Eliza. It was almost as if their girl day hadn't happened at all.

"Thank you. Megan. That would be wonderful. And perhaps something for the boys." By the boys, she meant the vampires, but she wanted to keep things civil at present, even though she felt an intense need to ram a wooden stake into the heart of every vampire in the castle.

Megan hurried from the room, returning with a mobile tray of tea, coffee, and blood substitute for the "boys," which she dutifully unloaded onto a sideboard. The dishes rattled alarmingly as she set them out, and at one point, she even dropped a teacup, which shattered on the hardwood floor.

"Oh, my," Megan commented, looking nervous. "I'm so very out of practice with this, I'm afraid."

Eliza ignored her. She collected a coffee for herself, then returned to her seat to wait. Megan chose tea and sat down on the divan across from her. For the first time, Eliza realized Megan was dressed simply in a summery lace gown, her hair properly pinned up and glittering with the antique comb that Eliza had given her. It was rather formal wear for so early in the day. Then she remembered that Megan was going driving with Mickey today, that they had set the date after hitting it off so well down at the pub. But then, finally, she reminded herself that that wouldn't be until Mickey got off his shift in the evening, so her formality was for some other reason.

After a half hour or so, Megan's wolf boys wandered in, both wearing suits and waistcoats with honest-to-god cravats. They bowed to her and took their place on the chaise lounge to either side of Megan. They drank tea and ate English biscuits noisily but otherwise said nothing, though both looked uncharacteristically subdued.

Edwin wandered in next, with Cesar on his heels like a good dog. Eliza chose not to immediately acknowledge either one of them. She had dutifully wound Edwin's heart up this morning, but because she was so sore from injury and full of frustration, she had neglected to hang about their suite. Normally, she laid out his clothes for the day, but this morning, she had left him to fend for himself. Edwin had done the best he could, pairing a dark hunter green suit jacket with black trousers, which was acceptable, but then he added red braces and a tartan bowtie, which was not. She tried not to let his poor fashion sense get to her. There were other things she was much angrier about today.

Edwin approached her and sat down on the end of the divan just as far as he could without actually falling off the cushion. He gave her a formal good morning but no kiss. She returned his greeting because it was the proper thing to do. Then she requested that Cesar take the seat beside her since he was hovering rather indecisively in a corner of the room near the sidebar. Cesar poured himself his breakfast and joined her on the cushion, wedged like a buffer between her and Edwin.

She asked if he was well. He looked tired.

"I'm good," he said, trying on a cheery smile that did nothing but accentuate his teeth, which looked strong and rather sharp. He was dressed in black up and down, the only spot of color on him being a red tapestry waistcoat and the blood-red pin cinching his collar. Count on Cesar to have good tastes in clothing—*unlike someone else.* The black made him seem older, more clerical. Cesar was Edwin's Enforcer, after all, his bully, his bad guy—a point of contention between the two of them. Cesar was only a baby. She set her hand on his arm. He couldn't have bullied someone out of a paper bag.

Lord Ian Severn came lastly, followed by his Enforcer, Baldy, and then, seconds later, by his wolf, Malcolm—the Werewolf of Whitby. Ian looked different this morning, though Eliza couldn't rightly say how. Perhaps it was his stronger gait, the way he leaned less on his walking stick. Or it was his clothing, which up until now had seemed darker and unnecessarily old-fashioned. He had eschewed the older fashions for a worsted suit in light summery grey. It put color into his face and made his eyes look keen.

Malcolm was another story. The moment he stepped into the room, all eyes turned to regard him with something close to awe, or perhaps terror. And for good reason. The young man stood well over seven feet, dwarfing even Edwin, who made most men look like Hobbits. He was dressed in a deep green tartan suit that looked very much borrowed because the cuffs of his trousers ended approximately half an inch above his boots, and his waistcoat strained his wide, lean chest in a way that most girls would have described as disarming.

Eliza stared and stared, unable to pull her eyes away from the werewolf. He was surprisingly young looking, but she'd learned with Megan that looks could be very deceiving where werewolves were concerned. He was actually hundreds of years old, and as if to attest to that, there were white strands in his jet-black hair. There was power and sex and darkness in his every move, and that was something a young stud his age didn't usually have. His hair was loose and long and curling, framing and softening an otherwise intense face and those very green eyes that made her want to catch her breath when she looked into them.

While Ian and Baldy availed themselves of breakfast, Malcolm made a round of the room, making strange, almost silent introductions to the denizens of Whitby Hall.

The wolves, including Megan, knelt to him, trembling slightly—whether in awe or fear, Eliza did not know. Malcolm spoke a few words over them in a rough brogue, touching their heads with his enormous hand like the benediction of some kind of priest. That was all.

There was no other show of animal pecking order, but perhaps that would come later, in a time of intimacy reserved only for werewolves. To Edwin and Cesar he was formal, aloof, not touching them. He used simple greetings. They were neither wolves nor his master; therefore, they were of little concern to him.

And then he came to her.

Eliza looked up, their eyes met, and her entire body flushed embarrassingly as if they had some long, sordid history between them. She felt a familiarity with Malcolm, something she had never experienced with anyone so early on in a relationship. Then again, this was the man who had shielded her from the Sidhe, who had licked her tears. They had shared a peculiar kind of intimacy within seconds of meeting; she couldn't shake the feeling that some bond had been forged between them, suddenly and violently.

He took her hand, completely obliterating it in his own, and said over it, "Miss Eliza Book. I am so very pleased to make your acquaintance." His speech was stiff and extremely formal.

"Thank you, Mr…Whitby." She was unsure how to address him.

"Please call me Malcolm." His steady, deep, forest-green gaze weighed against her with a near physical force.

"Then you should call me Eliza."

He stared at her a long moment before moving his free hand to brush her bandaged cheek where a shard of glass had struck her and caused a particularly deep gash. The same place where he had tasted her tears and her blood. "If it pleases you, my lady."

"It would." She felt Edwin's eyes on them, analyzing them. She slid her hand out of Malcolm's and returned it to her lap.

Ian took up his station in his chair with Baldy standing beside him. "I'm glad you have all chosen to come," he announced formally. "We have much to discuss."

None of them had planned this meeting, yet all of them had gathered instinctively for answers.

Eliza sat quietly and listened while their host spoke. Ian began with the events of the night before, then went on to explain about Lady Catherine's life alchemy lab and the Preservation Unit, built to heal and preserve the Werewolf of Whitby, who had suffered extreme torture at the hands of the Churchmen during the Fifteenth Century. He went on to explain about Malcolm's legend, which Eliza had read briefly about in the travel books. And then he explained about the Sidhe, the creatures that attacked Eliza the night before.

"Fairies," she said, sounding incredulous even to herself. "Sidhe are fairies."

Ian looked at her poignantly. "They are what you would call fairies, yes. We contemporaries call them Fae."

"For fairies, they were horrible," she said, thinking of every fantasy movie she had ever seen. She didn't know about the deer feet or the Glasgow smile full of teeth. They certainly were no Tinker Bell.

"They are the distant cousins of vampires," Ian explained. He briefly described the relationship between the Darkness and the Light, and how the Darkness must always pursue the Light. Yet, neither of those forces was to be admired or embraced, as they were both agents of chaos. He then talked about the Fae. He explained how they could divide their tainted souls from their bodies when they achieved a higher form of consciousness like sleep, hypnosis, or some forms of meditation.

Eliza soaked in the information. She had read about how the Fae wandered in Catherine's journals. Catherine called them Sleepwalkers. Eliza didn't feel terror, not just yet.

"We were a relatively happy people after the Light left the Village of Whitby. This castle was full of life and humanity. I had human servants back then...or, I believe I did." Ian paused as if it to consider and clutched his head.

Cesar leaned forward and asked the inevitable. "How can you not know if you've ever had human servants?"

Eliza wondered if Ian Severn suffered from a form of vampire dementia.

Ian thought a long moment, then forged on as if Cesar hadn't spoken. "But when the Light returned some years ago, all that changed. The Fae amassed and returned as soldiers to this castle. They touched everyone here, and only I, Baldy, and the wolves of the Bloodthorn Pack have survived their passing, and only because we are all a part of the Darkness, and the Light cannot completely extinguish its counterpart."

"I don't understand," Eliza interrupted. She did not care that the others were looking oddly at her for taking charge of this conversation. She was tired of secrets. "Cesar's right. How can you not know if you've had human servants? What happened to them? What's happened to you?"

Ian looked uncomfortable. "The Light came and the Fae touched all those who live here in the castle," he repeated. "I can only believe I've had human servants because I know my own nature, and I believe I would have kept them. Catherine loved the vitality of life all about her, and we had kept human servants in centuries past."

He paused and took a deep breath before continuing. "You must understand that when the Fae touch the living, they absorb every part of them, their bodies, their minds, and their very souls. Everything they are or will ever be—their whole potential—is absorbed by the Light. The Fae completely extinguish their victims and remove them for all time. The human being ceases to exist and their entire timeline is rearranged by default."

Eliza felt the shock down to her toes. "So, the Fae didn't just kill your human servants, assuming you had any. They destroyed them so completely that no one here even remembers they ever existed?"

Ian nodded once. "And they did this to me." He drew a finger down his dry, aged face. Eliza recalled the portrait in the lab. Ian Severn had not always been this grey old thing.

"I'm dying, Miss Book. I cannot ride my beloved horses. I cannot even walk very far without exhaustion overwhelming me. The Fae who touched me extinguished far too much of my lifeforce. And, although I do not believe I will be 'Erased,' as we call it, I do know that it is a continuing process—an unstoppable, terminal cancer, if you will. It's as if my entire body is being eaten through."

Beside her, Cesar opened his mouth as if to speak, then stopped himself. He stood up suddenly. Without excusing himself, he made for the door of the study.

"How very rude," Megan said.

"Leave him," Ian insisted. "He's young. These matters have upset him." He looked to Edwin.

Her boyfriend had remained quiet up until this point, but now he said, "I'll speak to him later." He narrowed his amber eyes on

Ian. "Now, tell them the rest." The serious tone of his voice made Eliza afraid.

Ian seemed to gather himself. Finally, he said, "There was a Wild Hunt many centuries ago to extinguish the Fae before they spread out into the world. I rode that hunt. I was the Master of the Hunt, and Malcolm"—he nodded to the man standing at the side of his chair—"ran with me as my hunting dog. Lady Catherine chose us both. Between us, we slaughtered most of the Village of Whitby and halted the tyranny of the Light. But we erred, and now there is a need for another Hunt—a Hunt I cannot ride. The Fae, in their machinations, have seen to that."

He stared down into the teacup sitting in his lap atop an embroidered Battenberg napkin. "That is the reason I invited Lord Edwin here to Whitby Hall. Lord Edwin has agreed to ride the huntin my stead."

Eliza felt the coffee in her stomach surge into her throat. She had to swallow to keep it down. "Why?" she said, her voice far more panicky than she wanted it to be. She turned accusing eyes on Ian. "Why Edwin?"

Ian raised his head and pinned her with keen eyes. "Edwin is strong, Miss Book. And his hands are not without bloodstains. He can ride the Hunt, and he *will* hunt well. He *will* finish what we have begun."

Edwin sat solemnly, eyes closed, the topic of conversation, but unwilling to meet her gaze.

"He won't do that," she said, standing up. She thought about the people she had seen at the market and then at the auction—even little, rude blonde girl with the dolly. The people who had not liked her or Megan. Their ignorance had made her angry for a time, but she did not want them dead. She didn't want *anyone* dead.

And, more importantly, she did not want Edwin responsible for their deaths!

"Miss Book, he has already agreed to it."

"No!" she shouted and saw Malcolm's eyes flare as if he were considering going to her. To do what, she didn't know. "Why would he do that?" She turned to her uncharacteristically silent boyfriend to ask him. "Why would you do this? Edwin, answer me."

But before Edwin could say anything in his defense, Ian's next words stopped her dead in her tracks. "He is doing it for you, Miss Book. He is doing it because if he does not, I will have my servants kill you. And Cesar."

She stood there, looking around the circle of familiar faces, her friends. People she had spent time with, shopped with, and played strip poker with. People she had—god help her—trusted.

None denied it.

It was all a ruse, she realized. She was nothing but a pawn. Painful tears filled her eyes.

Ian sounded tired, so endlessly tired. With eyes closed, he said, "I am so very sorry, Miss Book, but I have no other choice. I will kill you if you try and leave. This is far more important than you or me. Or anyone living or undead in this room. The Light has to be extinguished. This is the only way."

She had unconsciously started moving toward the door, but then she spotted Baldy standing near it, drinking his breakfast out of a teacup, watching her casually but intensely. She glanced elsewhere, but the windows weren't real and there were no other exits, not that she would ever reach it in time in a room full of vampires. There was nowhere to run. Nowhere she could go that they wouldn't find her.

So, she returned to her seat, sat down, and bowed her head while they watched her. "All of you?"

"Yes, Eliza," Megan informed her, her voice cold. "All but Edwin, of course. I am so very sorry, ducky. But we have no choice. None at all."

Eliza picked up her teacup from where she had set it on the little table beside the divan and sipped from it. The coffee was cold. Her cup clicked against the saucer because her hands were shaking so badly. A web. A fucking spider's web.

"And Edwin?" she asked. "What of him?"

"Edwin, too, is a prisoner," said Megan.

"Edwin will ride in two days," said Ian. "I have already begun the preparations."

She looked at him beside her. The nightsteeds. Edwin's strange behavior. She waited for him to speak, to say something in his defense, but he kept his silence, looking more like some pretty statue in a spotty outfit than a real man. He didn't say a word. But Malcolm watched her, his heated gaze tracking her every move.

"I'd like to go to my room now," Eliza finally announced. "If you don't mind."

"Go on, ducky," Megan said. She did not add that they would be watching her. Closely.

| viii |

Cesar, sitting cross-legged on a divan in the library where the wi-fi was strongest in the castle, was staring down at his glowing note book and reading about vampire etiquette when Edwin let himself into the vast room. He crossed to where Cesar was sitting and leaned against the wall under a huge painting of an English hunt.

"Ian was going to come round and update you, but I told him I would handle it as your Lord. You and Miss Eliza are to be confined to the house for the remainder of the week...until we sort things out."

Edwin briefed Cesar on the Wild Hunt, but when Cesar didn't immediately say anything, he stepped forward to close Cesar's laptop. "You can go anywhere you like in the castle or bailey. You only can't leave the premises. However, you have my word that nothing will happen to you or to Eliza, whatever Ian says."

Cesar was silent a long moment before rising to leave, the laptop tucked under his arm. He could finish his reading in the privacy of his own quarters. But before he left, he turned to Edwin. "So...you're going to protect us."

"Aye."

Cesar nodded but then bit his lip. "Maybe you shouldn't make promises you can't keep, *Prince*."

He tried to walk away, but Edwin grabbed his arm. Cesar stiffened and tried to throw off his master's touch, but it was like being held in place by some god. He was helpless to resist. Edwin could not possibly be that strong. Then Cesar realized his power was probably as much psychic as physical. Cesar's body was under Edwin's control and had been from the first moment he was remade into a vampire.

Well now...that sucked—big time.

"Let g—!" he began, but Edwin cut him off.

"You are my Heir, my Enforcer. And I am your Lord," Edwin explained, narrowing his eyes. "And the main responsibilities of a Vampire Lord are the protection and expansion of his Court. It may not always seem like it, lad, but I take those responsibilities seriously. Do you understand me?"

Cesar turned, his pulse racing, and managed to say, "Why?"

Edwin looked confused. "Why...what?"

It took Cesar a moment to ask the question that had dogged him since the beginning, when he first met Edwin McGillicuddy in The Clocks casino. "Why did you choose me? Why did you make me your Heir and Enforcer?"

Edwin's face remained stoic and unreadable. "I needed you."

"Needed me to fight the Hive for you. But you don't *like* me. You don't like having me around interfering in your little romance with Miss Eliza, pestering you all the time."

Edwin frowned at that. "Cesar, I welcomed you into my Courts...into my home."

"To dust your books and serve your tea. But I'm just your Jeeves."

"I don't follow," said Edwin, looking confused. "What are you saying exactly?"

Did he have to spell it out? He felt like some undead version of Alfred Pennyworth, there only to run Edwin's errands and pick up his dry cleaning.

Sniffing under a mighty swell of defeat, Cesar sighed. "Never mind. It's not important." He tugged, but Edwin wouldn't let go of his arm.

Their eyes met and Edwin let out a rattling breath. "I know what you're feeling, lad. We're connected, remember?"

He seemed to cast about for a better explanation. After a long, silent moment, he blinked his fierce amber eyes and said, "I needed you, aye, but..."

"But you weren't ready for an Heir," Cesar offered.

Grunting with frustration, Edwin said, "You're nothing like Mouse! Directly after I made her, she went her own way. We never had anything that resembled a real relationship."

Mouse, his Enforcer for almost a hundred years. Over the past six months of their relationship, Cesar had learned some things about her, but only from bits and pieces of conversation. Edwin was otherwise cagey about their relationship. His first Enforcer had been born into extreme poverty and despair. His Inheritance had freed her to become so much more than she would have been had she remained human. From what he had gathered, Edwin really did love her in his own way, and Cesar was certain her death aboard the *Gypsy Queen* had ripped a hole in his soul that had still to heal properly. But they weren't lovers—not in the traditional sense, anyway.

Cesar frowned. "What about others?"

"What others?"

"Your other Heirs."

"There are no other Heirs."

That surprised Cesar. "None? In two hundred years?" He found that hard to believe. "Do you mean to tell me that other than Mouse, I'm the only Heir you've ever made?"

Edwin gave him a suspicious look. Cesar took that as a yes.

"What about your Brides?" Cesar persisted. He'd read plenty about that on the vampire gateway website. There was even a section dedicated to classified ads to help vampires find their one eternal companion, their Bride.

It took Edwin a moment to answer. "There's Eliza."

"Other than Eliza."

Finally, Edwin just looked plain uncomfortable.

Cesar gaped at his master and maker. "So other than Miss Eliza and me, you've spent over two hundred years without a single working relationship with *anyone*?"

He saw Edwin almost say Foxley, then stop himself. What Edwin had with his maker wasn't a relationship; it was a toxic mire of contempt, manipulation, and old-fashioned murder. Edwin had terrorized people for Foxley, and a relationship that did not make.

Edwin's eyes darkened. "You don't know what it was like working for Foxley as his Enforcer. I had a reputation to maintain. Responsibilities. I didn't have time for…Brides or Heirs. They weren't good times."

Cesar let out his breath in a puff. He knew about Edwin's reputation, of course. Other vampires called him the Prince of Hell. An Enforcer so brutal that no vampire would dare cross Foxley for fear of him setting Edwin on their tail. But this was news.

"So, Miss Eliza and I are the only ones in your life."

Edwin's eyes darkened further as he threw up his now-familiar emotional barriers. "Oh, fark off!" He smacked Cesar across the chest, separating them, but it wasn't a hard push. Cesar barely felt it.

Cesar stumbled back but caught himself against the back of the divan. The gesture didn't impress him at all.

What a horrible existence, Cesar thought dismally, his heart breaking for Edwin. To live more than two centuries isolated with that sociopath Foxley. Always alone. No love. No friendship. No wonder Edwin was an arse sometimes. He literally didn't even know how to function properly in a non-toxic relationship.

Edwin started turning away, but Cesar lunged and grabbed him by the arm, pulling him back around so they were eye to eye. It almost felt like a dance they were doing.

Edwin's eyes turned dark and feral. Fearful. "Let me go."

Cesar didn't. He pulled his master closer, leaned in, and placed a soft kiss on Edwin's lips—barely more than a touch. The contact ignited both of their hungers, just not for blood. Before Cesar even knew it, he was pressed against the shelves of books, with Edwin doing the most amazing—and amazingly wicked—things to him. Things that left him gasping and clutching at Edwin's clothes.

"I'm sorry," said Cesar against his master's lips as they made out. "I'm so sorry..."

"About what?" Edwin said. They'd made it to the cushions of the divan. There, Edwin sat, dragging Cesar into his lap. It was a positively endearing gesture and allowed Cesar to hug as much of his master's body to himself as he could. The feeling was both thrilling and strangely comforting, like hugging his pillow in the morning.

A true professional in the amorous department, Edwin repositioned him so he could take him fast and hard, Cesar riding his lap while his open mouth moved over the column of Cesar's throat. Cesar closed his eyes and reveled in the sudden, almost heart-stopping waves of pleasure spiraling through his body. He growled and strained like an ensnared animal, clutching his master with hands powerful enough to bend steel rods.

"What...what happened to you," Cesar managed to squeak out. "It wasn't fair. It wasn't even like me and Ian...ah!" He cried out when Edwin hit his sweet spot perfectly.

"Ian is much too old for you," Edwin grunted suddenly.

"Are you *really* forbidding me from dating older men like you're my dad?"

"I'm not your dad. And Ian's not old, he's ancient. You have nothing in common with him." Turning his head, Edwin gave him a quick bite, which took Cesar over the edge.

Afterward, they settled down, Cesar kissing him and licking a particularly tasty spot. Edwin turned his head, giving him to take. Cesar sank his teeth in the side of Edwin's throat. Edwin gave a little moan of pleasure and clutched the back of Cesar's neck, giving himself over to his Heir. Edwin's blood was dazzling and delicious, everything Cesar wanted...everything he dreamed about.

"What he did to you," Cesar managed after a few frantic swallows. "How Foxley treated you. It wasn't fair—"

"It was a long time ago," Edwin insisted. "A lifetime ago."

Edwin's blood amplified their connection. A quick flicker through Edwin's memories made Cesar feel like his heart was being squeezed to death inside of him. Edwin had lived in a literal hell for almost his entire existence as a vampire. He was nothing but a blood-splattered puppet that Foxley trotted out anytime he needed a heavy to do his dirty work. The images that Cesar saw made him want to cry, and some of them even made him want to throw up.

Slowly, Edwin settled down on the divan with Cesar atop him. Cesar couldn't cry, but he sure as hell wanted to.

"You don't have to pretend, you know," Cesar explained in a soft whisper. He was lying against his master, both of them wriggling a bit awkwardly, the divan being too small for them, and looked deep into his pain-filled eyes. "You can tell me what he did to you. I'm here. I'll listen. I won't judge..."

The darkness shifted behind Edwin's eyes again. Cesar could tell Edwin was flicking through the library of Cesar's traumas as well. Their bloodlink flowed both ways. Edwin said after a few silent moments, "What I experienced wasn't as simple as being kicked out of the house because my father didn't like the company I was keeping."

Edwin probably meant it to hurt him, to get him to get up and off him, but Cesar recognized it as a defensive gesture. Not the first time for them. Besides, Cesar had long since come to terms with the pain his family had caused him. A father who hated him. A mother too cowed to stand up for him. It hurt, yes, and that hurt never really went away, but it also no longer controlled his life. He had a new and different life now.

What he had seen in Edwin's memories—the atrocities that Foxley forced him to commit—were horrible beyond compare. Real nightmare fuel.

Cesar held onto his master, and they watched each other for what seemed an eternity.

Edwin finally said, "You're not even afraid of me, are you?"

Cesar swallowed hard and told the truth. "No. You're not the things Foxley made you do. You had no choice. And you're better than that. I know you don't believe that..."

Edwin guffawed.

"...but you are. And you're better than Ian," Cesar persisted. "Better than all of them."

"You're a fool, lad."

"I'm your Enforcer, Edwin. Your Heir. Your creature. I wish you'd let me help you with this."

Edwin shook him off finally and stood up, fixing his clothes, but he kept his attention squarely on Cesar, still lying rumpled on the divan. "What are you going to do for me, little vampire? Ride the Wild Hunt for me? Be my villain?"

"I'll do whatever you ask me to do." A thought occurred to Cesar then, something so natural, it didn't seem at all odd that he should push himself up and take Edwin's hand. There was no ring to kiss, so Cesar made do with his knuckles.

"If you want me to ride, I'll ride. If you want me to kill Lord Ian, you need only command me…my Lord."

Edwin seemed equally impressed and saddened by the gesture. Moving his hand, he set it on the crown of Cesar's head and stroked his fingers through his hair, a surprisingly tender gesture. "You're still so innocent. Virginal. Like some newborn kitten."

"I may not have done all of the things you have, and I might not have much experience, but I'm hardly *innocent*. I was a soldier once. You know that?"

"Aye."

"So, teach me how to be a proper vampire. Teach me, and I'll serve you and be the greatest Enforcer you have ever made."

Edwin considered that a long moment.

Cesar smiled wryly. "I'm a right pushy bitch, as you've said. I don't give up so easily. Deal with it, *Prince*."

Edwin managed to look angry, amused, and bewildered all at once. Finally, he grunted. "Spoken like a true Enforcer."

* * *

Eliza had spent most of the day down in Catherine's lab, cleaning up the mess from the night before, righting the machines, and fixing all of the connections. It wasn't that she felt somehow obligated to repair the lab, only that she needed busy work to keep her mind occupied and quiet.

At home, she could spend hours typing up Edwin's latest book or planning the details of his next book tour. Here, she had to make do with what she had. Thus, she found herself sweeping up broken glass, mopping the flagstone floor, and going to work on all of the computers, making certain they hadn't sustained too much damage.

None of it had been as severe as it seemed last night. Most of Catherine's computers were pretty well insulated against age and water damage. Only the Preservation Unit lay in ruins. Once she had all of the overhead lights working again, she spent some time examining Catherine's lovely invention.

She was surprised to learn there were no mechanical parts to the Preservation Unit. The unit was not computerized like the rest of the lab. It was older than anything here and completely self-sustaining. It was the fluid inside that had kept Malcolm alive these many years. She used a microscope to analyze a sample of the fluid, but she could not identify it.

That annoyed her. She started going over Catherine's vast library of notebooks, impressed by the woman's advanced studies in science and alchemy. Catherine had written no less than six volumes on the processes of life. Eliza sat on a stool near the library shelves, munching on an apple from the platter of fruit that Megan had brought her, and read all about Catherine's version of machine-men by the light of an old-fashioned oil lantern. She found herself glancing at the metal man standing dustily in the corner. The machine-men were something her old and now very dead friend Dr. Grott had postulated about back in New York City, a way for the great cities to run on the work of artificial beings as opposed to enslaving Poppets like herself.

Someone closed his arms around her shoulders, hugging her against him. She'd never even heard him creep up on her. She jumped, screamed like a little girl, and swung around, shoving the light of the lantern into Edwin's face.

He blinked and shielded the light with his hand. "Lovey, please…"

"Don't *lovey* me, Edwin! And stop creeping up on me! *Jesus!*" She thought about throwing the antique lantern at him, but that would likely damage it, and it was a fine piece of craftsmanship.

She looked Edwin up and down. He had changed his clothes. "What are you doing here? Shouldn't you be upstairs, fighting with Cesar or riding for Ian?"

"I was worried about you," he said, sounding hurt. "You've been down here all day. I thought you might want dinner."

"I've been cleaning Catherine's lab. And I don't want dinner, thank you very much. I'm not hungry." She was still cross with him.

All his damned vampire secrets…

"What's that?" he asked, indicating the book on the workbench.

She turned and showed him Catherine's journal, the page with the schematics for the machine-men on them, though Catherine didn't call them that. "Catherine theorized about the machine-men centuries ago. She thought she could power them the same way she'd powered her Preservation Unit, with this elixir she'd invented. I think it's some kind of volatile molecular fluid that carries its own electrical charge."

"Ah." He looked over the book, obviously not following.

She picked up a beaker of the brown stuff she had been examining and swirled it. "Catherine created a fluid with its own renewable energy source. It's how she powered this castle in the middle of the moors in the time before the castle was wired for electricity. I'm not sure how she did it, exactly, but it does work. It's like Gatorade for machines. Machine-aid, if you will."

Edwin watched her. "You're sexy when you talk tech. And those glasses really turn me on."

Even though she was still angry with him, Eliza had trouble suppressing a smile. She hated it when Edwin made it hard for her to be angry with him. "Let's call it 'Elixir.' That's what Catherine called it."

Edwin watched her swirl the Elixir and then examine Catherine's notes. After a long silence, he said, "I'm sorry. I should have told you about Ian, about the Wild Hunt...all of it."

"Yes, you should have. You didn't." She took a deep breath to steady her voice and her nerves. "You know, you betray us and what we have when you do that. You have no idea how much it hurts when you belittle me, Edwin."

Looking deep into his aggrieved hazel eyes, she added, "I'm not a vampire, but I was a Poppet who worked in a vampire's Court. I'm not stupid. Or naïve. Don't ever treat me like I am."

"You're right," he admitted, his voice barely louder than a whisper. "I wanted to protect you, but in doing so, I disrespected you."

"I don't need to be protected, Edwin. I'm more than capable of protecting myself."

"I know that."

"Then why do you insist on doing it?"

He looked at a loss for words. "I'm sorry. I can't help it." But then he looked angry, not at her specifically, but at their current predicament. "I had *no* idea that Ian would force me into this. I trusted him, loved him once...his behavior is completely unacceptable, and I know that Catherine would be ashamed."

"Why don't you fight him, then? Why don't we just leave? Surely, you're stronger than he is...?"

"I owe him," Edwin said.

Eliza waited, her heart thudding hard up near her throat.

He took a deep breath. He let it out. He was shaking. He leaned against Catherine's workbench as if he might collapse. It took him a moment to gather himself. "When I met Ian and Catherine in 1963, I was on the run from Foxley and his agents. But, even knowing that, they took me in. Protected me. They made me welcome when no Lordin his right mind would. They weren't afraid of Foxley, like so many others—but they should have been."

He glanced over at the half-sheeted portrait sitting in a corner of the lab, Lady Catherine forever stern, forever alive, on the canvas. "They were foolish, Eliza. They thought they could lock horns with Foxley. And you know the consequences of *that*."

She grew very still. "What happened?"

Edwin looked away. "Foxley sent Chimera to retrieve me. That's when all of this business began between him and me, this...game of ours."

Chimera was the vampire assassin who had shot Edwin through the heart, nearly killing him some fifty years ago. Eliza knew the story. He then dragged Edwin back to his master, who gave him the clockwork heart he had now. Chimera was also the only vampire Eliza had ever heard of who could shapeshift into the form of almost any person, dead or alive.

Edwin killed him six months earlier, during the debacle with the Hive. At least, she *hoped* he had. They never did recover a body.

"I'm sorry, Edwin," she whispered softly. "I had no idea."

He let out his breath in a quick puff and closed his eyes. "Chimera came here to Whitby Hall in disguise. He tried to take me back, but Catherine had grown fond of me by then and intervened." He paused again as if experiencing it once more, then looked up. "She died at his hands, Eliza. Died defending me. As a result, I owe Ian a blood debt. I got his wife bloodied murdered. That's why I had to come when he summoned me. Why I had to be here."

She felt her heart breaking into little pieces for him. "Why didn't you say something?"

He stood up straighter and looked stoic, clasping his hands behind his back. "Honestly? I was ashamed. I've done a right job of hurting every single person in my life—those who haven't bloodied died, that is. Still...it was wrong of me to bring you and Cesar. I know that. I should have come alone. But I wanted you here. If Ian meant to kill me at last to settle our blood debt, I wanted you by my side. I wanted to be able to say goodbye to you proper and all." He hung his head. "I made a mistake. Again."

Tears filled her eyes.

"I did not mean to hurt you," he said very seriously, staring down at the flagstones between his feet. "I've never meant to hurt you..."

Eliza took a deep breath. "And yet, you have. Don't you understand what I'm saying, Edwin? He threatened you. He hurt you. And still, you didn't come to me. You didn't tell me. Do you know how that makes me feel?"

He didn't respond to that.

She swallowed against the tears in her throat. "I'm your *woman*, Edwin. You said so yourself. Not just your Courtesan or some brainless Poppet. You are supposed to tell me when someone is hurting you!"

Edwin leaned back against the nearby wall. He looked frightened and defensive. He could be so volatile. "As if you tell me everything."

"What's that supposed to mean?"

He had that look, as if he wanted her and yet wanted to run away from her. "At home, you never talk about your life at Court. You never talk about *him*, what he did to you all those years ago. It's like that part of your bloody life doesn't exist. You never let me in. And you accuse *me* of being dishonest?"

Eliza swallowed. "What do you want? A written account of what it's like to be a Poppet at Court? All the gory details?"

"I want you to be honest with me! I don't want you smiling when you're falling apart. I don't want you making me hurt you because it's the only way you can come when we're making love. Jesus!" He turned and faced the wall, his shoulders shaking.

Eliza hovered in space, in darkness, barely able to breathe. "Why would you want to know such horrible things about my life?"

Edwin turned. "For the same reason you want me to tell you everything. Because they're things that make you hurt! And I want to protect you from them!"

"Protect me from my own trauma?" she shouted. "How are you going to do that? Build a time machine and go back in time?"

He stared at her speechlessly.

Tears filled her eye. She held up her hands as if to ward him off. "You're acting like a child, and I'll have no part of it." She closed Catherine's journal, set it down, and started to get up, but Edwin swung around, grabbed her by the upper arms, and turned her to face him squarely.

She tried to shake off his hold, but his grip was like steel. "Let go! You're hurting me. Stop hurting me!" she screamed, surprising even herself.

He moved closer to her until he had her pinned against Catherine's workbench, no place to run. "Is that what he did to you?" Edwin asked, his voice an intimate little whisper. "How did he hurt you?"

She trembled but didn't answer.

"What did he do to you?"

"I don't want to talk about it." She was starting to cry.

She didn't know why he was doing this to her, why he was making her hurt all over again. "It's over, Edwin! It happened a long time ago." She tried to shake him off, but he wouldn't move. "Unhand me!" she cried.

"Tell me something he did to you. One thing."

"No," she said savagely, baring her teeth. "Fuck you."

"Then we'll stay here until you do."

"Let me go!" she screamed at him, sounding like some hysterical madwoman. A burst of fury animated her. Twisting her wrists, she managed to break his hold, surprising them both. She raised her hand and hit him hard across the face, her fingernails cutting across his cheek.

He flinched but then pinned her with the calmest of looks. The wound on his cheek mended itself in seconds.

It infuriated her. His terrible calm. His power and invulnerability.

These vampires.

She struck him again, harder this time, the scratches deep enough to draw his unnaturally dark blood. It filled the marks she made, then dissipated as his body quickly reabsorbed the precious blood it needed for him to survive, not a single drop wasted. The scratches disappeared.

It wasn't fair.

None of it was fair.

A keening noise she barely recognized rose up in Eliza's throat. She struck him hard across the shoulder with her unnatural Poppet strength. She struck him again and again. Her hands went numb with the strikes, but she couldn't seem to stop herself. She was outside herself, watching this ridiculous melodrama unfold from afar. She couldn't make herself stop as she cried and hit him repeatedly, hating him so much it hurt her whole body. She hit him until she couldn't anymore and the strength went out of her.

Edwin caught her at the shoulders and steadied her. She leaned against his shoulder and wept hysterically until she was all used up. It felt both good and horrible at the same time, and she decided in that moment that she never felt more naked and raw and human than when she was in Edwin's arms.

When she had quieted some, Edwin used a handkerchief from his pocket to wipe the tears off her face. "Better?"

"No," she said, unable to meet his eyes. "It'll never get any better."

"Yes," he told her, "it will. You're stronger than this. Tell me."

She shuddered, gasping for breath. "I hate him. He made me afraid. I still dream about him all of the time." She was talking like a little girl afraid of the dark, she realized. She didn't care. He wanted to know, and so he would.

She was wringing her hands by the time she finished the long laundry list of violations she had suffered at her master's hands—the way he had hurt her, inside and out. She even told him about the surgery she'd needed a few weeks after being sent to his Court. It had left her with so much scar tissue inside that she sometimes couldn't even feel it when Edwin was making love to her.

"I wish I hadn't told you," she said at the end, her tear-stained face resting against his chest. She sounded hoarse and old, far older than she should. "I feel so...tainted. I feel so filthy. I feel like I'll never be clean again."

"It wasn't your fault."

"I know that. But it's as if he took me and broke me and remade me, but it's all wrong, the way he put me back together. All the pieces don't fit right anymore." She sucked back on the terrible tears burning her throat and nose. "I'm not the girl I was. I stopped being her a long time ago."

She took a shuddering breath, her throat clotted with tears. "I wonder if he'll find me one day. I think about that all of the time. I dream about it. I think about what he'll do to me when he does, and I know I'd rather die than go back to that place and be that...*thing*."

Edwin was silent a good long time. She appreciated that he was listening but not offering useless advice or making promises she knew he couldn't keep. Despite their arrangement, she was not truly Edwin McGillicuddy's Courtesan. He had no legal recourse—no way to protect her—should her master return to collect her, and they both knew that.

He let her cry herself out. It seemed to take forever. But after a while, he whispered, "I have something for you. I was going to wait until a more appropriate time, but I think this is that time."

Eliza edged back and waited, her heart thudding painfully in her chest.

Edwin rummaged through his suit pockets until he found it. It took a few moments because he wasn't very well organized. "I've been carrying it around with me everywhere, afraid you'll find it." He turned and presented her with a small, oddly shaped metal ring box. He opened the clamshell lid.

It was a ring, but not one she would have ever expected to receive from Edwin—or anyone. It was a thick, white gold band topped by a small, heart-shaped ruby—no, not a ruby, she realized. It was a strange, exotic purplish-pink diamond.

A bloodstone, she realized, a red diamond, the rarest gemstone in the world. It was probably worth millions of dollars. She looked at it, too afraid to touch it.

"I don't understand," she said after a moment.

"It's a bloodstone."

"I know. I just don't understand why you have it."

Edwin studied it. "It's part of my Inheritance from Foxley. It's belonged to me, mounted in one form or another, for over two hundred years." He hesitated. "One of the few remaining bloodstones in the world."

She felt a dull shock as she stared down at the terrifying little ring. "That's a Covenant ring. Ian wears one of those. And Mr. Stephen, Foxley's Poppet. Do vampires even do that anymore?"

"Not really. Not unless they're very old. Or just old-fashioned." He took the ring from the box and went to one knee. She watched him, captivated by the gesture. "I'd like you to wear my Covenant ring, Miss Book. But I want you to wear it as my engagement ring. Will you accept it?"

She felt dizzy and it was very hard to think. She sat down on the edge of the workbench before she fell down. Covenant rings were medieval expressions of love, a wedding ring for eternity. When a Favorite wore a Covenant ring on his or her finger, it meant he or she had accepted her Lord's proposal. It meant the Vampire Lord would grant that Favorite an Inheritance at some unspecified point in the not-too-distant future. By accepting Edwin's Covenant ring, even under the pretense of marriage, she would be surrendering herself entirely to him. She would be Edwin's Courtesan and wife, and, eventually, his daughter and Heir.

He watched her, carefully. "If you need time..."

"I..." she answered uncertainly. "I...are you sure?"

He stood up and held her eyes as he said, "Aye. I have never been surer of anything."

He took her hand and drew her close against him. "Eliza, I would like you to be my Bride, my wife, and my Heir. Will you accept my Covenant? Will you wear its sigil?"

Her heart was thudding harder now, so hard it hurt. Edwin's whiskers tickled her as he waited for her response. Finally, she told him the only truth she knew. "Yes to the wife part. As for the other things—I don't know, Edwin. I just don't know."

She held her breath, wondering if she had offended him.

Edwin smiled, undid the clasp of the chain around her neck—the one she wore for the key to his clockwork heart—and slid the bloodstone ring onto it, then re-clasped the chain around her neck. The key, weighed down by the ring, hung at a place just over her heart.

It seemed a fair compromise.

She bit her lip. "Not angry?"

Edwin kissed her lightly on the forehead. "I'm...incredibly honored."

She smiled, too, and gave him a shy look. "Will you love me?"

"Here?"

"Yes."

"Are you all right?"

"Yes." She swallowed hard and ran a hand over his shirt, the places she had struck him. She didn't like that she had done that, but at the same time, she was happy they were finally being honest with each other.

The bloodstone winked in the lights of Catherine's lab.

A wedding. *Marriage.* Should she, a Poppet, even dare to dream of such a thing?

"You're very strong," Edwin said.

"I don't feel strong."

He lifted her chin and kissed her, the ring pressed between their two bodies. They made love slowly, with Edwin touching her in different ways to heighten the sensation. His bite was incredibly potent. Afterward, she sat curled against him on the workbench, her head on his shoulder. It was getting cold, the fire in the hearth burning out, but she didn't want to move just yet. She wanted to stay here with him just like this.

| ix |

The following morning, Eliza rose early, groomed, dressed, gathered up all of Catherine's notebooks, and called for an audience alone with Lord Severn. Of course, Edwin wanted to be there with her. She could see that in his eyes when she told him her plan, but he chose not to fight her when she insisted she do this alone.

"Give me a half hour. That's all I ask, and I'll let this go. Then I'll let you do whatever it is you need to do, Edwin."

He had been brushing his impressive set of teeth and spat into the sink. He watched her in the bathroom mirror. "You think you can alter everything by talking to Ian?"

"I think I may be able to, if you'll let me. If you'll trust me." She hesitated, searching for the answer in his eyes. "Do you trust me?"

He stood up straighter. "Aye. I trust you."

"You won't come to my rescue or protect me or anything?"

His eyes moved, the toothbrush clamped in his teeth. "It's him I don't bloody trust."

"A half an hour."

"And then I come to get you."

She smiled and hurried off.

Lord Severn was waiting for her in his private study. She burst in, glasses on, hair up, very businesslike just as if she were starting a new day at work. But her focus was on Lord Ian Severn.

"Where's that Cockney bastard?" Lord Severn asked. "We have training with the horses today." He sounded bored. He sat in his favorite chair, sipping his breakfast from a teacup. Behind him, near the mantel, stood Malcolm Whitby, dressed in a suit that fit him much better today. The suit was extra-large, and it would have hung off Edwin's bones. On Malcolm, it barely contained his solid linebacker body.

As she approached, Malcolm watched her in that way he had, as if it would be very dangerous to be alone with him. Not predatory or bloodthirsty. Something else.

"Edwin is busy," Eliza told Lord Severn coolly, turning her attention back on him. "And he's not a Cockney bastard. Do not address my Lord as such."

She did not wait for his response. She came around the seating area and set the dusty journals on the mantle beside Malcolm. The heat he gave off was like a blast furnace, or she was only too used to the cool, negative presences of vampires. She turned to face Lord Severn, conscious of how close the werewolf stood, of how his presence filled the room.

"You speak like a Favorite," Lord Severn said, raking his eyes over her in an unfriendly way.

"I am his Favorite," she said, standing close enough for Lord Severn to see the bloodstone ring hanging on the chain around her neck. "Does our love really hurt you this much? Is that why you've chosen him to ride? Because you hate what we have and what you have lost and will never have again?"

"I don't hate Edwin." The vampire's keen old eyes tracked the glint of the Covenant ring around her neck. "He merely disappoints me. The way he allows his women to run his life for him. He looks foolish and weak."

"And I'm here to talk about Catherine. The woman who was *your* Lord and master before you became *her* Heir."

Lord Severn's eyes flared. "I do not wish to speak of Catherine to you..."

"I found her journals," Eliza said, cutting him off. "I read them. She loved you immensely, Lord Severn. She loved you more than life, though I can't fathom why."

He glared at her. His gaze was like a laser, burning through her clothes and into her flesh beneath. Even so, she stood her ground. She would not be cowed by this broken, embittered old man.

"Have you seen Catherine's lab? Her inventions? There's a Golemi down there."

"You have no business rummaging through my wife's lab..."

"That's tough shit, you old bastard," she said.

She sensed Malcolm stiffening. She glanced up and thought she spotted the slightest glint of admiration in his eyes. "I learned things, Lord Severn. Catherine did not want this to happen again—not to you or anyone else. And that is the reason she created the Golemi. There is only one in the lab, but according to Catherine's notes, she created others. Many more, in fact—"

"You dare?" Lord Severn spat. "You dare come into my house? You dare upset my household...?"

"I dare," she answered simply. "I'm not afraid of you. I'm not afraid of the vampires."

"You should be."

She nodded. "I was a Poppet in another life," she admitted bitterly, surprised by her own admission. She hadn't planned on telling him that, but now that she had, she was willing to roll with it. "They made me afraid. They hurt me as much as they possibly could. Now, there is nothing you can say that will frighten me."

Lord Severn sat stunned in his seat, staring up at her. "Well, they certainly aren't making Poppets the way they used to."

Eliza took a deep breath as she worked on getting her temper back under control. "She died before she could tell you, but Catherine built the Golemi so you would not have to ride another Wild Hunt. She didn't want anyone to have to do that, should the Light return." She showed him one of the open journals, the lovingly drawn illustrations. "Where are they being kept?"

Lord Severn looked at the illustration, his face suddenly overwhelmed with sadness. "I do not know. She never shared that information with me or with anyone. Catherine was very secretive about her work." He smiled at her, grimly, bitterly. "And now, the Light has returned. And there is no way to fight it except to destroy it."

"Catherine believed there were other ways of defeating the Light. And so do I."

"And, pray tell, little Poppet, what are these secret ways?"

Eliza hesitated as she felt her bravado wilt. "Well, I don't know, exactly. But Catherine had faith that something could be done. Isn't that enough to make you stop this madness?"

"Now you're just boring me," said Lord Severn, his face blanked of all emotion. "It's obvious you're here to beg me to let your lovely but immensely stupid Vampire Lord go. You wish for me to let this cup pass him by." He flicked his hand at her. "So beg, little Poppet, and let me explain how that is entirely impossible, and let's be done with this theater already."

She clenched her teeth as a spike of anger rose within her. She could not afford to lose her temper now, not when Edwin's future depended on her next actions. "I thought Lord Foxley was the worst of you lot. But I question that now."

"Vampires are not pleasant creatures," Lord Severn said nastily, showing a hint of teeth. "Cry me a river!"

Eliza ignored his display. "Give me a day to find an answer. Give me today to find another way." She gave him a solemn nod. "I want to return to Whitby Village and discover the names of the Fae."

Lord Severn watched her for a long, silent moment. "You're insane. The Fae are the entire village, Miss Book. They are the Light and the souls of the people. The ones who attacked you in the lab were not even pure Fae. Just Sleepwalkers. In fact, the Fae within them was so diluted it was a miracle they were able to do anything at all, yet they did. That is how determined they are. And it is *all* of them."

"I disagree," she protested. "I can't see how that's possible in this day and age, not with how people migrate. Some of the people down in the village are transplants. *Human.* I want to discover the names of the two Sleepwalker women who died by Malcolm's hand and then trace them back to their circle of friends."

She raised a hand and tapped Catherine's journals. "Catherine says the Faestick together. They stay in tight groups. That's why they're strong. I know I can discover who the Fae are, and when I have the list, then you can hunt them in secrecy. You can hunt those people *specifically*."

She waited expectantly, hoping her words made sense to him. Admittedly, her idea did not sit well with her, and she was the first to admit it was flawed as hell, but it was better than the wholesale slaughter of a village of people, many of whom were probably untainted by the Light.

But Lord Severn just sat there, watching her. Finally, she could take the silence no longer. She gestured wildly. "Isn't it better than killing every man, woman, and child in your province?"

"They have to die, Miss Book," Lord Severn said softly. "All of them. We cannot allow any escapes this time."

Eliza clutched her hands together in front of her to keep from wrapping them around Ian Severn's neck. "All those people...all those *children*. And when you've completed your little crusade, my fiancé will be a murderer of both Fae *and* humans, and the High Vampire Courts will condemn and destroy him for that. He'll be put to death as a menace."

Lord Severn looked insulted. "It is better a village full of humans and Fae and a single vampiredie than the whole world be torn apart by the war between the Darkness and the Light."

She took a bold step toward him. "You would sacrifice Edwin? A vampire you loved? One Catherine loved?"

Lord Severn grew very still in that way of vampires, as if he could hold that pose forever, a living statue. "If Edwin were given the same choice, do you not think he would choose to sacrifice himself, or me, or you, rather than the whole world?"

He had a point. But Lord Severn hadn't given him that choice. Not even that. "And if I said I could save him? Save you?"

"Save the world?" Lord Severn mocked her.

She didn't know what else to do, how else to bargain for the time she needed, so she said, "What do you want in exchange for my failure?"

Lord Severn looked interested, finally.

"Give me one day. If I fail and Edwin must ride the Hunt, I'll give you whatever you want."

"Anything?"

"That's what I said."

"Even yourself?"

She hedged on a response, but only for a second. "Even that."

Lord Severn smirked. "You would give yourself to me as my Poppet?" He looked her up and down, making a lascivious show of it.

She ignored his silent threat. "If Edwin is gone, what do I have left, Lord Severn? I won't want to return to the States. I'll have nothing left for me there."

"You'll be my Poppet," he warned. "With all that entails."

"I understand."

"And Cesar—"

"Not part of the deal." She glared at him, at his audacity. Not that she was surprised. If it was two things that vampires excelled at, it was lust and greed. "Cesar goes free regardless of the outcome."

Lord Severn thought about that for a long moment. He looked unconvinced.

As if he'd been summoned, or perhaps listening at the door, Cesar burst into the study and looked directly at Lord Severn. Eliza turned to say something to him, but his face was so serious, so somber, her voice caught in her throat. She wondered if Edwin had sent him in or if he was acting under his own will. From the determined look on his face, she was willing to bet the latter.

"No, I am part of the package," Cesar insisted. "If Miss Eliza fails, you get us both. Miss Eliza as your Poppet and me as your Enforcer." He hesitated. "Or whatever you want me for."

Eliza glared at Cesar, trying to ward him back with just her eyes, but he ignored her and simply stood there, soldier-straight, hands clasped in the small of his back, waiting on Lord Severn's answer.

The old Vampire Lord's eyes gleamed, the bait too great to ignore. "Your offer is acceptable. You'll have until tomorrow night, the night of the Hunt, to present an accurate list of the Fae. That's approximately thirty-six hours. If there's no list, Edwin rides and you two stay with me. Forever." He hesitated to let that last sink in.

Eliza swallowed hard and then nodded.

Ian Severn narrowed his eyes on her. "You'll be my Heir. My child. Perhaps my second wife."

She felt cold. "I understand."

Lord Severn shifted his reptilian gaze to the boy. "And I'll find a use for your talents, lad. If nothing else, you'll be my plaything. My bed warmer."

Cesar's cheeks paled but, to his credit, he never flinched.

Ian's eyes drifted up to take in Malcolm, standing nearby. "My wolf goes with you, Poppet. To aid you. And to scout the area for the Wild Hunt that will most certainly take place in two days."

"And to watch me."

"That too." Ian smiled. It was a very hungry smile. A vampire smile.

* * *

At the first signs of trouble, Baldy retreated to what he liked to call the "entertainment lounge."He knew his master wasn't pleased, and by the sounds of the raised voices coming from his study, he didn't think this was going to end well for anyone.

The lounge was the only room in the whole castle with a fifty-inch television and a full satellite and entertainment system. Most of the denizens of Whitby Hall were not really couch potatoes—at least, not like he was. Megan and her boys were always preoccupied with running free through the forest and other werewolf rubbish like that, and Lord Ian looked down his nose at human endeavors in entertainment.

The boss could be quite a snob at times.

Baldy sank down on the sofa, an old brown thing of that particular type of buttery leather that molds to your ass over time. Baldy and the sofa went way back. It was here when he first come to Whitby Hall on vacation in the late 1940s.

Back then, Baldy was a trusted underboss, one of many who belonged to the Chicago division of "Lucky" Luciano's vast crime syndicate. Actually, Lucky wasn't all that lucky, when Baldy stopped to think about it, seeing how he was caught, imprisoned, and then deported late in his life. After that, most of Lucky's holdings were seized by other, younger, and more ambitious members of La Costa Nostra. Soon after, the old guard began to fall apart. Baldy was forty-one by that time, not a young stud anymore, and for the first time in his life, he was looking at a massive reorganization. He didn't think he'd survive it. He was small, ugly, and secretly Jewish. No one respected him. His underlings were barely aware he even existed.

Baldy decided to take a vacation abroad, see the world, and put his head together. The broad he was seeing at the time was from East Anglia, so, natch, they went there. He soon learned that things were even weirder here than they were back home. For one thing, there were vampires and werewolves everywhere. For another, a vampire couple owned this big, drafty castle on the moors and pretty much controlled the whole village of Whitby, which was so small and inconsequential that you couldn't even find it on a map.

The broad quickly ditched him—she'd just needed a ticket home, he learned from the note she'd left him after he woke up alone one morning—so Baldy decided to visit the castle and see the vampires. He'd always liked vampires, and he'd seen all of the movies. Bela Lugosi's interpretation of *Dracula* was a particular favorite of his. So, one night, he broke into the castle, using the same lock picks he normally used for safe-cracking back home. Unfortunately, Lord Ian Severn was a terrible host and told him to get lost. He didn't even have a cool accent.

Baldy couldn't figure out why the vampire seemed so resistant to warm-blooded visitors. "I've decided," he told the vampire that night, standing in the study, his hat in his hand as if he was attending synagogue. "I want to be like you guys. I want to be one of you."

"Any particular reason why?" the tall, thin, male vampire asked. He and the female were making love on a divan.

The male looked like a young, trim, black-haired buccaneer, maybe a fruity version of Errol Flynn in *Robin Hood*. It made Baldy jealous. He hated exercising and had lost half of his hairline by the time he was twenty years old. He would never look like this cat, he knew. But Lady Severn was one hot dame.

Suddenly, Baldy realized this was the reason he was here. This was what he had come for. "My life is over in the States. My boss is gone. My girl ran away. My family died in Treblinka. There's nothing left to live for. I want to try things as a vampire."

He thought about what else he could say to convince them to make him their Heir but decided honesty was indeed the best policy. "I'm not rich or handsome, and most folks think I'm not too bright, either, and they're probably right. But I know how to take care of my boss. Yeah, that's it." He held up a finger. "I have nuthin' to offer you but my loyalty."

For reasons he never understood, Ian and Catherine Severn accepted his covenant. Baldy went into Catherine's embrace and never again left the castle on the moors, proving that you should never go on vacation unless you're willing to change your life. Now, he spent his days drinking the house brew, taking care of his boss's meager needs, and watching his stories. He liked being a vampire. It suited him, fit him like a good suit. He'd never really been alive until after he'd died.

He was taking tea and watching *Blood Lies* on telly (he loved British slang) when the esteemed Miss Book appeared in the doorway of the room. She came and sat down beside him and looked at the TV. Her corseted body was rather distracting. Baldy looked her over, letting his mind wander a bit. She was a bit shorter than he liked his dames, but she had beautiful dark blue eyes, soft brown skin, reams and reams of wildly curling jet-black hair, and the most amazing rack he'd ever seen. A guy could fall asleep and dream forever on something like that, that's for sure.

The sight of Miss E. depressed him somewhat. It made him think of Star, his lady friend down in the village. Her real name was Dorothy Wick, and she was a big woman like he liked them, well over two hundred pounds and standing almost six feet tall. She had red hair and two children.

Star had moved to Whitby from London because, despite her great size and impressive personal strength, her husband beat her and her children, which just goes to show you that appearances didn't mean anything. For instance, Baldy was a foot shorter than Star's husband, but he'd had no problem dispatching the bloke and sinking the completely bloodless body into a bog up on the moorland. Only an archeologist would ever find the remnants of Star's husband, and that would be in about ten thousand years. He figured he didn't have anything to worry about until then.

Baldy called her his Star because that's what she was to him. His guiding star. It wasn't until he'd met her six months ago that he'd given serious thought to making an Heir. Maybe not right now, while Star's children were still living with her, but one day. He imagined teaching Star to fly (a shooting Star!) and then making love to her under the full moon. Star knew all about him but wasn't afraid. Of course, Star didn't know her abusive husband was feeding the worms. Baldy wondered if he should tell her or if that was a deal-breaker.

Two days ago, Baldy stopped ringing her. He did not want to see Star. How could he bear to look at her now, knowing what his boss planned to do to her and her children? A part of him wondered if he should send her and her children away to the States. But no, she wouldn't go. She'd come round and ask him if he was angry with her. And then Lord Ian would know about Star, and he would also know Baldy loved her so much that he was willing to betray his boss and the covenant they had between them. You didn't betray your boss in La Costa Nostra. That was doubly true among the Vampire Courts.

Miss Book looked drained of color. He knew about the deal she'd cut with Lord Ian because he'd been listening at the door for a while. In a way, he was proud of her, but also afraid for her. If she failed to stop the Wild Hunt, she would become Lord Ian's second wife, and the boss was becoming increasingly erratic in his old age. He might hurt her, and Baldy wouldn't like that much.

"Where's my husband, Baldy?" she asked. "It's very important."

Baldy looked back at the telly where *Blood Lies* was playing. The vampire Gabriel had been discovered in the bed of his best friend Mitchell, a human. Gabriel's human wife had yet to discover she had married a vampire or that Gabriel was gay and wanted a divorce. Their situation was so impossible that it was giving him anxiety. "He went out to the stables to make friends with Boyo." He tried not to look her in the face.

Boyo was the boss's prize stallion, the nightsteed that would lead the charge during the Wild Hunt. The Master of the Hunt would ride him while he slaughtered the Village of Whitby—including Star and her children.

Miss Book frowned. "I see." She sounded cold and remote. She wasn't Baldy's friend anymore, not since the boss had commanded him to make certain she stayed put—or else. But Baldy didn't want to have to do this. He didn't want to have to threaten her. He knew Megan felt the same way. Miss Book was sweet and funny, just like Star. The whole situation was impossible.

"I don't agree with what he's doing," Baldy said at last. His voice was soft and sad. "I mean, he's my boss and my master. But I don't think this is the way." He wondered how it was you killed women and children and then lived with yourself the following day. When he worked for Lucky Luciano, he never killed children. Or women. He didn't do it as a vampire, either.

"This is so hard, Miss Book. Impossible. You have no idea what this will cost me." He looked over. But she had already gone.

The phone rang and he looked at it on the end table beside him. Star's number came up on the caller ID, but he didn't answer it.

* * *

She found Edwin in the corral, putting Boyo through his paces. Boyo was a huge Thoroughbred field hunter standing at least seventeen hands, slim and chiseled, and yet he managed to loom as big as an elephant. She stopped at the gate and watched Edwin drive the horse around the course, surprised by his riding skills when he jumped the horse over a series of gates. She probably shouldn't have been, though. Edwin had lived much of his early life in a time when everything was horse-driven.

Edwin turned the horse and rode toward the gate, the big horse's head bobbing slightly as he approached her. He looked slim and a little bit foxy in his scarlet hunting jacket and tight breeches, no helmet or hat, his hair tied into a messy ponytail with a hank of black rawhide cord. His face looked paler and more intense the closer he drew as if he could see the bad news written all over her expression.

"What's happened?" he said, sliding nimbly off the horse, a crop in one hand.

"I'm going down into the village, Edwin," she told him. "I want you to know." She had decided on the direct approach, no lies, no subterfuge.

He looked alarmed. "Does Ian know?"

In the past, she might have made up an excuse so he wouldn't worry or try to stop her. But she couldn't do that any longer. If they were to be married, she owed him this honesty. She explained the deal she had brokered with the Lord of the Moors, and even explained how Cesar had unexpectedly offered himself as chattel.

"I know you're angry with me. I would be if I were you. I'm sorry." She bit her bottom lip but carried on. "The situation is impossible, but I'm trying to level the playing field in our favor and give us time to find Catherine's Golemi. I hope you can understand."

He looked at her bleakly, almost eerily, but he remained composed, though his hands tightened like twin vices around the crop.

She waited, her heart thudding painfully in her chest.

Edwin closed his eyes. She knew he was doing it because they were flashing black with his anger and he didn't want her to see. She had only seen it a few times, usually at the top of his bloodlust. It was absolutely terrifying.

"I understand," he said at last. His voice was calm, but a kind of electrical current seemed to be flowing through his body and, after a few seconds, his hands snapped the crop he was holding. "I understand, and I trust you."

Tears filled her eyes to overflowing. "I know you're cross with me, but I need you to have faith. I can do this, Edwin. I can save you. I can save us. I just have to find a way."

She swallowed hard. She felt like she was choking on a walnut. "I love you, Edwin, and I need you to have faith."

She didn't wait for an answer. She turned, shaking like a leaf in a storm, and headed back to the castle.

| X |

It was generous of Lord Ian to give her thirty-six hours, but she knew they would fly by like nothing at all.

Eliza fairly flew up the stairs to their suite and tossed some clothes randomly into a valise, then swung around and found her utility bag. She double-checked to make certain all of her tools were there, snatched up a parasol, then hurried down the stairs to Ian's study. She grabbed Catherine's stack of journals and added them to her valise, then hurried for the door.

Megan had her Slipstream running for her down in the bailey. Eliza slowed as she approached Megan, a woman she'd liked—a woman she'd thought she'd had a relationship with. But, as it turned out, she was just another lackey of Ian's—like Baldy. There was no escaping the influence of vampires, she decided. Like giant cosmic puppet masters, they controlled everything and everyone from their vast ivory towers in the sky.

Megan slid out of the car. "The clutch sticks. Just give it a moment and it'll be fine."

Eliza looked at her. "That's a sign that the clutch master cylinder is low on fluid."

Megan looked surprised. "You know about cars?"

"I know about a lot of things."

Megan stared down at her feet, her face and ears burning red. "I would never want to hurt you, ducky. I like you."

"But you will if I try to escape the village."

Megan bit her lip. "I owe Lord Severn my loyalty. All of us wolves do. Without him, the pack would have been hunted to extinction a long time ago. I'm sorry, but try to understand."

"I'm sure your loyalty to Lord Severn is well worth the price of your soul."

Megan looked away as if she might cry. But Eliza felt not an iota of sympathy for her. They'd been friends. Or Eliza had thought so.

Malcolm was heading toward her across the parapet. She had hoped she might escape the castle without seeing him. He was dressed in a long grey trench coat and carried a valise of his own. The coat was open, and the wind was blowing it back. It framed his dark worsted suit and imposing physique.

Megan turned back to her. "I've been talking to Mickey every night on the telephone. That was all you, Eliza. I would never have been able to do that without your help."

Eliza ripped her eyes away from Malcolm's approach to fix them on Megan once more. "I want you to know something, Megan."

Megan looked up. "What's that, ducky?"

"If anything happens to Edwin or Cesar while I'm gone...if they're harmed in any way...I'll come for you and your boys. If this fails, I'll be Ian's Bride, his Heir. And my first act after my death will be to cut your fucking hearts out. Do you understand me?"

Megan blanched and took a quick step back, almost buffeted by Malcolm as he moved past her and slid into the passenger side of the car.

"Watch your back, *ducky*." Eliza got in the running car, ground the gears a few times until she got the hang of the old car, then drove off for the village.

***

They rode for ten minutes in silence before Eliza said, "You're not one for many words. Big, silent type?"

Malcolm looked uncomfortable. He also looked sexy as hell in his snug-fitting grey pinstripe suit, his long black hair carefully combed back over his ears and secured at the nape of his neck with a cord. He filled the car to capacity and then some and made it seem tiny.

"The language is strange to me now," he said, speaking with a weird, clipped dialect that sounded like it was stuck somewhere between Great Britain and the Scottish Highlands. She had lived with Edwin long enough to recognize some of the more popular British dialects. Edwin's was definitely Bow-bell, circa 1800. But Malcolm's she couldn't place at all.

"I am afraid I will misuse it," he added shyly, looking down.

His insecurity was unaccountably sweet. It was like learning a football player liked to paint flowers or play guitar or something.

He watched her in the reflective glass on his side of the car, making her want to squirm in her seat. She kept her eyes on the road as she piloted the old, rambling sedan along the curving, alien-looking landscape of the moors. They passed the occasional dairy farm, and sometimes an old, crumbling stone church that seemed to sit in the middle of nowhere. She kept her gloved hands at two and ten on the wheel.

Finally, she said, "I'll help you. I mean, if you misuse a word down in the village, I'll correct you. If you want."

"Thank you. Why?"

She was confused. "Why would I not?"

"I am your enemy. Why should my lady care?"

She frowned through the glare of the smeary windshield. "You saved me from the Fae. I owe you."

"No," he answered. "It was duty. My lady owes me nothing."

She sighed. "It's 2022, Malcolm. We don't do chivalry like that anymore. You saved me, so I owe you one—as we say in the States."

Malcolm looked like he was ready to argue—or maybe he was only contemplating using the right words—when he turned to look out the windshield instead. "What are the States?"

"Oh, Jesus," she muttered. "You have been sleeping a long time." She took a deep breath. "It's the country I come from. It's a new country—in central North America." She went on to try and explain about America and what it was like, wondering if any of this made any kind of sense to him.

"The colonies," he said finally.

"Yes," she agreed. "Like that."

He put out a hand and touched the cool glass of the windshield, then moved it to the dashboard of the car. She thought he might be feeling for the engine.

"It's not magic. It's electricity," she explained. "You know about electricity?"

"Lady Catherine made electricity down in her lab. Aye, I know."

"It's an…electric coach. Only, don't call it that. We call them automobiles. Or cars. 'Car' is the right word. This one is an older model from around twenty years ago called a Slipstream sedan."

"So, it is not powered by invisible horses?"

She thought he was being serious until she glanced over.

He was smiling. "Megan had me watch your cable channels all last night. The History Channel, and then the Discovery Channel. I learned much. Not everything, but much."

"And you let me go on," she said, trying not to smile in return.

"I enjoy listening to you speak," Malcolm told her. "Are dogs still hunted? Are wolves? Tell me."

She had to work to keep up with Malcolm's erratic thought processes. "Dogs are pets now. But some are still used to herd animals like down in those farms." She pointed toward a field full of grazing sheep. "Wolves were hunted long ago, but not anymore. They are gone from most places."

"That is sad but expected," he said, then seemed to think of something. "Is it all right if I say 'aye' or has this changed?"

"No, it's all right if you say it here. I've heard it used down in the village."

"Aye. Many thanks to my lady." He was smirking again.

"But don't call me 'my lady' or anybody 'my lady' or whatever. My name is Eliza Book."

"Lady Eliza Book," he said.

"No, just Miss Book."

"But you are betrothed to your Lord." Malcolm frowned. "He has chosen you to be his Heir and his Favorite." He glanced down at the ring on the chain she wore.

With one hand, she slid it back inside her coat. The last thing she needed was trouble from the natives or anyone asking questions about her bloodstone.

Malcolm continued by saying, "You will be Lady McGillicuddy's Heir one day, aye?"

She thought about that. Malcolm was both astute and observant. He might look like a teenage boy and have slept half a century under an ancient, crumbling castle, but he was a quick study. She would need to be careful not to underestimate him. "Perhaps. But I'm just Miss Book now. I won't be a Lady until I choose to be."

"Until you choose?" He sounded surprised. "Your master is letting you choose?"

"He is not my master."

"Edwin is a Vampire Lord and you are his Favorite."

"But he's not my master. Mostly, he does what I tell him to do."

Malcolm blew out his breath. "So much has changed."

As they approached the village, she thought it might be time for a female empowerment talk. She didn't need him saying or doing something embarrassing.

She talked about women's suffrage first, which lead to other things. Soon, she found herself talking about the rights of all marginalized people. Malcolm nodded but said nothing as she explained about the new same-sex marriage laws. She then moved on to the nonhumans, explaining that they were the last minority group to be struggling for human rights. Malcolm was, naturally, very interested in werewolf rights and suffrage.

She didn't think he was ready to hear how the vampires had come to control—or at least influence—at least half of the businesses and governments in the world, or that it was that fact more than anything that had helped passed the Vampire Bill the year before.

"Your people—the humans—have accepted the vampires before the wolves?" Malcolm sounded bewildered.

"Yes." She felt uncomfortable suddenly. "I guess they figured the vampires are more human than the werewolves."

"Then they do not know the vampires. They are much less human than they seem. And *more* human. If devils are permitted to walk the world, it is in the guise of vampires."

His statement surprised her. "And yet you call a vampire master."

Malcolm was silent for a long moment. "Lord Ian and Lady Catherine are unusual among their kind. They were kind to my people when the humans—and other vampires—were not. They gave us sanctuary when the Church hunted us. They protected us when the humans came with their swords and nets and guns. Without them, my people would be extinct in all of East Anglia, perhaps all of Britain." He narrowed his eyes. "I wish to honor Lady Catherine's legacy. That is all."

"By listening to Lord Severn."

He didn't answer, but he seemed to pick up on her concern, because after a few moments of hesitation, he said, "Lord Ian has changed. I am aware." He clasped his hands in his lap and stared down at them. They were large, roughened hands, nothing like the delicate, white, glove-like hands of vampires that she was used to. "But I owe Lord Ian a blood debt. I must obey his word as long as I remain his hunting dog."

"Lord Ian is very good at collecting blood debts," Eliza pointed out as they reached the outskirts of the village. "And do you actually like that? Being called a 'dog?' It sounds…derogatory." When she realized he probably didn't understand what "derogatory" meant, she added, "Offensive and uncivil."

Malcolm looked up, his electric green eyes alert. "It is a great honor to be called as a hunting dog in the Wild Hunt."

"You wolves have some strange customs."

"Humans, too." He smiled at her. "But I like that the dark-skinned humans have been accepted and are no longer slaves. That brings me great joy."

It took her a moment to realize what he meant. Then it took her a moment more to respond. "I don't know about 'accepted.'"

He kept his eyes on her, which was just a hair too flirty for her tastes. Not that she minded, exactly, because it was flattering to imagine that someone as sexy as Malcolm found her attractive. But she didn't want him getting the wrong idea about this trip.

They parked in the lot behind the Wolf's Head Inn and Eliza got out with her valise. Malcolm insisted on carrying it. She thought about protesting, but he seemed so eager to do the gentlemanly thing that she wound up giving in.

They went inside and talked to a young female concierge at the front desk. She was very thin, with long brown hair tied back in two braids, which made her seem younger still. The nameplate affixed to the front of her shirt said ANNIE.

"Help you fine folks?" Annie asked in a dialect that suggested she'd never seen the outside of Whitby. She gave Eliza a professional smile, then her jaw dropped when she saw Malcolm standing just behind her.

"We'd like two rooms, please," Eliza said, half-hoping Annie would quickly move past her sexy werewolf shock and do her job. She was living on borrowed time here.

"I'm afraid we're booked solid," Annie replied, finding it difficult to tear her attention away from Malcolm, who didn't seem to notice. He was too preoccupied with a little spring toy on the counter shaped like a frog.

"Booked?" Eliza said.

"We have folks coming in from all over for the funerals at St. Catherine's." She finally dropped her eyes to Eliza. "You're not local, aye?"

"No, we're American," Eliza said, hoping Malcolm wouldn't ruin it by speaking.

"Well, since you're not local, you might not know. Two fine old ladies passed on the night before last."

That would be the Fae who had attacked her at Whitby Hall. She recalled Catherine's notes. The town was burying the Faes' physical forms since Malcolm had killed their spiritual forms down in Catherine's lab.

Eliza tried to look innocent and said, "I'm sorry to hear."

Annie looked over her computer. "Let me see if anyone has canceled. Won't be a moment!"

While she checked, Eliza glanced around the rustic walls of the inn. Like the Wolf's Head, it was mostly made of stone and sported a wide variety of medieval weaponry and animal heads. She wondered if any of the weapons had once belonged to Malcolm—or maybe his family, if he had any.

He kept playing with the toy frog, so she put a hand over his to stop him. He glanced up at her and smiled a little at her touch.

"I have one cancellation, so we do have a room, but only the one." Annie looked over at the two of them with great disappointment.

Eliza was about to suggest to Malcolm that they leave, but her big, brawny werewolf guardian suddenly spoke up. "Aye, we will take that room."

* * *

The room was on the second floor, at the end of the hall near the bathroom, something Eliza wasn't especially pleased about. The hallway outside would likely see a lot of traffic in the night, which was apt to make her nervous. Luckily, they weren't going to be here long, and the single, uncomfortable-looking bed was more for Malcolm's convenience than her own.

"I think it would be wise for you to stay here while I explore the village. You're apt to draw too much attention." She thought about the concierge girl who looked as though she wanted to jump Malcolm's bones.

Malcolm looked insulted as he set their valises down. "I go where my la...where Miss Book goes."

Eliza flipped one of her valises open and stacked Catherine's journals on the desk beside it. "Though I appreciate your concern, Malcolm, that won't be necessary..."

"The Fae already know we are here. You cannot go out without protection."

She turned to face him. Just what she needed, another guy stuck in outdated chivalry mode. "Have you detected any Fae up to this point?"

Malcolm smirked. She decided she disliked his smirk. It meant there was stuff going on in his little lupine brain that she probably wouldn't like very much. "We faced the Fae two nights ago, and the Fae have a hive mind. They already know who we are."

"Oh, Christ." She threw her hands up. "Not another hive mind."

"You have fought the Fae before?"

"No, but I did fight something similar just last year." She thought about the Hive, the giant group consciousness that belonged to the revolting Poppets. Being one of them, she might even have felt some pity for them and supported their cause, but the Hive tried to use her as their nuclear weapon, and they had exploited her powers as a techkinetic. Well, she had no intention of putting up with that nonsense again.

They would need to move fast, she decided.

She started sorting together her utility bag for her research mission, including the journals, a notebook, and her computer tablet. She would need to travel light and fast. She was just debating whether she would need her lock-picking tools when she realized that Malcolm was standing right behind her.

She turned, finding him much closer than she'd anticipated. He was practically standing on her hem, and his heat immediately soaked into her clothes. Malcolm leaned down, his powerful hands resting on the desk to either side of her, and sniffed at her hair.

She pushed against him to make space. "What are you doing?"

He drew back, but not far. "I want to know your scent so I can always track you. It is my duty as your protector." He went back to sniffing her, even raising his hand so he could tangle his fingers absently in her hair.

"Malcolm, stop. That's enough!"

He touched the side of her face, brushing it with his fingertips. His was rougher than a vampire's hand, but his touch was gentle and exploratory. She went to remove it and was struck by the raw, urgent hunger in those very green eyes.

She was all but mesmerized by them.

"You told me about women's liberation," he insisted. "You said that sex was no longer something to be ashamed of."

He was right. She did tell him that back in the car, except...

Just wonderful, she thought. She was stuck in a hotel room with a big, handsome, horny werewolf who hadn't gotten laid in five hundred years. What was she supposed to do with that?

"Malcolm," she said, trying to sound reasonable. She put both hands upon his brawny chest. He was so thickly muscled that he felt like a rolled-up mattress in a fancy waistcoat. "Many things have changed, yes, but we don't just do as we like, even now."

His face remained impassive, but he said, "You are beautiful and healthy, Miss Book, and I can tell from your scent that you want to mate with me." It took him a moment to find the right words. "I am not...averse to that."

Her face flushed hotly. "That's...inappropriate."

"Why?"

"We only just met."

"You would like me to court you first?"

She stared into his faintly glowing emerald eyes, wondering if he was being serious or not. She waited for a smirk to indicate that he was joking—"taking a piss with her," as the English would say—but he only continued to stare at her in his fixed, ravenous way as he waited for her answer.

He was being perfectly serious.

Oh, Lord. Was she going to be able to handle this mission? She no longer knew. Deadly fairies...machine-men...giant, horny werewolf boys...she felt so hopelessly out of her depths.

Reaching blindly behind her, she grabbed up her utility bag on the desk and slid sideways away from Malcolm. "I think we should get on with business."

***

Their first port of call was the minimart adjacent to the inn. There, Eliza purchased a local paper and they sat together at the counter where the owner was making chocolate and strawberry sodas for the local children coming in.

Malcolm was unaccountably quiet. She figured he was feeling how weird things had gotten between them since their arrival. She wondered if she should discuss it with him, then dismissed the idea. She wasn't ready to deal with a giant werewolf's bruised male ego.

She found the names of the dead women on the front page of the local paper rather than in the obituaries. Whitby was a small village. Two women dying on the same night was big news. She marked their names down in her notebook.

"Mary Elizabeth Finley and Jillian Carbuncle," she said. "Now we know who the dead Fae women were." She pulled out her tablet and did a quick web search of the names.

Malcolm strained as he tried to see what she was doing. "What is that?"

"It's a tablet. I'm searching for the women's social media to see who they are related to." She thought for a moment and then began explaining again, showing him the screen. "I am looking their families up in a huge database of names on the Internet. That's sort of like a virtual connection between all the computers in the world..."

Malcolm looked confused.

This wasn't working. Malcolm predated the Internet, computers...hell, pretty much everything. She tried again. "The Internet is like a giant invisible ledger with the knowledge of almost everything that has ever happened on all of these different pages, and anyone can access it if you have one of these devices." She held out the tablet.

Malcolm took it delicately in his big hands. "All of the world's knowledge is contained in this small device?"

"Yes."

He looked it over. "It says *Facebook*."

"You can read," she said, surprised. Then she wondered if she had insulted him. She knew not many people in his time could read. Such things were usually reserved for monks and royalty.

"Lady Catherine taught me." He gave the tablet back to her. "I should like to have one of those. Are they difficult to attain?"

Eliza bit back a small smile. "No. I'll buy you one."

"Do they contain books?"

"Yes. All kinds. We can fill your tablet up with as many books as you like. Hundreds. Thousands."

"I can own thousands of books with that device?"

"A whole library's worth. A hundred libraries' worth."

For the first time, Malcolm looked stunned. He sat back on his stool, trying to absorb all of that.

She didn't like the way the owner of the shop was watching them.

They returned to the car, and Eliza jotted down all of the names related to the two dead Fae women. Then she brought up a Wikipedia page about werewolves and showed it to Malcolm.

Malcolm frowned over it, then pointed out the picture of Lon Chaney Jr. as the Wolf Man. "This is not accurate. We don't look like that."

"There's a lot of stuff on the Internet that isn't accurate. You can't believe everything you read."

She drove them to a little tea house that looked especially touristy. She thought it was best to avoid the local hangouts. She ordered two cups of Earl Grey tea, and then she and Malcolm sat in a corner booth with a generous pile of digestive biscuits between them. Malcolm liked the biscuits very much. He ate ten while she was still nibbling on her first.

It occurred to her that Malcolm might be hungry. She imagined that five hundred years of suspended animation could work up quite an appetite in a young man like he was. The way he ate the biscuits, with such gusto, made her smirk.

Malcolm stopped swallowing the biscuits and wiped the crumbs away from his clothes with the cloth napkin in his lap. "Forgive me. These are very good."

The uncomfortable iceberg of weirdness between them was melting, and Eliza said, "Did Megan give you any food at all today?"

He nodded. "She gave me four roast chickens."

"Four?" Holy Jesus, Malcolm was going to eat Whitby Hall out of house and home by the end of the week!

He smiled, not offended. "They were good."

She smiled too, despite herself. "Do you want some more chicken?"

He shook his head, though his eyes wandered to the serving bar across the room where a glass cake dome covered some chocolate-covered croissants. "May I have some of those?"

Eliza called the waitress over, and Malcolm started ordering everything on the pastry menu.

"You are going to have a bellyache if you eat all of that," Eliza pointed out.

Looking worried, Malcolm ordered just the croissants and another round of biscuits. While Malcolm tested the food, eating them with his fingers and with an enthusiasm she wasn't used to seeing, Eliza went over the names and addresses she had written down in her notebook, trying to determine who they should visit first.

"What will you do when you approach the villagers? You cannot ask them forthright if they are Fae," Malcolm said. He looked sad after he'd eaten the last croissant, but then he was back at the biscuits, eating them quickly, his face lit up like a little boy at

Christmas. It was cute. Edwin never looked like a cute little boy, especially when he ate.

"I'll think of something," she said. "You said the Fae have some common characteristics?"

"Yes," he said, eyeing up a pile of scones on another table. "They are tall and usually very fair and delicate. They look almost breakable."

She felt sorry for Malcolm and asked the waitress to bring them some scones. She gave both of them a dubious look but went to fetch the order.

When some of the jelly from the scones got on his fingers, Malcolm dutifully wiped them on his napkin, then stared longingly at the napkin. Eliza had a distinct impression that if Malcolm was alone, he might have licked his fingers clean—and maybe the cloth napkin, too. The thought made her stomach jump in a funny way.

Their waitress was leaning against the serving bar, watching Malcolm and giggling into her mobile phone. Just great. They were making waves all over the village now.

"We shouldn't stay here too long." Eliza glanced around at the quaint, cottage-like interior of the teahouse. She clapped her notebook shut.

Malcolm, losing interest in the scones, watched the waitress. "Why is the barmaid talking to herself?"

"Don't call her that. And she's not talking to herself. She's talking on a mobile phone. It's a long-distance communication device." She paused as she thought about that. "Goodlord, just wait until you see someone playing an Xbox."

"I am not a Lord, good or otherwise," Malcolm said, his voice pitched low as he contemplated his remaining scones, the jelly leaking from them like stage blood. "I am Freki, the king of my kind, and the Hunting Dog of the Wild Hunt." He licked jelly off his thumb, looking very proud of himself.

Eliza sighed. She had a feeling she had a very long day ahead of her.

xi

Megan was wending her way down the stairs of the castle, the day's laundry in hand, when she heard a ping from the electronic gate. Sighing, she set the load aside and went to the monitor in the computer room adjacent to the Great Hall. She was mildly surprised to find the female driver of a late-model sedan had gotten through the gates, probably using the security code that only she, Baldy, and Lord Ian knew. Since she hadn't let the visitor past the security checkpoint, and Lord Ian didn't normally entertain company, that left Baldy the prime suspect.

A few moments later, she opened the front door to find a very large woman in a sheepskin coat standing there. She was nearly as tall and wide as Megan, was very red-faced, and her hands were chapped, probably from working as a dishwasher in one of the village eateries. Megan felt mildly proportionate for once in her life.

"Hello there, dear. I'm Dorothy McNeil. Do you know if Baldy is about?" the woman inquired.

Despite her otherwise imposing size, the woman spoke softly and kept her eyes meekly pinned to the floor.

Megan slammed the door in the woman's face and looked at it. This was very, very bad. Her first instinct was to go and fetch Lord Ian and let him deal with this mess that his Enforcer had wrought, but considering his capricious moods of late, Lord Ian might just kill the woman to vent his frustration with his friend Lord Edwin. Megan did not want Baldy's lady friend's blood on her hands like that.

She didn't want *anyone's* blood on her hands. Oh, this whole situation was impossible! She stood wringing her hands, staring at the door, and trying to decide what the right thing to do was. Eliza thought she was a mindless slave of Lord Ian's. She had lost a good potential friend because of this silly drama. She didn't think she could weather Baldy's contempt if she got Star killed on top of everything else!

She took a deep breath, soldiered herself, and opened the door again. "Sorry, ducky," she said as pleasantly as she was able. "I thought I saw a mouse."

"A mouse?" Dorothy looked her up and down. "Aren't you Baldy's friend? The lady werewolf?"

"Yes." She shook Dorothy's hand. "But I don't like mice. Come inside before you catch your death."

"I need to speak to Baldy. It's very important," Dorothy announced. She looked over her shoulder at the sedan parked in the bailey. "Would it be all right if I brought the children in? It's rather chilly, and the car doesn't heat right."

"You brought children," Megan said with false cheer, feeling her figurative tail droop. Oh, this just got better and better!

***

Edwin and Ian were riding across the five miles of marshy moorland that grew around the castle when Ian's horse encountered a snake and bucked him off rather suddenly. Ian landed hard in a creek. Edwin reined Boyo back before he wound up trampling Ian, then wondered why he had afforded the vampire such a courtesy. It would serve Ian right if Boyo crushed his skull in.

Ian scrabbled around the rocky banks of a creek before dragging himself with some effort onto the flattened, muddy grass. He did not ask for Edwin's aid, nor did Edwin offer it. They both knew where they stood.

"Getting rusty, old thing," Edwin said with a smirk.

Boyo danced back, but Edwin put a hand on the horse's neck and told him mentally to be still. Ian's horses were just a little bit psychic. Boyo stopped but continued to paw nervously at the ground as if trying to decide if bucking Edwin off would be a wonderful idea. Despite their training, the horses still did not care much for vampires, not that Edwin could blame them. He wasn't keen on them himself.

Ian crouched on his hands and knees for a long moment, his hair in his face as he gulped air like a wounded animal. His shoulders looked like blades even through his padded crimson hunting jacket, and his backbone resembled a prehistoric ridge.

"What did the Fae do to you, exactly?" Edwin asked more out of morbid curiosity than concern.

It took Ian a long moment to speak. "They touched me."

"Just touched you."

"They have the unique ability to absorb life energies. Everything a human is or will ever be—their whole potential—which is the reason the human ceases to exist. They steal everything alive. But there is nothing alive in us to steal—nothing but our youth and our energy."

He pushed his hair out of his face and climbed unsteadily to his feet with the aid of a crooked nearby tree limb, one of the few with roots deep enough in the peat to weather the blanket bogs here.

"How long have you been dying?"

"Just over a year. Since they laid siege to the castle one night."

"You were beautiful in your time, Ian," Edwin said, then realized he hadn't meant to be so brutally honest.

Ian smiled bitterly up at him. He had even lost a few teeth, Edwin noted. "The first time she laid eyes on you, Catherine said you looked like some fallen angel to her. She called you a Wandering Devil."

"She was right." Edwin looked away, toward a stand of barely surviving hickory, and waited for Ian to remount his horse. He was having some trouble, so Ian unbuttoned his riding jacket, tossed it aside, and extended his great, black wings, which afforded him lift as he got back on his steed.

"I wonder where the boys are."

They had left Cesar and Baldy about two miles back. Baldy hated riding, and Cesar, though not exactly a virgin horseman, looked reluctant to follow his master as if he sensed the fission in the air.

"There is a storm coming. I can feel it." Ian squinted up at the sky. "There are times I wonder if the shields are really working. Too often, I feel the sun hunting me these days."

"It's not the shields," Edwin said. He felt nothing. "It's because you're decaying."

Ian laughed at that and had to steady himself, lest he fall from his horse again. "I don't think you have to worry too much about your woman, Edwin. I very much doubt I'll live long enough to make her my Heir."

"That's something, at least."

"You really hate us," Ian said with that same bitter smile. "You have always hated your own so much."

"I'm pragmatic," Edwin said as Boyo pranced nervously forward and back at the edge of a long, rough ravine that led down to yet another peat bog. They pocketed the land dangerously here. "We're bottom-feeders, Ian. Rapists and murderers. Monsters at the best of times."

"Yet you gave her a Covenant ring, Edwin." Ian turned his horse's head toward home. "You would drag her down into this with us."

Edwin didn't answer for a long, breathy moment. Then he said, "I gave her a choice."

"And if she says yes? If she chooses to become your Heir? What then?"

"It won't matter. I won't survive this." He turned Boyo's head and cantered off toward the castle.

* * *

"So are you and Edwin...you know?"

Cesar looked up from his mobile. Baldy was sitting on the ground beside him, feeding his horse some wild alfalfa. They had given up riding the nervous horses about two miles back.

He hated the burning in his cheeks and throat. "Are we what?"

"Together. A couple." Baldy looked interested. "I mean, how do you make something like that work? You, him, his woman..."

Cesar almost laughed. Baldy was perfectly fine with vampires, werewolves, and evil fairies, but he had problems with the idea of a trupple?

"What about you, Ian, and Catherine?" he shot back.

Baldy looked offended. "What do you take me for, a Bohemian?"

Cesar was trying to decide what to say to that when Baldy's phone went off. He picked it up. "Megan?" He listened for a few minutes, then his entire face changed expression. "Don't let her wander around! I'll be right there!"

He put the phone away and jumped to his feet. "Sorry, kid. Business to attend to. Gotta fly."

Before Cesar could ask for any details, Baldy spread his wings and shot straight up into the air like a bottle rocket, proving once and for all that fat, unattractive vampires were still better at flying than his own master, who was absolutely terrified of heights. In mere seconds, he was a mere speck on the horizon. It was pretty impressive.

Cesar jumped to his feet and started trying to figure out how he was going to get the two nervously snorting horses home. That's when a pain as big as a mountain hit him and drove him, nearly retching and gagging, to his knees.

Cesar, said his master's voice in his head. *I need you. Now!*

* * *

They had set a trap for him. Later, he wondered why he hadn't noticed anything out of the ordinary among the trees, just the shadow-dappled ground and the spare beech and firs shivering minutely around him. Boyo was nervous, of course, but he was always nervous around Edwin. That wasn't unusual.

His senses were greatly enhanced, and he still didn't detect the Fae until they were upon him. He never expected them to be so audacious.

He smelled the blood and Boyo stumbled. Blood was gushing from his horse's side from where someone had sunk a large, sharp knife between the horse's ribs. The cut had been so deep that as Boyo passed a fir, the knife had caught in the branches, further ripping apart the wound.

Part of Boyo's intestines stuck out like strange, bloody tentacles. Boyo stiffened and dropped over sideways onto the knife. Edwin slid the opposite way, landing hard in the pine needles and blood. He automatically lunged to his feet. He was now on full alert, but something slammed into the small of his back, propelling him forward. He automatically vomited blood all over his riding jacket. He figured it must be another knife.

Boyo was screaming the way animals do when they realize they are about to die. The sound of the horse's suffering galvanized Edwin as much as the sudden pressure and pain in his back. He rolled over in the leaf litter, thankful that his spinal cord had not been entirely cut and he could still move, and, almost instinctively, sent out a mental cry for help.

Cesar! I need you! Now!

Then there was no more time to think as shadows swarmed through the trees and a hoarse voice commanded the shadows under his control, "Restrain the Dark Fae and bring him to me!"

Edwin whipped around and bared his bloody teeth at a number of the shadowy figures surrounding him. "You *so* did not call me a fairy..." he snarled, scrabbling uselessly against the ground. If he could just get some leverage, he knew he could throw these tossers around like old laundry, but the knife wound must have been deeper than it seemed. He felt like the knife was literally draining the energy out of him.

"It is a special kind of athame," the same hoarse male voice explained as if he sensed Edwin's confusion. "Endowed with Fae Light. An anathema to something like you, Lord Edwin, Disciple of the Dark One."

Edwin stopped struggling and looked up. A tall, older bloke properly dressed in a grey chevron suit and deep blue cravat stood looking down upon him from his great height. He looked irritatingly innocuous, like a grandfather or great-uncle. He wasn't smiling, which at least would have helped Edwin hate him a little bit more.

In fact, the leader of the Fae looked quite grim, as if this act of violence had caused him no pleasure at all. Aside from his height, he looked human and didn't seem to follow the stereotypical Fae— whatever that looked like.

"Who the bloody hell are you?" Edwin demanded to know.

The man inclined his head. "They call me Mr. Cummings down in the village. Of course, that is only my human name. My Fae name is Corcoran. It is a name of Gaelic origins which means 'The Red One,' if you wanted to know."

He paused dramatically when he realized his name meant almost nothing to Edwin and he was not impressed. "It also means 'The Bloody One.' I earned the name among my people after slaying a dozen of your kind with my knife." Then he added, almost as an afterthought, "If you are having trouble placing me, I drove you, your woman, and your Heir here."

The driver. Ah. Edwin stopped struggling and pushed himself back into an awkward kind of animal-like crouch. Anything to make the knife in his back hurt less. "So, essentially, you're an old fairy."

Mr. Cummings, or Corcoran, smiled, showing teeth that were less than straight but looked almost metallic in the bright light of day. "I am Sidhe. Not much, mind. My blood is greatly watered down, but it is enough."

"So you're part fairy and part tosser."

Corcoran laughed. "They said you are amusing and full of wit, Prince. They were right."

Edwin narrowed his eyes at the tall man. "Thanks, I guess?" He glanced around at

Corcoran's circle of friends—farmers, herdsmen, young modern women influencers with mobiles, people from all walks of life. Most looked surprisingly human to him. The only thing they seemed to have in common was that almost all of them were tall and lithe, and most were fair of face and eye.

"We are Fae enough for you," Corcoran said, and the others gathered close, nodding in appreciation of his words like some kind of supernatural clique. "And yet, you would kill us just for that little bit of our blood, Prince. I hardly think you can blame us for taking the initiative and acting in our own self-defense."

Corcoran frowned sadly. "We really do not want to do this to you, our distant cousins, but you leave us with no choice. The Sidhe are great warriors, and we will not die without a fight."

Edwin struggled to get to his hands and knees. He even managed to succeed, though none of the Fae looked especially impressed. Corcoran's knife was doing its job. From the waist down, he just felt...dead. No pain. Nothing. He felt that was probably a bad thing. "If it's any consolation, I don't want to do this anymore than you do."

"Then you understand that it's nothing personal. Under normal circumstances, we might be friends. Allies, at the very least." He signaled to one of his people, and a tall, older man who smelled of sheep stepped forward.

The man grabbed the knife in Edwin's back and pulled it out of the sucking black hole it had made in his flesh. Edwin screamed—a scream of relief as much as pain. Agony filtered back into his lower extremities, but before he could act, or even try to escape, the man kicked him onto his back and raised the Fae knife high so it shimmered in the daylight. Edwin tried to roll away to safety, but his body felt like a series of concrete sacks tied together, too heavy to move.

The sheepherder plunged the knife down into his belly. Edwin's entire body erupted into spastic convulsions around the magical, vampire-eating athame. He felt his clockwork heart stutter as it struggled to cope with the sudden trauma. Blood bubbled up into his mouth, and he was suddenly terrified he was going to choke on the synthetic blood substitute he'd drunk only that morning.

As he tried to sit up, the old man kicked him nimbly in the face. Edwin fell back onto the ground, staring up helplessly at the sky with Corcoran standing above him, his face upside down.

"I am truly sorry about this, Lord Edwin," Corcoran said and nodded to his fellow Fae.

The old fairy reached down and pulled the athame from Edwin's body. Edwin hiccupped when it came out but felt nothing this time. Then Corcoran grabbed his head by the hair and dragged his chin back to fully expose his throat.

Edwin would have panicked had he been able to do anything but lay there like a helpless wanker. Unfortunately, the Fae knife had taken even that from him. He felt nothing. And he'd very soon *be* nothing, he realized.

A low roar filled Edwin's ears, and, a moment later, Corcoran was ripped from the ground by something positively dragon-like flying high above. Edwin's body dropped bonelessly to the ground as he watched a large bronze shape carry Corcoran and his poison knife away.

It carried him as high as the treetops before letting him go. Corcoran screamed for a remarkably long time before he hit the ground with a dull thunk on the other side of the hill.

The Fae broke into a disorderly rabble as the creature returned, darting so quickly above their heads that Edwin had difficulty recognizing it as Cesar at first. He just looked like a bronze blur. If it was one thing Cesar could do, it was fly. He swooped low, his wings close to his body, and scattered the crowd before stumbling to a running parachute landing on the ground beside Edwin.

He collapsed to his knees, breathless and windburned, then leaned over Edwin with bright-eyed concern. "Are you all right?" He sounded panicky. "Edwin? Master?"

Edwin convulsed in an effort to get to a sitting position. "Behind...you," he whispered hoarsely.

Cesar spun around just in time to see the sheepherder who had stabbed Edwin charging him with another Fae athame. "The knife...is poison..." Edwin warned, struggling to get out every word even though he knew Cesar had no intention of being stabbed if he could help it.

As the man reached him, Cesar shot skyward, his wings outstretched like tawny fans. It was more of a knee-jerk reaction than anything else, and he likely didn't mean for it to happen, but his wingtip clipped the man under the chin. Vampire wings, full extended, were like sharpened blades—literally. The motion nearly decapitated the man. The man stumbled back, an arc of blood gushing from the place where his head had once been and now lay flipped back against his shoulder blades like a lid, his knife falling harmlessly into the tall grass.

Cesar, looking more frightened than ever, dropped back down to the earth in a crouch. He seemed horrorstruck by what he had just done and crouched there in the tall, bloodied grass, unable to move. He even ignored all of the spilled blood.

That was when someone jumped him, a woman. She raised her hand. In it was another knife. Cesar whimpered around and twisted, the women clinging to his back. The woman lost her grip and started sliding down the nearly metallic slope of Cesar's wingroot, her fingers raking along the shiny, overlapping scales, a petrified scream slipping past her lips. Cesar, still in a haze of panic, flapped his wings to dislodge her.

It was a recipe for disaster as the edge of his wing cut into her shoulder and tore downward diagonally, slicing the woman neatly in half as if a giant Ginsu knife had been driven through her. The bisected woman dropped, still screaming, into the blood-soaked grass, pulling Cesar down on top of her.

Seeing an opportunity, the other Sidhe moved in as if they were sharks alerted to a feeding frenzy. As well as he'd been doing, there was no way Cesar was going to be able to fend off a crowd this large. Surprised and confused, Cesar started to scream.

Edwin forced himself to his hands and knees, his wings ripping right through the back of his riding jacket as he tried to steady himself. The last thing he was going to allow was a bunch of bloody *fairies* tearing his Heir apart.

"Fight them," he snarled at Cesar as he willed the strength back into his body. "Fight them, damn you!"

Cesar, still screaming, began to fight.

He was much stronger than he looked. Stronger than even Edwin expected. He grappled the Sidhe who were dogpiling him, using muscle memory from his time in the service, Edwin reckoned. At first, he did a series of throws and punches that were mostly military-inspired, but as the seconds ticked by and his desperation mounted, his vampire body started taking over. He crushed the windpipe of one of his enemies, and then, in a motion so simple it was like twisting a cap off a bottle of water, he ripped the head straight off the Sidhe's shoulders in an arc of hot, fresh life. Blood splattered his face and mouth and seemed to galvanize him. Soon, he had graduated to plunging a fist into a chest or grabbing an arm and wrenching it from the shoulder. The bodies piled up around him, squishy and broken.

Edwin had crawled to his feet at last. But he was forced to stand down as Cesar tore blindly into the Sidhe like some hydraulic machine gone amok, each swipe of his hands tearing away pieces of flesh or chunks of bloody hair. The Sidhe screamed in pain and frustration and, finally, the survivors began to fall back.

They had only a small percentage of Fae blood in them, after all. Cesar was one hundred percent bloodthirsty vampire. A few who were not too badly damaged began to stumble around, searching either for Corcoran or some avenue of escape.

Finding their organization tattered and their leader missing, they started fleeing into the woods in the general direction of where

Corcoran had fallen. In seconds, they had melted into the spaces between the trees, their passage so swift and graceful they stirred neither the moorland grass nor the leaves on the trees.

Unlike them, Cesar continued to stumble around like a wounded water buffalo, surrounded on all sides by a stinking hot soup of blood, bodies, and muddy, overturned earth. He kept lashing out, mostly at nothing, until Edwin moved in front of him and raised both hands.

Cesar, growling like a wild animal, lifted one bloody hand to rip Edwin's face off, but then stopped suddenly as if someone had thrown up a force field between them.

"I'm your master. You cannot hurt me," Edwin told him.

Cesar bounced back and dropped to his knees. He took a good look at the bloody mess he had made—the chunked, steaming carcasses, the endless blood, and the limbs scattered about. From experience, Edwin knew that none of it looked real. More like horror movie props. He clamped both hands over his mouth and started dry heaving, which didn't work out. He just started horking violently through his fingers and into the tall grass.

Edwin stood over him, waiting until he was empty. Then he said, "Can you get up?"

Cesar wiped his mouth and sat back on his heels, his face as white as paper. "I don't know...I don't know...I don't know..." He kept chanting those words in a mindless mantra.

Edwin felt for him. He knew how horrifically confusing this all was, but before he could offer any words of vampire wisdom, the world took a half turn around him. He felt like his skin was crawling...burning...like the UV shields weren't working. He looked at the backs of his hands where something resembling a dark tattoo of twining tree branches seemed to be growing. Fae toxin, likely from the cursed athame he'd been repeatedly stabbed with.

He opened his mouth, then dropped like a lead sack to the ground.

That snapped Cesar out of his hysteria when nothing else could. He crawled to Edwin and put his arm under Edwin's shoulders, helping him to sit up. The sudden motion made the deep, unhealed wound in his belly froth over with fresh, stinking black blood. It didn't do a lot of good for the wound in his back, either.

"Bloody hell," Edwin said very calmly as his eyes rolled up into the back of his head. He could feel spider webs of Sidhe poison crawling across his face and other parts of his body. "I think I'm fucking dying."

Before he passed out, he said one word.

* * *

Cesar sat there with Edwin's head in his lap, shaking and gulping air while in the throes of a good, old-fashioned panic attack—something he hadn't experienced since his service days. This was worse than frontline combat. He was so shell-shocked that he could barely think straight.

Blood. That's what Edwin said before he passed out.

Blood.

What the hell did Edwin mean? *His* blood? Cesar's blood? The blood all around them? That had to be it. Cesar didn't have enough blood to sustain Edwin.

He glanced around at the slaughter in the grass, but all of that was dead blood. It would be no good to Edwin.

Panic washed over Cesar. He worked on getting his breathing back under control and then dug out his mobile. It squicked in his fingers, his hands too full of blood, making it hard to find the keys.

If he called the castle, maybe he could get Megan to bring some blood substitute.

Cesar lurched, gasped, then dropped the phone as a huge pain seemed to tunnel right through his chest. His heart hurt like someone had kicked him in the breastbone. Not a panic attack. This was something else, something *worse*. Gasping and clutching his chest, Cesar spat up blood onto Edwin's clothes. He realized—belatedly, and with an awful certainty—that Edwin was dying. His master was dying!

Cesar felt the shock of the slow disconnect. It felt like someone was cutting off his limb very slowly and painfully. For the first time, he was afraid, really afraid. What if Lord Edwin died? What would happen to him? Would he even survive it?

He forced himself to breathe in and out, in and out. He couldn't afford to panic. He had to find living blood for Edwin. He had to save his Lord before he was gone, leaving Cesar an Orphan. If Edwin died...well, he didn't even want to consider what would happen to him.

Where could be get living blood? There was nothing of use at hand. Nothing but the horse, lying on its side a few yards away. It breathed roughly, its legs occasionally pedaling. Cesar knew it was dying. The wound in its side was too great.

Shifting Edwin's head to the ground, Cesar moved to it and knelt by its head. He put his hands on its burning, jumpy skin. He wondered if he was going to cry again. He didn't want to watch another beautiful animal die. He snuffled back the tears and snot in his nose.

No. He didn't have time for this. He had to focus. Edwin.

He leaned down, extended his feeding teeth, and bit deep into the horse's flesh just above the shoulder. The horse screamed and bucked. Cesar rested a hand on its neck, holding it down as blood pooled into his mouth. When he thought he had enough, he moved back to Edwin's side, leaned over, tilted his head back, and gave his master the kiss of life.

Nothing happened. Edwin remained as cold and lifeless as a stone. Cesar moved back to the suffering animal and took another mouthful, then repeated the exercise, trying to get as much blood into his master's mouth as he could.

Time passed. He didn't know how much, but slowly, ever so slowly, Edwin seemed to grow warmer to the touch, and the toxin running through his body seemed to fade and retreat. Cesar kept going until Edwin's eyes flared open and he gasped awake, his mouth roughed in the horse's blood. He coughed, struggling to sit up. Cesar braced him on his knee.

"Th-thanks," Edwin managed. He looked terrible, paler than usual (which was saying a lot, considering he was a ginger) with deadly black rings under his eyes. He looked like he wanted to say more. Instead, he curled up in Cesar's lap. The wound in his belly had stopped bleeding, at least. That was something.

Cesar drew his wings close about his sleeping master, held him fiercely for a long, silent moment like some demonic and blasphemous Pieta, and then remembered the mobile lying in the grass. He scrambled to call the castle for help.

| xii |

They were driving out of the village and into the countryside when Eliza was hit with a spasm of nausea. She jerked the car to one side, narrowly avoided hitting a telephone pole, and then hit the brake. Leaving the car to idle and her driver's side door open, she fairly stumbled into the weeds at the side of the road to throw up. Then she threw up again. Thankfully, her stomach was pretty empty. She'd only had tea and a biscuit back at the café.

Slowly, she became aware of Malcolm hovering with concern behind her. She gagged and then sat stunned in the tall grass, staring down in shock and horror at the mess she'd made.

"Are you well, Miss Book?" Malcolm asked after some time.

No, she decided. She was most certainly not well. She was confused. "I have no idea."

He offered her his handkerchief in a gentlemanly way. She wiped her mouth before standing and allowing him to guide her back to the car. Eliza turned the engine off and sat for a long moment in her seat, wondering if another spasm would hit her.

"Has anything like this ever happened to you before?" Malcolm asked.

She shook her head but kept his handkerchief clamped over her mouth just in case. She wanted to brush her teeth, and she desperately wished she'd thought to bring some breath mints with her in her utility bag.

"Are you with child?"

She glared at him. "Certainly not!"

He looked at her in that way he had, a strange commingling of concern...and something else. "Forgive me. I had sisters. And Mother was frequently with child."

"I'm not pregnant." She wasn't sure of many things in life, but she knew that to be impossible. Edwin was dead, and, as a Poppet, she had no working ovaries. There was no way she was pregnant.

"Perhaps—" Malcolm began, but she immediately cut him off.

"I can't have children."

Malcolm's eyes darkened. "Forgive me. I meant no insult. I was merely going to suggest that it was your bloodlink to your Lord."

Suddenly, she felt bad about snapping at him. He had a good point. She and Edwin were still feeling their way through their connection. A cold wave of panic passed through her as she dug her mobile out of her utility bag and rang him. After seven rings, she got his voicemail. She hung up.

"He's not answering his phone. He probably left it in our suite when he went riding with Ian." She didn't want to tell Malcolm the truth: that Edwin was likely too cross with her to take her calls at the moment. They were so very angry with each other right now. She tried Cesar next. Same thing.

A bad feeling tickled at the back of her head, and she had to suppress the impulse to turn the car around and drive back to the castle...except that what she was doing was far too important to all of them.

She felt so overwhelmed that she hit the steering wheel hard with the heels of her hands, startling Malcolm. "Sorry," she said, checking the watch pinned to her suit jacket. The morning had passed and she only had two names on the list. She was wasting too much time!

And she was running out of it.

With a deep breath, she cleared her mind, started the car again, and they drove out to the Finley farm, the first name on her list.

* * *

Cesar had put Edwin on a stringent feeding schedule. Every half hour, Cesar drank down at least six twelve-ounce bottles of the house brew—a potent combination of werewolf blood and blood substitute—and then had Edwin drink from him for approximately two minutes. He thought about plying Edwin with the drink directly but decided the added benefit of drinking from their bloodline would help him recover faster.

Edwin had no complaints. At the moment, he was willing to sink his teeth into anything that had blood in it, which made the process tricky and not as romantic as, say, what they'd shared the day before. It wasn't fun, there was no sex involved, and the truth was, it hurt—a lot. Edwin buried his teeth in the crook of Cesar's arm and gnawed at his flesh and blood until Cesar was dizzy with the pain. After that, Cesar was sick and famished and had to drink plenty of the house brew to replenish himself. Wash. Rinse. Repeat. If he had to continue doing this much longer, he decided, he was going to throw up all over himself.

By late afternoon, Edwin was sitting up in bed and the spidery veins of toxin that had been creeping under his skin had completely receded. He had dozed on and off all day, wrapped in Cesar's sheets, but now he looked almost painfully lucid.

"Did you bring me here?" he asked, glancing around Cesar's suite with bleary eyes. His voice was hoarse and crackled as if his throat was dry.

Cesar, sitting beside him on the bed, nodded. "I thought you were going to die on me."

Edwin raised his arm, and Cesar sank down against him. The touch of his master's hand on his face made the deep tension loosen inside of him. "You did well, my Heir."

"Are you better?" Cesar asked, hating the pleading, childlike quality of his voice. "Will you be okay now?"

He smirked. "Worried about me, were you?"

Cesar lay with his wings wrapped almost completely around the two of them. They were lying so close that you couldn't have slid a playing card between them. He thought about being brave and saying no, but Edwin would know better. "Yeah. I thought you were going to die and leave me and Miss Eliza alone." He squirmed. "I should call her."

"Don't. Please."

Cesar felt like crying, as stupid as that was. "You scared the hell out of me. And whatever they did to you made me sick as hell."

Edwin swallowed and gathered his strength. "Our blood..."

Cesar thought about that. "We're connected forever."

"Hell of a thing, aye?"

"Do you still...I mean...is it like that between you and Foxley? Even now?" Edwin clenched his eyes in frustration. "I still feel his pain, but I don't answer his summons any longer." Edwin smirked. "Foxley's likely very ill right now because of me. He might even call if he's not feeling too pissy at the moment."

Edwin's mobile went off as if to prove his statement. But when Cesar picked it up off the nightstand, he saw it was Miss Eliza. "Should I answer it?"

"No."

"What if she's in some kind of trouble?"

"She's not. I would know if she was. She's sick from my mark. It'll pass." Edwin sighed tiredly. "Let her get on with what she's doing."

Cesar looked regretfully at the phone. "Are you two still mad at each other?" He felt uncomfortably like a child caught between warring parents.

"I'm not mad at her." Edwin still looked pale and unwell, and the skin of his chest under his open shirt was coated in a fine sheen of sweat as if he had a fever. "She has to get that list. Both of you are dependent on that. I can't summon her away at the moment to come baby me."

Cesar thought about that long and hard. "Do you want me to kill him? Ian? Because I will." He thought about all of the Sidhe blood he'd shed in the last few hours. He could no longer claim any reasonable facsimile of virginity. He'd lost that in the battle, and Ian was at least partly responsible. If Edwin wanted him dead, Cesar, as his Enforcer, would make that happen.

"Do that and the High Courts will try you for the murder of a high-ranking Vampire Lord," Edwin said. "They will burn you alive."

"He deserves it," Cesar bit out angrily.

"But you don't."

"Court etiquette is really fucked up, do you know that?"

Edwin looked about to say something when he stopped. He was staring down at his forearm where his shirtsleeve was rolled up. Slowly, he raised his arm. Scrawled across his white skin in quickly fading Sidhe toxin was the word TONIGHT in that scrawling, spidery script.

"Corcoran," Edwin said.

Cesar examined it. "They're coming back, aren't they?"

"It would seem so."

"Doesn't that mean Miss Eliza's in danger down in the village? What if they take her?"

Edwin considered that. "If they are coming here tonight, she's better off away from here. The Sidhe don't want her. Anyway, she has Malcolm looking after her." He lowered his arm and used it to push himself up. It took some doing. "We need to arm ourselves and prepare."

"You're not strong enough," Cesar said because it was pretty obvious that Edwin was still recovering from whatever the Sidhe had done to him. "*We're* not strong enough."

Edwin moved like a slow old man to the end of the bed, then hung his head as he got his bearings. "We don't have a choice."

Cesar thought about what he could do to stop all of this and get Edwin back in bed. That was, essentially, impossible.

"Fuck!" Cesargot up, went to one of the viewing portals, and looked down over the bailey far below. The sun was setting across the moorland.

He swallowed hard. Things had been so much easier back when he was human. The biggest crises he'd faced back then were getting to work on time, paying bills, and navigating a shitty dating life. Now, he was dead, a vampire Enforcer, and he had to defend his Vampire Lord against hordes of life-threatening fairies. How in fuck's name had he gotten to this place in his life?

"They're going to be much more dangerous tonight, aren't they?"

Edwin dragged himself to the window and ruffled his Heir's hair. "Well, now, you're not afraid of a few bloody fairies, are you?"

"This is worse than the Hive zombies. We had guns then. We could defend ourselves, at least."

"We'll do it again."

"How?"

"I'll think of something." Edwin paused a long moment as he considered. "We'll check the battalion reserves and basement. I'm sure Ian has *some* munitions tucked away somewhere in this old pile. We'll organize everyone."

"Four vampires and three werewolves against a village full of Sidhe in spirit form with the power to kill vampires and make living things cease to be."

"That's about the size of it, yeah."

Cesar grimaced and stared out over the moorland. "Christ. We're going to be slaughtered."

Edwin must have realized the extent of his panic. He turned him around and cupped his face. "Do you remember what I said about being your Lord? How I'll never let harm come to you?"

"Yeah."

"Do you trust me?"

Cesar bit his lip and thought about that. "I guess."

"Your vote of confidence in me is just amazing."

Cesar straightened up. He was a soldier, after all. "No, I do."

"That's all you need, my love."

* * *

The farmhouse was a large, two-story brick affair surrounded on all sides by enormous pastures where at least three hundred head of sheep grazed. As Eliza drove up the dirt road to the house, a collie mix darted out of a nearby barn and started to bark excitedly. Eliza parked on the gravel drive and shut off the engine.

The dog bounded right up to the car. But the moment the dog spotted Malcolm, it started to growl. Malcolm frowned. The collie immediately flattened its ears, tucked its tail, and raced back to the barn.

"That was impressive," she said.

Malcolm shrugged and followed her up the gravel path to the door.

Eliza availed herself of the big, brass doorknocker in the shape of a bull with a ring in its nose. She waited, glancing around furtively for the dog—or maybe a Sidhe. Then she reminded herself that Catherine wrote that the Fae could only divide themselves into their dangerous spirit forms while asleep or in some form of altered consciousness. Since she didn't think anyone slept on a busy farm in the middle of the day, she hoped she was safe.

"Oy," said a man a few steps behind them. Eliza turned, not expecting the voice to come from that direction, and saw a tall, work-stooped, middle-aged man walking toward them from the direction of the barn, a dirty rake resting on his shoulder. The man smelled like horse manure, and he wore dirty coveralls and a down jacket. His eyes were sharp, grey, and keen. "Canna help you folks?"

The words were probably meant to sound friendly, but his expression was guarded.

Eliza cleared her throat. "I'm looking for the owner. Mr. Finley?"

"Found him." The man didn't offer his hand.

Eliza ran through her prepared speech. "My name is Alisa McGillicuddy. My husband and I are writing a book on the local legends of Whitby Village. I was wondering if you had time to speak with us." She glanced briefly at Malcolm, who'd remained stoic and silent as she had asked him to be. Her story sounded reasonable without being overly suspicious, she thought. After all, Whitby had some of the biggest concentration of local legends in all of East Anglia.

When Mr. Finley didn't immediately answer, she added, "We were hoping you could enlighten us on the more infamous legends."

She watched Mr. Finley carefully, half expecting him to transform into a white demon right before her eyes and try to stab them with his rake. Instead, his expression softened and he almost looked...flattered. "Why don't you come inside, Mrs. McGillicuddy?"

He herded them into a huge kitchen done all in stone, with an actual hearth and a large cauldron boiling in one corner. It looked positively medieval, except for the modern appliances scattered about. Eliza glanced at Malcolm, but he looked pleasantly composed.

The lady of the house, Mrs. Finley, was just coming up the basement stairs with a load of laundry in her arms. She was tall but not especially thin, ginger and freckled and wind-burned like her husband. She wore similar coveralls and a heavy lamb's wool sweater. Along with the laundry basket, she carried a toddler in a sling around her middle. The toddler was crying and pawing at Mrs. Finley's breast.

"Visitors?" she said, sounding surprisingly pleased about it. Eliza hadn't expected that. "Let me just get the kettle on."

As she went about the task of efficiently preparing them early afternoon tea, Mr. Finley took his jacket off and knocked the mud off his boots and onto some newspaper on the floor. Mrs. Finley moved so quickly around the kitchen that Eliza gained the impression that in the Finley household, no one stood still for long. She learned why when two more red-haired, be-freckled children charged down a flight of stairs, battling to reach the front door first.

"Take your hat, Ewan!" Mrs. Finley called to the boy in a surly, commanding voice. "And be sure your sister keeps her jacket on!"

"Yeah, yeah!" called the children, yanking open the door, their coats and hats in hand.

Mrs. Finley turned to smile politely at Eliza. "They're a cheeky lot."

When she turned to face her, Eliza realized that Mrs. Finley was expecting a fourth child. She stared at the baby bump under Mrs. Finley's coveralls and said, "How far along are you?"

Mrs. Finley smiled, showing teeth that had not known proper dentistry in some time. "Five months. John says he'll be a biggie." She let Eliza touch her tummy.

The toddler began to scream.

"Hang on a tick. Mikey's due his milk," she said, sitting down near the hearth to nurse Mikey. At the same time, the kettle started going off. Mrs. Finley looked at it with tired eyes.

"Let me," Eliza offered, seeing to the tea.

Mrs. Finley looked grateful for Eliza's help. As Eliza transported everything to the table and set up tea, including covering the teapot with a knitted cozy, Mrs. Finley bounced the now full and sleepy Mikey and said, "You're American. But you know how to make English tea."

"My husband is British."

Mrs. Finley glanced over at Malcolm, who had seated himself at the table and folded his hands, trying to look invisible, which was impossible for him. She, like every other female in town, got a dreamy look in her eye, probably due to Malcolm's romance novel-cover good looks.

Mr. Finley stepped back into the kitchen, sans dirty jacket and boots, while Eliza was sitting down beside Malcolm. "Tea, John," Mrs. Finley said, trying to juggle a suddenly fussing Mikey as she reached for the teapot.

"Let me take him," Eliza said suddenly. She didn't know why she said it, only that she wanted to. But then, glancing over at John, she wondered if she had overstepped.

"Are you sure?" asked Mrs. Finley.

"He's no bother," Eliza insisted.

Finally, Mrs. Finley liberated the squirming Mikey from his sling and handed him over. Eliza had never handled a baby before—it was not exactly something they taught you at the Scholomance, the Poppet academy—but the moment he was in her arms, it seemed the most natural thing in the world to her. She cradled him against her body and he seemed to calm, his small hands pawing at the key and bloodstone around her neck.

"My! You're so good with him," said Mrs. Finley. "And he doesn't often take to strangers."

Eliza felt a few wayward sparks jump off her skin and kiss him. That made him laugh.

While Mrs. Finley served tea and biscuits, Eliza retold her cover story. She was a little worried that Malcolm would eat the whole plate, but he was every inch the gentleman, taking only two and laying them on his napkin properly.

"Well, now, 'tis a sad day you've come upon, Mrs. McGillicuddy," Mrs. Finley said, rubbing her belly. "We buried one of our own only this morning. John's mum, in fact."

"I'm sorry to hear that," Eliza said, pretending to scribble notes in her notebook while Mikey grabbed at her pen. "Should we be on our way? Is this a bad time?"

Mrs. Finley sighed tiredly and rubbed at her belly again, her eyes going to the door. Mr. Finley had gone back to the barn. "The old bird was good to us, but she was a cagey old thing. So, you're writing about the legends of Whitby Village?"

"The village has such an interesting history. My husband and I would love to know who the founders were and if their descendants are still alive today. We plan to include a chapter about the history of the people who settled here."

"In that case, you might want to visit the town hall. The Archbishop's Bible is kept there, and it holds the genealogy of almost everyone born in the village in the last four hundred years. It's a tradition, you see." She rested her hand on Mikey's head. "On a babe's christening, their name is written down in the Good Book."

"How wonderful. But that must be a huge book," Eliza said in wonder.

"A large book with many pages. I doubt the curator will let you lot handle it, but I reckon it wouldn't hurt to ask." She paused. "I remember me grandfather telling me stories about the castle. Now, there is a lot of history and folklore to be had."

"Lord Ian's castle?"

"And Lady Catherine's. I remember me granddad telling me about the Golem he encountered when he was a wee boy out hunting conies. One of the great lady's, he said. Was just wandering the deep woods, breaking through the trees like a juggernaut. That was when the lady was still alive, conducting her experiments, you understand…"

Eliza scribbled and scribbled. A half hour later, she climbed back into the car, drove a half-mile down the road, stopped on the shoulder, and stared out of the windshield at the moorland. "Were they of Fae blood?" she asked when she trusted her voice not to crack.

It took Malcolm only a moment to answer. "Aye. The man more than his wife. I do not think he has told her."

"The children, too?"

"Aye."

She rested her head on the steering wheel, taking deep, slow breaths to keep the tears at bay. "Did you see them, Malcolm? They're a family. And we had tea, and Mrs. Finley tried to help me. And now I have to write their names down in my book."

"Aye."

"And Edwin has to kill them."

He didn't say anything to that.

She had a bad moment while the pain surged deep inside of her like a hot knife twisting her guts into a knot. "I can't do this, Malcolm. I can't send those people to their deaths. And Ian. He treats all of this like it means *nothing*."

"It hurts him, too."

"He's a vampire! He's fucking dead! He doesn't feel anything!"

She clamped a hand over her mouth to keep from sobbing. Christ, this was supposed to be her holiday, the first time she had ever been outside the States, yet it seemed that all she'd been doing for the past week was hurting and crying.

Malcolm put his big warm hand on her knee, a rather obvious gesture. "We could drive all night until we reach London."

"Why would we want to do that?" She looked at his hand.

"On the TV, I saw there are ways out of England. Ways to fly. We could go to your country."

She turned her head and looked at him sitting there so composed with his curling black hair and fierce green eyes. "Are you saying we should run away? Leave all of this to Ian and Edwin?"

He slid his hand up just a little. "It is an idea."

To her shame, she considered it for a moment. But while she did, her hand instinctively went up and caught the ring around her neck. Baby Mikey had found the shiny stone fascinating. But Baby Mikey had to die because he was part Sidhe. How would Edwin ever live with what he had done? How would she?

She couldn't stand this anymore. She opened the door of the car, scampered down the embankment on the side of the road, and raced to the edge of the deep woods, beech and fir trees rearing up like a wall in front of her. She held the chain the ring was on, tilted her head up, and breathed deeply of the piney cold air. It smelled sweet and refreshing. She wished she could think. She wished she knew what the right thing to do was...

She never felt the wind stir, just a light electrical buzzing against her skin as something flickered past her. Her heart thudded as she turned, wondering what it was—and then she spotted the suit and cool green eyes in the shadows cast by the trees. Malcolm. She didn't know what he was up to, but she had no energy to call to him. She started back to the car, but the shadow moved with her as if they were playing a game. Then it caught her up in its embrace and carried her deeper into the trees.

Malcolm had her. She started to cry out, but he pressed her suddenly against the scratchy bark of a willow, cupped the back of her head, and, before she could protest, leaned down to kiss her. It was a light kiss, inviting. But the moment she tasted him, she wanted more, she wanted his all-consuming kiss, his mouth wet and hot and pungent on hers. Her heart thudded so hard that she wondered if he could feel it against his chest.

He kissed and she kissed him back. He breathed roughly into her, nearly panting. His cheek was smooth—he was so young!—but his sharp teeth caught her bottom lip.

She started to say his name, but he whispered, "Quiet" in a commanding, masculine voice.

So, she was. His warm breath plumed white in the dusky light of the forest. His hands moved around her, grappling her. He kissed her almost frantically, his mouth tracking along her chin to the edge of her ear. He licked her there, sending up waves of gooseflesh.

She felt as though she was melting, truly becoming one with him.

He said, "I could make you like me. We could be mates."

His voice was a breathy whisper. She could barely hear it over the frantic beating of her heart. He licked the skin all around the pulse in her throat invitingly, making it jump. Then he lowered his hungry mouth until it was level with her bosom. He licked her there too, gently through her coat and clothes. The sensation made her writhe for him against the tree.

"Malcolm..." she managed.

"I'm alive."

"I know that." She could feel every part of him, from the low growl in his throat and his roughly calloused hands holding her all the way down to the pressure in his trousers. She could smell his hair, like the forest at night, and his breath had a slightly minty, carnivorous taste. He was so very alive. And gorgeous. And everything a woman might want in a dream come true.

But this couldn't go on. "Malcolm, please…" she began, lifting her chin to look him in the eye. But that only put her in alignment with his mouth. He kissed her silent, a kiss so bruising it left her mouth numb and tingling. She felt dizzy with the feel and taste and smell of him.

He lowered his head and nipped gently at her neck.

"Malcolm…no!" She pushed against him a little and he finally stepped back, though he turned his head and spoke in her ear.

"You excite me. You have the wolf in you already, my lady." He smiled against her throat.

Just one bite, she thought, a small one, and she would be like Megan, like Malcolm. She would never belong to the vampires then, never again be subject to their Courts, their games, their awful machinations.

"You would savor the change. You would enjoy the hunt with me. We could rebuild the Bloodthorn Pack. We could be great."

She entertained the thought for a moment. It sounded like a fantasy come true. Malcolm was the king of his kind. She could be his queen. He was right. They could be royalty. They could be great.

Then she reached up and touched Malcolm's cheek. "If things were different…"

"He's dead," Malcolm growled.

"I love him."

"He cannot give you children. He cannot give you life. There is no life in him. He makes you sad, and he can only bring you sorrow."

"Sometimes. You're right, but…"

"He can only take life. He will take yours in time." He gripped the Covenant ring around her neck. "He has promised you this."

She closed her eyes and looked away, tears spilling over her cheeks. "And I still love him. If he asks for my life, then I must give it to him."

With a disgruntled sound in his throat, Malcolm eased his weight off her. Anger sprinted behind his eyes, something uncatchable. She was afraid of what he would do next, but he only touched her cheek with the back of his hand. His expression was returning to that unreadable nothing he usually wore.

He was resigned to her decision, at least. "You will make him a beautiful, dead vampire bride one day, my lady."

He was gone in seconds, leaving her alone to breathe in the woodsy air and compose herself. She ran a hand over her face and fixed her hair before returning to the empty car. She sat alone in the driver's seat for almost five minutes, crying softly, until Malcolm returned. She wondered what he had been doing in the woods.

Perhaps he killed something in his rage. Or, maybe he needed a few moments of alone time to think.

She dried her eyes and then shoved the car into drive. Neither of them spoke for close to ten minutes—not until they'd reached the outskirts of the village where the church was located. As she parked, she glanced over at Malcolm, but Malcolm's eyes were far away as if dreaming.

| xiii |

Edwin stepped into Catherine's lab where the others had gathered. He wore black trousers, knee-high combat boots, and a long, dusty buckskin cavalry coat over a very shirtless chest. In his experience dealing with the enemy, the poor control he had over his temper usually resulted in more shredded shirts than an angry Dr. Bruce Banner. Sometimes, his wings even got caught in the fabric.

The others turned to look at him as if he'd suddenly appeared before them like an angel of war. He looked them over, keenly. "We all know why we're here."

That solicited concerned looks from everyone in attendance. He started moving around the long, plankwood bench in Catherine's lab, pointing out the various weapons they'd scrounged up over the past few hours. "Ben Franklin 800," he said, picking up an impressive, forty-inch cannon gun and resting it against his forearm to show his audience its impressive length. He sighted down the barrel. "Otherwise known as the Rainmaker. It emits free radical particles from static electricity."

The denizens of the castle, all summoned here by Edwin for this exact purpose, glanced at each other. Some looked toward Lord Severn, standing in a corner of the lab near the remnants of the Preservation Unit. The gun had come from his own barracks. But he looked blankly ahead as if this demonstration was of little interest to him.

Edwin hefted it. "That's the stuff that makes your hair stand up when you walk on a scratchy carpet."

Megan raised her hand like a student in class. "And this can actually harm something?"

"It emits one-hundred-twenty kiloampreas. That's five hundred megajoules of electricity, or enough energy to power a one-hundred-watt light bulb for just under two months." When he saw that she wasn't following, and quite obviously didn't appreciate gun facts the way he did, he added, "Roughly the equivalent of a bolt of lightning."

Her eyes lit up. "Oh, my." She swept forward to take the Rainmaker and then sighted down a random target with it. "I used to be good with a rifle."

"Just make certain you're grounded before you shoot someone," Edwin advised. "Rubber boots. Otherwise, you'll set yourself on fire."

The next two weapons that Edwin reached for looked like a pair of ornate flintlock dueling pistols from roughly the mid-Eighteenth Century. Edwin said, "Looks old, but they're not. These are primitive forerunners to the sonic boomer gun, the firearm that almost brought down the *Gypsy Queen* last year. They work by emitting high-frequency sound waves that can disrupt molecules. I have no idea if they'll work properly. Ian purchased them at auction last year but has never fired them."

Baldy, who had eschewed his cowl in favor of his old suit from his Prohibition days, stepped up. "I'll try 'em. They look sexy."

Edwin gave him a concerned look.

"I read all about 'em in *Guns & Ammo*. I can handle it."

Edwin handed the twin boomers to Baldy, who smiled broadly, then turned to their remaining firearms and hefted the first of a bunch of big, mismatched rifles. "Remington rifles armed with blooding bullets." His audience again looked confused, so he added, "That's bullets made from a lead compound mixed with vampire blood. Since vampire blood is incompatible with virtually every other blood type, spiked ammo will kill almost anything that breathes."

Megan's two big werewolf boys grinned at each other as if to share a private joke.

Edwin tossed them over and, as expert gunmen, they immediately started looking the rifles over, checking the ammo and discussing how they were going to blow the Fae away.

After the remaining firearms were divvied up, Edwin gave his troops their marching orders. He told Megan to take the west side of the castle and Baldy the east. The twin werewolf brothers would cover north and south. Cesar would watch the roof. Edwin passed out CB radios so everyone could stay in touch—big, clunky devices you had to wear on your belt, but still.

Cesar, still unarmed, was the only one who didn't immediately file out of the room. "What weapon do I get?" He looked despondently upon the empty workbench.

"Are you a bloodkinetic like me and Foxley?" Edwin asked him.

"I don't even know what that is!"

Edwin came around behind Cesar and held him in place, a hand in the small of his back to steady him. With his free hand, he took Cesar by the wrist and brought his fingers up to his lips. "A little pinch," he said and bit his middle finger.

A few drops of Cesar's blood pattered to the floor at their feet. Edwin waited, but the blood just lay there, hissing a little as it slowly turned to black powder. "I don't think you're a bloodkinetic," he announced. "Your talent must lay elsewhere."

He drew his favorite handgun Belle from the inside pocket of his coat. "Take this," he said, slipping her into Cesar's hand. "She's loaded with blooding bullets. And keep in mind that your blood is toxic even if you can't command it, so if you get into a tight spot, just bleed everywhere."

Cesar closed his hand around the grip of Edwin's old-fashioned handgun. It looked like something out of the Wild West, and it felt like a prop, something not real. He swallowed nervously. "What will you use?"

"Don't worry about me. I'm a professional." Edwin leaned forward, hung his arm about Cesar's neck, and kissed him. It was a sweet kiss that Cesar felt down to his toes. Then Edwin slapped Cesar's cheek—harder than he probably had to. "Yes," he said.

"Yes...what?"

"I'll teach you everything I know. Assuming we live through tonight." Edwin turned his Enforcer, aimed him toward the door to the tower, and slapped his rear. "Now, off with ya."

After he was gone, Ian said, "A lovely display of a loving relationship between a Lord and his Heir. Was that for my benefit?"

Edwin turned back to Ian. "Suddenly, I'm finding it a little bit fun, being a *dad*."

"You are perverse, Edwin, do you know that?"

"Absolutely," he said, checking his pocket watch for sundown.

"You have a great deal of gaiety for a Vampire Lord about to lose his Courtesan and his Heir."

Edwin looked up. His eyes, he knew, had turned to a solid, tarry black, with no irises or whites. Ian shifted a little in place at the sight.

Edwin stalked Ian back across the lab until the backs of Ian's knees hit the edge of an old, handmade wooden captain's chair.

Then he sat down. Edwin rested his arms on the chair, boxing Ian in, and leaned forward so only their breaths separated them.

Edwin's mouth was suddenly deep with teeth. "She will get you your list, my Lord. I trust her."

Ian laughed. Rather nervously, Edwin thought.

"You are so much like Foxley, Edwin," Ian complained. "Your stubbornness. Your highhandedness. Your faith in your own meager power. But you don't really know how to play the game, do you? You never have. You're not a vampire. You're a human being trapped inside a vampire's body."

When that solicited no reaction from his adversary, Ian looked vaguely annoyed. "The horses will be in danger as well. There are only two left now."

"I'll bring them inside the Hall and guard them," Edwin said. His eyes cleared. He smiled, once again the devil-may-care rake. "And you won't touch her. I'll kill her before I'll let you touch her. I'll kill you."

Ian smiled slyly, and his eyes darkened. "You won't kill her. And you won't kill me, Edwin. Not after what you did to Catherine. I *know* you." He reached up and snatched Edwin by the front of the coat. "After tonight, after the Sidhe finish with you, she'll be mine. They both will." He licked his lips lasciviously, his tongue churning in his mouth. "An eye for an eye. And when I'm inside them both, when both of them are pleasuring me, I'll make them scream. And while they're screaming, I'll be sure to remind them every day of how very dead you are—"

Edwin never lost his smile as he drew his fist back and then punched it soundly through Ian's chest, right into the place where his heart ought to be. The motion was so sudden, so brutal, Ian blinked but otherwise didn't react at all, even when Edwin's fist was buried to the wrist in his ribcage. There was little blood. But that wasn't unusual with vampires. The little bit in Ian painted Edwin's face. Some speckled the portrait of Ian and Catherine that was lying against the wall beside them.

Lord Ian and Lady Catherine forever watching the world from the safety of their canvas, their eyes grim and ageless.

Slowly, ever so slowly, Edwin withdrew his fist, his knuckles scraping along the old vampire's shattered rib bones. Once it was free, he showed Ian his black, shriveled, and barely beating heart. A pulsing mound of quivering black jelly. It didn't look human at all. They watched together as it quickly dried out and turned to black dust in Edwin's hand. He closed his fingers, the powder sifting between them.

"Devil," said Ian, knowing it would be the last thing he ever said.

"You never knew meat all," Edwin answered as the light flickered out of his old friend's eyes forever. "No one threatens my pretties."

* * *

On his way to his station on the east side, Baldy detoured up the stairs to his suite on the second floor of the castle. He let himself into his private quarters and closed and locked the door.

"Star?" he called softly into the still darkness of his rooms. He had requested that she and the children keep the lights turned off while he was gone. The last thing he needed was Lord Ian or the werewolf brothers stumbling upon his guests.

There was a rustling in the next room, followed by a faint glow. Baldy felt an irrational fear grip his throat. He made his way to the door and found Star sitting on his settee with the children on the floor. They were sharing a box of pretzels and the children were coloring pictures with crayons while Star read from one of their bedtime books. Star looked up and said, "Baldy! You're back!"

The children immediately rushed him. Baldy got down on one knee as the girl, Annamarie, gave him a strangling bear hug around the neck. Star's son Tim, who was just slightly more standoffish, said, "Uncle Baldy? You got any candy?"

"I didn't bring any candy, son, sorry. But whatever you can find here is yours."

"Can I watch TV downstairs?" Annamarie asked, rubbing her eyes sleepily.

Baldy looked up at Star. "Sorry, darling. I can't risk anyone noticing you're here. You're being here is a big secret."

The children's eyes lit up. They liked big secrets.

Star stood up, less enthused. "Are we in danger here?"

Baldy stood as well, with Annamarie clinging to his leg. He didn't mind. He loved Star's children. In a way, they were his now. The only children he would ever have. "No. Actually, you're much safer here than in the village."

"You keep saying that. But what does that *mean?*"

Baldy shushed her, afraid Star's agitated voice would alert someone. "Can I talk to you alone?"

Star settled the children with their coloring books, and then she and Baldy stepped into his adjoining bedchamber, the place where they had made love on many a night. "*What* in bloody hell is going on?" she whispered hoarsely when he had closed the door. "You weren't answering your phone or texts. I thought something bad had happened to you!"

"I'm fine, Star, as you can see."

"Baldy, you're dead. You're always fine." She gave him her imperial mother face and set her fists on her generous hips. "Enough games. I want you to be honest with me! Right now!"

Baldy sighed, pulled Star away from the door in case the children were listening, and led her to the bed. They sat down on the edge, with him holding her hands. He thought about what he could say, then decided on the truth. He was never a very good liar.

He started telling her a truncated version of the Sidhe story and the Wild Hunt. Thankfully, Star was familiar with most of the local legends. But when he reached the point where he was explaining how the Fae would be descending on the castle tonight, Star looked dubious.

"Is this a joke?" she asked.

Baldy blinked. "Have you ever known me to joke?"

She looked worried, finally, and bit her bottom lip. "You're serious about all of this."

"Deadly. You can't go back to the village, Star. Not tonight. Maybe not tomorrow. I don't know when it will be safe again."

Star looked toward the door to his antechamber where she could hear her children talking amongst themselves. "I don't understand any of this!" she hissed. "Can't you stop it?"

"No. I mean, I wouldn't know how, doll-face."

She stood up suddenly. "Why don't you just kill this vampire? This...what's his name? McKinney? If you kill him, there won't be any Wild Hunt..."

"McGillicuddy," Baldy corrected her. "His name is Lord Edwin McGillicuddy. And I can't kill him."

"Why?"

Baldy stared at the pattern of the bedspread and thought about that. "Well, for one thing, he's my friend."

Star looked appalled. "You're going to let him slaughter my entire village...all of our friends, all of our *families*...because he's your *mate*?"

Baldy winced and looked up at Star, the woman he loved. The most beautiful woman in the world. The woman he would do almost anything for. At a loss as to what to do to protect her, he reached for one of the sonic pistols in the double armpit holster he was wearing under his suit jacket.

"Here," he said, offering the pistol to her butt-first. When she didn't immediately take it, he pressed it into her hand and closed her fingers around it. "Take it. It looks like a traditional pistol but it's not. You cock it back like a regular handgun, then wait for it to charge. When the red light stops blinking, it means it's fully charged. It emits a sonic pulse that can kill virtually anything."

Star looked with horror at the gun. She was not squeamish, but she had children, and she did not like the idea of guns around them. "I don't want this, Baldy," she said in a low, trembling whisper, trying to give it back to him. "I don't want to kill anything."

"Things could get rough tonight," he confessed, hoping he wasn't frightening her too badly. "I'm just making it easier for you to defend yourself...and the children."

A long, breathless moment passed. Finally, Star checked the safety—she was not unfamiliar with firearms; her dad was a bailey cop back in London—and then put it in her purse on the bed beside her.

Baldy pulled her close so her warmth soaked into him. He luxuriated in it. He clutched the back of her neck and put his face in her hair. "You stay here with the children. Don't come out, no matter what you hear or see. And if anyone tried to get in here, you shoot to kill. Do you understand me, doll-face?"

It took Star a long moment before she nodded. He touched her face and kissed the side of her mouth. "I'll come back for you and the children just as soon as I can."

"Baldy."

"Yes?"

"I love you. Marry me?"

He smiled. "Yes."

And then he left her to join the battle.

***

Your talent must lie elsewhere.

What did that mean? What talent? And if he did have some superpower he was hitherto unaware of, like some fumbly teenage Clark Kent, how was he supposed to find it?

Cesar stood on the rooftop, surveying the rolling, rocky hills of the moorland far below, and wondered. The sun was going down, but with his vampire's eyes, things never really got dark anymore. They just changed to shades of grey as if the entire world was leaking colors but increasing in clarity and contrast. The grey was sharp-edged, defined. He saw better in the night than he ever had in the daylight.

The wind raked over him, but he didn't really feel it. Another thing he'd had to get used to. He knew, intellectually, that it was a strikingly cold wind slicing across the rigid, lonely landscape, but it didn't seem so to him. His impervious flesh was dead; he stood apart from the rest of the world. He unbuttoned his coat—it seemed ridiculous and impractical to be wearing it—and dropped it to the rooftop. That allowed him to stretch his wings to either side, the rustling wind tickling across his scales.

Behind him, the door to the roof opened. He knew who it was without turning. He could always feel Edwin like a constant hum at the back of his brain. In the beginning, it had made him feel watched, but he knew now that it was his own blood calling back to its fountainhead. It wasn't Edwin seeking him out. It was *himself* calling out to his master.

"You holding up, soldier?"

He turned to glance at his Lord, faintly horrified by the smell of vampire blood on his clothes and exposed skin. Edwin looked so remote, so intense, that Cesar felt his skin crawl. "What happened?"

It took Edwin a moment to answer. "I killed Ian."

Cesar swallowed against a knot in his throat. For a moment, he thought maybe Edwin was making a joke in poor taste. But after a few moments of contemplative silence, Cesar had his doubts. "You're not kidding."

Edwin glanced aside at him, his eyes steady and very dead. "No."

He didn't know what to say. All he could think of was, "I thought you said if I killed Ian, the High Council will know and burn me alive. Won't they do that to you?"

Edwin clasped his hands behind his back and looked out over the moorland. "I lied. There is no way for them to know he's dead or that I killed him."

Cesar felt a cold numbness filter through his body, and that had nothing to do with the wind. "Why did you lie? I would have killed him for you."

He knew Lord Ian was Edwin's friend. Once. They had a lot of history between them. Cesar would have done it to save Edwin that pain.

"What were you like back in the service?" Edwin suddenly said.

Cesar watched Edwin light a cigarette from the stash he kept under his coat. It was an odd question, but he still answered it. "In Afghanistan, I was stationed on an Air Force base outside Rigestan. I dropped supplies mostly, but sometimes I worked with the flight medics to get the soldiers medevec-ed." He stopped and stared at the ground between his feet as Edwin passed him a cigarette.

Cesar smoked it down to the butt before realizing he'd never smoked a cigarette in his entire life. Even though he had never personally killed anyone in battle, he sometimes still dreamed about those messed-up soldiers he'd flown back to the field hospital. But he didn't tell Edwin that.

Edwin was silent for a long time while he smoked. Then he said, "So, you have never killed anyone innocent. Or anyone you ever cared about?"

Finally, Cesar caught on. "I didn't love Ian. We didn't have...what we have, Edwin. I would have done it. For you."

Edwin looked up with somber eyes. Cesar shuddered as if someone had raked a sharp knife up his back. "Yes, you would have. For me."

Cesar got angry suddenly. "I told you. I'm not a child. You don't have to protect me!" Cesar blew smoke through his nostrils like a dragon, disappointed that Edwin would think him so weak. But the truth was, under his bluster, he couldn't help but feel a great surge of relief. He knew he would have done it, but he also knew it would have hurt him to kill Ian. Maybe it would have even broken him.

He bowed his head, remembering what he had done to all of those Sidhe earlier that day, how he had destroyed them utterly. At the time, it had felt like it was happening to someone else, or like something he was watching on TV, not something he was actually doing. But he had. And he didn't know how he felt about that.

Was he a monster now? Like Edwin? Like Ian?

The real curse of vampirism, he thought, was that you had to live forever with being a truly shit-awful person.

"How do you cope?" Cesar asked at last. "How do you deal with the things you do?"

Edwin considered that as he lit a new cigarette with the butt of his first one. "I found someone better than me. Someone...who held me accountable."

"Miss Eliza."

He looked like he was about to say more, then stopped, his attention refocusing on the moors.

Cesar looked too. In the far distance, he could see half a dozen tiny flickers of light like little white flames, only they seemed to be moving toward them. "What's that?"

Edwin gritted his teeth, the cigarette caught between them. "*That* is showtime." He didn't look afraid. Then again, what was there to be afraid of when *you* were the monster? When *you* were the enemy?

"They're here, my Heir," Edwin said, taking the smoke from his mouth and crushing it out. "The Fae have come."

| xiv |

Mrs. McCormick's office was probably very tidy underneath all of the dust and carelessly stacked books. The walls were wood-paneled after a fashion that had been stylish in 1979, and the carpeting was of a garish blue-green that Eliza didn't think had ever been in style. Mrs. McCormick had run out of shelf space long ago and had opted to stack most of the books on various surfaces—desks, worktables, end tables, and every chair within her small workspace. The woman herself looked like someone from a spy movie or maybe an old British war drama where characters stood around a sand table, talking about the Nazis. She was small and neat, dressed in a conservative brown suit. Her graying hair was piled atop her head in a corporate beehive, and she wore an authentic pair of cat glasses, complete with rhinestones.

"Shall I be mother?" she asked as she moved around her desk and sat down in a mothy-looking swivel chair to pour Eliza and Malcolm each a cup of tea. Her voice was clipped, and she used the right expressions, but her accent had started to wander in the last fifteen minutes. Eliza thought she detected something very East Coast-y now.

"Thanks for making an allowance for our visit," Eliza said to be courteous. She sat beside Malcolm and glanced around the office.

"I don't usually stay this late, but your book sounds so interesting, Mrs. McGillicuddy!" She paused dramatically as if Eliza was expected to say something, then continued in a rush. "You're American. I don't see many Americans here. The tourists are too busy checking out the vineyards or the pubs. That's all we have here—vineyards and pubs. And sheep. Lots of sheep. And a castle. But you don't want to hear about the castle. If you hear about the castle, you'll want to visit it..."

She paused again and blushed. "I'm sorry. I'm prattling."

"That's quite all right," Eliza told her. "You're American, too?"

"British citizen. Now. I came to live here with my husband Roger over thirty years ago—bless his heart. Roger passed on three years ago. I was born in New York State, though I guess you could call me a genuine East Anglian now."

"I thought I recognized the accent." Eliza nodded. "Thank you for seeing us on such short notice, Mrs. McCormick."

"Call me Betsy, and, yes, of course. Tea?"

She took the cup and nodded. "My husband and I are concentrating on the local legends of East Anglia. We've made it something of a working honeymoon, you see." To accent her point, she slid her hand over Malcolm's arm. Malcolm covered it with his free hand and patted it, smiling harmlessly at Betsy without speaking.

Betsy stared at them both over the top of her glasses, making Eliza squirm in her seat as though she were a teacher examining her. "Your husband is East Anglian, yes?"

They had discussed this in the car. If he slipped or someone suspected, he was not to deny it.

"That's correct, madam," he said, and Eliza was incredibly proud of him. Not only did he sound sincere, but he also didn't sound archaic. "I met my wife while on holiday visiting New York City. Alisa will deny it, of course, but from the moment I saw her, I knew we were destined to be together."

He glanced over at her and smiled with genuine conviction. Eliza returned the smile, trying to make it seem sincere even though what she wanted to do was kick him in the nuts for that.

Betsy smiled. "You make a very attractive couple. And you remind me so much of myself and Roger when we were young!" Betsy hunted out a clean handkerchief from inside the top drawer of her desk and dabbed her eyes behind her glasses. "Very sweet."

Eliza smiled nicely. "Now, about the Whitby Bible. We were told you were the caretaker?"

Betsy sat back in her chair. "Forgive an old lady her nostalgia." She bounded up and moved with surprising speed to a door at the far side of the room.

Eliza and Malcolm stood up and followed.

"It is wonderful that you want to see it. Hardly anyone comes to see the Whitby Bible anymore!" She fumbled with some keys until she found the proper one.

The door opened to a perfectly black room. Betsy flicked on some fluorescent lights that buzzed and spat. Moths fluttered inside the tubes. Much like Betsy's office, this room was also covered in bookshelves, but all of them were encased in glass cabinets. The tomes displayed inside looked positively mummified. On the far side of the room, Eliza spotted a number of glass display counters. She moved toward them, studying the well-preserved scrolls and stone artifacts.

"These pieces look Proto-Celtic," Eliza said.

"They are," Betsy said, beaming with pride for her work. "Urnfield and Hallstatt Iron Age cultures. Whitby was one of the original great Anglo-Saxon settlements as defined by the Twelfth Century writings of Henry of Huntington." She nearly swooned with excitement. "This region was considered the great beating heart of East Anglia for centuries. Known as 'Annwyn Aes Sidhe,' by the locals. Annwyn, in Druid traditions, is similar to the 'Summerland,' the

Land of the Light. Interestingly enough, the name also translates as..."

"The Land of the Fae," Eliza finished for her.

Betsy stopped and covered her mouth to prevent a squeak from escaping. "You're very well versed, madam! But, I must be boring you something silly with these stories!"

She wasn't. Eliza was finding all of this rather educational. Annwyn was Ground Zero for fairies.

Opposite the glass counters was a dais upon which a tall, dusty glass box stood. Inside the box was an archaic, leather-bound book, open and tilted slightly up so it could be read. She approached it carefully, noting that the book was at least five feet tall, as big as a person. "Is this it?" she asked. "The Whitby Bible?"

Betsy glided up beside her, again moving with that particular grace. "Yes. Would you like to examine it more closely?"

"Please."

Betsy offered her a pair of latex gloves from a box kept on a nearby shelf, then went to work unlocking the display. Eliza said, "I'm particularly interested in seeing the first few pages, if that's all right."

"Of course." After the display was open, Betsy carefully turned the massive, parchment-thin pages of the Bible to the front matter. The Whitby Bible was written entirely in a Celtic script, with ornate borders and fearsome mythological creatures dancing around every page.

"The Bible belonged to the first settlers of Whitby, a gift from the Holy Roman Empire herself." Betsy stood back to let Eliza see more clearly.

Eliza looked at the swirling Celtic script of the front matter, turning pages until she found the Whitby Village family tree. It covered two whole pages and was the only thing in the tome written in discernible modern English. Malcolm moved up beside her and glanced down at the scrawling mass of names and hand-drawn lines. There had to be at least a thousand names on the tree, all written in a painfully small, monkish script.

Betsy said, "The Great Whitby Tree. It was a magnificent tradition once. Parents used to write down their newborn's name in the Good Book on the eve of their christening, but I'm afraid that's fallen out of style of late."

Eliza fished out her glasses and slipped them up. She squinted at the tree. "When did the tradition stop?"

"Not long ago. Maybe ten years? The new mothers have decided it's a bad omen to write their child's name down in the book. They're afraid a fairy will come for the child if the fairies know its name." She laughed. "The people of this region can be very superstitious!"

Eliza let out her breath. The names were still useful; she could extrapolate by looking up the surnames on the online white pages or on social networking. She used her mobile to snap off a few shots of the family tree.

Betsy said, "I should like to show you the athames next. They were used by Druids in pagan rituals…"

Eliza let Betsy lead them along a tour of the private library, trying silently to hurry the old curator along. About ten minutes later, Betsy clapped her hands together and said, "I'm afraid that's all there is. You must be very disappointed in our village."

"Not at all." Eliza smiled, taking a few extra pics of the athames just to maintain her cover. "There's a wealth of information here that I think anyone would kill for."

* * *

Back in their hotel room, Eliza showed Malcolm the screen of her phone with all of the names. "I put them all on my mobile."

He took the phone from her, staring at the screen so intently that she almost thought he was X-raying it with his eyes. "Every family I must kill."

"Malcolm…"

He handed the mobile back to her. "No," he said. "I will not."

"I don't understand."

"I will not kill the people of Whitby." For the first time, he looked truly afraid. "Those names…they are my people. My clan." He shook his head very slowly. "Before I was harmed by the churchmen and Lady Catherine put me to sleep, I had a son. I will be killing my own descendants."

It never occurred to Eliza that Malcolm might have had children, but it made sense. People often had children very young back in his day.

His face clouded up, and then he just stayed that way, very still. Eliza felt her heart clench in sympathy. She had no idea what to say, what to do. How in hell could she comfort this man?

And then, a heartbeat later, she had an epiphany and became enraged. "You will *not* leave this task to Edwin! You're his dog and he's your master! He's our Lord, Malcolm! He's the head of our Court, and you owe him your loyalty!" She clenched her fists, surprised by her outburst. "You won't abandon him to this. You won't because I won't let you!"

It seemed to take a long time, but finally, Malcolm turned to glance at her, his face like a rock. "You are correct. Forgive me."

She swallowed and reached out to him, setting her hand on his massive shoulder. She felt like her heart was lodged in her throat and wriggling around like a panicked fish. "I know it's hard. I know you did this once before. But I know you're strong."

He stared at the floorboards between his feet. "Do you know what it feels like to kill your own family because it is the *right* thing to do?"

"It's not the *right* thing to do, Malcolm. It's the *only* thing we can do."

Malcolm nodded, not happy but resolute. "You are right, of course. I will do it. Edwin is master now. I must do as he bades me. We all must—"

His statement was cut off when someone smashed a burning bottle through the window of their hotel room.

The bed clothes immediately went up in flames, and Eliza jumped in response. She couldn't help but wonder what it would have been like if they'd come back earlier and had gone to bed. Malcolm grabbed her and swung her out of danger. He was casual about it even though the tail of his coat was on fire.

"Malcolm!"

He gently set her down, dropped his coat, and stomped on it to snuff the flames out.

The room was quickly filling with smoke, and the flames had jumped from the bedclothes to the drapery and were crawling along the wall of their room as if they had a mind all their own. Eliza lurched back and studied it, realizing that it did have a kind of animalistic form, and that the fire periodically shifted to a lurid shade of blue. Fae magic, she thought even as she started to look for a means of escape.

And then she saw the Fae face in the flames like an old man laughing at her, and it was all she could do to keep from screaming like a little girl.

Malcolm shoved the highboy away from the wall and into the center of the room. It created a barrier for the flames to work through, but it wouldn't last. The flames were so hot that they were melting the glass of the broken window. The room quickly filled with plumes of grey smoke, and she knew that was going to kill them long before the flames got them.

"Miss Book!" Malcolm cried as he edged to the door. The flames were etching a path across all four walls at a truly supernatural speed. He held out his hand.

Eliza, meanwhile, had detoured to snatch at her utility bag on the desk, dragging it back seconds before the flames reached it. It contained Catherine's journals. She couldn't afford to lose those! But as she ripped the bag off the surface, a single flame jumped to the carpetbag fabric as if it knew how precious it was to her.

"Leave it!" Malcolm insisted.

"No! I can't!" She started beating the bag against the floor to try to extinguish the flames that were quickly spreading and eating up the material.

"Are you mad?" Malcolm cried.

The bag was a goner. She ripped it open just as a backdraft of faintly laughing flames spat their fury at her. For one second, her entire world burned, and Eliza felt like the skin was baking on her arms and face, but she had managed to grab at least two of the four journals out of the burning material before Malcolm yanked her away and they headed for the door.

"We need to get to the car!" she said, choking on the smoke reaching them even in the hallway.

They flew down the back stairs together. Eliza noted how empty the hotel was. No guests, no desk concierge. She wondered what had become of Annie, and if she was one of *them*. It was like being stuck in a movie about a secret alien invasion, she realized. She had no idea who to trust.

She and Malcolm piled into the car, the faintly smoking journals between them. The gears stuck, of course, as Megan said they would. Snarling with frustration, Eliza tried putting the car in reverse to see if she could unstick it. And that's when the lorry plowed into the back of them.

* * *

Malcolm crumpled the whole dashboard under the forward momentum of his body. Eliza, much smaller than he, hit the wheel, her lower half never reaching the dash, and the car horn blared imperiously. Then the two of them were snapped back into their seats.

The lorry had come out of the dark so fast, headlights off and engine silent, that Eliza never saw it. After what felt like the longest moment of her life, the terrible crunching noise stopped and she turned to Malcolm. He was slumped over, unconscious, in the passenger seat, his legs buried to the knees in the shattered dashboard of the car.

She screamed his name and started to claw at him, but she was quickly cut off. The lorry revved in the dark, sounding like a roaring dragon, and again they lurched as it began pushing them forward along the darkened country road. The car was locked in reverse, but the lorry was huge. It pushed the old Slipstream ahead of it like a mother bear herding along her cub.

Eliza's hands scrabbled over the steering wheel and the gearshift, trying to steer them out of the way of the enormous truck, but the impact must have damaged something in the steering column because the wheels remained locked even after she managed to get the sedan into drive.

The lorry kept going and they went with it, faster now that the car was in drive. Lights and noise blared behind them, encapsulating them, and she realized the lorry had switched on its brights, probably to blind her, which it did.

"My...lady..." Malcolm whimpered groggily as he struggled to sit up in his seat. "Run...you...run..."

"No!" she cried, angry as hell now.

Malcolm groaned. There was blood in his lap. There was blood everywhere in the cab of the car like a slaughter. He wasn't going anywhere, and neither was she. She grabbed his bloodied hand.

The lorry ground its gears, pushing them on, slowly at first but with increased momentum. Eliza hit the brights so she could at least see where they were headed, then wished she had not. Even in the daylight hours, she hadn't realized how steep the ravines were on both sides of the road. They were traveling along the shoulder, but at an angle. She could see the drop-off sloping ten or fifteen feet down to the edges of the moorland. A drop that would surely roll the car.

Eliza panicked, then told herself to stop it and do something constructive. She threw the car back in park. That slowed them down. The lorry pushed them on, but at a much slower rate. She had bought them more time—but not much.

At the slow rate they were going, she could probably wiggle out of the car, but Malcolm was wedged *inside* the dashboard. There was no practical way to get him out. But as he came around, he fixed his eyes on her. "Please...you must escape. You must take the list back." He pulled his hand away from her.

"I don't want to leave you," Eliza said, crying through the blood on her face.

"I will not die," he told her. "But I *will* be dangerous." His eyes clouded over and looked wilder. Small fissures opened up along his face and neck like cracked fine porcelain, black fur crawling forth from them. He was on the verge of changing.

"You should not be here, my lady," he snarled in a voice full of ragged teeth.

Resigned, Eliza opened her door and slid sideways, sickened by the speed of the ground passing beneath them, but the sight of the fast-approaching ravine gave her the courage to jump from the moving vehicle. The last thing she saw before the rocky ground came up and pummeled her ribs was the skin splitting along Malcolm's human face.

* * *

Eliza rolled down the side of the ravine. Each impact felt like a giant hammer pummeling her bones. She grunted and jounced along until she hit the bottom, where a drainage pipe let out a thin, cold stream of water. Eliza landed squarely in it.

It was cold enough to revive her and just disgusting enough to ruin her clothes forever. She scrambled up, cold and aching, and then cringed as Megan's car slid nose-first down the steep incline less than a hundred feet away, bits and pieces spiking off it as it smashed into the bottom of the ravine, tipped arse over kettle, and landed upside down, the crumpled wheels spinning uselessly.

She covered her mouth at the sight, wondering if Malcolm had been able to free himself of the dash in time—or if he had simply been smashed to pieces. She waited, her heart thudding so hard it hurt to breathe—not daring to breathe.

Far above, the lorry's engine revved and sputtered in the gravel as the driver put it in reverse. The headlights dimmed as the lorry backed up. Eliza waited, trying hard not to panic and do something stupid like run off and get caught in the headlights. She knew she had to wait it out until the lorry had gone.

After what seemed an eternity, a screech of tires sounded as the truck turned on the road. Eliza climbed unsteadily to her feet and raced to the passenger side of the very upside-down Slipstream. It was dark inside, and she smelled gasoline. She grabbed the door handle on the passenger side but the door was crumpled shut from the fall.

"Malcolm!" she cried. "Can you hear me? *Malcolm!*"

Something powerful hit the door and she cried out and backed up a step.

Pressed against the window was a matting of bloody long dark fur. Malcolm thrashed inside, whimpering and snarling in panic. A huge paw-hand scraped the window, leaving a crimson smear of blood on the glass.

"Oh, Malcolm." She forced herself to swallow her panic, grasped the door handle with both hands, set her feet, and pulled. She was a Poppet, not a human. She was not weak. After a few hard tugs, the door cracked open crookedly on its hinges. Almost immediately, something clawed at her.

Eliza lurched backward, falling down in the cold, muddy drainage water again.

Malcolm snarled, his nearly fluorescent green eyes rolling wildly in his head. He was in his transitional phase, a huge, befurred creature that looked more ape-like than anything else, except for his head, which was an elongated snout filled with huge, yellow, bone-sharp teeth. Blood and saliva poured from his gaping jaws.

Eliza let out a sharp breath. She had no idea how much of the Malcolm she knew was still in that black-furred, snarling beast. He had warned her that he was dangerous. She scrambled up, clinging to the door of the overturned car for support. She made certain to stay just outside the creature's grasp.

"Malcolm! It's me! It's Eliza."

The creature writhed in the seat, snapping its jaws reflexively. Then its green eyes fixed on her, and she saw it relax a little. She saw it consider her and *think*, or the closest thing to thinking that an untamed animal can do.

"Malcolm," she said in a softer voice. "Malcolm, I need to get close to the car. Then I can get you out. Do you understand me?"

The creature calmed down inch by inch until she found it staring at her with pleading, pain-filled eyes. It wasn't Malcolm, but it was the closest thing she was going to get to him.

Eliza slid in the mud, gripped the crumpled car door tighter, and moved toward the werewolf, keeping her eyes locked on it for any signs of trouble. She made soothing noises as she leaned across Malcolm to put her hands on the crumpled remnants of the dash.

Though the car was old, Megan had cared enough about it to install a new electrical system and computer. She'd seen that plainly in the display as she was driving it. That meant she could conceivably communicate with the wreck.

But as she stood there, seeking a connection, Malcolm put his big, clawed paw over her arm, his nails clicking. Eliza stiffened but didn't jerk her arm back, afraid Malcolm would rip her arm right out of the socket. She concentrated on breathing and not panicking. Malcolm breathed as well, but more roughly. She moved one hand and laid it carefully against the side of his face. That seemed to help.

"Easy," she said.

Malcolm quieted and slowly released his deathgrip on her arm so she could put both hands back on the dash. "I'll get you out. Just give me a moment." She hoped he understood her.

She took a deep breath as she felt a spark from the car. In her head, a whole diagram opened up, showing her every part of the engine and dashboard. She realized she had to somehow uncrumple the dash without hurting or upsetting Malcolm. She had only done this once before, while she was repairing the gyroscope of the failing *Gypsy Queen*. She wasn't even sure if she could do it again.

Closing her eyes, she concentrated on getting the car to do what she wanted it to do. Malcolm struggled, then grunted as the dash suddenly untwisted, metal crunching and screaming. Eliza jerked back just in time as his jaws scissored closed compulsively. He began to thrash, further loosening the metal.

She quickly danced back as the werewolf tore himself loose from the totaled car and fell to the muddy ground. Her panic was back, the fear that he'd be in so much pain that he wouldn't care how he lashed out—or at whom. He might even kill her, she thought and turned, prepared to flee into the nonexistent safety of the trees.

But he hit her, knocking her to the hard, boggy ground. A scream stuck in her throat, Eliza twisted around, facing him, and raised her hands. But he was too fast. He stood over her, his breath meaty and hot, and licked her face and neck like an exuberant puppy.

She couldn't believe it! Her scream bloomed into a laugh as he brushed a particularly ticklish spot. She reached for his face, clenching great handfuls of his soft, wild wolf fur, and gave it a gentle tug. "You're welcome."

Malcolm edged back, shook himself all over, and then bounded off into the woods so quickly she had difficulty following the motion. She let out a sob of relief and fell back on the damp earth, too tired and overwrought to even move. When she looked up, she spotted a large, orangey, gravid moon.

A blood moon, she realized.

Her mobile went off.

She thought maybe she was dreaming. She turned her head and spotted it lying in some mud a few feet away. It must have been thrown from the vehicle when the lorry pushed it down the ravine. Somehow, though, it had survived the fall. Not a crack on it, she noted.

She had programmed her mobile to play a unique ringtone for each person in her Contacts list. Right now, it was playing "Sympathy for the Devil."

She scrambled for the phone. "Edwin!"

XV

Cesar stood on the roof and sighed down on the white flickering figures, but they were still too far away for him to get a decent bead. He'd worked with military-issue firearms on the practice field, and he knew at this distance, air friction would knock his shot off-center. An idea struck him. He took to the air with one great flap of his wings, the gun in his hand and the wind raking back his hair. He stopped a hundred feet up, hung in the air, and glanced down the sight at the encroaching enemy.

The first Sidhe to reach the outskirts of the bailey was a tall, willowy creature. In full Fae form, the creatures looked strangely androgynous, more like an alien than anything that had ever been human. It stared impassively at the castle until Cesar flew down to engage it.

Then its mouth broke into a grim smile full of jagged, hooked teeth like something from the deep sea, and its eyes turned into black, cat-shaped tarns within which he thought he could see the universe sparkling. He dive-bombed the creature with the hopes that he could clip its head off with his wingtips as he passed, but it turned sharply and with a speed he didn't expect and delivered a very well executed sidekick with a delicate but sharply hoofed foot.

Cesar crashed down to earth, momentarily stunned by the blow. He touched the left side of his face where the skin was curling down in a carpet-like flap. Thankfully, there was no blood. He was a vampire; he didn't have that much inside to spare. So, he pressed the skin back into place with his hand. It hurt like his face had been set on fire, but after a moment, it began to itch as it healed. Good.

Sitting there, he took Edwin's gun and aimed it at the Sidhe in a secure, two-handed grip. "Bitch…bastard…whatever you are!" he breathed out and jerked Belle's trigger. The creature went down screaming as something milky and foul gushed from a hole in its throat.

He was mildly surprised to find the Fae had gone down so easily. Edwin was right; the Fae couldn't tolerate vampire blood.

"Dark Fae!" someone called to him.

He turned. Another Sidhe was closing in on him, moving quickly on its little deer feet. It looked vaguely like a young boy, or so he thought. Unlike the one he had just shot, this one had a pair of coiling horns rising from both sides of its head like a ram. Its voice came garbled out of its Fae throat like a man speaking through crushed glass underwater.

Cesar swung around to face his enemy fully, the gun raised.

"You are an abomination!" it screamed, lunging at him.

"Well, fuck you, too!" he told it, firing the gun.

The Fae sprang into the air, missing the bullet as it spread huge, luminescent, dragonfly-like wings. It crowded Cesar, blinding him with its light as it fell upon him.

Well, fuck! he thought in the seconds before its claws went for his eyes. *Edwin didn't mention they could fly!*

* * *

Edwin lowered himself to the kneeler in the castle's medieval-looking Lady Chapel and lit two tall, white votive candles on the altar before the statue of the Blessed Virgin Mary. He noted that she was surrounded on both sides by two stone guardian archangels. One was Michael and the other Gabriel, both powerful warriors in their own right. Edwin hoped it was a good omen.

He crossed himself, then fingered the small silver cross he wore under his coat. He kissed it, then sent up a prayer of contrition, one for the living and one for the dead, wondering how many warriors before him had done this same act before a battle. He was not a good person, and, in truth, he was a terrible, mostly lapsed, Catholic. He knew that, had fully accepted that a long time ago, but he hoped that God would overlook his shortcomings and stand with them regardless—if not for his sake, then for Eliza and Cesar's. They were innocent. He needed God to understand that.

Behind him, the two remaining night steeds he had brought in from the stables stomped nervously and blew air through their nostrils as if they were fully aware that trouble was coming. He finished his prayer, crossed himself once more, and stood up, gathering the horse's halter leads in his hands.

"I know, my loves, I know," he told them, hoping the sound of his voice would calm them.

Out there, beyond the walls of the castle, he heard the distinctive crack of a Remington going off.

He immediately brought his wrist to his mouth and bit, then stretched his arm out and let his blood patter down to the stones of the chapel floor before using his power as a weak bloodkinetic to coagulate it into a long, thin, and exceedingly agile chain whip. Edwin grasped the end loosely in his hand and snapped the manriki up around his shoulder. It hissed menacingly.

"Sorry about that, My Lady," Edwin said, turning contrite eyes upon the statue. "Didn't mean to disgrace your place of worship." As he pushed the doors of the chapel open and stepped out to engage the Fae, he dearly hoped God was willing to overlook that as well.

***

Megan stomped out of the west door of the castle and took up her position on the frontlines. She wore heavy rubber galoshes over high, tough riding books, a long duster, and a straw sunbathing hat to keep her hair back. She hoped there was enough rubber insulation between herself and the ground to keep her hair from catching on fire. She did not like the thought of that. Fire frightened her.

A hundred years ago, a great number of lambs had been found ripped to pieces in the farms surrounding Whitby. A week before, a circus had been though, and one of the dancing bears had gone missing, but the angry townsfolk of Whitby thought it would be a good idea to smoke out the Bloodthorn werewolves, whom they assumed were responsible. On that terrible night, they set fire to the cottage that Megan shared with her mate and pack members. She and the twins, her sister's pups, were the only three wolves to make it out alive.

It had been hard on them all. Her mate Jonathan had been the pack leader. She was little more than a country bumpkin and hadn't the self-confidence to fill her role as the alpha female. After the fire, Lord Ian took her and the twins in. Over the years, they had talked extensively about rebuilding the pack, but with Jonathan's death, their momentum had died.

Megan saw no point in making more werewolves in a world that despised their kind. In recent years, the twins had discussed going native—that is, shifting into their wolf forms and not coming back. Megan was torn. She knew they were all greatly disliked in the village, but she still liked being human some of the time. She didn't want to be forced to go feral.

She took a deep breath and reminded herself that she was a wolf of the Bloodthorn Pack. She was Jonathan's mate, a position of honor. Alpha female. She wondered how her boys were faring, and she feared it wasn't going well. They were probably frightened half to death and as likely to race off into the woods as to fight the Fae. She had to be strong for them all. She had to be the pack leader.

Setting her feet shoulder-wide, she hefted the Rainmaker onto her shoulder, wondering why it was called that. She knew, intellectually, that even a grown man would have had trouble lifting it. But for her, it might as well be a plastic water gun. She was strong. She was a Bloodthorn wolf.

As the first Sidhe crested the hills, she sighted down the barrel, clicked off the release, and took careful aim. The bloody sod spotted her and started to charge, looking like some ghost displaced from a haunted house in a bad horror movie. Lord Ian had once theorized that most ghostly "hauntings" were caused by the Sidhe in their sleeping forms—Sleepwalkers just mistaken as ghosts.

"Bloody fairies," she said as the female closed the distance between them, her eyes black and mean and as dead as shark eyes.

She squeezed the trigger and was momentarily bewildered by the lack of recoil. She had expected the thing to kick like a bloody mule. Instead, it offered a polite cough…and then a charge of blue-white lightning lit up the Sidhe's face. It looked vaguely insulted. Then it exploded into snowy white flotsam as if it was some kind of giant white Christmas toy shaken by an angry dog.

Megan screamed victory at the dead fairy. "Can't even bleed right!" she shouted across the battlefield. Every hair on her body stood at rigid attention, but whether from the static electricity of the Rainmaker's discharge or fear, she did not know. She aimed and fired again, making another of the fairies do the electric boogaloo before bursting into marshmallowy gunk.

A few seconds later, she heard the first clap of thunder far above. It made her skin jump. Then the rain started, not a good English rain, light and airy, but a 'bad soakin',' as her mum used to call it, the kind that happens only in the Highlands or in American gangster movies set in Chicago.

So, that's why it was called a Rainmaker...

From afar came the blast of a gun, then a wolf howled, not a hunting call. Rather, it was a higher-pitched scream of distress. Megan lost all focus, tilted her head back in the rain, and answered the call of the wild, howling as loudly as she could so it would travel over the long distance.

She wished Malcolm was here. If the Werewolf of Whitby were here, at least they would have a leader. But they didn't. They had only her.

Her howl said, *I'm coming, my darlings.* Throwing Edwin's gun aside, she ripped at her clothing and went down on all fours to join the Bloodthorn Pack in her more natural form.

* * *

Baldy, dressed in a white zoot suit and Fedora, twin gun holsters strapped across his shoulder, stepped out onto the bailey and into rain so fierce it sparked on the stones. He lifted a sonic pistol and sighted down the nearest Sidhe. He smoked a cigar while he squeezed off a reverberating sonic blast.

The Sidhe screamed as it disintegrated.

That pleased him. A lot.

His smoke was soaked through in seconds. That didn't please him. In fact, it downright annoyed him. He crossed the bailey, searching for more fairies, which wasn't all that difficult. The Sidhe were cresting the rise of the twin stone bridges that led to the castle, their numbers increasing as the night wore on and more children were put to bed.

Children. He was shooting children. He let the thought permeate his skull for approximately three seconds before wiping it away. He couldn't afford to go soft, not when his Court needed him. Not when Star needed him.

He marched to the end of the bailey, to the place where some privet shrubbery was getting flattened in the rain, and took cover behind the parapet wall. There, he took careful aim once more.

In the distance, he heard the mournful cry of a wolf.

Rain dripped off the edge of his Fedora. He shot another Sidhe, spit out his wet smoke, and then got ready to shoot some more.

* * *

Inside Baldy's quarters in the castle, Star jumped in the dark when she heard the wolves howling in the night. Blimey, she thought, it was like a bad horror movie. Except these weren't cheesy horror movie sound effects; these were honest-to-god werewolves howling as they tangled with whatever was laying siege to Whitby Hall.

She sat straight up on the divan she'd been dozing on and looked around the cool darkness of the room. Baldy had given her instructions. She was to keep the lights out to keep the other vampires away from his quarters. God knows what *they* would do to her or her children. Besides, there was that terrible ginger vampire with the devil goatee she had spotted from the window. He was currently ripping into Sidhe with the use of what looked like a black, medieval chain-whip. *He* made vampires like Baldy look like angels.

Her heart thudding uncomfortably in her throat, she fumbled in the dark until she found the hand torch—it had somehow rolled under the divan—and switched it on, shaking it until the light flickered on properly. She could never understand that. It was a new torch, and yet it acted unreliably. She sighed when she realized she was so much like the torch. Small, weak, shining only interminably, and only for a short burst of time.

At least, that was how she felt in the years before she met Baldy. That's how her ex, Franklin, made her feel. Franklin was a monster, a hundred times worse than the ginger vampire, she decided. Or Baldy. Baldy was the most human inhuman she had ever met. He had the best hugs, and he always said the perfect thing when she was done crying her eyes out like the fool she was.

Getting to her feet, Star crossed to Baldy's bedchamber, aiming the light ahead of her like a sword to cut the dark. Inside, she found Annamarie and Tim lying dead asleep on Baldy's massive, four-poster bed. They had slept through the wolf howls the way they slept through thunderstorms. She wished she could be more like them, so innocent and trusting.

She moved closer to them, brushing some hair off Tim's forehead. Tim had her ex's looks, but Annamarie looked nothing like Franklin. Annamarie, almost twelve years old now, had been from her boyfriend at the time, a boy named Matthew that she had met down in the village when she was a young girl and her parents first transplanted them here from London.

They had moved to Whitby because the crime rate was so low, and her parents were tired of worrying each time she left the flat. She never told Baldy that. She was too afraid Baldy would think she'd been a loose, dirty lass. But it was true. She'd had a tryst with a Whitby boy when she was only fourteen years old. And then, when she moved back to London to study at university, she'd met Franklin. The rest, as they say, was history.

Well, she was some hot mess, Star decided. Despite having two human boyfriends, she had never really known what love was until she came back here and met Baldy, who was neither English nor human. A man she had asked to marry her. A man who might even make her his wife forever. His vampire Bride.

She took a deep breath and thought about that. She wondered whether she was ready to make such an enormous sacrifice of life for love. She decided that she did. She loved Baldy. She would always love him. And, as a vampire mum, she would be more than capable of protecting her children.

She stepped out of the bedroom, back into the antechamber, and gently closed the door behind her. From outside, she heard a threatening belly growl of thunder. The rain was coming down, silvery and sharp, making everything glow hazily through the window. Undecided about what she should do, she sank down on the divan and waited for Baldy. But she grew tired from worrying, and it wasn't long before Star fell asleep.

* * *

In Baldy's room, Annamarie slowly sat up. Not her body, but her soul.

She whimpered but did not scream. It hurt to separate her two selves—like skinning her knee, only worse, because it she was skinning her entire body. But this was something that Corcoran had warned her about. He told them all about how much pain was involved in shedding their human skin. For their people, it was often the source of their anger. Pain transforming into a rage as only pain can.

Corcoran usually spoke to her in her mind late at night, after Mum put her to bed, but tonight, he was quiet. He must be very busy, she thought. She knew he was hunting the Dark Fae. Vampires like Uncle Baldy.

Her anger at Uncle Baldy helped her push the pain aside. He wanted her mother, wanted to make her like him, one of the Dark

Fae. She realized that now. She'd heard their conversation, the one she wasn't supposed to hear. In that way, he was just like Franklin, preying on her mother like that. Well, things would stop. They would stop *now*.

She turned to Tim lying beside her. Her half-brother, though Mum didn't know she knew that. Corcoran had told her.

Tim was human and she was not. She realized she needed his lifeforce, his strength, or she would never succeed in stopping Baldy. So, she reached out and touched his cheek in her true Sidhe form, and in that moment, everything that Tim was, had been, or would ever be became hers.

Her brother's young, fiery energy filled her. The timeline shifted. *She* remembered Tim, of course, but no one else in the world would, including their mother. Tim had ceased to exist.

Rising from the bed and leaving her body behind, Annamarie went to the door and let herself out.

Mum sat nodding on the divan, the hand torch on one side of her and the sonic handgun on the other. Annamarie went up to her mother and stood there, looking at the gun. The weapon could hurt her kind, she knew, so she took it. For one moment, she thought about kissing her Mum, taking her life force. Then Baldy would never have her. But Corcoran had warned her about such things. She could not touch any human being in direct genetic line to her. To do so would cause a paradox. That person would disappear along with all of the Fae/human hybrids she might have birthed in her lifetime.

Annamarie would cease to exist as a consequence. Shame.

Turning on her heels, Annamarie went to the door. She was afraid the sound of its opening would alert Star, so she phased right through it instead.

***

Out on the moors, Edwin busied himself with cutting down Sidhe whenever they grew too close to the castle by lassoing them with the manriki and zipping off an arm or a leg. Sometimes even a head. The manriki, constructed of his blood—vampire blood—was deadly poison to the Fae, and he was not unskilled in his use of the weapon. It was a good weapon as weapons go, allowing him to kill the bloody tossers without getting too close to them or their cursed athames.

They did their customary scary hissy fits, stomped their ugly deer feet, and threatened him en masse, but he'd been a monster for over two hundred years; they would need to do a lot more than that if they wanted to get under *his* skin.

Somewhere in the dark, the wolves were howling—a high, screechy sound of distress that did not sound like they were winning this war.

"Hell," he cursed, stopping to catch his breath while the rain poured through his hair and over his face. After a quick breather, he used the manriki to tear another Fae in half before it could reach the bridge he was guarding. He rushed to the top of the next rise in the moors and looked down.

Far below, in a boggy valley, the Sidhe had tossed a heavy fishing net loaded down with lead weights over one of the werewolf boys. The wolf lay pinned while his brother, half-transformed into a kind of ape-like man-wolf shape, circled round undecidedly, too afraid of the encroaching Sidhe to rush in and help.

Distantly, another werewolf howled as it rushed toward them. Edwin recognized it as Megan. It was a large wolf, but not as bulky as the boys, and it had ginger fur. She snarled as she closed in on her packmates. Edwin was big on loyalty. In that moment, he hated Megan just a little bit less despite the way she had betrayed Eliza. She was an arse and had spent far too many years being Ian's puppet, but at least she was a brave warrior who looked out for her own, and that meant something to him.

The little hairs on the back of his neck stood on end, and Edwin swung around, coming practically nose-to-nose with a half dozen Sidhe flying straight toward him, their long, slim wings buzzing like insects in flight. Blimey, he wished someone had mentioned they could fly!

Surprised, he stumbled back, lost his footing in the mud, and tumbled down the hill. Only his quick reflexes saved him. As he fell, his wings speared through the back of his coat, which gave him some much-needed lift and a chance to right himself. But the wind had kicked up considerably with the storm brewing high overhead, and when it caught under his wings, he was effectively airborne. He could use a manriki very well, and he was trained in the use of most handguns. He even knew a little bit of martial arts. But flying was not his forte.

Edwin crashed straight into the Sidhe who were marching up the hill, scattering them like bowling pins. He cursed under his breath as he landed, skidding and scrabbling in the mud. He reached for his manriki, but it was gone, melted away. Bloodkinetic powers were only as good as the mind that wielded it. He had lost his concentration and, thus, his weapon.

As he lay there in the mud, a Sidhe stomped on his hand with her sharp little deer hoof, making him bark in pain. "Look at the clumsy vampire," she snickered to her comrades. "Funny, that never happens in the movies."

"Sod off!" Edwin said. "Bloody poofers, go dance off into the woods!"

The Fae who had spoken glared down at him.

"Don't like stereotypes?" Edwin asked with a grim smile full of rain and teeth. "Bloody shove off."

They dogpiled him.

* * *

Oh god, Cesar thought as the Sidhe raked his impressive claws across his eyes, he was such a fucking noob! He felt like he'd just stepped into a brand-new guild in one of his favorite online multi-player RPGs. You don't know anyone, don't know the rules, and generally feel like an uneducated dweeb. And, just like a noob in a monster-fighting guild, he was about to get his ass kicked well and good. By a goddamned fairy, no less!

Blood and pain blinded him. The Sidhe wrapped his hand around Cesar's throat, his fingers pressing so tightly against his Adam's apple that he couldn't breathe. Together, they rocketed upward to the level of the roof, the sensation sickening. Cesar would have blown chunks had he had access to his throat, which he did not.

He just sort of hung limp in the Sidhe's hold, although that wasn't even the worse part of it. Because he could feel the Sidhe leeching his strength, eating his power right out of his soul with a kind of psychic spork, and he couldn't help but wonder if this was what Ian had felt when the Sidhe touched him. *Christ.* He did not want to end up like Ian, dying slowly, disintegrating cell by cell.

"You are no Dark Fae," said the fairy. "Just a shadow. A pup. You are nothing but a receptacle for your master's waste, bottom-feeder."

"What...ever," Cesar choked out, struggling to pronounce every word. "I got...more creative gay-boy jokes...in high school!"

"A gay vampire, how original," the Sidhe said.

As his eyes gradually repaired themselves from the effects of the creature's claws, Cesar noted the fairy's rather impressive, silvery, hook-like teeth. "How does it feel to be Queen of the Vampires, poofer boy?"

Okay, that did it. He'd had enough from this joker. He bared his teeth. "Closet case!" And as a killing rage began filling his body, that's when it happened. That's when he discovered what his secret superhero power was.

One moment he was dangling from the fist of a bitchy, repressed Sidhe, the next his enemy disappeared with a scream and a sparkle of almost blinding white light.

Cesar dropped to the roof of the castle and just sat there, confused, too stunned to move for the moment. Slowly, he gasped for breath as his windpipe repaired itself. Then, gathering his courage, he looked down at himself, terrified he'd become an old man like Ian, his life essence sucked away.

But it was worse than that. So very much worse.

Because he wasn't old, which would have been bad enough. No. He'd become the bitchy, repressed Sidhe.

Things got very weird after that.

* * *

Baldy stopped shooting Sidhe when he heard the screams coming from within the castle walls. They weren't human screams, but they still made his blood—what he had of it, anyway—run cold. The horses! There were only two night steeds left, and they were screaming in panic. Without the horses, there would be no Wild Hunt!

Abandoning the Sidhestill amassing over the hills, he raced back across the bridge, crossed the bailey, and skidded to a halt outside the north entrance of the Lady's Chapel. He gripped the great oaken double doors in both hands and threw them open. His heroics were immediately rewarded by a stampeding horse that nearly collided with him as it fled in a blind panic out of the castle. He shifted aside just in time as it charged past him and headed out into the bailey.

He turned to follow its motion and watched as Grey Molly, the boss's oldest horse—kept more for sentimental reasons than anything practical—took off across the bridge and headed for the deep woods. The sight of her dusty retreat made something in his heart fall.

Baldy turned back slowly, already acutely aware of the presence in the chapel. He glared at the Sidhe girl standing over the body of the dying horse lying on the chapel's cobblestones. She was eyeing him contemptuously. She had broken a crystal vase and had used a long spear of the broken glass to spear the horse through the heart.

The horse lay, pedaling uselessly, as great gouts of its blood poured onto the stones. It was a young, barely broken-in stallion—Grey Molly's son. The horse that Edwin would have ridden to replace the deceased Boyo. The Sidhe's arms were gloved in the horse's blood up to the elbow, and more blood was splashed across her long filmy nightgown and over her face.

Even so, Baldy recognized who she was. He wondered how it was possible but then realized the whys and wherefores didn't really matter. It was obvious that Star had kept secrets even from him. "You won't win," he told Annamarie. "Even if you wipe all of us out, doll, you won't win when the Darkness comes."

Annamarie waited until the horse stopped struggling, then sighed long and loud before stepping over it and taking a few careful steps toward him on her awkward little deer feet. She pulsed with her own ethereal glow.

"Uncle Baldy, the Darkness always recedes in the face of the Light," she said in her sweet, lilting soprano. She sounded so innocent, as if she were explaining the history behind her favorite doll or the plot of her favorite cartoon. But her eyes burned. Her eyes were bright blue Fae eyes.

"Do you really believe that?" Baldy asked, trying to remain calm. He was at a total loss as to what to do. He wondered if he should shoot Annamarie with the sonic pistol. He wondered if he could even do that. "Who told you that?"

Annamarie seemed to consider the question. "Corcoran."

"Who's that?"

"The All-Father."

"Your boss?"

"Yes." Annamarie smiled, sweet and harmless.

"Well, then," he said, hoping to forestall her progress, "Corcoran lied. He doesn't know anything about the Darkness. Because when it comes, doll, you can be sure it'll swallow you the same as me."

"I don't believe you," Annamarie said, sounding cross. "Corcoran has been right all along. He would know."

"How would Corcoran know? Was he here the last time the Darkness came to this place?"

The girl hedged on a response.

"Yeah. I thought so. You mooks planned all this, but you have no idea what you're messin' with."

The girl, steadily moving toward him, stopped inches from him. She suffused the whole chapel with her light. Her lips were pressed together solemnly, although that was hard to tell when the Sidhe assumed their true form. They didn't have much in the way of lips—or faces, for that matter. They were oddly featureless.

"You would say anything to save yourself. We know you, Dark Fae."

"Then you know I'm right," Baldy assured her. "You have my word—as a man, a vampire, and one of the Dark Fae. This shit's gonna go all sideways on ya, doll."

Behind Annamarie, the stallion struggled one last time to rise. Annamarie turned her head to follow its movements. Baldy tried to take advantage of the distraction. He lunged forward, hoping to knock her out with the butt of his pistol like in all the gangster movies, but he'd never been very fast, or very graceful. He'd been a fat, graceless man when he was alive, and now that he was dead, he made a fat, graceless vampire.

He slid in all of the horse blood all over the floor. That gave Annamarie a chance to turn back and slap him away. Baldy landed hard on his belly on the stones at her feet, grunting from the impact, the sonic pistol bouncing away. It was like being hit by a machine.

"Do not do that again," she warned.

Baldy tried to recover, tried to find his feet, but Annamarie's hoofed foot came down hard on the back of his neck with the force of a stone mallet, severing his spine with a sharp, sickening crack. All the feeling immediately went out of Baldy's body as he was rendered as useful as a sack of concrete.

She lowered her eyes to him. "I believe you, Uncle Baldy," she answered with grave concern. "I believe it will all go sideways. For you." And then she touched him.

* * *

The Sidhe had gathered round and were treating Edwin to a good *Casino*-style beat down, something he hadn't experienced since Prohibition. He assumed this was their way of playing with their food before they ate it.

They kicked him in the face, the chest, and once (much to his unhappiness) the nuts. After he ran out of expletives, they casually laid into his already well-broken ribs, making his half-mended bones do all kinds of calisthenics. Things didn't hurt much after that. At least he had the presence of mind to buckle under and try and protect himself from being disemboweled by their daft little hoofed feet.

Finally, after what seemed an eternity in hell, a new Sidhe arrived, one who apparently had no command of its powers. He landed atop them all—more like fell, really—scattering them far and wide and giving Edwin time to re-form his manriki.

Pushing past the mind-numbing agony in his body, Edwin lashed out at the Sidhe slowly killing him, dispatching them one by one by grappling arms and necks and ripping through their soft, white Fae flesh so they bled snow-white blood into the muddy ground. One by one, they went down until only one remained, and that was the latecomer standing a few feet away and looking over the battle with confusion.

Holding his wounded side, Edwin let out a pain-filled growl and lashed out at that one, too, snagging the male by the ankle and knocking him down. Edwin then dragged him through the mud toward him despite all of his protests. Pain had made Edwin mean, and he wanted this one to suffer. He jumped atop the creature and raised his hand, curling his fingers into a claw.

He was fully prepared to plunge it deep into the creature's chest when it croaked out, "Lord Edwin!" in an American accent.

Edwin stopped and just looked at it for a long moment as the rain fell around them, turning the hole they were lying in into a muddy, overflowing pit. "How the bloody hell...?" he began.

"It's me!" the Sidhe croaked.

"Cesar?"

"Y-yeah." The creature cowed away from Edwin's upraised claw-hand.

Edwin wasn't convinced. Who knew what tricks the Fae could play? Growling in frustration, he said, "Prove it!"

The Sidhe thought a moment. "We met in Foxley's casino. I gave you the best head of your life and you never even bothered to thank me. Asshole!"

Finally convinced, Edwin lowered his hand and stood up, pulling Cesar up with him by one long, white, faintly glowing hand. "Want to explain how this happened?"

"I have no fucking clue."

"What did you do?"

"I don't know!" Cesar cried, touching his body with only the tips of his glowy fingers. "I was fighting this fairy guy—very well, I might add—and then…poof."

"Poof?"

"I don't know…somehow I *became* him."

Edwin blinked. "You turned into the fairy you were fighting."

Cesar nodded, then changed his mind and shook his head. "No. I mean, I *look* like a fairy, but I still operate like a vampire. I'm *still* a vampire. I'm just trapped inside a fairy body." He looked at Edwin with terror-struck eyes. "You never told me about any of this! What do I do?"

"How the bloody hell should I know?"

"You've never seen anything like this?"

"Never."

"Well, fuck me!"

Edwin looked Cesar's new physical form over. "We'll have to sort it later. Can you fight? Kick like those bloody tossers?"

Cesar narrowed his glowy, pale eyes. "Do I look like Bruce Lee to you?"

"Fine." Edwin sighed. "Can you look after Eliza for me? I'm going to be very busy with these blokes for a while."

Cesar looked around, frightened. "Is she in trouble?"

Edwin's expression remained neutral, but Cesar could feel the dread creeping up his back through their bloodlink. "Aye. She's being hunted down in the village."

"Sure. Um...now?"

"Yes, Cesar. *Now.*"

Cesar stomped around in the mud for a few seconds on his crazy little deer feet before spreading his dragonfly wings. He looked scared and confused, but he still shot straight up like a bottle rocket on Edwin's orders.

Edwin watched him head north toward the village. But even as he was glancing up at the sky, he noticed an unbelievably strange thing through the sheets of nonstop rain: The stars seemed to be winking out one by one. It was a little like a lunar eclipse, except it seemed to be encompassing the entire bloody sky.

He felt a spike of irrational fear, and then he thought, almost irrationally, *The Darkness is coming.*

He dug his mobile out of his muddy clothes.

| xvi |

"Edwin!"
"Hello, lovey."
"Oh, Edwin. I'm having a *hell* of a night."
"What's happened?"
"I got the list! Tell Ian that. I got the list! And…oh, my god, it's almost everyone in the village! But the Sidhe know who I am. They tailed us, Edwin. They burned us out of our hotel room, then forced us off the road. Malcolm was injured…the car accident made him change. I got him out of the car after they wrecked it, but he's hurt and now he's run off into the woods, and I don't know *where* he's gotten himself off to. Edwin, I'm stuck here. I'm just sitting here in the woods…"

"Are you hurt? Eliza…"
"No. I'm banged up, but it looks worse than it is. No, I'm okay."
"Eliza…"
"Don't fret. I'm all right. Really. It's nice to hear your voice, Edwin. It really is. You have no idea. Are you still mad at me?"
"I'm not mad at you, Eliza. I promise. Are you crying, lovey?"
"No…I'm just…Christ, I guess I am. I miss you so much, and I'm wet and cold and tired. Can you come get me? Please…?"
"I want to. I do. But I need to ask you to do something for me first, and I wish to God I didn't have to rely on you to do it after all

you've been through, but I have to. You're all I have left, love, the only one I trust."

"Edwin...tell me what's happened."

"The Sidhe are here. They're laying siege to the castle. Everyone here is fighting..."

"Dear God..."

"...but there's too many, and more are arriving every hour. We're swamped, love. They're getting through. It's better that you don't come here...and...I think the Darkness is here. I think it's moving toward us, chasing the Light—"

"What can I do? Edwin, tell me."

"Can you create some form of distraction? Something that would wake up most of the village? The Sidhe can divide their form when they're in an altered state of conscience, but—"

"REM sleep. Yes, I know about that from Catherine's notes."

"They can't become Sidhe if they're awake—"

"REM sleep occurs all night long for young people, Edwin, but it takes longer the older people get. Most adults only experience REM sleep close to morning..."

"Then we need to act quickly. This night won't last, and if more are coming, we'll be outnumbered."

"Understood. I'll call you when I've figured something out."

"I love you, Eliza. I should have been more understanding, trusted you...."

"I know, Edwin. Wish me luck, ducky."

"Bloody hell, you did *not* just call me 'ducky.'"

Eliza hung up, looked up at the blood moon, and smiled.

* * *

By the time Eliza climbed the bank to the shoulder of the road, she was soaked through, disoriented, and on the verge of tears. No part of her didn't ache. In the dark, she had no idea where she was, and only a vague notion of where she needed to go. The only thing she had to guide her was the dim, far-off glow of lights from the inn burning to the ground on the outskirts of Whitby. Far off, she heard the wail of sirens as police and the fire brigade descended on it.

She was terrified to go back. The lorry might be waiting for her, and if not them, then the rest of the villagers who wanted her dead. But the moorland stretched in the opposite direction—miles of scrubby wasteland pocketed by blanket bogs that were impossible to see in the dark. If she fell into one of them, she was doomed. She seriously thought about sitting down on the road and just crying her eyes out, but that wasn't her way. That wasn't constructive.

Giggle-sobbing with fatigue, she stood in the rain and fingered the Covenant ring around her neck. It seemed to give her a much-needed jolt of energy. Maybe it was silly, but she felt stronger for wearing it. Edwin had worn it, touched it, for centuries. It was like a little piece of him. Taking a deep breath for courage, she started back toward the village, more focused on the task at hand. Soon, she was marching with such determination that she almost didn't see the swish of lights coming up behind her.

She jumped and was mildly shocked to see it was Betsy McCormick driving an older model classic roadster with the top up. She pulled to a halt beside Eliza and rolled down the window, looking overtop her cat glasses. "Mrs. McGillicuddy? What are you doing out in this weather?"

"Oh, Betsy, I'm so glad to see you!"

"Get in the car, lass. Good Lord, you'll catch your death."

Eliza grabbed the door handle and slid, sopping wet, onto the leather passenger seat. She glanced down at the squishy mess she was making.

Betsy waved it away. "Don't worry about that! I drip all over the car on nights like this." She turned the heater on full blast, then reached into the back seat and produced a big, folded tartan blanket, which indicated to Eliza just how prepared Betsy was for the almost schizophrenic East Anglian weather.

"Thank you," she said in relief, taking the blanket and wiping her face and all down her neck where the rain had dripped. She wrapped it around herself. The heat in the car enfolded her, stealing away the worst of the chill.

"A dog's night!" Betsy exclaimed, looking out the windshield. She put the car into gear and they started motoring along the muddy ruts in the road. "Can I ask what you're doing in it? Not research for your book, I hope!"

"No," Eliza answered uncertainly. "My car broke down on the way out of town and I..." She let her voice peter away, unsure of how big she wanted to weave her web of lies. Instead of continuing, she concentrated on patting her hair dry, then noticed Betsy staring at her. Or, more precisely, the ring around her neck where it was catching the glare of the headlights.

"That's a lovely ring," Betsy said. "A Covenant ring, isn't it? I haven't seen one of those in ages." She looked back toward the road. "Lord Ian wears one."

Eliza decided she needed to come clean. Betsy didn't come from here, at least. She wasn't Sidhe and she wasn't a danger to her. "My name isn't Alisa. It's Eliza. And I'm not married to Malcolm, Betsy, the man you met at the museum. He's my...bodyguard, you might say. I'm engaged to be married to Lord Edwin McGillicuddy, an Heir of Lord Foxley's."

Betsy's posture stiffened. "Your fiancé...is a vampire."

"Yes."

Betsy nodded, almost imperceptibly. Eliza was glad she didn't ask further questions about her relationship. Instead, she kept her narrow gaze on the road. "Why do you need a bodyguard?"

Eliza hesitated, then reminded herself that Betsy wasn't one of them. Her information might even save the woman's life. So, she told Betsy a very truncated version of the Wild Hunt story and explained how Lord Ian had trapped them all and was forcing Edwin to ride the hunt. Betsy listened with rapt attention, her face like a solid porcelain mask, betraying no reaction until Eliza finished by telling her about the Darkness. Then, and only then, did she look concerned.

Finally, Eliza just stopped. "You must think I'm insane."

Betsy pressed her lips together. "Well, I always suspected there was something wrong with this town. I mean—but I never really *knew*."

Eliza nodded and swallowed. "You should leave. Go back to the States. It isn't safe here, Betsy."

Betsy thought about that, her eyes clocking across the road. "I don't think so."

"Why do you say that?"

Betsy swallowed hard before saying, "I was born in New York, Eliza, but my mother was from here. From Whitby. That's why I chose to move here with Roger in the first place." She turned her head and stared blindly at Eliza. "My entire family comes from Whitby. Doesn't that mean I'm Sidhe, too?"

Eliza didn't answer until they reached the outskirts of town.

There, Betsy pulled the car to the side of the road and killed the engine.

"Betsy..."

Betsy leaned forward in her seat, suddenly overcome with realization, and breathed out an "Oh, my god!" into her hands.

Eliza waited, her heart ticking, for her friend to compose herself.

Finally, Betsy sat back in her seat, moonlight glinting off the lens of her cat glasses. "I've never slept very well. Had nightmares my whole life. I was even medicated for them for a while. But nothing helped. Having Roger helped a little. But after he died, the nightmares came back, and they were worse than ever."

She shook her head as if she were trying to toss something unwanted off. "Sometimes, there's a man in my dreams. He walks in a desolate red moorland, the sky pitch black above me, no stars, no moon. I used to hate that dream." She looked over at Eliza. "Do you think...I mean, is it possible I become one of them at night? Do I...sleepwalk...or whatever? Do I wander?"

Eliza saw the pain in the older woman's face and her heart clenched inside of her. She thought about touching her hand, but she was afraid. "I don't know, Betsy."

Betsy nodded. "You said you have to sleep?"

"I read Lady Catherine's journals. She believed that it...sort of liberated the Sidhe within, I guess."

"So, if I become Sidhe, it's only when I sleep."

"I guess. Though the activity of the other Sidhe may have some impact. I'm not sure. I don't know all of the rules."

Betsy forced a mirthless smile. "So, what you're saying is—I shouldn't go to sleep tonight."

"I wouldn't recommend it, no." She reached out then and touched Betsy's hand. She felt exceedingly human to Eliza.

"You're being very nice to someone who's your potential enemy," Betsy pointed out.

"You're not my enemy."

"Until I am."

"Betsy..."

Betsy laughed miserably, then nodded, looking determined. "So, what now, enemy of mine?"

Eliza turned and stared out the windshield at the inn burning down in the distance. Eventually, she got out of the car and went up a steep hill. From the top, she could see the small collection of buildings that made up Whitby Village, maybe a hundred buildings in all, a town so small it was only about the size of two or three city blocks at home in New York. She bit her lip as Betsy joined her, then nodded slowly to herself.

"I have to wake this town up. It's the only way I can save my fiance, my friends, and everyone else. Any suggestions?"

"You could run through the streets, clashing pots and pans together."

Eliza smiled. "That would get me shot." The fire trucks gave her an idea. "Does this town have anything like a fire alarm? Maybe if the whole town thinks it's burning to the ground, that'll be enough."

Betsy shook her head. "We have a fire station, but no alarm. For the past two hundred years, everyone's just used the bell tower for emergencies."

Eliza felt a spark so powerful that her techkinetic power actually jump-started the engine of the car in front of them. Betsy flinched and stared in shock at the dashboard as if trying to decide how the car had roared to life all on its own.

"Betsy," Eliza said, "I would very much like to visit the bell tower."

* * *

The bell tower was located on the edge of town, which, if not an ideal location, was at least convenient. Eliza jumped out of Betsy's car almost before the woman braked and made for the door of the little stone Angelical chapel.

It was locked! She cursed and kicked at the door as Betsy followed behind at a more ladylike pace, holding an umbrella over her head against the drizzle. Betsy shook her head. "The key's with the vicar, but I'm not sure if he's still awake—or if we should even approach him."

"Probably not. Is there another way in?"

"No, but the rear window is often left open to fight the mold…"

Eliza had disappeared around the back of the church before Betsy had even finished her statement. She found the window inadvisably propped open by a stick, with a big green dumpster parked just beneath it. That made it somewhat more convenient as she scrabbled up the cold, wet, metal side, sliding several times in her now hopelessly ruined walking boots. By then, her skirts, along with the rest of her, were dripping wet again. *Wet knickers.* She wondered if she would ever feel dry again.

She scrambled through the window, finding it just a tad too small and her bust a tad too big before dropping to the very wet, green-tiled floor of a tidy if outdated washroom. Then she was up and racing through the door to find herself in a rustic rectory inside a two-story, modestly furnished, and rather impoverished church. A wooden catwalk encircled the upper story, leading up to what she hoped was the bell tower.

Eliza started up the winding stairs, her wet boots clattering on the old steps. Behind her came Betsy, disheveled from her struggles of window wrestling and glancing around furtively as if she expected the Sidhe to burst out of the ancient woodwork.

Eliza, reaching the top, found the bell tower cold, drippy from the rain, and musty. A thick, knotted rope hung down from the belfry high above. Eliza grasped it and pulled, expecting it to be easy. It wasn't. The bell barely moved, and she wondered how the vicar or choirboys managed it.

Betsy clattered across the wet floorboards, dropped her umbrella, and joined Eliza at the bell. "Are you sure this will work?"

"Absolutely not."

"Mother of Mercy. I must be mad."

They each took a spot on the rope and braced themselves. At first, they started pulling in the wrong directions, but Eliza managed to sort them out, and just as they got it going and the huge, rusty bell began to peal, a man dropped his hand on her shoulder, halting her.

She never noticed him standing there in the tower with her, but when she turned her head, she saw other townies lurking in darkened corners as if they were part of the shadows—or, more likely, they were slowly *emerging* from the shadows.

Eliza only had time to scream as they yanked her and Betsy away from the rope and then dragged them back toward the walls of the tower where the un-shuttered windows were wide open, letting in sparks of rain that danced on the floorboards as they fell. The wind buffeted her, and she had a terrible moment when she realized what the townies meant to do, how they were likely dragging them both to their deaths.

Betsy started to scream and twist in her captor's hands, then stomped backward, right onto his foot. Eliza felt a surge of victory. Then the man cried out and swung Betsy into the wall with truly preternatural strength. Betsy's head collided with a wood beam, and there came a sickening crunching noise. Suddenly, shining blood darkened the floorboards.

"Betsy!" Eliza screamed as the older woman slumped down into a broken doll pile on the floor at her captor's feet. Eliza kicked at her assailant, twisted as Betsy had, but he was one of the local pub boys, huge and beefy, and he just hauled her back until she was face to face with Mr. Cummings.

Mr. Cummings, of all people!

"What did you do?" she raged at the old, grey-haired man. Her wet hair fell in snarls around her grimace of pain and horror. "How could you hurt Betsy like that?"

Mr. Cummings only smiled serenely. He stood in one of his natty grey suits, leaning heavily on a cane. He didn't move much, so she suspected the cane was more functional than decorative. Her assumption panned out when she realized there were bruises all along his face and jaw like he'd been in a fistfight and lost.

He traced one nasty bruise near his mouth where several of his teeth were missing. "A gift from your fiance's Enforcer."

"Good," she spat, getting angry now. "You deserve it for what you did to Betsy!"

"Miss Book," he said patiently, "what makes you think she's dead? Look again, please."

Eliza turned her head and looked.

Betsy's crumpled body trembled as if she was lying on a fault line. Then something that glowed as fiercely as a flame rose from within the still form, pure white and shining. At first, Eliza feared she was witnessing Betsy's soul leaving her body. But it was a solid being, tall and thin and strangely androgynous—entirely unlike Betsy.

"I haven't murdered her, Mrs. Book," Mr. Cummings explained with a giant smile. "I have *liberated* her."

The Fae thing looked at Eliza with its large, black alien eyes. And then it smiled, its mouth stretching wider and wider over its long, uneven rows of shark teeth. Very soon, and despite Eliza's protests, it began approaching her, its arms outstretched, ready to embrace her.

* * *

Through Edwin's mark, Cesar was able to hone in on Eliza, though it wasn't an exact science. It was more art than anything else, if he was being honest. He found himself zigzagging around the village through sheets of pelting rain, even glancing in upstairs windows, before his internal compass drew him to the belfry of the local church.

The belfry of a church, of all places!

* * *

"I'm not your enemy!" Eliza pleaded with Mr. Cummings as he held her tightly, his hand fisted in her wetly tangled hair as he drove her to her knees on the floor at his feet.

Betsy drew nearer. At first, she'd seemed certain about her target, but after a moment or two, she became confused, almost agitated. She looked frightened as she wandered around the belfry like a dancing flame, touching the walls as if she was looking for something she couldn't find.

"I disagree, Miss Book. You and your vampire boys have conspired to destroy this village. That hardly makes you innocent."

Eliza twisted in his hold but only succeeded in hurting her hair. She tried scratching at his legs like an irate cat, but Mr. Cummings grunted and started to glow. His legs grew longer and hard as bone in his trousers. His fingers in her hair seemed to grow longer and sharper. Then his feet ended in large cloven hooves that tried to stamp her fingers flat.

She jerked her hands back before he broke both of her hands. "We can work this out," she panted hoarsely as Betsy turned to look at her once more with those horrible black cat eyes. "We can make a compromise…"

"Oh, yes? How? Do tell."

Eliza scrabbled for something, anything, any weapon she could find. If Betsy touched her, she would die—or worse. According to Catherine's journals, she would never exist at all. "We can break up the village. We can send the Sidhe people away. If we do that, the Darkness won't come and your people can live and prosper elsewhere..."

"Leave Whitby," Mr. Cummings laughed. "How dare you. This is *our* village. We are a family. *You* are an outsider. You know *nothing* about how we live here, how we care for each other!" His fist shook with rage and he yanked on her hair, making her cry out.

Finished with waiting for the aimlessly wandering Sidhe to find them, Mr. Cummings grunted and tossed Eliza down on the floor.

Eliza landed hard at Betsy's burning white feet. She scrambled to her knees and immediately backed away, careful not to touch the creature.

"End her!" Mr. Cummings insisted, pointing at Betsy. "I am your Lord, your master. I am the All-Father. Erase this woman who would see us all die!"

Betsy looked down at her. She looked confused, torn. Eliza could see the war playing out on the little bit of face she had. But before she could make any decisions for better or for worse, a new Sidhe came bursting and full of bright white light through the belfry window.

He was big and lean, with curling horns. He was frightening, oh so frightening. He landed on the windowsill, hooked his arms around Eliza's waist, flapped his big, insect-like wings, and then the two of them slid across the floor and out the window on the opposite side of the bell tower.

Eliza screamed as the tower dropped away beneath her and she was carried up and out into the darkness of the night and the punishing rain. The speed at which they were going was sickening, and the height terrified her. She couldn't even see the ground, and everything around them was a mere blur. She'd always found Edwin's fear of heights amusing, but the truth was, she was no fan of them herself.

She twisted around, desperately clinging to the Sidhe carrying her away despite how grotesque it was—how dangerous. The motion caused them to dip dangerously, and she screamed again.

The Sidhe's flight went all erratic before he straightened himself out. "Christ! My ears!" he cried in a familiar voice.

"Who are you?" she said.

"You wouldn't believe me if I told you!" the Sidhe whimpered.

* * *

After a short flight over the darkened landscape, Cesar and Eliza landed atop Whitby Hall's battlements, under a carven stone overhang. They were both soaked through, clothes and hair, and his landing caused them to more or less skid across the wet parapet. Cesar's weird, cloven feet kicked up some sparks as he tried to slow them down, but he didn't have full control of this weird Sidhe body just yet, and he'd explained that to her while in flight.

Finally, he lost his balance altogether and they both pitched forward, with Cesar landing atop her. Thankfully, his reconstructed body was somewhat lighter than his old one, so it didn't hurt her quite as much.

Cesar panted, his long white hair hanging in his eyes as he pushed himself into a kind of push-up and stared down at her, trapped beneath him. "Jesus," he said inches from her face. "This body isn't as strong as a vampire body. I'm *wasted*."

Eliza wriggled out from under him, feeling angry even though she knew it was mostly the fear working on her—that and the exhaustion. "Tell me again, Cesar, why you just happen to be a fairy?"

"I decided vampires were so last year?" He smiled at his witty repartee. It wasn't a pretty smile, and it was full of those godawful teeth. She liked his other smile better.

Eliza shakily stood up and took his hand, helping him to his deer feet, which were clicking in a peculiar way on the stones. He looked like a paler, slightly glowy version of a satyr from Greek myth, just not that attractive. If it weren't for his shy eyes and the cadence of his voice, she never would have believed it was him.

She reached out to touch his arm. Nothing happened. "You have no Sidhe powers," she pointed out.

"That's because I'm *not* a Sidhe. I'm a vampire." He looked himself over sadly. "What if I'm stuck this way? It's really awful, isn't it?"

Eliza looked him over sympathetically. "No, not at all," she lied.

He looked like he was going to cry, then a strange look came over his almost featureless Sidhe face. "Ohhh..." he said as if he was suffering a heart attack. He gripped his chest, dropped to his knees, and bowed his head so the crown nearly touched the wet stones of the battlement's parapet.

"Cesar!" Eliza dropped down beside him, but the truth was, she didn't know what to do, how to comfort him.

Cesar's skin looked like it was moving on its own like a thin coating of white paint rippling away to reveal darker streaks. He put his hands on both sides of his head and moaned long and loudly as if in pain as his skin seemed to develop small cracks everywhere. As the rain came pouring down, it started washing away the little pieces of Sidhe, thick, milky white Fae fluid swirling away until Cesar looked up at her—the Cesar she knew, the one she cared so much about.

"That…that was almost cool," she said as she watched as his Sidhe skin was washed by the rain across the rooftop.

He looked sick like he might throw up.

She was about to help him up when she spotted pinpricks of light on the horizon like a scattering of white jewels. She and Betsy never got the bell run properly, and Mr. Cummings and his group of toadies had probably gone all through the village, braining sleeping people to release their inner Fae. She wouldn't put it past him at this point, especially considering what he'd done to poor Betsy. She owed him one for *that*.

"Where's Edwin?" she said, watching the encroaching army of Fae.

"I don't know," Cesar stated, standing up. He sounded hoarse and he weaved on his feet. "Probably riding the Hunt at this point." He pointed out over the moors, not that she could see anything in the darkness and the pounding rain. "He just told me to protect you."

"Cesar, we have to do *something*."

"Like what? I'm so done." Cesar slumped down to his knees again.

Eliza stood in the rain and thought about that. Far above, a flicker of lightning painted the whole landscape in lurid colors and long shadows. She caught a brief glimpse of something more than black and frighteningly solid creeping catlike across the sky. Cesar looked too, then immediately turned away.

She couldn't blame him. The moment she saw it, she felt her heart lurch into her throat as if it was trying to escape, her stomach turned over, and something—some primal fear *thing* as close to an instinct as she'd ever had—pinged in the back of her brain. She knew two things at once: Whatever was up there was alive. And it loved them not at all.

"Edwin said the stars are going out." Cesar averted his eyes. "He said the Darkness is coming."

Eliza closed her eyes as the rain shushed down over them. She'd glimpsed a sky only half-full of stars like something was blotting them out...or eating them. She did not want to look upon it again. "Star-eater," she said, more to herself than anyone.

"What?"

"That's what Catherine's note said it was. And what the vampires call it. Star-eater. The Thing out of Space." She felt the contents of her stomach rising up on a wave of her nausea, along with her pulse and her panic. "We need to do something, Cesar. And we need to do it *now*."

Another flash of lightning illuminated Cesar's young, frightened face. The last of the Fae skin washing off like corpse paint. He was shaking, his eyes wide open. He leaned over and dry heaved on the stones.

She waited until he was finished. She thought about what Mrs. Finley had said about Catherine's Golemi. She felt it was their last and only hope. Turning to Cesar, she took his hand to steady him. "Come with me. I need help down in the lab."

xvii

When Edwin spotted the horse—an old, spotted grey mare named Molly—he didn't think. He moved fast, catching her halter before she could disappear into the forest beyond the castle and sliding up onto her back. He had no saddle, so he had to hang onto her mane to anchor himself.

Molly stamped and backed up a step, then calmed as Edwin made soothing noises to calm her. "It looks like it's just you and me now, old girl," he told her. She was the oldest of Ian's night steeds, and the absolute last horse he would have chosen. But, somehow, she had managed to escape all harm. Ian had taken to riding Molly because she was old and slow. And now, an old, slow Molly was his last hope.

Up ahead, just beyond the ridge of the forest, he sensed something watching them. Molly stamped and he backed her up, mindful of the rough terrain.

"Who's there?" he called, purposely making his voice sound more fearsome than he felt. He bit into his wrist and created a new manriki just in the event something rushed him. "If someone is there, show yourself."

He caught the glint of green eyes before a very handsome—and very naked—bloke stepped out of the forest. He looked rough, like someone who hadn't slept in a week, and his body was caked with animal blood, mud, and dirt. Sticks clung to his ragged black hair.

"Malcolm," said Edwin, working to control the horse now. It was obvious that Molly disliked the werewolf from the way she was blowing her nostrils in alarm. "I spoke to Eliza. She said you were injured..."

"Is she all right?" Malcolm asked, looking genuinely stricken. He stepped fully from the trees with no concern whatsoever for his nakedness or the fact that the wind and the rain were assaulting him. He was a handsome feller, but Edwin had decided some time back that he did not like Malcolm Whitby.

Edwin hesitated to answer. He wasn't a fool. Malcolm, he knew, had more than a passing interest in his wife. Through his and Eliza's bloodlink, Edwin had experienced almost everything she had in the last twenty-four hours.

"She's fine. Cesar is with her." Edwin clenched the end of the manriki, making it slither dangerously in the mud. A part of him wanted to destroy the Werewolf of Whitby for what he had done—how he had tempted his soon-to-be-wife. It was the same part that needed to establish that Eliza was his woman. His Bride. But that part was a monster.

Malcolm looked up at him, fearlessly unsurprised, almost challenging him to act on his impulses.

Edwin closed his eyes, stuffed his inner psychopath back inside, and coiled the manriki up over his shoulder. *Not today, Satan,* he thought.

Malcolm picked up on his thoughts relatively easily. "She refused me," he offered. "She loves you and is loyal to you...my Lord. As am I."

Edwin swallowed and opened his eyes. He looked Malcolm up and down. His wounds—assuming all the blood on him was his and not some animal's—seemed to be healing. He was strong. A good ally. But he also knew that they would never be friends.

"Run with me," he said.

And Malcolm nodded one. "If it pleases you, my Lord."

"It does. But listen to me, wolf. Eliza and Cesar are mine. If you touch them, I'll kill you. If you harm them, I'll rip your world apart. Do you believe me?"

Malcolm lowered his head but raised his eyes, a sign of both contrition and aggression. "I understand, my Lord."

It wasn't the best reaction, but it was good enough for now. Edwin took a deep breath. "Lord Ian is dead and your loyalties now lie exclusively with me. I offer myself as your Vampire Lord, and I present my Court as your Court. Do you recognize me as your sole and only master?"

He waited.

Malcolm blinked, showing no reaction to the news of Ian's death. Then he went to one knee in the way of the old-fashioned Court greeting. "I accept your terms and I recognize you as my Lord-at-Court, as well as my exclusive and only master."

"Join me on this Wild Hunt, Malcolm of Whitby."

Malcolm, never taking his burning green eyes off Edwin, said, "As you say, my Lord." His bones began snapping apart and his human skin shredded off his muscles as he surrendered himself to the change.

***

Eliza moved the stack of paintings away from the wall and started pounding against the flagstones, looking for any changes in sound.

"What are you doing?" Cesar asked, looking a little sideways at the psychedelic painting of Edwin as the Devil.

Eliza tapped the wall, moved a few steps, then tapped again. She didn't hear anything that sounded hollow. "Catherine's notes mention a sub-lab, but I don't see any obvious way into it."

"Like a secret passage?" He went to the huge bookshelves and started playing with books and bottles and other objects, moving them around. That seemed a bit too obvious to Eliza, but when she heard a sharp click, she stopped what she was doing and turned.

A narrow panel of the bookshelves had slid back dustily to reveal a dank, cobwebby flagstone tunnel barely large enough for a grown person to enter. It edged downward into darkness at a questionable angle.

"Whoa," said Cesar, looking impressed. "I didn't think that would work, but Scooby-Doo was right." Then he cocked his head at it with some concern. "Do we really need to go down there?"

"It's probably where Catherine's sub-lab is located," Eliza explained, moving toward the ominous opening. "The place she hid the Golemi. You're not afraid of a dark passage?"

Cesar glanced over at the machine-man standing in the corner and shivered. "Stuff like this always goes wrong in the movies. What if there are monsters down there?"

"Cesar," she said as patiently as she could, "you are a monster."

Picking up an electric torch, Eliza moved past him and started down the tunnel. After a few hesitant seconds, Cesar dogged her. He breathed very loudly in the close space, and she decided it was probably his claustrophobia at work.

As she moved along the dusty tunnel, she held her hand torch out in front of her to ward off the shadows and anything...well, untoward. *Like monsters.*

"This is really spooky," Cesar admitted, shadowing her steps.

"How is it spooky when you can see in the dark, Cesar?"

"Being able to see everything doesn't mean things are less spooky. Actually, things are spookier when you can see everything."

She sighed, then stopped when she realized the tunnel was opening up into a gigantic underground cavern naturally hewn from the bedrock under the castle. The air was stagnant and bitter, and when she aimed the torch upward, she saw the domed ceiling was full of spiraling shark-tooth stalactites. She moved the light down. Before her lay a landscape of rocky ground and stalagmites like teethy outcroppings. Next, she flicked the light right and left...and nearly jumped.

It was not an empty cavern.

An army of Golemi stood dustily at attention like soldiers waiting to be called to war. At first, she was afraid they were humans or something *human-like* at the very least, but as she approached the soldier standing closest to her, weighed down in webs of dust, she realized they were not even that. They were shaped like primitive machine-men, their features mere imprints pounded rudely into their metal heads with a large, flat mallet, their bodies made of some kind of dull, armored steel alloy the color of rusted copper. They had massive forearms and hands, and their fingers were frozen around long black iron staffs with spheres at the end. The Golemi, a hundred or more grouped in clusters of ten, looked strong, their metal skulls connected via ancient insulated wires into the ceiling, but they stood lifeless as she flashed her torch over them.

Cesar whistled under his breath. "That is really cool. What are those?"

"Primitive, medieval robots. According to Catherine's notes, she had metal forgers and blacksmiths create at least a hundred of them so that Ian would never have to ride another Wild Hunt, but then she hid them away. She was afraid the Sidhe would discover them and destroy them. That's how much she loved her husband."

"Ian's dead."

Cesar's words paralyzed her for a long moment, though she wasn't certain if it was with relief or concern. Finally, she asked, "Edwin?"

He didn't answer, which was all the answer she needed.

She swallowed hard, wondering what the repercussions of this would be. "Stay here," she told him. Turning, she hurried back up the tunnel to the lab and flipped the large hand switch in the main power console, then stood back and called down the long tunnel, "Is anything happening with the Golemi?"

"No!" Cesar called back. "They're just standing there."

She tried more switches, a lever, everything on the unfamiliar monitor. But each time she called down, Cesar responded the same way.

"Are you sure? Nothing?"

"Nothing!" Cesar shouted back.

Exasperated, Eliza leaned over the computer console and ran her hand over her face and tired eyes as she stared down at the unfamiliar controls. They were archaic, an ancient Antikythera mechanism similar to the one on display in the National Archeological Museum of Athens. Eliza had never seen it up close and personal, but she had read extensively about the "first analog computer" created in roughly 100 B. C. by the ancient Greeks. She wondered if this ran anything like that.

At a loss as to what else to do, she set her hands on the console and absorbed whatever information was in the old, battered database. She learned Catherine built this particular Antikythera about a hundred and fifty years ago. It was not the same as the one in the museum. This one was moderately upgraded and constructed of a number of huge, rusted gears that worked together like a giant clock to create "ticks" that the mechanism then translated into primitive binary code—which was really clever, she decided. It also controlled virtually everything in the lab, including the power source for the Golemi, though it seemed the spark of life had long since fled them.

Cesar ducked out of the tunnel and started toward her, looking defeated. He spread his hands. "No lights, no movement. Nothing. Maybe the wires are too old, or just not connected. Maybe Catherine died before she finished the system."

Then he brightened. "Can't you...you know..." He indicated the computer console with a whirlybird gesture. "Do that thing that controlled Foxley's gyroscope?"

Eliza shook her head sadly. "My talents are pretty useless if there's no actual juice, Cesar. If I can't power up the computer, I can't do anything."

"What about the castle's generators?"

She knew the generators were pretty weak, just enough to light the castle and perform a few basic functions. The wiring didn't even reach down here, as she'd discovered several days ago.

"They won't be nearly enough. I need..." She stopped and listened to the distant rumble of the storm far above them. An idea sparked inside of her, literally and figuratively, an idea that would have made Thomas Edison proud. She glanced at Cesar. "Could you find some coaxial cable? Fiber optic would be better, but coaxial will do. A lot of it. *All* of it..."

"Sure," he said after she explained what it looked like. He started hurrying off toward the stairs, then stopped and looked back. "Whatever you're going to do, is it dangerous?"

"Very."

He bit his lip but still ran off to get her cable.

* * *

Baldy would have screamed in agony if he could scream at all. But Annamarie had taken even that from him.

He lay on the floor of the chapel, writhing as the Sidhe knelt over him, her hands on his face, sucking at his life force as if she were a giant industrial vacuum cleaner. He watched his own lifeforce writhing into her—crackling branches of light that passed through her hands and arms and over her face like a creature caught in a lightning storm.

"Baldy!" someone screamed in alarm from far off. It sounded like Star's voice, and that, more than anything, roused him from the tide of almost dizzying pain overwhelming his body.

He managed to turn his head a few inches. Star standing in the doorway of the chapel, her hand clamped over her mouth to keep from screaming. Tears poured from her eyes. "Baldy..."

Summoning what he feared might be the last of his strength, Baldy lifted his arm, clenched his hand into a rock-hard fist, and swung it. He wore three rings on that hand. All of them, plus his knuckles, crunched into Annamarie's cheek and sent the girl sprawling across the chapel floor.

It took a moment, but he rolled over onto his belly and just lay there like an overweight turtle, his hands scrabbling over the stone floor until he was able to push himself up to his hands and knees.

Star raced to him, her soft, perfumed flesh pressing into him, her arms about his shoulders. "Baldy? Oh, dear god, Baldy! Can you hear me, love? Can you stand up?"

"Trying..." he mumbled. A few bubbles of blood formed on Baldy's lips.

Star leaned down and kissed them. It was like a life elixir enlivening his dead body.

After a few seconds, Baldy raised a hand to touch Star's tear-stained face. "Dollface," he said. He almost got to his knees before he fell back down.

Across the room came the clicking of little deer feet on stone. Baldy's heart fluttered with panic. He grabbed Star's arm so fiercely that she cried out. "G-go…" he said while he felt a little of his strength filtering back. Annamarie hadn't taken it all, thank god. "Get away from her…she's Sidhe!"

But Star didn't hear. She was crying and shaking her head. "My daughter is gone, Baldy! She's gone!"

Star didn't recognize Annamarie in her Fae form!

"She," he said, pointing at the quickly approaching Fae, "*is* your daughter. And if she touches you, she'll erase you from existence."

Star lifted her head and looked with confusion at the monstrous *thing* stalking them from across the chapel. Annamarie slowed and then came to a halt a few feet away. "Get out of my way, woman!" the creature roared, spreading wide its insect-like wings as if in an attempt to make itself look bigger and even scarier than it is. It advertently knocked over a stone angel that smashed on the floor.

Star stood up, slowly. Then, unbelievably, she moved to stand between Baldy and the Sidhe. "No," she stated simply.

"Give me the vampire!" the creature garbled.

"No."

"Star!" Baldy pushed and pushed harder, finally achieving a kind of wobbly push-up. But he was still much too weak to stand. He had no idea how long it would be before he recovered from this.

Star turned her head and looked at him. The pain on her face was heartbreaking to see. It made her beautiful, finally. "I know what you did for me, Baldy. I know what you did to Franklin."

Baldy felt his heart twist like a giant had his fist about it. "No, Star…don't…!"

"I only wish you'll be able to remember me," she said. And then she threw herself at Annamarie.

* * *

Megan tore through the ranks of Sidhe, quickly and efficiently jumping from one to the next. Her enormous, slavering jaws clamped down like, quite literally, a wolf trap over throats and arms and sometimes—if they were small—whole bodies. She shook each body, tearing the extremities from it before dropping it to the earth like shreds of wet toilet paper. Then she swiftly moved to the next.

The whole battlefield smelled of death and spoiled milk. She'd thought it would be difficult to kill them, but the Sidhe were frail and fell apart like ragdolls full of loose seams. Their strength was in their numbers. But she moved steadily across the moorland toward her boys, ripping a path of sticky white death as she went.

The Sidhe had dropped a huge fishing net atop the twins, and now they were jabbing long, pointed sticks through the holes in the net. Each time they did, her boys howled and snapped at the sticks, but they couldn't move, couldn't defend themselves.

They were so young, she thought with tears burning her eyes. They should not have been doing this. Howling, Megan fought her way through toward them.

She was nearly there when a tree moved, its roots erupting through the earth in an explosion of earth and rocks. The falling limbs tripped her up and she fell hard on her face, her jaw cracking with a sickening pain she felt all through her body. She tried to dodge left, but the roots only followed and closed about her like a giant hand. The last thing she saw before the roots encircled her neck and closed like a fist, snapping her vertebrae, was Corcoran standing under the enchanted tree, smiling pleasantly.

* * *

Edwin rode straight into the thickest part of the fray. There must have been a hundred Sidhe, maybe more. And still more were appearing all the time. He rode Molly hard through the rain and mud and chaos, uncoiling his barbed manriki anytime he encountered one of the enemy.

They snarled at him like animals and tried to kick him off the horse. But he deftly avoided their reach, the manriki allowing him to attack at a safe distance. He let the chain whip split the night air, and the moment it had snaked around a Sidhe and the barbs had sunk in, he yanked on it hard and the creature exploded, screaming, into a puddle of white light and muck.

Still, there was a problem. A big one.

It was an effective way of killing from a distance, but also very slow, requiring that he isolate each Sidhe and spend far too much time killing it. In the time he'd killed ten, at least fifty more had replaced them over the next ridge like a video game you simply cannot win.

Malcolm was doing minimally better than he was. The giant werewolf had reverted to a kind of halfway point between wolf and man. It gave him the formidable size, bulk, and ferocity of the wolf, but left him with human-like hands that made grabbing Sidhe for quick disposal that much easier. And Malcolm was strong. Edwin had to give him credit for that.

He watched the werewolf king snatch a Sidhe woman by the throat, his hand so big he could have wrapped it twice around her delicate neck, and rip her head off her body with little more effort than it would have taken Edwin to uncork a bottle of wine.

In the time Edwin took to dispatch one Sidhe, Malcolm had disposed of four. It was rather bruising to the ego, but he had to admit his hunting dog was made for this. Not to mention, he had the experience of killing the creatures that Edwin did not.

Edwin turned Molly's head and charged her toward a new group of Sidhe just waiting to die. He expected them to turn their attention on Malcolm as the bigger and more looming threat, but something had changed. The creatures seemed more interested in him than in the werewolf ripping through their ranks.

Perhaps they sensed he was the weak link, the inexperienced Master of the Hunt, the young Vampire Lord; he didn't know. He only knew that this time, when Molly reached his new targets, they were smarter and started working together. Two Sidhe yanked an unseen fishing wire across Molly's legs. It cut down to the bones of her knees and pitched her forward. She fell awkwardly right into their numbers—along with her master.

* * *

Eliza stiffened at the sound of rapid footsteps on the stairs leading to Catherine's lab. She couldn't tell if they were Sidhe hooves or vampire footfalls.

She looked down at the many tools she had taken from her utility bag and spread across the console. She had a laser screwdriver, sonic wrench set, and a high-frequency scalpel. She grabbed the scalpel. As puny as it was, she could inflict the most damage with it. Her scalp prickled and she felt the little hairs on the back of her neck lift as the footsteps rapidly approached. She turned.

Cesar rushed into the room, carrying a thick tangle of black coaxial cable over his shoulder. Eliza let out her wheezing breath and set down the scalpel before she hurt herself—or him—by accident.

Cesar stared at her, cringing a little. "Are you okay?"

She put her hands over her face and just concentrated on not crying. She was so tired, so goddamned tired, and she had no idea if this would work. This was supposed to be her holiday, goddamnit!

She stayed that way until Cesar come to her and put his arms around her. She buried her face in the side of his neck, smelled his aftershave and the warm, chocolaty scent that was just him, and let him hold her. He was so painfully young a vampire that he still felt almost human. Still, she reminded herself, he was becoming more like Edwin every day, more stoic and self-assured. More the Enforcer that Edwin had come to depend on.

"Okay, now?" he asked after some quiet moments.

"Yes."

What a time to have a meltdown!

She drew back and gave him a somber, determined smile. "I'm fine. I'm okay." She rubbed at her eyes, stood up straighter, squared her shoulders, and nodded. "Let's get to work."

* * *

The Sidhe descended upon Edwin, hissing and clawing at his face.

Edwin, sitting on the muddy grown, half-buried under his dying horse, swung the manriki around. Except it wasn't a manriki anymore. He had altered it into something halfway between a Gaelic broadsword and a long Japanese Tachi. The blade cut through three throats, shaving away one head while the other two sort of flopped to the sides of their bodies like white fishes, gushing more of that pale, milky, non-blood. The Sidhe with their heads mostly decapitated fell back into the mud, shrieking in rage.

More Sidhe shoved in, ready to take a swing at Edwin, who was almost too tired to fight. But then a calm, familiar voice said, "No!" and the Sidhe fell back obediently to reveal the visage of Corcoran.

He stood placidly in his human form, leaning on his cane. He inclined his head as if they were attending some posh dinner party instead of meeting on the battlefield for the first time and said, "Lord Edwin."

Edwin climbed out from under his dead horse and scrambled to his feet, holding his sword close against his hip, the tip pointing down and resting against his instep. He was covered in mud and blood—his own and the Sidhe.

Corcoran passed a dubious eye over the hybrid blood-sword that Edwin was struggling to hold the shape of. The truth was that bloodkinetics worked better if you had experience forging a weapon. One's mind was better adept at designing a blade that worked, or so Foxley had explained to him long ago. But Edwin had never had much interest in such things. It seemed such a bloody waste—studying swords and warfare when there were so many beautiful men and women in the world to love.

Corcoran narrowed his eyes at his weapon, which was nearly pulsing in his grip. "What the bloody hell is that?"

Edwin leaned on it as he sought to catch his breath. "A back-scratcher. What do you think it is, you bloody tosser?"

Corcoran shook his head very slowly and returned his attention to Edwin's face. "I had hoped you'd died from your injuries." He withdrew the athame that had nearly killed him and showed it to Edwin. It glinted in the spare moonlight.

Edwin tried not to show how uneasy the sight of it made him feel. "I'm annoyingly hard to kill. Shoot me, stab me, and I bloody keep getting up."

"I noticed. Like a cockroach."

Edwin looked the blade of the knife over. "Mine's larger than yours."

"Size hardly matters, Lord Edwin."

"Only blokes with small equipment say that."

Corcoran grinned nastily. His teeth gleamed long and sharp like his knife. "Now you're just getting annoying." He pointed the knife at Edwin. "My people will kill you and your lot, make no mistake, vampire. You are in the wrong. You are the evil. And for that, you'll pay the price."

As he spoke, the Sidhe began to gather round, making a loose, Fight Club-style ring around the two of them.

Edwin stood in the beating rain and looked around. "An audience. Lovely." He looked back at Corcoran, the movement shaking water from his hair. "How about just you and me, fairy? Your knife against mine."

Corcoran smiled a shimmering grin full of anticipation. "Why not? I would love to humiliate you before all of my people, Dark Fae."

And saying that, he produced a small, nickel-plated gun from his pocket.

"Oh, please," said Edwin, looking disdainfully at the gun. "You do know I'm already dead?"

Corcoran, still smiling, stuck the gun in his mouth and pulled the trigger.

***

As she worked on splicing the cable into the Antikythera mechanism, Cesar started rolling out the coaxial cable. He kicked the large blackroll of cable so it traversed the length of the lab and bumped against the foot of the stairs.

He looked at it dubiously. "Is this going to work?"

She had no idea, but she didn't want to say as much and jinx any chance they might have. "Can you run this cable to the roof?"

"Sure." He picked up the heavy roll—it must have weighed close to three hundred pounds and would have required a handcart, were Cesar human—hefted it over his shoulderas ifit weighed nothing at all,and started bounding up the stairwell.

Eliza followed him.

When they reached the battlements, Eliza zeroed in on the power box connected to the utility tower that was responsible for controlling such things as mobile signals, the Internet, and Ian's UV shields. Unfortunately, the power box was locked and she didn't have her lockpicks on her.

"Cesar," she asked as the rain came down hard and the stars above continued to flicker and go out one by one, "can you open this?"

He made it look criminally easy, ripping the steel door right off the hinge of the power box in one casual swipe. Eliza started attaching the cable fibers to an outlet, shoving sopping wet hair from her long-dead coiffure out of her face with her sleeve. "The castle runs on static electrical energy. It farms power from the elements and channels it down to the generators."

"Like solar power."

"Like that, but more stable. Catherine rigged the castle to draw power from static electricity using this tower. And with this storm, we have a *lot* of power to use."

After all the connections were secure, they rushed back down and Eliza took up a position at the control deck of the Antikythera mechanism. She checked her connectors one last time, squinting through her magnifying glasses, then told Cesar to stand back. She wasn't sure what would happen, but there was no point in electrocuting them both. She rushed to the wall where the main electrical box was located and grabbed the control lever. She pushed it up as far as it would go.

Cesar glanced around apprehensively as the lights flickered and the whole lab hummed with a sudden jolt of power. The generators buzzed as if they were hives full of angry bees, and then the sound great louder as they went into overdrive. Down in the tunnel leading to the cavern, a ghostly blue light flickered to life.

They both looked at each other, then rushed down the tunnel, Eliza in the lead and Cesar close on her heels. She stopped abruptly when she reached the ancient cavern and that caused Cesar to more or less plow into her, almost knocking them both to the floor where cables full of liquid fire seemed to be writhing like snakes. Pulses of pure, undistilled power crackled along the floor and walls, casting everything in a lurid neon blue light and making both of their hair stand on end. The whole cavern stank of burning ozone, and, for one moment, Eliza could see every artery of power flowing through the cavern and into the Golemi standing like patient stone statues hoping to live again.

"Should it be doing that?" Cesar asked, staring at the walls and ceiling.

"Catherine must have rigged the whole cavern like a giant battery." Eliza watched, wide-eyed and faintly horrified, as one of the Golemi about a hundred paces away turned its head, its metal gears grinding, and *looked* at her with its bright, blank, robotic eyes. Meanwhile, just beyond the army, a door in the actual cavern wall slid back, letting in the cool night air of the distant moorland.

Cesar sucked in a sharp breath, and in his spookiest voice, he said, "It's alive!"

The army was alive and ready to file out into battle...

...and then the power suddenly died, plunging them all into darkness once more.

"Shit."

| xviii |

The All-Father stood up in full Sidhe form.
Corcoran was at least twice as big as his fellow Sidhe and milky white all over, his body covered in arcane glyphs that glinted like a constellation of scars. Two huge, coiling horns rose from his misshapen skull like a crown.

Edwin shifted uneasily at the sight. As Corcoran dropped his head and started to charge him, Edwin tried to sidestep, but the creature was remarkably agile as well as fugly as sin, and he managed to snag Edwin about the waist as he sailed by. The two of them went down so hard in the mud they skidded twenty feet up a slight incline and left a sizeable rut before finally sliding to a halt with Corcoran on top.

Corcoran punched him so hard in the jaw that Edwin tasted blood and the chips of his broken teeth. He snarled through a foam of blood, but Corcoran reared up, grinning (rather literally) from ear to ear. He snorted and aimed those deadly sharp horns straight at Edwin, driving them downward. Edwin cried out at the sight.

Only the fact that Corcoran's horns were incidentally spaced farther apart than Edwin's shoulders saved him. Corcoran wound up driving his horns deep into the earth to either side of Edwin. Thankfully, they stuck good and solid in the mud. It gave Edwin a chance to grab them, so when Corcoran ripped them from the earth in his fury, Edwin was able to cling to them.

He arched over Corcoran's head in a backward somersault, drove his boot heels into Corcoran's back, and delivered what he hoped was a punishing blow to Corcoran's spine. He expected to be rewarded by at least a modest crack.

Instead, he got a grunt. A bloody grunt! Then Corcoran rammed his elbow into Edwin's side to dislodge him, and the impact knocked him back down into the mud behind him.

Edwin groaned as he sat up. He gripped his dislocated shoulder and snapped it back into the ball joint. "Ow," he said.

Corcoran swung around, swaying slightly. Edwin hadn't crippled him, but maybe he had hurt him just a little. His catty black eyes observed Edwin with cool indifference as he tossed his enchanted athame from hand to hand. "Dark Fae, I'm going to pluck your bones loose and grind them for my gris-gris."

"Whatever, wanker," Edwin answered as he struggled to his feet.

Corcoran tossed the knife expertly at him like an acrobat in a circus aiming for a target.

Edwin tried to shift away, but he was ankle-deep in mud and didn't move fast enough. The knife bit deep into his upper thigh. Edwin screamed as agony poured afresh into his body. He gripped the handle of the athame, but even that was an anathema to him, and his hands quickly began to burn. He let go and spat and swore until Corcoran leaped forward, sinking one giant hoofed foot into his belly and pushing him back down into the mud.

Despite Edwin's struggles, Corcoran held him there, struggling like a writhing fish, and then reached down to yank the knife loose. Edwin screamed again in mindless pain and outrage, his wings ripping through the back of his coat and beating helplessly in the muddy bog, spattering them both with mud, rain, and blood.

Corcoran stood over Edwin and held the bloody knife aloft. "See here, my children, the blood of the Master of the Hunt. The Prince known as Lord Edwin McGillicuddy—"

There was nothing for it. Edwin brought his knee up sharply, crunching it into Corcoran's nuts. He'd learned long ago that honor meant nothing in a good old-fashioned brawl. Winning—and surviving—was everything. He was determined to survive.

Corcoran screamed like a little girl and then dropped like a pile of bricks into the mud, clutching his bruised equipment. Edwin climbed slowly to his feet, shaking himself like a wet dog, the rain washing the blood and mud down his face. He limped forward, watching Corcoran roll around in the mud a bit.

From behind him, one of the Sidhe roared with rage and kicked him squarely in the back of the knee, snapping his good leg and sending the jagged shard of his femur bone bursting through his flesh. He splashed down into the mud once more, this time clutching the shattered bone, dizzy with agony. He flailed and twisted as Corcoran rolled over on top of him, the creature's face clouding over with a bestial rage.

"You are pathetic," he cried, spitting on him. "You are not worthy of being called an Englishmen, vampire." He reared up, and, with both hands wrapped around the hilt, drove the cursed athame at Edwin's face.

Edwin, forcing himself to ignore the almost mind-crushing pain in both of his legs, clapped his hand over Corcoran's blade to halt the knife. Immediately his hands burned. Edwin groaned, grunted, and then whimpered as he watched the little pulsing arteries of his own life force flowing up the blade of the Fae athame and into Corcoran's hands and body, but he couldn't let go. He was dead if he let go. He stared at the bloody tip of the knife hovering only inches above his face, and in that moment, he realized that the blade still held traces of his own black blood on it.

He grinned.

"What's so funny?" Corcoran barked. His black eyes were wild, his wings fully extended and buzzing with agitation.

With his last remaining strength, Edwin twisted Corcoran's wrists at a bad angle, breaking both of his hands. Corcoran screamed. With a laugh, Edwin turned the athame around, gripping the handle even though it was like holding a boiling black skillet in his hands, and sank the blade deep into Corcoran's windpipe.

Corcoran looked surprised. "You...no..." His whole body started melting around the knife in his throat. "How...?"

"My blood," Edwin said and smirked.

Screaming, Corcoran exploded all over him.

* * *

Back on the roof, standing in the pouring, silvery rain, Eliza checked the connectors in the power box once more while Cesar tried to shield her from the worst of the storm with his wings. A spark bit into her hand and Eliza dropped her sonic wrench. "Oh, bollocks!"

"What's wrong?"

"I think the initial power surge burned out Catherine's Antikythera...that's the primitive computer down in her lab, the one that controls the activation of the Golemi," she explained. "It was too old. I don't think it could handle the overload. That's probably why Catherine never succeeded with this. The computer technology just wasn't there at the time."

"Okay," Cesar said, adjusting his wings like an umbrella as he tried to keep the rain from getting into the power box. "What do we do to fix that?"

Another spark made her cry out and swear. "I need a computer, a huge computer to bypass the Antikythera mechanism...!"

Cesar grunted and then bowed his head, nearly falling against her as if someone had hit him hard from behind.

Eliza gripped him by the shoulders to keep him upright. "What's wrong? Cesar...!"

Cesar shuddered as if he were bracing against invisible blows. He cupped his hand over his mouth to keep from vomiting all over her. "I think Edwin's in pain," he managed. "This happened before."

"Dear god," she said as Cesar slowly slid to the ground at her feet, shivering in the rain. He scraped along the stones as he tried to find purchase but then lay still as Edwin's pain overwhelmed him.

She was alone now.

She didn't know what to do.

And then she did. She turned, looked at the power box, hesitated only a moment, and then plunged her hands straight into the circuitry.

* * *

In retrospect, killing Corcoran had probably not been the best idea.

The Sidhe, rather understandably upset by the loss of their leader, slouched forward as one, and Edwin backed up, crawling brokenly in the mud to try to escape the rising tide of glowing, angry beings with black eyes and screaming open mouths.

Unfortunately, he quickly found his route cut off. Down a sharp incline behind him lay the wolves—or, rather, what was left of them. The Sidhe had clobbered the werewolf brothers into pools of red soup and fur, and Megan lay nearby, a number of snakelike roots twined about her broken body. She had reverted to her human form in death. He would get no backup from them.

Distantly, he heard Malcolm's howl of triumph as he continued to tear through the Sidhe ranks—not that it was going to do him any good. Just over the ridge, a skirmish line full of glowing Fae was flowing on like a frothy wave of deadly water. He was effectively hemmed in on all sides.

He tried to stand up, but his injuries would have none of that, and his legs, not quite healed yet, spilled him to the muddy ground once more. He sat there in a muddy hole and thought about what to do, not that he had a lot of options to choose from at this point. He bit into his wrist in a last-ditch effort to summon the manriki, his last and only defense, but no blood emerged. He was running on empty, literally and figuratively.

This was it. The end...

"Eliza," he said, his voice full of regret.

But then, just as the first Sidhe reached him, its eyes dark and smiling, everyone on the battlefield came to a halt, stopping in whatever pose they were in and just stood there, listening. Over the darkened hills came the dull, thudding, rhythmic sound of what sounded like huge, power-driven machines at work. The muddy water in the hole where he sat jumped and rippled with each jarring thud. The Sidhe slowly turned their heads—a strangely coordinated orchestra of gestures—and looked to the east, toward the castle. The thudding was growing louder, nearer, like a heartbeat that wouldn't quit.

"...the bloody hell?" Edwin asked no one in particular. And then, a few seconds later, the first of Catherine's army of machine-men crested the hill. Edwin stared, speechless, as the Golemigathered at the ridge, assessed the situation in seconds, and then started marching down the hill, their even, mechanical gaits motoring them through the mud at an impressive rate for such enormous creatures.

They were each at least eight feet tall and made entirely of a coarse, gunmetal grey alloy blackened around the edges with age. They looked only vaguely human, with barrel bodies and punch-marked faces, all their parts riveted together with ship seams.

Catherine, a practical woman rather than an aesthetic one, had taken special care with the limbs, he noted. The legs were short and sturdy, the arms long and as massive as missiles, giving her Golemi an almost ape-like gait as they approached. Each carried a long spear with a heavy black ball topping it.

Edwin wondered how effective their weapons could be—the spears certainly didn't look sharp enough to penetrate flesh and bone—but then it happened. As the first Golem reached a Sidhe, it extended its arm, an arc of what looked like cloud-to-ground lightning jumping from the black ball to the creature's skull, the Sidhe exploding with the stench of sour milk and pungent electricity. Then the Golem moved to the next.

The Sidhe quickly forgot Edwin as they turned their collective attention on this new threat. They stamped and hissed and clawed at the air menacingly, but the army of Golemi wasn't alive in the conventional sense and had to fear. Their heads swiveled to and fro as they took in the sight of the battlefield, marching forward like tanks down the incline of the hill and pouring into the basin where the Sidhe were the thickest.

Not night, nor rain, nor deepening mud seemed to slow them as they and the Sidhe clenched together like two gigantic ancient armies locked in mortal combat. The Sidhe immediately threw themselves upon the Golemi, but since the Golemi were automatons and generated no energy of their own, the creatures' touch-magic was useless. Their attempts to absorb the static electricity off the Golemi only made them writhe and explode. The Golemi were immediately coated in simmering white innards as the fragile-looking creatures combusted around them. At least half of the Sidhe army imploded in the first few minutes.

Some of the Sidhe—the smarter ones, perhaps—hung back and adopted a wait-and-see approach. But when they saw how useless their touch was, they turned tail and started hop-running on their bizarre little hoofed feet toward the forest, hoping to find cover. That's when the Golemi lifted their staffs and aimed them at the fleeing creatures. The discharge from the weapons was like a white-hot bolt of ambient lightning hitting them. The Sidhe burst into burning flotsam. The Golemi moved on.

From a distance, Malcolm screamed in rage and pain, a hoarse animal sound tinged with human terror. Edwin, finally mostly healed, shuffled to his feet and turned to face the sound. The weave of white Sidhe and dark Golemi figures stood like a wall between him and Malcolm, making it impossible to see what was happening. Plus, there was no way he could walk, never mind run, while his compound fracture was still mending—bones always took the bloody longest to heal.

He knew what he had to do, and yet he hesitated, his clockwork heart ticking along much too loudly in his ears. This was much worse than facing the Sidhe orCorcoran. Hell, he'd rather take high tea with Foxley than have to do this again, and he couldn't help but wonder why God conspired to put him in this position again and again. Perhaps it was to keep him humble or teach him a lesson.

He stumbled back, got his balance, spread his wings as wide as he could, crossed himself, said a brief prayer, then took a wounded hopping leap, shutting his eyes in the process. The rest was left to providence.

* * *

The explosion from the power box tossed Cesar the length of the rooftop. He hit the flagstone wall of a battlement, the only thing that kept him from flying right off the roof, and then slid down to the stones, groaning as he felt several bones crunching loosely underneath him. Pain flared up in his body, mostly from what he suspected was his mangled neck and spine. It was all he could do to keep from passing out from the pain.

He lay very still for a while with his back to the wall as the worst of his breaks slowly reknitted themselves, and during that time, he watched the stars above flicker and go out as if someone was turning off a series of light bulbs somewhere. It took him a moment to realize he was staring into emptiness. Not emptiness as in the lack of light, but emptiness as in the lack of *anything*. Emptiness like some great creature was eating its way cancerously across the sky.

As he watched it, the creature—the Darkness—seemed to slow down, to consider him, to recognize him as one of Its own, to *look* at him. He had become aware of *It*, and so *It* had become aware of him. Cesar was suddenly very afraid.

It was a primal, basic fear—the Darkness, the emptiness, the aloneness, and the things that hunted in it. He heard a whimpering, childlike noise echoing up from his own throat. He found in that moment that he wanted his family so, so bad—his mom, his dad. He didn't care if they loved him or hated him, just so long as they came for him, protected him. For the first time since his mortality had died inside him, he realized *he* was the thing being hunted, *he* was the thing that could be hurt, could be consumed...

The Darkness moved again, this time away from him.

He blinked and groaned and closed his eyes to the brilliant white light that seemed to be encompassing the whole rooftop. It was like staring into the watery, blinding power of the sun, the whole castle and surrounding area illuminated like noontime by the massive explosion of power hanging over it. Even though his closed eyelids he could see it. Vaguely, through the painful brilliance, he made out a slightly darker form, that of MissEliza suspended at its center, channeling the power of the storm down into the Golemi far below.

***

Edwin landed hard and awkward upon the group of Sidhe pinning Malcolm to the ground. The impact scattered them. His landing wasn't graceful, but it did the job. It stopped a Sidhe from plunging one of those toxic daggers into Malcolm's back.

He bounced upward, taking the Sidhe with him, and the two of them were suspended in the air for a moment, then rolled like Jack and Jill down a steep incline before landing at the bottom in a puddle of mud. The Sidhe woman, her athame lost, immediately bounded to her feet and lashed out with her hoof. Edwin skittered backward in the mud, staying just out of reach.

"I'll kill you, vampire!" she screeched hysterically. "You killed Corcoran!"

"And you got my trousers muddy!" he shouted back. "My best pair!"

The Sidhe stopped and stared at him as if she wasn't sure if he was being serious or not. That's when Malcolm sailed overhead and clipped her head right off her shoulders.

Edwin saluted him as Malcolm splashed down in the mud and shook himself, casting a sheen of rain off his long, muddied black fur. "Thanks, mate..." Edwin started, then noticed Malcolm standing at full attention. Looming over Edwin, he was as large as a grown Shetland pony and as black as a moonless night—though the night wasn't very black any longer. If anything, it had turned brilliant.

Edwin climbed shakily to his feet and scrambled to the top of the next incline for a better look at the phenomenon unfolding before him. And there he stopped, perplexed. Hanging over WhitbyHall was a fiery white sun casting its relentless, eye-watering light down upon the battlefield where a hundred Golemi were systematically slaughtering the retreating Sidhe.

His mobile rang and he dug it out of his suit pocket, wiped the mud away, and answered it. Keeping his eye on the castle, he said, "Cesar, what in bloody hell's going on? What the hell's causing this?"

There was a long pause. Then Cesar said, timidly, "It's Miss Eliza."

"What about her?"

"She's doing this. She's powering the Golemi...and I'm afraid it might be killing her."

* * *

Edwin and Malcolm joined Cesar on the battlements of the old castle, and, together, the three of them watched Eliza burn in the center of a holocaust of white light.

Edwin was the first to move, to grab Cesar by the front of the jacket. Cesar groaned as his feet left the ground. "How long has she been like this?"

"I don't know! About five minutes, I guess."

"Shut it off!" he said, his voice barely more than an animal's growl. Every ache and pain in his body had dissolved with his fear.

"I don't know how! I don't even know what she did!"

"Shut off the main power supply! Shut it all off! The whole castle!" He realized he sounded more than a little hysterical, even to himself. He let Cesar go and shoved the boy stumbling backward toward the door that led down from the roof.

Cesar turned to go, then looked back at his master fearfully. "But won't that stop the Golemi?"

"I don't care!"

"We can't do it, Edwin. We can't cut the power to the Golemi!"

Edwin lunged at him.

Malcolm grabbed Edwin around the shoulders to retrain him, but Edwin whipped around, teeth bared like a lion, and snagged

Malcolm's throat in his hand. "Let me go, dog!" he cried, his fingers dimpling Malcolm's skin there.

"No," Malcolm stated with infuriating calm. He glanced up at Cesar, and something seemed to telegraph between the two men, a kind of mutual understanding. He then glared down at Edwin and said, to his extreme horror, "We mustn't."

"You don't tell me what to do, dog! I am master, I am Lord...!"

"Edwin, stop!" Cesar came up behind him and wrapped his arms around Edwin's waist. Edwin began to fight in earnest. Cesar found it was like trying to restrain a hydraulic machine that was out of control. The only thing keeping Edwin from ripping them both apart was his conscience—what he had of it in that moment. He certainly would have broken free were it only Malcolm holding him back, but Cesar was a vampire, too, and nearly as strong as Edwin himself.

Sandwiched between the two men—the vampire and the werewolf—Edwin began to weaken and then to sag.

"Let...me...go!" Edwin sobbed.

"Hush," said Malcolm. "Be still, vampire. This is what Eliza wanted. What she chose. What she must do. Her sacrifice. You mustn't interfere..."

Edwin writhed. "Don't tell me what she chose!" he cried, eyes wild. "She's my woman! I know what's best for her...!"

"Don't, Edwin. Stop!" Cesar said, his voice clear and strong and very close to his ear.

But Edwin continued to fight. He would fight forever to get back to Eliza...

"Give him to me," said Cesar.

Malcolm's eyes flared with concern. "Are you sure?"

"Give him to me!"

Malcolm let go and Cesar spun Edwin around and clenched him.

* * *

For one heart-stopping moment, Cesar wondered if Edwin was going to kill him. Kill him as he had killed Ian. He could do it. A claw to his heart, his teeth at his throat. But something of what they were must have penetrated Edwin McGillicuddy's enormously hard Cockney vampire skull, because he sobbed, then went limp in Cesar's arms and slid to his knees on the parapet, clinging to Cesar's legs.

Cesar collapsed with his master, pulled him close, wet and muddied, and rested his chin on Edwin's shoulder. Edwin grew very still in his arms, though his shoulders shook like a man suffering a seizure.

His terror and his love and his helplessness and his years washed painfully through and over Cesar for what seemed like forever...until the castle's circuits could take no more of the overload and every fuse in the old pile blew, and until the lights—and the Golemi—went out for good.

* * *

The moment the power died, Eliza dropped to the battlements like some lifeless rag doll. The boys standing at a distance, kept there by the sheer ferocity of power coming off her, immediately rushed to her side. Her eyes were wide open, and she stared sightlessly up at the rainy sky. A long, wet spiral of her black hair had turned stark white, and the tips were singed and smoking. The hem of her gown was burning fitfully. Edwin immediately shucked off the remnants of his cavalier coat and used it to extinguish the flames. He used it to wrap her body and then lifted her easily into his arms.

He turned, finding Cesar and a naked Malcolm hovering uncertainly. "Don't touch her," he said even though he knew full well they meant well, that they cared about her, too. But he couldn't be bothered. There was only one focus in his life now, and that was the woman slowly dying in his arms. He carried her below to their suite, and when one of her limp arms fell from the bundle of his coat, he noticed, peripherally, that she was wearing his Covenant ring on her ring finger.

She'd said yes.

Far, far above them all, the Darkness began to unravel.

* * *

In the early hours of the morning, the storm passed. And while the night was at its darkest, Cesar and Baldy walked the battlefield full of mud, blood, and shattered bodies. The Golemi were substantially moored in the mud. Cesar had tried to move one, but it was like trying to shove around a suit of armor filled with concrete. The Sidhe lay dead, or mostly dead. When they came upon one that was only mortally wounded but not quite ready to move on, they helped it along, mostly by crushing its throat under their boot heels, or, in Baldy's case, staving in its skull with the cane he was using to walk with.

Baldy seemed particularly keen on killing the survivors. He had awakened in the Great Hall, badly injured but able to move around once his strength had returned. He had been full of rage and sorrow, though he didn't rightly know why. He thought perhaps the Sidhe who had somehow gotten inside the castle had insulted him in some way.

One Sidhe they came upon he impaled through the heart, letting her writhe upon his cane for some moments before finally stamping out her face with his boot. More of that sour milk substance poured forth.

Cesar watched from a careful distance. "I'm sorry about Ian," he said. "And about Megan."

"Yeah," Baldy answered and frowned, looking away as if he were trying hard to remember something. "But I'm glad the stars didn't go out."

***

Baldy seemed to want to say something more but then lost his train of thought. That had been happening all morning, Cesar noted.

Since he was less than pleasant company, the sun was slowly rising, and the shields were offline for the moment, Cesar crossed the bailey and ducked back inside the castle. He was only inside a few moments when he heard Baldy release a scream over the moors—a barren, frustrated sound that echoed up and down the valleys and sent chills up his back.

He decided to leave the man to his grief. Upstairs, he stood before Edwin's door, his fist raised to knock. But then he lowered it and tried the door instead, finding it unlocked, much to his surprise. He cracked it open a bit, then a bit more.

He slid inside the darkness.

Edwin and Eliza occupied the large canopy bed. Eliza lay on the sheets with Edwin kneeling over her body. She looked like some lifeless doll in her torn and muddied dress, the tips of her wet hair singed by the shock of pure, unbridled storm power. Cesar searched for signs of life, but her skin looked waxy and grey, and her breathing was fitful. She looked dead, or undead.

While he watched, Edwin seized her cheeks in both of his hands and kissed her, the blood from his freshly bitten tongue bubbling up around the seal of their mouths. He stopped, breathed, and kissed her some more, feeding her yet more of his life force. He had been doing this for hours, Cesar knew.

Finally, he turned to glance at Cesar, blood smeared across his chin and cheeks, his hair and clothes in disarray. He looked a pale fright.

"Is she...?" Cesar couldn't finish. But it didn't matter, because Edwin was too preoccupied with trying to save her to pay attention to Cesar's question.

So, instead, Cesar settled on the edge of the bed and just watched them. Would it work? Would it save her? He had no idea. He doubted Edwin knew, either.

Edwin tongued a bit more blood into her mouth past her dry and cracked lips. He hung his head and his voice came scorched out of his mouth. "She was so afraid he would find her. That he would take her away. Take her back to his Court."

Cesar waited, saying nothing.

"She was afraid of him," Edwin continued. He touched Eliza's cheek tenderly and tried to smooth her hair away from her forehead. "But she should have been more afraid of me."

"She loves you."

Edwin sat back on his heels and stared down at his fiance for a long, hard moment. Finally, putting an arm across his face as if he might cry, he spoke again. "She loves me...and I want her to die."

Cesar swallowed and waited.

"I want her to die," he repeated. "That's how greedy I am. I want her to die and come back to me." He turned to glance at Cesar again. "That's the kind of monster she loves."

Cesar didn't know what to say to that, what was appropriate. He slid to the floor, his back to the wall beside the bed, and sought and found Eliza's hand. It was small and very cold, like the porcelain hand of some doll. He stroked her fingers and touched her Covenant ring. She must have removed it from its chain and put it on at some point while they were running frantically up and down the castle steps. He never noticed.

His heart clenched inside of him like a fist.

"I'll trim her hair. I'll make it right," Cesar told his master. He didn't know what else to do to help, how else he could comfort either of them. So, like Edwin, he sat in silence and darkness and waited to see if Eliza would live or die.

Three days later, she opened her eyes.

* * *

...eliza.

In the beginning, the world was nothing but pain. It was like being born. Light carved a burning path into her eyes, and that made her sad because she was happy in the darkness where there was no pain and no fear. But the light drew her inexorably out of the darkness, and as it did so, the pain in her body made her want to scream in agony, and the scorching air she sucked into her tattered and tired lungs made her want to choke.

"Eliza?"

"Oh," she answered, unwilling and unable to force more than that out of her parched lips.

"Open your eyes, lovey."

But she didn't want to. She wanted to sleep. She wanted to go back to the place where the pain was nothing but an abstract concept, not real.

"Eliza."

The voice was familiar and commanding, and it simply wouldn't let her be, so she finally gave in and cracked open her eyes. She immediately felt nauseated, surreal, outside herself. She gulped against the nausea but it refused to let her be.

Edwin held a basin under her chin and Cesar held her hair out of her face as she ralfed rather ingloriously until her sore belly hurt from the convulsions and she was afraid all of her organs had been displaced by the trauma. Then her boys helped ease her head back onto the pillow.

They sat on either side of her, caging her in. It felt good and familiar to have them near, Edwin on her left and Cesar on her right. She reached for them and they each took one of her hands.

"What...?" she began. She knew something had happened, but her mind was blank and spinning. She had a vague memory of rain running down her face, and the cold and the terror ripping through her...

"You had an accident," Edwin explained as he dabbed her lips with a handkerchief soaked in cold water. "You were hurt, but now you're fine. You're alive."

It seeped back into her slowly, the rain and the storm—the almost heart-shattering power that had flowed through her brain and down into her body and bones...and from there down into Catherine's lab, into her machines. She remembered the Golemi. She remembered controlling them on the battlefield like puppets without strings. She remembered cutting down the Sidhe one after another, weeding them out fearlessly like a bad crop, the anger and the power...oh, such angry, unstoppable power.

She had done that. She had animated the machine-men, and they had been full of strength and fury. She remembered glancing up and seeing with perfect mechanical eyes the Darkness receding slowly, slowly, even as the Sidhe died screaming. Soon, the stars glinted once more.

"You saved me," she said after a few moments of trying. Her lips were so cracked that they tasted of blood. She remembered a taste in her mouth like that, a taste both familiar and new. She had gone to other places, seen other people. Some she had never met, would never meet. Some had died centuries before she was ever born...

Edwin. He had given her his blood. She had tasted it, bitterly sweet, like death and chocolate.

She sat forward slowly. She understood the gravity of the act even as she lifted her hand and touched the side of his face. "You made me drink."

He looked embarrassed, afraid. "You wore my ring..."

"I know," she answered. "I know." Slowly, she moved a hand to her shoulder, searching for the telltale scrape of scales, of wings.

But there were none.

| xix |

One week later

"Really, Edwin, you're being very silly," Eliza complained as he carried her up the long staircase to the tower room. "I really can manage on my own. The doctor gave me braces."

"I know," he said but still didn't set her down, which frustrated her to no end.

The doctor and chemist that Edwin had lured out here—they were the best of the best that London could offer and he had spared no expense—believed she had suffered cerebral cortex damage due to macroshock. In other words, a major stroke due to the high voltage her body had conducted down to Catherine's Antikythera mechanism. Edwin's blood had helped her, maybe even saved her life, and it had certainly undone most of the damage to her body, but it wasn't like some quick, movie-inspired fix. Vampire blood wasn't a cure-all. They had warned her it would be several months before she could walk without braces, and she might have suffered permanent memory loss. So far, though, she felt unchanged.

When they reached the top of the stairs, Eliza spotted the small landing crowded with a collection of handsomely dressed men—Baldy, Cesar, and Malcolm. Her boys.

Baldy folded down an antique wicker wheelchair for her. He was smartly dressed in a black suit and white tie that positively screamed gangster. Since becoming the new master of Whitby Hall, he had decided to look the part of the young Vampire Lord.

It surprised them all that Lord Severn had made provisions that the castle and estate be passed onto Edwin in the event of his untimely death, but he and Eliza had both agreed that Baldy was the true Lord of the Moors now. Besides, they had no desire to live in a castle out in the middle of nowhere, surrounded by townsfolk who distrusted them. New York was their home—and this place held too many bad memories, Edwin admitted. So, they had passed the estate to Baldy.

He grinned at them both. He had taken to wearing the sonic handguns in armpit holsters under his suit jacket. He said it was in the event the Sidhe ever returned, but Eliza suspected he'd simply grown fond of them.

"You're *all* being very silly," she insisted after Edwin settled her in the chair. She glanced around the faces of her boys, smiling and trying not to tear up at how they had dressed for this very special—and secret—"engagement," as Edwin had called it.

Cesar and Malcolm looked smart as well, Cesar in his aviator jacket and buccaneer trousers, and Malcolm in something all-over black and leather. Since deciding to return to the States with Edwin, Eliza, and Cesar, Malcolm had begun working to refine his look so it was polished and modern. Unfortunately, he was gaining rather a lot of inspiration from the late-night action films he watched on cable TV. Cesar jokingly referred to it as Malcolm's "biker from hell" look, usually accompanied by a droll roll of his eyes. Some days, Eliza wondered how all this would work out between them once they were settled back home. Edwin's Court was quickly expanding and the townhome was only so large.

"You wanted to know what was in the tower room," Edwin insisted with a smirk. "You even snuck around behind my back to find out."

Eliza sniffed. "I wasn't sneaking. I don't sneak. I was *investigating*."

"*Miss Book Investigates*," said Edwin. "I like that title. I might use it as inspiration for my next book series."

Baldy furrowed his brow at the news. "I thought you only wrote trashy books about gumshoes and slutty dames, Eddie."

Edwin put a finger to his lips. "Shhh."

"You had better not turn me into a slutty dame!" Eliza insisted, sniffing again.

Grinning, Baldy opened the tower door with a flourish and waved them all in. Edwin pushed Eliza's wheelchair forward.

The tower room was round and airy like a belfry without a bell and constructed of white flagstone. It was much brighter and cheerier than she expected. Daylight beamed in from four opposing windows, illuminating the garlands of white paper roses hung from the ceiling beams, the streamers, the ornate brass candelabra, and the antique silverware and delicate platters that covered a long trestle table sitting squarely at the center, lit candles marching down the length of it.

Standing directly in front of her were Juliana and Robert. Juliana was wearing one of her big, boisterous traveling outfits, a long, pinkish swishy gown with a tartan coat and a giant buccaneer hat with an ostrich feather. Robert was dressed a little more conservatively in his dark evening suit and long wool coat. Juliana immediately squealed and raced to Eliza, clenching her where she sat in the chair.

"Leeza, dear!" she cried, hugging her best friend. "I heard about you. How are you? Are you well? Say yes."

"Yes," she said, so overwhelmed for a moment that she felt giddy. She gave Juliana another squeeze, the familiarity of her long coils of red hair and heavy Egyptian perfume putting her at ease. Juliana was everything that was home, and she was missing home very much right then.

She then turned to give Robert a hug, as well. "I missed you guys so much! What are you doing here in England?"

Robert chuckled and pointed at her boys. Juliana glanced up at Edwin and something passed between them, a look that hinted at many past discussions she had not been privy to.

Eliza saw the look. "You guys have been conspiring, haven't you?" She glanced around the tower room, but she couldn't make heads or tails of it all. It looked like someone was putting on a fancy dinner party.

Juliana deftly shifted to one side. Her dress was so huge that she'd completely eclipsed the object behind her.

It was a wedding gown on a dressing dummy. It was long and Gaelic, sewn in cream linen and overlaid with eyelet lace, with an embroidered bodice and long bell sleeves that flowed to the floor. It was tastefully simple and yet, the little antique embellishments made it fantastic, dreamlike—and, by the authentic look of it, hardly inexpensive.

"It's...oh, my god, it's beautiful," Eliza said, a hand at her mouth. She wasn't sure if it was possible to sum up her feelings for the dress in just those few words. "So, who's getting married?" She glanced around the room of familiar faces, then back at Juliana.

Her BFF leaned forward, her hands on the armrests of the chair, and kissed Eliza on the cheek. "You are, dear." She grinned mischievously, running a finger through the white witch's streak in Eliza's black hair. "You're going to have a proper wedding to your Edwin. Isn't it exciting?"

"Now?"

"Yes now!"

Eliza glanced around at the faces of her circle of friends—Juliana, Robert, Cesar, Malcolm, Baldy, and, finally, Edwin. It took a moment for it all to sink in, that this was all for her.

They must have been planning this for weeks, if not months. Every part of it, from the gown and decorations to Juliana and Robert's being here. In that one moment, she felt so loved and cherished that she had to fight to hold back the overflow of tears in her eyes. She turned the Covenant ring on her hand nervously, a habit she'd newly acquired. "I don't understand. All of this is for me? How long have you guys been planning this?"

Edwin came around and slid to one knee beside her chair. "A bit of a surprise, love, yes?"

"Yes! But...I mean...now? Right now? I can't walk an aisle like this." She looked down at her legs.

"I'll carry you."

"You will not carry me!"

He put his hand on her arm. The feel of it calmed her, but also sent a pulse of electricity into her, and she felt many things at once. His hunger, his cynicism, the fierceness of his love for her. She knew he thought of himself as a bad man. He had killed Ian. She had seen that clearly in his head even though he was deftly avoiding the subject with her. Unfortunately for him, the blood he had given her had only strengthened their link; there was nothing he could hide from her now, no secrets she could not unravel.

She wished she could tell him the truth: that he was both a good man and a bad man all wrapped up in one package. He was like every man. And, like every man, he struggled.

"I wanted to make our last day of holiday special, give you the wedding you deserve." He hesitated. "If you don't mind marrying me, that is. I know this engagement thing is sudden. It's also been hard on you, love..."

Edwin then bit his lips nervously. "If it's too much, too sudden, we can take it all back to the States, do it some other time…"

"It is sudden. But, I'm ready." She looked down at the ring on her finger.

He brightened at that.

She squeezed his hand to reassure him. "And you guys planned all of this? All of you worked together?"

"Actually," interjected Baldy, "it was mostly Megan who planned it. We were just her little helpers."

"I helped." Cesar raised his hand as if he was in class. "I did the decorations."

"You did wonderfully!" Eliza told him as everyone gathered around to congratulate her and Edwin. Drinks were passed out and everyone paused to reflect on those who could not be there. Edwin popped a bottle of champagne for those who could drink it and a bottle of house brew for those who could not.

"Actually, most of us were pretty useless with this wedding stuff…at least, until Juliana got here." Cesar nodded to her in thanks when he had finished a circuit of the room and was again standing by Eliza's chair.

Baldy nodded. "She's been a real doll!" And he lifted his glass to her.

Juliana blushed, then undid her coat and did a little spin as if she was on a New York catwalk to show off her Gaelic bridesmaid gown. It seemed to glow in the daylight streaming in, the same shade of the blush on her cheeks. "What do you think, Leeza? It matches your ring!"

She grinned despite herself. "It's simply lovely."

"I chose the dress," Edwin explained, then frowned. "You always pick my outfits, so I wanted to do it for you for a change." Then he stared down at the floor, looking worried. "I shouldn't have done that, I reckon. Ah, well, we can always visit the dressmaker…"

"It's perfect." The truth was, in all of her years, she never believed she would have a wedding or a wedding dress. Or a wedding ring. Or friends. Or any of this. She looked around her circle of friends. "So, you guys *did* take my dress!"

Edwin grinned sheepishly. "We needed the measurements for the dressmaker. Sorry about that, lovey."

Juliana, who was good at organizing all manner of engagements, clapped her hands and told everyone that the ceremony would begin as soon as the sun started to set.

"I love all of you," Eliza said, tears in her eyes. "Thank you for this." Suddenly, it was too much and Eliza covered her face to keep from making a fool of herself in front of her friends.

Juliana chased everyone out of the tower room. "Nervous bride," she explained rather gaily as she shooed everyone out of the tower and then returned to help Eliza dress for the marriage ceremony.

Later that night, when they were finally alone, and wed, Edwin sat in bed and let Eliza cry happily on his shoulder for a little while. And when her tears had dried, she took his hand and looked him in the eye and said, "Edwin, I think I'm ready now. I'm ready to become one of you" while the candlelight winked in the heart of her Covenant ring.

ABOUT THE AUTHOR

K.H. Koehler is the bestselling author of various novels and novellas in the genres of horror, SF, dark fantasy, steampunk, and young and new adult. She is the owner of KH Koehler Books and KH Koehler Design, which specializes in graphic design and professional copyediting. Her books are widely available at all major online distributors and her covers have appeared on numerous books in many different genres. Her short work has appeared in various anthologies, and her novel series include *The Kaiju Hunter*, *A Clockwork Vampire*, *Planet of Dinosaurs*, *The Nick Englebrecht Mysteries*, and *The Archaeologists*. She is the author of multiple Amazon bestsellers and was one of the founders and chief editors of KHP Publishers, which published genre fiction from 2001 to 2015. She has over fifteen years of experience in the publishing industry as a writer, ghostwriter, copyeditor, commercial book cover designer, formatter, and marketer. Visit her website at https://khkoehler.net.

www.ingramcontent.com/pod-product-compliance
Lightning Source LLC
LaVergne TN
LVHW031609060526
838201LV00065B/4791